THIS PUBLICAN

THIS PUBLICAN

By

DORNFORD YATES

> *Two men went up into the temple to pray; the one a Pharisee, and the other a publican.*
>
> *The Pharisee stood and prayed thus with himself, God, I thank thee that I am not as other men are, extortioners, unjust, adulterers, or even as this publican.*
>
> ST. LUKE xviii. 10, 11.

WARD, LOCK & CO., LIMITED

LONDON AND MELBOURNE

First published .	**1938**
Reprinted . .	**1940**
Reprinted . .	**1942**
Reprinted . .	**1943**
Reprinted . .	**1944**
Reprinted . .	**1946**
Reprinted . .	**1947**

MADE IN ENGLAND
Printed in Great Britain by Butler & Tanner Ltd., Frome and London

To

That great ring-master, Satire.
who plays so big a part in the
circus of Life.

The characters of this book are entirely imaginary and have no relation to any living person.

CHAPTERS

PREFACE

IF they read this book, some of my customers may complain that they asked of me a fish (Berry) and I have given them a serpent (Rowena). I have only the maddening, if time-honoured, excuse to offer, that for the moment I am out of fishes, but am expecting more shortly.

DORNFORD YATES.

10   THIS PUBLICAN

THIS PUBLICAN

CHAPTER I

As Usual

THAT snow was coming was plain. A black frost
ruled all Essex and the north wind blew about
Jeffreys under a sky of lead, chilling the old, gray stone
of which the mansion was built : since there was no
central heating, the cold within the house was that of
the tomb. Certain fires did their business, but, because
their grates were old-fashioned, most of their heat was
rising into the air, and though a man sat to their blaze,
his back was cold.

The butler had rendered these truths for nearly
thirty-five years. In the servants' hall he was the
recognized authority upon the reactions of the body
to a winter at Jeffreys, and few things gave him more
pleasure than an opportunity of remembering, for the
benefit of a new-comer, the agonies of cold which he
had suffered in what was to be their home. Yet he
and the valet and the housekeeper stayed where they
were, because there are some masters you cannot leave.

If the three belonged to Lord Elvin, his lordship
belonged to them. It was less a case of affection
than of religion itself. There was no god but Elvin,
and they were his prophets. And now, to their
consternation, their god was ill.

" He didn't never ought to have lef' London,"
said Mrs. Mason. " If only we was back in the
Crescent . . ."

" Ah," said the butler. " If. But he don't go by
nothing excep' by the almanac. Law Sittin's in
London, vacations 'ere. That's his rule, Mrs. Mason,
an' you know it as well as me."

" He's broke it now," said the valet, miserably.

This was the sinister truth. Though the Hilary
Term had begun, for the first time for sixty years
Lord Elvin was out of Town.

He had not said that he was ill. He rose, as usual,
at seven ; worked the most of the day ; dressed, as
usual, for dinner : but he had not gone out. For five
days now, the law lord who never kept house had not
ventured abroad : yet prudence was not among his
foibles, although he was eighty-six.

So much the three servants knew. They suspected
that their master was failing. They could not know
that, because of the cold within him, the old judge
dared not go out until he had altered his Will.

He should have been in London on Monday. He
had had an appointment on Tuesday in Lincoln's Inn
Fields. But on Sunday he had thrown in his hand
and had written to Forsyth, solicitor, saying the Will
must wait.

Two days later he wrote to Forsyth again.

*I believe the Codicil should be made without further
delay. Can you come down to lunch on Friday,
bringing two clerks ?*

And now it was Friday, and Forsyth was on his way.

*   *   *   *

The library of Jeffreys might very well have been
that of a nineteenth-century club. It was a long, tall
room, heavily carpeted, lined to the ceiling with books.
Two mighty fires and four tremendous windows respec-
tively warmed and chilled such as ventured within

their range : a terrestrial globe neighboured its celestial twin : two massive writing-tables, not unlike altar-tombs, divided the room into three, and, midway between the two, a mahogany lectern was presenting *The Times* and *The Morning Post.* Leather-covered arm-chairs stood about, offering less comfort than ease : and in one of them was sitting the old life peer.

Such men are not bred to-day. The pace is too hot. The fine, clean-cut features, the piercing eyes, the thick, snow-white hair—these things may severally survive : but the quiet dignity of countenance, the classic excellence of mien belonged to another world. But, then, Lord Elvin was fifty ere cars came in.

He was carefully groomed and was wearing a country suit and well-polished, brown walking-shoes. No slippered pantaloon here—at eighty-six. Still, he was sitting at ease, before noon, in a high-backed chair. And that was out of order . . .

The law lord took out his watch and glanced at its dial.

Two minutes to eleven.

He slid back the watch with a frown. Then with a manifest effort he got to his feet, steadied himself for a moment by holding the arm of the chair and crossed the floor to the lectern six paces away.

When the butler entered the room at eleven o'clock, his lordship was standing, as usual, reading *The Times.*

As he set down the sherry and biscuits, his master looked round.

" What ?   Oh, thank you.   Weston."

" My lord ? "

" Serve the Methuselah brandy after lunch."

" At table, my lord ? "

" No.   Up here."

" Very good, my lord.   I've arranged for the clerks to have lunch in the housekeeper's room."

" Very well.   Don't forget the chauffeur."

" No, indeed, my lord."

His master turned over a page and the butler passed
to the fires, there to sweep the hearths and garnish
the grates. Not till this duty was done did he make
himself scarce. As the tall door closed behind him,
Lord Elvin swayed to a chair and let himself go . . .

After five minutes, perhaps, he got again to his feet
and, making his way to the table, poured out a glass
of sherry and drank it off.

The medicine revived him at once.

As he set the glass down on the tray—

" Just about do it," he said.

* * * *

John Galbraith Forsyth was an attractive man.
That he was also a fine lawyer goes without saying :
otherwise, he would not, for instance, have been
solicitor to Lord Elvin. His honesty and wisdom stood
out : his astonishing adaptability was not apparent.
The fact remains that his clients swore by his name.
Subalterns and archdeacons, débutantes and financiers
sat in turn in his room and went easy away. His
counsel was so manifestly good. The shrewd solicitor
was as other men are.

He had cancelled seven appointments to lunch at
Jeffreys that day. But when Lord Elvin sent out an
S.O.S. . . .

" Just about do it, Forsyth."

The solicitor smiled.

" I'll remind you of that, sir," he said, " next time
you're in Lincoln's Inn Fields."

" Then why did you come ? It must have been
damned inconvenient."

" I came," said Forsyth, " to set both our minds at
rest. The unmade Will's like Macbeth. It murders
sleep."

The judge took a sup of old brandy and crossed his
legs.

"Listen to me, Forsyth. The boy—my boy was married ten days ago."

"Yes," said Forsyth, "I saw it. Miss Howard, I think her name was. Her parents were dead."

"That's right. Rowena Howard. He brought her to lunch, to meet me, the week before." Lord Elvin set down his glass and fingered his chin. "I liked her—anyone would. I liked her immensely, Forsyth—a most attractive girl. And when they'd gone I thanked God that the boy had made no mistake."

"I'm terribly glad, sir," said Forsyth. "I know——"

"Wait a minute. There's more to come. The instant I saw the girl, I knew that I'd seen her before. Not her herself, but her double—same face, same figure, same charm . . . same little trick of putting a hand to her throat . . . And when they were gone and I was alone again, I began to try to remember —for curiosity's sake." The old fellow picked up his brandy and cupped the glass in his palms. "I've seen so many people in eighty-six years—all sorts and conditions of men, as high as low, and over and over again I have proved the truth of the doctrine that those alike in body are also alike in mind."

"No doubt about that, sir," said Forsyth. "I've proved it, too."

"Then you will agree that the closer the physical resemblance, the closer the resemblance of soul."

"Certainly," said the solicitor, crossing his legs.

"Very well. If I could contrive to remember when and where I had seen her image before, I might or might not be able to form a further judgment of Miss Rowena Howard, now Mrs. David Bohun. Not that it mattered, Forsyth—understand that. That she was sterling stood out. She took me by storm—and, where the boy is concerned, I'm hard to please. Out of pure curiosity, therefore, I went to work—and the more my memory failed me, the harder I drove the brute. It should have been easy—you don't see women like

that every month of the year. But it wasn't easy,
Forsyth. It took me more than a week. And that
was because I had got my environment wrong. I
was looking for her double at dinners, at garden-parties
and balls—a long way back, of course, but I used to go
to such things. And then, eight days ago, I turned
to the courts . . ." Lord Elvin drained his glass
and set it back on the tray.   " I tried her for perjury,
Forsyth, some twenty-nine years ago—the foulest,
most treacherous lies that ever a woman told."

" Good God," said Forsyth, wide-eyed.

" It's true. The jury let her off. They couldn't
withstand her charm and her angel face. And they
hadn't before them the proofs that lay on my desk.
They were not ' evidence '. And so she went free—
in this world. But if I had done as she had—out-
Judased Judas, put out the eyes of Truth, I say to
you, Forsyth, I'd be afraid to die."

" Perhaps——"

" Perhaps be damned," snapped the judge. " She's
as deep as Hell." With a shaking hand he touched
the bottle beside him, and Forsyth, observing the
movement, refilled his glass.   " The boy's been fooled,
Forsyth : and so have I. He's married a brilliant
vampire, who knows no law but that of her own
desires, who's clever as sin, whose heart is of frozen
iron : and because he is honest and faithful and likes
to keep his hands clean, she's going to feed on him,
Forsyth, for as long as it suits her book. And he will
be—miserable . . ." He drank again. Then he set
the glass back on the tray and sat up in his chair.
" Well, the milk is spilt. She's Mrs. David Bohun.
But I'm not dead yet—and this is where you come
in."

" What can I do ? " said Forsyth.

" I'll tell you. As both of us know, I had left him
everything. I make it some seventy thousand, when
everything's paid. In fact, he doesn't need it. He's

doing well at the Bar and he has a private income of nearly a thousand pounds. And the house as well. And so I shall alter my Will and leave you half my fortune . . . upon trust . . . to do as I say."

"Upon trust," said Forsyth. "Yes? What trust will that be?"

"The words," said the judge, "will be these. *To employ the same as I may hereafter advise.*"

"Yes?" said Forsyth again, with a hand to his chin.

Lord Elvin leaned forward.

"You will use that money," he said, "to bring Mrs. Bohun down. It may take you several years, and stalking a woman like her is expensive work. It may very easily cost you five thousand a year. But I give you a free hand, Forsyth. Your job is to spend that thirty-five thousand pounds in catching out that she-devil and freeing my boy." He threw himself back in his chair and put a hand to his eyes. "If there's anything left when you've done it, give it to charity. God knows how grateful I'll be, wherever I am."

There was a little silence.

Then—

"You really mean this?" said Forsyth. "I mean, it's a secret trust—and I might be killed to-morrow, crossing the street."

"I know. I've thought of all that. But you are the only man, and this is the only way."

"Are you sure of that, sir?" said Forsyth, folding his arms. "I mean, it's a delicate matter. I'll do it for you, if I must: but I'd like, if I can, to—to go round some other way."

"You try and find one," said the judge, and picked up his glass.

For perhaps five minutes the two men sat very still, the one considering his brandy and the other with his eyes on the fire.

Then Forsyth raised his eyebrows and let out a sigh.

"You're right—as always," he said. "There's no other way." He got to his feet and stood looking into the blaze. "I wonder if such a strange duty was ever imposed before."

"Or accepted," said Lord Elvin.

The solicitor laughed.

"Why do I accept it?" he said.

"Not for my sake, Forsyth, but because you've a sense of justice which must be served." He smote an arm of his chair. "And so have I. That's why I impose the duty. I'm fond of the boy, of course: but it's more than that. Can you watch a man flogging a horse that's doing its best? And that is nothing to what's going to happen here."

Forsyth took a pen from his pocket and looked at the judge.

"*Humanum est errare*," he said. "Supposing I prove you wrong."

Lord Elvin frowned.

"You will take what is left of the money and buy her the finest diamonds that you can procure."

The solicitor nodded. Then he crossed to one of the tables and drafted the Codicil . . .

Some twenty minutes later this had been written out fair by one of the nervous clerks, and when the testator had read it, the second clerk was sent for, to see the document signed.

The law lord laid down his pen and rose to his feet.

"I'm much obliged to you both. I hope my people are looking after you."

The two stammered an assurance, glanced at Forsyth for instructions and made their way from the room.

"I'm more than obliged to you, Forsyth. Mind you're fair to yourself in the matter of costs."

"I always am," said Forsyth, "as a matter of course."

"I'm not so sure," said the judge. "But in this case remember it was my especial desire."

"Very well, sir," said Forsyth, obediently.

"And now we both know you must go. I should very much like to keep you, but you've given me a yard and I'm not going to take an ell. Are you going to lodge an appeal in that revenue case?"

"I can't make up my mind," said Forsyth. "I wish I could."

"If you do, you'll win. There's a case that's dead in your favour that's not in the books. *Gunther* v. *Borwick* in 1910. A very good judgment of Scrutton's. It's never been overruled."

The solicitor's eyes were shining.

"*Gunther* v. *Borwick*," he repeated. "I'm terribly grateful, sir. That revenue case has worried me out of my life."

"That's the worst of a sense of justice." The law lord moved to a fireplace and rang a bell. "And now good-bye, Forsyth. You've done a good deed to-day."

In silence the two shook hands.

Forsyth would have spoken if he could have trusted his voice : but the moment which he had dreaded had taken him by the throat. A giant of his world was swaying : a time-honoured elm was toppling : a peerless, full-rigged ship was going down. He was looking upon an old master, whose period frame would be empty within the week, with whom he had been familiar for thirty years.

The old fellow smiled and nodded, and Forsyth turned . . .

Arrived at the mahogany doors, he opened a leaf and looked back. His hand upon the head of a chair, Lord Elvin was standing, watching him, still with a smile upon his face. Forsyth put up a hand in salutation. Then he turned again and passed out of the room.

As the door closed behind him, the law lord moved

round the chair and sat carefully down. After resting for a moment or two, he got again to his feet and crossed to one of the windows commanding the drive. As he did so, a car emerged from the stable-yard.

Approaching the window-pane, he watched the car fetch a compass and come to rest. He could not see the front door, for this was flush with the window at which he stood, but by standing against the glass he could see the last of the steps. After perhaps two minutes, he saw the chauffeur descend and open the hinder door. Then Forsyth appeared, his hands thrust into his pockets, his fur-coat's collar lifted against the cold. For a moment he spoke with the chauffeur: then he stepped into the car. The senior clerk followed him in, the junior waiting to sit by the chauffeur's side. And then they were all within, and the doors were shut. At once the car moved off . . .

The law lord watched it until he could see it no more, and when it was out of his sight, he still stood looking after, as though he was taking in spirit the London road. So for perhaps two minutes: then he looked to and fro, to focus the empty park.

Remarking the graceless country, he found the house of Nature divided against itself. The hang-dog day was passing into a vicious night. The bitter wind was still whipping a sullen world; great trees rocked and bellowed, as though in pain; the bushes below them shuddered; the lake lay dead. Somehow the pregnant clouds withheld their snow, weighting the faltering twilight out of its humble race and making the hearts of all things fail them for fear. As well that darkness was coming to cloak the sheer unkindness that ruled the earth.

A sudden stab of pain reminded the aged peer that cold within him fed upon cold without. At once he turned from the window and made his way to a fire, but, now that he had no interest, he felt too weak to stand and after a moment he left the fire for a chair. As he laid back his head, again the pain shot through him and he began to cough . . .

Perhaps some instinct told him he must have warmth.

God knows what it cost him to drag his chair to the blaze, but ring for a servant he would not—he never had rung for a servant to move a chair. For the matter of that, no servant had ever seen him sitting beside a fire ; but that record went that day, when the butler came with the tea.

Still the warmth had done its work, and the pain was gone. He was able to speak to the man, as soon as the lights were up and the curtains were drawn.

" A cold night, Weston."

" Bitter, my lord."

" See that the postman has something to warm him up."

" Very good, my lord."

The butler saw to the fire and then, without inquiry, poured out his master's tea.

For a moment the law lord stared.

Then—

" Er, thank you," he said. " Much obliged."

The butler passed to the lectern. One minute later *The Times* and *The Morning Post* were lying beside the tray.

" Thank you, Weston, thank you. I—I'm quite all right."

" Certainly, my lord. But it's warmer here by the fire."

" You find it cold, do you ? "

" My lord, it's exceptional."

" Ah."

The second grate replenished, Lord Elvin was left alone.

The tea did him good. He even glanced at *The Times* before falling asleep . . .

When he awoke, he realized with a shock that the tray had been taken and letters left in its place.

"This won't do," he said shortly and got to his feet.

Two minutes later he was sitting at one of his tables, dealing with one of the letters which the postman had brought . . .

As usual, he dressed for dinner at half past seven o'clock. He could not know that, whilst he was in his bedroom, his valet was standing, listening, without the door.

He dined, as usual, at eight.

How he managed the stairs, I cannot pretend to say, but under the eyes of his servants he passed up and down. And then once more he was back in the library . . .

The pain had returned now, to lace his chest with irregular, savage thrusts. Perhaps the low-cut waistcoat must answer for that. It was not, of course, so warm as that which he had put off. Still, there was a roaring fire, and the butler had left his chair drawn close to the hearth. Out of all order, that. Still, Weston had said that the cold was exceptional. He supposed it was. He hadn't been out himself, so how could he know?

"All wrong," said Lord Elvin. "All wrong. I'll go out to-morrow, come snow. No reason now why I——"

Another slash of pain snapped the sentence off short, and the valet, stooping in the shadows, straightened his back.

His master was clinging to the chair. After a moment or two, he worked his way round its side and into its seat.

He sat, leaning back, with the firelight playing upon him, lighting the stiff shirt-front and the clean-cut face. This might have been cut out of marble, it was so pale : the lips were white as the rest, and the eyes were shut.

He sat so still for so long that a sudden apprehension

knocked at the valet's heart. He began to approach softly, finger to lip. Then the law lord lifted his voice, and he stopped in his tracks.

" Where was it I saw her ? Gunther v. Borwick's the name. You've given an old man pleasure. It's too late now. Good-bye, my boy. Up here with the coffee, Weston. There's no other way."

The valet was shocked—with reason, for the nonsense was naturally spoken and not by a sleeping man. At once he whipped to a fireplace and rang a bell.

In an instant the butler appeared . . .

The two men consulted together. Then the butler ran out of the room and down the stairs. At their foot the housekeeper was trembling . . .

" Delirious," vouchsafed the butler. " Is Lupton there ? "

" Here, Mr. Weston," said the chauffeur.

" Stan' by, while I talk," said the other, and fell on the telephone.

After a moment or two—

" Is that Dr. Riley ? " he cried . . . " Oh, this is Lord Elvin's butler . . . I'm speakin' from Jeffreys, sir. His lordship's took very bad. Can you come at once ? The chauffeur's here if you'd like me to send the car . . . Oh, very good, sir. Thank you . . . Well, I think it's the cold, sir, that's done it . . . In the library, sir . . . Very good, sir. Thank you. Good-bye." He put the receiver back and turned to the housekeeper. " 'Ot bottles at once, Mrs. Mason, to warm his bed. An' one to the library, Lupton, an' car rugs out of the 'all."

With that, he was gone . . .

Five minutes went by. The chauffeur had been and gone and Mrs. Mason had come to the library. Lord Elvin's voice was still speaking—intermittently.

" Just about do it, Forsyth. You won't get a bid. Where have I seen that face ? The post's very late. A very good judgment of Scrutton's. I'm much

obliged. That's a good boy. I've seen her somewhere. All wrong . . ."

Together the butler and valet removed his shoes,
set his feet on a bottle, swathed him in rugs. Sometimes the voice petered out and the peer seemed to
doze : then it would start again, investing its inco-
herence with such conviction as made their blood
run cold. Just before the doctor arrived, the brain
resumed control, and the law lord sat up.

" What's this, Weston ? "

He plucked at the rug on his knees.

For once confounded, the butler made no reply,
and Mrs. Mason, behind him, fell to her knees and
began to crawl out of range. The valet stepped into
the breach.

" You fainted, my lord. I think perhaps it's the
cold. When Weston answered the bell, he—he found
you asleep."

" I'm—I'm quite all right. I—I only rang for . . .
for some tea."

" Very good, my lord. Tea, Mrs. Mason."

" Mrs. Mason ? What's she doing here ? "

" She brought the hot bottle, my lord. Your feet
were cold."

" Very good of you, Mrs. Mason. I'm much obliged.
But I'm all right now. And don't bother about the tea."

There was an awkward silence.

Then—

" By your lordship's leave," said the butler, " Dr.
Riley is on the way."

" Dr. Riley ? Why ? "

" Er, we thought it a precaution, my lord. We're
—not used to your being ill."

" I'm not ill, Weston. I—Ah ! "

The pain had replied to the plea—and that, so
effectively that nearly a minute went by before its
victim could speak.

Then—

" Perhaps you're right. Where's Weston ? "

" My lord ? "

" You—you said it was cold, Weston."

" Exceptionally so, my lord."

" Ah." The white head fell back. " I tried her for perjury, Forsyth. I'm much obliged. See you in London, David . . ."

Mrs. Mason burst into tears.

Then the door was opened by the chauffeur, and the doctor entered the room.

The butler hastened to meet him . . .

Very gently he lifted one of Lord Elvin's hands, to take the wrist between his finger and thumb. After a little, he laid the hand back on the arm of the high-backed chair. Then he passed to the other side and lifted the other hand . . .

As he laid this back—

" I shouldn't move him," he said. " It won't be long."

There was a dreadful silence. The law lord had ceased to talk. Two fat tears rolled slowly down Weston's face. Mrs. Mason was sobbing quietly. On his knees by the chair, the valet hid his face in his hands. By the doors at the end of the room the chauffeur stood very still, with his eyes on the floor.

The doctor stood back, to set a hand on the marble above the grate.

With his eyes on the fine, old face—

" I might have done something," he said, " two days ago. But I very much doubt it. Eighty-five is full eighty-five in weather like this."

" Eighty-six," quavered the valet, " last Michaelmas Eve."

Unable to bear such inaction, the butler lifted his voice.

" But can't you do nothing, sir ?   Nothing at all ? "

" Nothing," said the doctor. " I'm sorry. His heart has practically stopped."

Twenty halting minutes dragged by, the doctor watching his patient, the weeping servants supporting their dying lord. Then a change came, and Lord Elvin was short of breath.

The unfamiliar condition disturbed his peace. For a moment his eyelids fluttered : then, at the second attempt, he lifted his handsome head.

" Is—is Kendal there ? " he said faintly.

" My lord ? " said the valet.

" I'm . . . rather tired . . . this evening. I don't know why. I . . . think perhaps . . . it's the cold. But call me as usual, Kendal . . ."

With the words, his head fell back ; and after the ghost of a struggle the law lord died.

By Dr. Riley's direction, the servants lifted his body and carried it off to his room.

Then Weston rang up Forsyth : and Forsyth rang up *The Times* to say that a great man was dead.

CHAPTER II

Knave and Fool

A MEMORIAL service for Lord Elvin was held in the Temple Church. The [life peer's funeral in Essex was private enough. David Bohun, great-nephew, was there, and so was Forsyth : so, of course, were the servants : and so was Mrs. Bohun.

The solicitor, watching her closely, could find no fault in the girl. Her demeanour was admirable : her discretion stood out : her taste was above reproach. She shed no tears—why should she ?—but comforted Mrs. Mason, who was in great distress. Afterwards she took care to leave Forsyth and her husband alone. They saw her from the library windows, proving the snow-clad park and walking with a tele-graph-boy who was telling her all he did. Mrs. Bohun did more than attract : at times she inspired.

Forsyth saw only two things which might or might not be straws indicating the set of a wind which he could not feel. One was that the chauffeur's mongrel, a friendly dog, denied the lady the homage he offered to everyone else : the other was that Bohun seemed pensive, and Forsyth was not quite sure that this was wholly due to Lord Elvin's death.

Together the two considered the law lord's Will. As Forsyth had known that he would, Bohun took the new Codicil very well.

" Why not, Forsyth ? " he said. " We both know he's done me proud : and how could I ever question wisdom like his ? "

" I shall miss him terribly," said Forsyth.

" I know you will," said David. " But you have the consolation of knowing that you were the only being on whom he ever leaned."

" That's absurd," said Forsyth, bending the documents flat.

" He swore by you," said the other, and left it there.

The Will itself was simple. The town house and Jeffreys and their contents were to be sold forthwith for what they would fetch. For the three older servants annuities were to be bought. A picture went to Forsyth, a bust to the Inner Temple, the silver to David Bohun . . .

At five o'clock that evening the Bohuns left in their car. Forsyth was staying the night—for the sake of the servants as much as anything else. Their occupation was gone. It would do them good to have someone they knew and trusted to be their guest.

Seated in his bedroom that night, the solicitor stared at the fire and fingered his chin. The duty which he had accepted was now alive, and Forsyth was not the man to let such a matter wait. Mrs. Bohun had to be cornered and forced to release her prey.

It was typical of the man that he would not let himself question the judgment Lord Elvin had formed. He assumed that the girl was guilty—against all reason, of course : but he knew that if once he looked back, his own opinion would tell him that that of Lord Elvin was wrong. And so the girl was guilty . . . What was she guilty of ? The judge had spoken of deceit—a vague enough crime. But this was so gross a case that under the threat of exposure the lady would do as he said.

Forsyth raised his eyebrows and got to his feet.

There was only one thing to be done. The present being obscure, the past must be discovered, to see if that shed any light. He would set on foot inquiries to-morrow—to find out who she was and whence she had come. A Miss Rowena Howard . . .

As the man had determined, so he did. Exhaustive inquiries were made. They took some time to complete, cost more than two hundred pounds and taught him nothing at all that he wanted to know. This was nobody's fault. Who should know that the leopard had changed his spots?

* * * *

Elsie Baumer was a precocious child. This was natural enough. Before she was eight years old, the fruit of the tree of the knowledge of good and evil had become her staple food. This, again, was natural. She had ' travelled the road ' with her mother almost from the day of her birth.

The provinces liked Mrs. Baumer, whom they knew as Cora Perowne. She never appeared in London, but starred for years everywhere else. Parts were rewritten to suit her—in musical shows. She never played a lead in her life, but, while leads come and go, Miss Cora Perowne went on. She was, as they say, a sure thing. For fifteen years a brazen mezzo voice stood her in stead : then the hot, vocal number came in, and she took on a new lease of life.

Whether Mr. Baumer existed is matter for doubt, but a daughter, Elsie, was born in 1914. Unknown to each other, two gentlemen paid for the *accouchement*, which the doctor did as a friend. Supported by these contributions, Cora stayed out of the bill for fully six months. Then she returned—with her baby, who became the company's pet.

The infant, conveniently, resembled no possible sire. Indeed, what strain it was that reappeared in Elsie I cannot pretend to say. She never resembled her mother, within or without. Mrs. Baumer looked the ' good sort ' she undoubtedly was.

The years slid by. Some sort of education took place, but Elsie Baumer's school was the grimy kaleidoscope of provincial, theatrical life. A noticing child, she knew rather more at twelve than nine out of ten girls know at twenty-six.

Then something occurred to wake the iron ambition she had not known she possessed.

Travelling to a town in the midlands, the company entered the protectorate of one of those fishers of men who choose to believe in humanizing the stage. They had been warned. As well warn the private soldier *en route* for the front. They came, they were seen, they were netted. Aware of their captor's good intentions, the company blasphemed in secret and rewarded his efforts openly. It sniggered when he jested in the wings, hid tumblers under towels when he knocked at a dressing-room door, submitted to photographic records of a jovial understanding which did not in fact exist. In an ecstasy of elation the bountiful angler concocted a luscious *bonne bouche*. The principals were formally invited to a private view of the parish Christmas Tree, erected in the brutal nakedness of the parish hall and enriched with tallow and tinsel to delight less fortunate eyes. Too good-natured to refuse, they accepted with wreathed smiles and, when they were once more alone, reviled their exalted host in terms which I dare not set down. That Elsie's education had never before included the inspection of Christmas Trees did something to leaven the lump.

The afternoon came. Whimpering with pleasure, the vicar received his guests. Elsie Baumer, entirely collected, was shown the tree.

She had, of course, been told to say how lovely it was. Every precaution had been taken, for Elsie was a critic who was not afraid of speech.

Gravely she surveyed the sapling, the last year's tinsel, the candles as yet unlit. Then she addressed her mother.

" Daddy's an angel, isn't he ? "

A startled Mrs. Baumer was understood to concur.

" Then perhaps he did some of that," said Elsie radiantly.

The vicar was transported and related the conjecture for weeks, with tears in his eyes. So did the principals —when they were once more alone.

Then Elsie was introduced to other girls of her age. These were present with their mothers. The principals and the mothers were then encouraged to mix.

It was Elsie's first experience of meeting girls of her age who did not work for their living or that of somebody else. She perceived herself to be their superior in every way. She was treated as their inferior all the time. These things inclined her to laugh—so many pots were calling the cream-jug black. Instead, she listened and watched, determined to discover the reason for a complacency which was as fantastic as it was universal. Before it was time to be gone, the secret was hers. *She was not as other girls were, because she belonged to the stage.*

From that time on, Miss Baumer had one idea. This was to sever her connection with the world to which she belonged. ' If thine eye offend thee, pluck it out.'

No opportunity offered for three long years, but Elsie knew what she wanted and knew how to wait. She was, of course, a most exceptional girl. She employed her time in preparing for her escape. She learned how to get something for nothing—a trick which had nothing to do with sleight of hand, and she took to absenting herself, for days at a time. On the first occasion or two hue and cry was raised : very soon, however, her mother and other well-wishers gave up making fools of themselves : at the end of two years she came and went as she pleased.

Then she met a dull girl, a Miss Howard, whom nobody liked, who had no idea at all how to wear her expensive clothes. The encounter took place at Reading, in the waiting-room of a dentist whom Elsie had

proposed to blackmail : but five minutes' study of
Miss Howard convinced the huntress that here was far
bigger game. She let her appointment go and took her
new friend to tea.

I imagine that Elsie's instinct told her that here at
last was the tide which she had been waiting to take.
Be that as it may, she played her game throughout as
though she knew what cards were going to be dealt.

Rowena Howard was an orphan, aged seventeen,
doomed to be ' finished ' in Paris in six weeks' time.
At the moment she was staying with sisters who
accepted, during the holidays, homeless girls. The
establishment bore a good name, but was, unknown to
its patrons, passing through a difficult time, for the
sister who did not drink was seriously ill.

All this Miss Baumer learned before tea had been
served. It was over the scones that she was made free
of the nightmare of which Miss Howard was now the unhappy prey. She dreaded Paris, of course. That was
for her The Black Death. But a more immediate peril
was haunting her waking hours. In eight days' time
she was to travel to London and travel alone—there
to encounter her guardian, whom she had never seen.

Elsie there and then determined to go in her stead.
And so she did.

The guardian, a City solicitor, found his ward a
highly promising girl. He gave her lunch at Scott's,
had her photographed for her passport and gave her
information for which Rowena Howard would never
have asked. Under his supervision, she opened a
banking account.

When she returned to Reading, she told a twittering
Rowena what she thought she might conveniently
believe. Miss Howard was consumed with gratitude.
The already luxuriant friendship burst into riotous
bloom. Elsie watered it with devotion. For the next
five weeks her victim hung on her lips. It was too easy.

When the time came to leave for Paris, Miss Baumer

accompanied Miss Howard—to do what she could.
The two left Folkestone together, one sad, September
night . . .

The wind was fresh to strong, and Miss Howard,
true to type, had begun to feel sick in the train. Before
the lights of England had faded, she cared no longer
whether she lived or died. This was as well, for,
attached to Miss Baumer's suitcase, she sank like a
stone.

According to plan, a Miss Rowena Howard was met
at the *Gare du Nord*. Of Miss Baumer nothing was said
and nothing was ever known. Her mother made
belated inquiries which naturally bore no fruit.

* * * *

From the foregoing facts two conclusions may fairly
be drawn. The first of them is that, when Lord Elvin
said ' She's as deep as Hell ', that estimation, if blunt,
was undoubtedly good. The second is that Mrs. David
Bohun was a lady who knew not God nor respected
man. Nothing counted with her but her own desires.
Nothing. Her outlook was that of the Pharaohs.
Could she have done so, she would have crushed a
people—if that would have saved her the trouble of
stooping to pick a flower. She remembered her bene-
factress with a hatred which never died. It was wholly
thanks to her that she had for ever to add two years
to her age.

* * * *

When Miss Howard met David Bohun, again she
knew in a flash that here was what she required. As
once before, something within her—the furtive nudge
of Instinct told her that here was the man.

In seven years she had developed, but she had not
altered at all. She had increased in wisdom and in

favour with man. She had studied most carefully the spirit and manners of the world which she now adorned, and she had at length perceived that a generous, faithful husband is a rock upon which one can build. (The verb is significant. Build. Not lean, or rest, or rely. *Build*. Rowena believed in construction.)

Of her fellows, all knew what they wanted. If you had asked them, they would have said, " A good time." So would have Rowena—if she had told you the truth. The difference was this—that Rowena could have defined that loose, if convenient, phrase. She was no fool. When you are seeking something, your chances of finding it are greater if you know in your heart what it is.

Where men were concerned, she watched other women striving and learned of them : she saw them rising and falling, fooling and being fooled : she saw the rich become noble, the poor become rich : she saw the limitations of money : she saw marriage fail and succeed . . . She could, of course, have defined the word ' success '.

Four times she served as a bridesmaid—at weddings worth going to : no mean achievement, that, for a homeless girl. She augmented a slender income by odd secretarial work. Most of this was done for a Mrs. le Bras, a rich, persevering woman who believed in house-parties and devoted more hard labour to their composition than her regular secretary could perform. The work was highly instructive. Rowena began to learn where Mrs. le Bras left off.

And then, at twenty-four, she met David Bohun.

She found him straightforward and simple—two valuable faults : she found him hard-working and generous—a useful contradiction in terms : the briefest acquaintance proved him as clean within as without. She learned that his private income approached a thousand a year, that he was making twice that at the Chancery Bar, that his parents were dead, that

he had a small house of his own. When she learned
that the house stood in Curzon Street, Mayfair, Rowena
could hardly wait for its lord to propose. Talk about
rocks . . .

They were married at the end of the vacation,
postponed their honeymoon till Easter and settled
down at once for the Hilary Term.

* * * *

At the time of his marriage, Bohun was twenty-
nine and as strong as a horse. By no means brilliant,
he, nevertheless, had a flair for equity—that intricate
dry-as-dust branch of the English law. His work was
good. Slow to pounce, when once he had hold of a
point, he would never let go. He did his cases as a
mathematician does sums, unravelling with infinite
patience knots which the careless had tied before his
father was born. He could not have cross-examined
to save his life, but the settlements he drew were
unassailable. He would never make law : but no
man would better apply the law which others had
made. Thanks to Lord Elvin's perception, he had
entered the chambers of a leader who had in his youth
displayed the same limited competency and, as a
result, was now making ten thousand a year. As was
to be expected, the two agreed together, and such as
instructed Mr. Beaver began to give junior briefs to
Mr. Bohun . . .

Brown, dog-like eyes distinguished his pleasant face,
and, for all his work within doors, his colour was
high. No one would have thought him a lawyer : he
had more the frank look of a sailor than anything
else. He was tall and well set-up, cared for his hair
and his hands and always wore well-cut clothes. So
much for his appearance. His nature has already
been declared. It should be added that he was a
practical man, that he danced atrociously, but handled

c

a car very well. He made the best of London, but gloried in unspoilt country of every kind. The greatest mistake he made was to take life seriously. The greatest weakness he had was that he was an idealist.

Those David Bohun liked he set up upon pedestals : and when they fell down, as sooner or later, of course, they always did, it was he that was chipped or broken because of their fall. For his wife he had no pedestal, but a niche. It had been waiting for years. Rowena fitted it—ideally.

The lady's appearance is very hard to describe. Her features were unattractive. Her nose was poor, her mouth was too wide, her dark-brown eyes were too close : yet a most charming expression much more than redeemed these faults and clothed her face with a beauty which nobody could deny. This expression was most of all naïve. *Summa ars celare artem.* Rowena had achieved artlessness. Here was no baby stare, but the playful, friendly look of a creature that knows no wrong. Lord Elvin had spoken in haste of her ' angel face '. Still, for such a description there is a great deal to be said. When Rowena was hurt, Rowena a saint could seem. Her wistful, far-away aspect remembered the glorious promise of more than one of The Beatitudes. Her size supported the illusion. She was ' a little thing '. For the rest, her hair was fair, her hands were passable, and her figure was nearly perfect in every way. Rowena was beautifully made. Add to this that she knew how to choose and to put her clothes on, and it will be immediately clear that the lady appealed to the eye wherever she went.

As was fitting, her husband was proud of his wife. Had Rowena been asked, she would have confessed that she was most proud of Bohun. This would have been untrue. She was neither proud nor ashamed. Her husband suited her book.

Before they had been married a week, Rowena had shown him gently how selfish and thoughtless he was, and he had cursed himself and had sworn before God, who made her, that he would correct these faults.

The credit must go to the lady. With everyone else, her husband was strong of heart.

* * * *

"What will it come to?" said Rowena.

"About thirty-five thousand," said David, and switched on his lights.

"You each get the same?"

"That's right. But, though it's left to Forsyth, it isn't his. It's only been given to him to hold for somebody else."

"Presumably you," said Rowena.

"Us," said David. "Or you. I hope that it's you. You know that he fell for you flat. It was after seeing you that he altered his Will."

Rowena raised her eyebrows.

"Possibly us," she said. "He certainly seemed to like me. Most people do—except you."

"Rowena!"

"You like yourself better, David."

"My sweet, you know I don't mean it. I've got into certain ways, through living alone. I've had nobody else to think of. And now sometimes, without thinking, I do as I've always done."

"'Without thinking' is good," said Rowena. "Are the Cadnams a case in point?"

Her husband put a hand to his head.

"My darling, I've told you——"

"God knows you have," said Rowena. "I know the recital by heart. The Cadnams are the best in the world. They're sober and honest and faithful and quite devoted to me. We shall never get anyone like them. You don't want to see me worried—a pretty thought. But you always omit the truth that you do not want them to go."

They drove for a mile in silence.

As working butler and cook, the Cadnams had been with Bohun for nearly three years. They were quiet, old-fashioned servants, who did their duty and took a pride in their work. Mrs. Cadnam was an excellent cook, and her husband had learned to clean silver when he had been a page. David was right when he said that Rowena and he would not get such servants again. And Rowena was right when she said that he did not want them to go.

To send them away seemed so wanton : and not only wanton—unkind. The Cadnams worshipped Rowena and served him and her so well. They were so good at their jobs and so happy in all they did. They were content and settled, gave every satisfaction, glowed with goodwill. It was certainly true that Cadnam's handwriting was poor : when he wrote down a telephone-message, his spelling was full of faults. But you couldn't make a case out of that . . .

Rowena could—and did. And she said that the man was too old—at fifty-two. She declared that his sight was failing—because he used pince-nez when consulting the telephone-book. She said that his wife didn't know how to send up a dish. She said . . .

" It's a question, David, of pleasing yourself or me. You can dress it up as you like ; but that's the truth, and you know it—and so do I."

" All right," said Bohun, at last. " Will you give them their notice ? Or shall I ? "

Rowena yawned.

" Well, you engaged them," she said.

" I don't know how to tell them," said David, miserably.

When, fifty minutes later, a beaming Cadnam received his master and mistress as though they were king and queen, David Bohun knew he had sold his soul.

That night he summoned the butler and told him haltingly that he felt he must make a change. Cadnam, all unsuspecting, misunderstood what he meant. He thought Bohun was referring to the housemaid lately engaged and very respectfully ventured to plead her cause. He thought, if he might say so, the girl meant well. Mrs. Cadnam was watching her closely . . . It was an awful business. Bohun had to tell him right out. All his life he never forgot how the dawn of understanding had crept into Cadnam's eyes.

The next day, when David was out, Rowena saw Mrs. Cadnam and told her how grieved she was. She said that she had pleaded with David to let them stay, but that he had insisted that Cadnam got on his nerves. She promised—and kept her word—to get them a first-class place . . . and wrote to a footman in the service of Mrs. le Bras. The man was awaiting the summons, which was not signed, and gave his mistress notice the following day.

* * * *

Though his wife was a knave, I hold no brief for Bohun. The man was a fool. The thing was this— he had fallen in love with Miss Howard : he stayed in love with his wife. ' For better or for worse '. The words were cut in the marble beneath her niche. I doubt if he realized this : but Rowena did—and traded upon her knowledge for all she was worth. She was not invariably brutal, but did as she felt inclined. She had only to toss him a smile, to bring the light into his eyes. It must be remembered that his faith in the girl was sublime. Bohun trusted his wife as he trusted himself. He would not have believed her false though one rose from the dead.

* * *

Because of Lord Elvin's death, the Bohuns attended no parties until a fortnight was past. David had suggested this course, and to his relief Rowena had quietly agreed. 'Night work' hit Bohun hard. He was in Chambers each day by a quarter to ten and held himself lucky if he could be home before six. Strong as he was, to dine and dance four times a week, severely taxed the resources his work had left. Had he had but the fitful practice of most of his peers, such a subscription to gaiety would have cost nothing at all : but, as has been pointed out, between Beaver's work and his own, Bohun had very nearly as much as a man can do. Then, again, at a party David Bohun had nothing at all of his wife. They came and went together : but that was all. Weary or no, he could have danced all night with her in his arms ; but to revel with comparative strangers, most of whom did no work which deserved that name, few of whom would rise the next morning before ten o'clock, only insisted on the virtue of a good night's rest. Still, his wife had to be considered—David saw as much for himself and did not oblige the lady to point it out. And Rowena gloried in parties—a natural exultation which her husband had not foreseen. To be perfectly honest, foresight was not his strong point.

Bohun had not hoped, but expected that his wife would breakfast with him at half past eight : that she would receive him with pleasure at six o'clock : that they would dine together and sometimes go to the play, but more often sit by the fire, each sufficient unto the other, letting the world slip. Of his marriage he had expected a new heaven and a new earth. He was not wholly disappointed. He got the new earth. But it was not the earth he had expected.

Parties, then, were a burden—as far as the man was concerned : dinner for two misfired : it was dinner for four that brought David his happiest hours. The explanation is simple. Dinner for four meant a quiet, comfortable evening, passed in a private house with familiar friends : he saw almost as much of Rowena as if they had been alone : and Rowena was as charming to him as she was to everyone else. When others were present—even Cadnam—Rowena never dissembled her love and respect for the man who had made her his wife.

Though the Bohuns did not go out, because of Lord Elvin's death, dinners for four were given in Curzon Street. The Leightons came more than once—to Bohun's delight.

Punch and Belinda Leighton were David's most intimate friends. He had met Punch Leighton at Oxford, and, during the years which followed, acquaintance had grown into one of those grateful friendships which are the salt of life. Leighton's marriage three years ago had actually strengthened the bond : Belinda and Bohun took to each other at once : as both of the men had hoped, the two became three. Now, though that phase was over, Rowena liked and was liked. The pairs agreed together admirably.

With no money to spare, the Leightons lived in Chelsea and paid their way. Their flat was small, but well found : such as they had and offered was of the best : the two dressed well. Always ready to share a taxi—and pay their share, when they were alone they would travel by 'bus or tube : they never cadged, but gave as good as they got : in a light purse they saw no shame—unless it inconvenienced their friends.

When the girls had left the table, the cronies, Bohun and Leighton, sat over some hunting port, and Leighton commended Rowena with all his might.

" Belinda's crazy about her . . . those big, brown eyes. She should have been called Madonna—I don't know what her parents were thinking about. I mean, it's so obvious. And you went and gathered her in . . . Never mind. How's the Chancery Bar ? "

" I can't complain," said David. " How's Mincing Lane ? "

" Foul as foul," said the other. " There's no other

word.   But we do our best, D.B.   We chug along knee-deep, and we're not broke yet.   Oh, and what about these ? "   He produced some superb cigars.   " A hundred, D.B.—one hundred, complete with box.   A present from a client, my son, who very wisely rejected my best advice.   You don't get thank-offerings like that in Lincoln's Inn."

" I wish we did," said David, helping himself.

Here Cadnam came in with the coffee.   As he withdrew—

" What a servant," said Punch.   " Remembers my weakness for sugar and actually leaves me the bowl."

Bohun frowned.

" He, er, has his faults," he said.   " We're making a change."

" Go on," said Leighton, staring.   " Why——"

" He's been here too long," said his host.   " He's all right on parade, of course : but we—I thought it better . . . And Rowena agreed."

" Oh, I can't bear it," said Punch.   " If I can't have my Cadnam, I shan't come here any more. Why, you've told me a hundred times——"

" I know," said Bohun, " I know."   He emptied his glass.   " But these things happen, Punch, and it's best he should go."

Leighton shrugged his shoulders.

" It's your funeral, D.B.—not mine.   And I have a dreadful feeling that you know best.   But what a soul-shaking thought.   I never suspected that Cadnam had feet of clay."

Bohun writhed in spirit and made a considerable business of pinching his big cigar . . .

Upstairs Rowena was saying her little piece.

" I can't discuss it, Belinda : but David thinks it's best and he's always right.   It was rather hard to tell them, but I hope and believe I've got them a jolly good place.   Meanwhile I'm doing my best to find somebody else. And now tell me about that dress. If only I'd hair like yours . . ."

As the Leightons went home that night—

" D.B.'s fired the Cadnams," said Punch.

" I know," said Belinda, slowly. " Rowena's too loyal to say so, but I can see she's upset."

" Poor child," said her husband, frowning.

" And now she's got to get down to finding a cook and a butler to take their place."

" She'll never do that," said Punch, " in a year of Saturday nights."

There he was out.

Within one month the two places were duly filled.

The new butler was an Eurasian, whose name was Anselm, whose manner was very reserved. The service he gave was undeniably good, but at times his Chinese blood was disconcertingly apparent. Infinitely correct, he never smiled : and he moved so silently that often you could not be sure whether he was or was not within the room. David found him inhuman, but Rowena's manifest rapture silenced the protests which he would have liked to make. Besides, within twenty-four hours, the man had produced to Rowena a truly excellent cook : and when later the housemaid left, as of course she did—" you don't get me muckin' in with one o' them Chinks "—the cause of her displeasure replaced her within the week.

With his coming, a change took place. The fact that the butler was present no longer prevented his mistress from dissembling her conjugal love. If she wished to rebuke his master, she did not wait until Anselm was out of the room.

CHAPTER III

Honeymoon

SINCE the Easter vacation was short, Rowena decided that Biarritz should make it sweet. Myself, I think she was right. When Winter is hectoring Spring, ten clear days on the shore of the Bay of Biscay can minister to the soul.

David found her decision a brilliant idea and plumed himself on the wisdom his wife possessed. To visit the South of France would never have entered his head. He had seldom been out of England and never so far afield. And this was no ordinary trip. 'The honeymoon will be spent at Biarritz.'

As the end of the term drew near, his excitement began to run high. The evidence, which Rowena produced, of tickets actually taken and rooms engaged stayed him through more than one party which ended at half past two.

Inspecting their luggage the night before they set out, he remarked Rowena's golf-clubs in some surprise. Bohun did not play golf. Surely she was not proposing . . . A cloud, like a man's hand, hung for an instant in the heaven about to be his. Then he forgot the matter—till he saw the bag at the station the following day.

" You won't want those, will you, my sweet ? "

" You never know," said Rowena. " Besides, I want you to learn. I must say you've got a good tailor. I only wish you could always wear country clothes."

The cloud, which had reappeared, dissolved there

and then. Ten minutes later the train slid over the river and into a squall of sleet.

David spoke private-school French. In other words, provided that time was no object, he could make himself understood. It had never occurred to him that the French which Rowena could speak was that which is spoken in France. The truth became apparent as soon as they disembarked. From that time on, a proud and marvelling Bohun took a back seat while the lady dealt with porters and customs, selected a restaurant and told a Parisian driver the way to go. Nor, when they came to Biarritz, was any difference made. After an effort or two, reception clerks, porters and waiters threw in their hand and spoke French. Bohun, standing by, picked up what he could.

The weather was more than kind, and Biarritz was at her best. What breeze there was was gentle, a summer sun was ruling a flawless sky, and a splendid suite was commanding such an ocean as Homer sang. A bath and a change and a breakfast before open windows handed Bohun into the heaven which he had known he would reach.

That morning they proved the town and strolled on the esplanade : after luncheon Rowena retired, and David went off in search of a private car. The quest took time ; but after a little he hired a fine *coupé de ville* for the whole of their stay. The price demanded was high, but the car was fit for—a queen. And the chauffeur might have been in service . . . (As a matter of fact he was. His mistress, whose car it was, had only left for Venice two days before. Rowena, who knew her France, suspected the truth the moment she saw the Delage : when she found the speedometer lifeless, there was no room for doubt. She took care to say nothing to David—the car was all right.)

Mrs. Bohun had not been idle whilst her husband was out of the way. Upon his triumphant return, he learned that they had been invited to join the

Chiberta Club and begged to proceed there for tea that same afternoon. This information was untrue. Rowena had rung up the club and had said that they wished to be members during their stay. Then she had summoned a manager of the hotel, inquired about casinos and night-clubs and said that, if Biarritz was dull, they should go on to Nice. She had also desired to be furnished with a visitors' list. Then she had changed and descended into the hall. By sitting where David could see her when he came back, she was seen by everyone else who entered or left the hotel.

"What is this club?" said David, returning the stare of a Frenchman who was sprawling three paces away.

"I've no idea," lied Rowena. "But as they mean to be civil, we can't very well refuse. What time is the car coming round?"

"Almost at once," said David. "The chauffeur's getting into his kit and filling her up."

"Well, you get into yours—your gray suit. It's lucky I changed. If she's half as nice as you say, we shall have to live up to this car."

Reflecting that they must have tea somewhere, David withdrew to their suite and did as Rowena had said. Half an hour later their car had joined twenty-two others, drawn up in rows, and Mr. and Mrs. Bohun were free of the country club.

The famous pleasance of Chiberta was fretted with black and gold. The sun, though low, was so brilliant ; the shadows, though long, were so sharp ; the emerald turf was so vivid ; the myriad pines were so still that the scenery seemed to be that of some monstrous stage. A ridiculous sense of unreality would not retire. On every side perfection delighted the eye : yet colouring, lighting and setting were all theatrical. The flash of a striking villa, sunk in the woods : a lawn like a magic carpet, its sprinkler's leisurely flourish jewelling the air : a bathing-pool like a mirror, framing with marble the elegance which it surveyed . . . Such beauty took David by storm : Rowena was much more inspired by the sight of the twenty-two cars.

Before they left Chiberta that evening, the Bohuns had met twelve people, three of whom were patently women, all of whom seemed to be French. Two of the men could camouflage a few words of English, but, though David and they both tried, the communion achieved was so worthless that further attempts were abandoned by mutual, if tacit, consent. Much was made of Rowena by men and women alike. Her clothes were commended, her style was pronounced charming, her speech superb. She talked very naturally, continually turning to David and translating what had been said, much as a pious daughter trumpets to a deaf parent such tit-bits of conversation as the latter must else have missed. David played the deaf parent and felt the fool of his life : but Rowena's devotion was unmistakable. An invitation to the Casino was presently served in this way, and David, of course, accepted because he could not refuse. Then the talk turned to golf . . . After ten minutes' discussion, husband and wife were invited to view a reach of the links. The offer was submitted to David, who did his best to express surprise and delight. The move was made. Thankful for any release, David followed the others much as a royal detective shadows a prince of the blood engaged with his friends. Now and again, Rowena would glance behind her and throw him a smile—just as she did at night-clubs, when she was dancing and he was sitting alone.

When the inspection was over, Rowena declared they must go, but cocktails were immediately suggested and David's consent was sought.

" I think, perhaps," said Bohun, " we ought to be getting back."

" My husband says ' no '," said Rowena, taking his arm. " I'm afraid he's rather bored and wants to go home."

As they were approaching the cars, one of his wife's cavaliers made Bohun some formal request which the latter could not understand. After a desperate flurry, the interpreter intervened.

" He's asking if he has your permission to request me to make up a foursome to-morrow at eleven o'clock."

" Oh, er, of course," mouthed David, and wiped his face.

Rowena turned to the other.

" My husband gives his consent."

The petitioner bowed to Bohun, who made himself smile . . .

That was the last of his efforts. He simply had not the heart to make any more. His pretty dream was broken. For an hour he had watched it cracking, and now it was smashed. Even he could see what was coming—what was to be the burden of the next ten days. ' The honeymoon will be spent at Biarritz.' He had thought that he was building a castle, and all the time he had really been digging a pit. And now he had fallen in.

As a man in a trance, he saw the car leave its station and steal to their side. He saw the chauffeur descend and open a door. He heard badinage and laughter—one of Rowena's escort was pretending to weep. A great many bows were made—he made some himself. And he shook hands several times, and Rowena's fingers were kissed.

And then they were alone in the car, and were whipping past the wonderful backcloth of forest and lawns and villas and bathing-pools of marble, sunk in the sward. The scene was not quite so striking —the sun was down.

Rowena went straight to the point.

" Well, now that you've got your way, what the hell do we do ? "

As a man who is dazed, her husband put a hand to his head.

" I don't understand," he said slowly.

" That's right. Play the village idiot," was the reply.

David made a gesture of hopelessness.

" I can only assure you," he said, " that I've no idea what you mean."

As one whose patience is threadbare, Rowena expired.

" We were given an invitation which you refused. It was very civilly made. To refuse it was grossly offensive—unless you had a golden excuse. But you didn't want to accept it, and that was enough—for you. You refused to drink with those people, alleging that we ' ought to get back '. And it's now a quarter past six . . . God knows where they think you were bred, but that is beside the point—which is that you've got your way. We are at liberty—for more than two hours and a half. I repeat—What the hell do we do ? "

" I don't know or care," said David. " Whatever you please."

" That's very easy—now that you've got your way."

" I'm sorry if you wanted to stay. You asked me my opinion, and I said that I thought we might go."

" You needn't have bothered," said Rowena, " to clothe your desires in words. Your boredom was painfully obvious to everyone there. You've always been the finest wet-blanket that I ever knew, but to-day you excelled yourself."

" I'm sorry," said David, again. " When you can't talk the language——"

" Two of the men spoke English : you could have talked to them."

" I tried to," said David, " but I couldn't understand what they said."

" I have noticed before," said Rowena, " a convenient inability on your part to do what you do not like."

David said nothing at all, until they approached the hotel.

Then—

" When shall I say," he said, " that you want the car back ? "

Rowena shrugged her shoulders.

" I heard you accept an invitation for half past ten to-night. Of course, if you don't mean to go . . ."

David ordered the car for a quarter past ten.

As the two gained their splendid suite—

" I wish to God," said Rowena, " that in public you'd try and play up. I always do my best, because I was always taught that to advertise domestic dissension was shocking bad form. Coming through the hall just now, you looked like a sulky dog. I suppose the idea is to excite sympathy."

" I'm very sorry," said David. " I suppose I'm—disappointed. That's all."

" Disappointed in me ? "

" Of course not, Rowena. But I'd looked forward so much to our ten days here. I'd hoped that we'd spend them together."

" I assume that we shall," said the girl.

She pitched her hat on to a table, flung herself on to a sofa and took out a cigarette.

" Alone together," said David. " You know. Going out in the car for the day, and that sort of thing."

" What a gorgeous prospect," said Rowena, closing her eyes. " In other words, you were proposing, as usual, to please yourself. What I might want didn't count—never entered your head."

" To tell you the truth," said her husband, " I hoped that you'd like it, too."

"Why lie?" said Rowena, shortly. "You never gave my wishes one single thought. You even tried to prevent me bringing my clubs."

"I didn't try to prevent you. I only asked if you'd need them."

"Exactly," said Mrs. Bohun. "It's called moral pressure, my friend. You were trying your best to squeeze me into leaving my clubs behind. They didn't fit in with your scheme . . . I'm mad about golf. For your sake—because you can't play, from the day we were married I've never lifted a club. Yet you grudge me a chance I might get of playing a round or two of my favourite game."

"You know I don't, Rowena. But I—I like to be with you, you know."

"No one would guess it who'd seen you this afternoon."

David put a hand to his head.

"I can't run with that crowd," he said. "I never could. Quite apart from not speaking French——"

"You mean you're not going to try. They may amuse me: they may amuse everyone else: but that is beside the point—which is that they don't amuse *you*. You see? Wherever we dig, we always get down to the same old stratum of rock. It underlies all we do: and I'm beginning to think that it always will."

There was a little silence. The man had nothing to say. Rowena was a masterly exponent of the best of all methods of defence. Not that David was an opponent: he was a prey. Her right hand was to teach him terrible things.

Presently he glanced at his watch.

"I think perhaps," he said slowly, "I'll go for a walk."

Rowena looked down and away.

"I suppose it's no good asking if you'd like me to come with you," she said.

D

The dog was at her side in a flash.

"My darling, you know I'd love it." He laid his cheek against hers and held her close to his heart. "It's just because I love you so much that I seem so selfish," he said. "You see, I want you all to myself. I——"

"I know. But you must go gently. I gave my freedom up when I married you. I knew what it meant, and I thought it was good enough. Don't make me think it wasn't."

"My sweet, my sweet."

"You've no idea what a change it is for a girl. I, who was free as you are, have given up my freedom and put myself in your power. If you want us both to be happy, don't ride me upon the curb. Let me sometimes taste the freedom I willingly threw away."

"I will, I will. I promise. I only want you to be happy. I love you so."

Rowena gave him her lips.

Satan rebuking Sin should be matter for mirth: but Satan forgiving Sin is a pitiful sight.

Rowena took David's arm as they strolled through the shadowy streets. Subtlest of navigators, she steered him towards the Bar Basque. He was not aware of its existence; but Rowena knew where it was. Together, they regarded its portal. Then—

"That's the best of a husband," said Rowena, pressing his arm. "Would you like to take me inside and give me a drink?"

A glowing David obeyed his heart's desire.

Within, they found two of the people whom they had met at the club. Since each was with a fresh party, more introductions took place and History repeated herself. Broken English and French were toyed with and laid aside. Further and better compliments were paid Rowena, and David munched olives and chips and radiated good humour until his face was stiff.

An hour and a quarter later they made their way back to their rooms.

They dined alone. They left the Casino at one and the night-club that followed at three. They were called at nine—which gave Rowena nice time to breakfast and bathe and dress and be beside the first tee at eleven o'clock.

* * * *

Three days and three nights went by.

Rowena played golf every day and danced every night. Her acquaintance grew very fast and she was in great demand. Almost all of her waking hours were spent with ' a crowd '. David was also present, except on the links.

On the fourth day husband and wife drove into the countryside. The venture was not a success. After they had been moving for nearly an hour, Rowena asked what they were doing and why they were there. David, who made a bad witness, submitted that they ought to see something of the country about.

" I don't think I ought," said Rowena. " It gives me a pain."

" You must admit, my darling——"

" I admit," said Rowena, " that I was a fool to come. If I'm to be comfortable, I can't see out of the car. If I sit on the edge of the seat, I can have a series of close-ups of some of the filthiest farms that I've ever seen. Unless you've a weakness for eyesores, I suppose you proposed to sit still and maul me about. Of course, you're within your rights, but . . ."

White to the lips, her husband picked up the mouthpiece and gave it into her hand.

" Tell him to turn," he said thickly, " and go straight home."

Eight hours later big trouble broke out again. They had left the Casino at midnight and had not 'gone on'—a sin of omission which David had dared to propose. The proposal had been instantly honoured by Mrs. Bohun. As always—in public, his slightest wish was her law. People said right and left that she hung on his lips. In the depths of the *coupé de ville* she had told him what he was fit for in measured terms . . .

" I'm tired," said David, and flung himself down on his bed.

" ' Because thou art virtuous, there shall be no more cakes and ale ? ' "

" I don't think that's fair," said David. " I——"

" What's your idea of fairness ? That I should do as you please ? I'm not your mistress, you know. I bear your name."

David sat up.

" Why talk like that, Rowena. You know——"

" Because you behave as if I was a woman you'd hired. I'm to lead your life—not my own, day in and day out. When you make a suggestion, it's always to do something *you* want. You never suggest doing something you know I should like. I have to suggest that myself—and go in fear and trembling lest you should decide, as to-night, that it isn't what you want to do. Then, again, if you can help it, you never let me out of your sight. I get away for my golf, but that's only because you can't play. If you dared, you'd walk round behind me the whole of the way."

The man started up to his feet.

" If it wouldn't seem funny, I'd do it—you're perfectly right. And why ? *Because I love you.* That's why I like to be with you as much as I can."

His wife expelled breath of contempt.

" That's lust," she said, coolly. " Not love."

" Rowena ! "

The lady shrugged her shoulders.

" If you can't see it yourself, it's obvious to every-one else.   Good God, it's the jest of the place.   ' Hands off my woman ' is written all over your face.   It isn't very pleasant for me : but——"

" Just because last night I said that that scented bounder should keep his hands to himself."

" Yes, and why did he treat me like that ?   Because *you* gave him his cue.   Because he could see how the husband regarded his wife.   He saw that I was your woman—and nothing more."

" You know it's untrue," cried David.   " You know that I love and respect you——"

" I don't.   Nor does anyone else.   For my own pride's sake, I play up.   I try to counteract the impression you always give.   I try to make out that we have an understanding that nobody else can share : and I see them pretend to believe me—and laugh in their sleeves.   Why d'you think they're so nice to me, one and all ?   Because they're sorry for me. Because they can see that I haven't got a square deal."

The man was trembling all over.   Because he had vexed her, because he had made mistakes, his wedded wife—his darling was adopting and using against him the vile conclusions a bunch of wasters drew.   She knew they were false—*knew* it.   But that did not matter to her.   She had need of a scourge.

With a shaking voice, he broke out.

" Rowena, how can you ?   How can you say such things ?   Let others think and say them—what do I care ?   But you know as well as I do how mad about you I am.   You know——"

" Oh, go to Hell," said Rowena.   " When you married me, you installed indoor sanitation ; but that's not love."

With that, she turned to her table, took off and bestowed a brooch, a ring and a wrist-watch, together insured for one thousand two hundred pounds, and then proceeded to fight her way out of her dress.

The man who had paid for all four considered her dazedly.

* * * *

For sickness at heart there are few remedies: but at eight o'clock that morning Bohun received the treatment he most required.

The man had not slept. His mind had defied his body for hour after hour, declining, like some morbid spectator, to move from the scene of his catastrophe. The spectacle was certainly rare. The bottom appeared to have fallen out of his world.

Had his nature been other than it was, had he been less loyal or less simple, less trusting or less sincere, his case would have been less bad. But Rowena had made no mistake. Unkindness might bruise his heart, but this was still hers. At a nod from her, the gulf between them would close. David Bohun was still in love with his wife.

When Sleep had rejected his addresses for nearly five hours, the man left his bed. He shaved and bathed and dressed, while Rowena slept. Then he put a note on her table, to say he had gone for a walk and might not be back before lunch. By seven o'clock he was well on his way to Bayonne.

Knowing no other way, he went by the woods.

Because the dawn is so natural, Chiberta seemed less unreal: but, though the rising sun was arraying the paradise with splendour, lacing the lawns with silver and gilding the gray-green plumes of a thousand pines, Bohun's eyes were too dull to mark the loveliness. He never smelled the fragrance which Night had left: the organ voice of the Atlantic fell on deaf ears. Still, when he had passed the club, he became aware of the virtue of having the world to himself, and when a lorry-load of workmen had rammed this home, he left the smooth highway and took a road that went curling out of his sight.

At the first of its bends, the surface of this became rude, and Bohun began to perceive that here was a slice of the pleasance, ready to be developed, but not yet touched. In this he was right. The roads had been roughly drafted, the mains were laid, but, though notice-boards were commending the purchase of lots, their counsel had not been taken and the lily was innocent of paint.

For half an hour the man wandered, careless of his direction and meeting no one at all to trouble the flow of the waters which were going over his soul. From time to time the drone of an early car would drown for a moment the murmurous thunder of the surf : now and again a cuckoo would make his exquisite boast : but for the most part the sounds which he heard were too distant to distract him from his distress. And then, at eight o'clock, he encountered another being whose acquaintance with grief was plainly closer than his.

Seated alone upon a patch of loose sand was a very, very small dog, that once had been white—a wire-haired terrier-puppy, some two to three months old. Gigantic pines stood over him, a malevolence of briers beset him round, the hollow stump of a tree gaped upon him with its mouth. Burrs were fast in his coat, blood was oozing from one of his tiny pads, the whole of his forehand was caked and plastered with dirt and, what was worse, with the needles the pines had shed. His forelegs propped him, like sheers ; his tongue was out ; and desperation peered from his frantic eyes. Come to the end of his tether, the scrap could go no further and do no more. When David addressed him, he took no notice at all, and when the man stepped to his side, he only bowed his small head, as though in resignation to inhumanity.

"Poor little boy," said David, picking him up.

Some part of the trouble became immediately clear. The pines had been slashed for resin, one and all; and the puppy had had to do with their glutinous yield. His muzzle and paws had passed their fatal plunder to ears and head, and when he had sought relief by wiping them on the ground, he had gathered unto himself whatever he touched. Then he had turned to flight, and, doubtless already lost, had driven along in frenzy, wild to outrun an unkindness of which he had never dreamed. And now the last state of that dog was worse than the first.

"Poor old fellow," said David, wiping the crust of filth away from the hopeless eyes.

As though unable to credit that he was not to receive the *coup de grâce*, the puppy looked fearfully up into Bohun's face. Then, as though asking for mercy, he touched the strong hand with his tongue.

"There's a good boy," said Bohun, removing some more of the filth. "You want some water, don't you? First and foremost, a drink. Nice, cold water, old fellow. And then a good wash and brush-up. My God, you are in a mess . . ."

By now his handkerchief was corrupted. The resin had rendered it viscous. It stuck to his sleeve and his fingers—whatever it touched.

"It's hopeless, old chap," said Bohun. "Water's the only wear. God knows where on earth we'll find some. I know—we'll make for the club."

Assured by the comfortable accents that here at least was a being that meant him no ill, the puppy licked a button of Bohun's coat and settled himself in the crook of his saviour's arm . . .

Together they set out for the highway, Bohun taking his direction from the sound of the passing cars. After a quarter of an hour he saw the tarmac ahead.

As he stepped on to the roadway—

" Now we're all right, old fellow. Another ten minutes, and you'll be out of the wood."

This time there was no response. Now that the danger was past, reaction had set in amain. The poor little scrap was drowsy, if not asleep.

David had sighted the club, when a coupé moving towards him, swept to his side and stopped. A door was flung open and slim bare legs were swung out. Then a girl was standing before him—a girl with rumpled hair and immense blue eyes.

" Oh, Tumble," she cried, " my precious, where *have* you been ? "

At the sound of his mistress's voice, the puppy-dog opened his eyes. Then he gave a delighted wriggle and let out a miniature bark.

As the lady made to caress him, a smiling Bohun put out a warning hand.

" I shouldn't touch him," he said, " until he's been washed. He's quite all right, but he's mucked about with some resin . . ." The girl recoiled. " Exactly. I tried to get some of it off, but you know what it is."

" What a shame. It's all over your coat."

" That's all right," said the man. " We were on our way to the club. They'll give us some water there, and he'll be glad of a drink."

A charming smile swept into the great, blue eyes.

" Tumble and I," said the girl, " can do better than that. Our home is five minutes from here. Besides, we want to thank you. You know what you've done for him, but you've no idea at all what you've done for me."

A moment later the three were within the car.

As this was being turned round—

" Where did you find him ? " said the girl. " They woke me at half past seven to say he'd got out, and when I questioned them they said he'd been gone half an hour. Half an hour's start . . . in these woods . . . Of course I just fell out of bed and into the car. I've been all over the place . . . But I'd next to no hope—he's only a baby dog, and he hardly knows his name."

Bohun told what there was to tell.

When he had done—

"What's the good of trying to thank you? I only hope that one day I'll be able to pay you back. I've only had him three weeks, but he's got me down. He's always so pleased to see me, and—and all his ways are so sweet."

"I'm only thankful," said Bohun, "that I was there. The merest chance, you know. I haven't been out before breakfast for months and months."

"Have you got to get back?"

The eager question flicked David upon the raw.

I will not say that he winced, but the light went out of his eyes.

"Er, no," he said slowly: "I haven't. I'd meant to go on to Bayonne."

"Then do breakfast with us," said the girl; "with my mother and me. I know. If you'll wash Tumble, as you were going to do, I'll have my bath and get up as quick as ever I can. By the time you're through, I'll be ready. We always breakfast at nine."

"All right," said David. "I'd love to. My name's Bohun."

"Mine's Helen Adair, and my mother is Lady Persimmon. She's rather a dear."

With that, she swung off the roadway and into the speckless drive of one of those sparkling villas which Bohun had so much admired.

The 'close up' revealed no fault. The garden was swept and garnished; the hedges were trimmed to a hair; the smooth, close pile of the lawns was perfectly cut; a sash of magnificent tulips girdled the marble basin from which a fountain sprang. As for the villa itself, this might well have been painted the day before. White walls, green shutters, red roof were all without spot or stain. *La Belle Issue* was almost too good to be true.

As the car came to rest on the apron, a bright-eyed *femme de chambre* came pelting out of the house.

" He is found," said her mistress, in French. " We have him here." The other praised God. " This English gentleman found him. But he has played with resin and must not touch or be touched."

" The poor little one."

The maid fussed over Tumble, wriggling in David's arms.

" *Monsieur* is going to finish the work which he has begun : so take him to the spare bathroom and give him all that he needs. And clean his coat. Are the others all out ? "

" But all, *madame*. They have all gone different ways. The *chef* has gone off in tears towards Chambre d'Amour."

" The first to return must go and find the others and tell them he's found. And now take *Monsieur* to the bathroom. He stays to breakfast, of course."

Five minutes later, the bright-eyed maid and Bohun were giving Tumble a bath, Tumble's mistress was staring out of a window, and Lady Persimmon was brushing her soft, white hair.

Her daughter spoke over her shoulder.

" You'll like him, Mo. He's white. But there's something wrong. Some woman, of course. I think he's been hit pretty hard. Between us, we may do something. He saved Tumble—himself he cannot save."

CHAPTER IV

Behind the Scenes

THOUGH Bohun had eyes for no woman except his wife, he would not, I think, have been human if he had not responded to the charm of Helen Adair.

' For beauty lives with kindness.'

The lady was twenty-four and looked twenty-six. This was the sum of the mischief which two bitter years had done : indeed, out of tribulation Helen had drawn a beauty that had not been hers before. Her brow was not lined, her golden hair was not dull ; but the cast of her excellent countenance had been refined. Misfortune had chiselled her features from temple to chin. A steadier light looked out of her glorious eyes ; her gaze itself was more level, the lift of her head more proud. Her nose was more sensitive ; the mould of her cheek was less full ; but the masterstroke had been reserved for her mouth. This very lovely member had taken an exquisite curve—which painters, the moment they saw it, wanted to draw. The impulse of the average layman was more material.

She was slim and supple of body, and not too tall : her head was well set on and her carriage was good. Her limbs were shapely : her legs and her feet were her mother's, her beautiful hands were her own. These were especially fine. Even Bohun remarked them at once. As though to flout the true faith, their nails were not painted red.

He never forgot that breakfast so long as he lived. This was natural. The man was ripe for comfort :

mother and daughter laid themselves out to be nice. So one woman sowed the furrows which another had ploughed.

Lady Persimmon was charming, in blue and white.

" Still life is here our portion, Mr. Bohun. We look to you to make it a conversation piece."

" It is like a picture," said David. " The first time I saw Chiberta, I couldn't believe it was real."

" In weather like this it isn't," said Helen Adair. " It's just a shade too perfect. We three seem to be here, but I doubt if we really exist."

" I exist," said Lady Persimmon. " And very comfortably, too. I lead an existence here. It's a very pleasant change from leading a life. You're staying at Biarritz, Mr. Bohun ? "

" That's right. We've been there for four days and we're staying till Sunday next. You see, I'm a barrister, and I've got to get back."

" Of course," said Lady Persimmon. " Though I have known young men at the Bar whose absence would not be remarked if they were a week or two late."

David laughed.

" I'm in very busy chambers," he said. " It isn't all my own work. But as the time was so short, my wife suggested that we should go and look for the sun."

" Wise girl," said Lady Persimmon. " What have you done with her now ? "

David, who should have been ready, did what he could.

" She's playing golf this morning—not now, you know. But—well, I don't play : so, if I wait till eleven, it—it does my morning in. And I've wanted to see all this part. I've gone by it time and again, going down to the club. But I wanted to walk it, you know."

" And so you decided to do it before the heat of

the day ? How very prudent. And who is in Biarritz now ? And who goes to the club ? "

" I really can't tell you," said David. " I've met quite a lot of people, but I hardly know any names. I'm introduced, you know, but I can't speak French, and—and I find them so hard to get hold of. There's a Madame . . ."

Though Bohun did not know it, the name he contrived to pronounce was a household word. So notorious was its bearer that Lady Persimmon found herself at a loss. Her daughter whipped into the breach.

" I know her by name," she said. " But I may as well confess that we have met next to no one since we've been here. If you'd known how quiet we were, you'd have handed Tumble over and gone on your way to Bayonne."

" No, I shouldn't," said Bohun. " Before you'd had time to invite me, I should have asked myself. I—I simply love being here."

Helen addressed her mother.

" I believe he's like us," she said.

The light came flooding back into Bohun's honest, brown eyes . . .

After breakfast they proved the garden and sat on the sunlit terrace at the back of the house. Helen and David and Tumble enjoyed a three-ball match. Lady Persimmon remembered Lord Elvin well, and David spoke of Jeffreys and his work at the Chancery Bar. Coming to Curzon Street, he magnified Rowena —with a hunted look on his face. Helen led him away to the country which he had hoped to see—mountains and falling water and hanging woods, and baby cities, set on the tops of hills. Then travel by air was discussed. David had his pilot's certificate : but for his marriage he would have had his aeroplane. But Rowena was not ' air-minded '. Helen had flown for years.

At eleven he got to his feet and said he must go.

Helen Adair, brushing Tumble, looked up from her task.

"Where to? Bayonne? I'll take you. I've got to go in."

"You're terribly kind."

"What rot. I'll tell you what. While I'm doing what I've got to do, you can look at the town. Then I'll drive you back to Biarritz the other way."

"I can't let you do that," said David.

"Three miles out of my way. What an awful thing."

"Good-bye, Lady Persimmon."

"Good-bye, Mr. Bohun. I wasn't too bad before, but you've done me a world of good. You must bring your wife next time. We'll send her a note."

The shining visit was over . . .

As they passed the club, Helen Adair saw David peer at the waiting cars : with the tail of her eye, still talking, as women can, she saw him discover the car he was looking for : and, as he discovered it, she saw the light in his eyes flare up, as the flame of a candle, and then go out. The lady set her white teeth—and had brought the light back to his eyes before they had reached Bayonne.

They did not part in the town. The good-looking *coupé* berthed, they made their way together down busy, cobbled channels that once were streets, threaded low-pitched arcades and watched an aged bookbinder doing his patient work. The bench which he was using must have been old and worn when the bayonet received its name. Helen matched some tapestry wool and procured a glass for her watch. Slight as her purchases were, the tradespeople sprang to serve her and seemed to sleek themselves in her friendly smile. She had not Rowena's accent, but plainly spoke French very well. Something to his surprise, David found himself able to comprehend what she said.

When they had surveyed the cathedral, they strolled on the pleasant ramparts for half an hour—a place of lights and shadows and sudden airs, of the gray of old stone and the tremble of tender green.

"You like all things old," said Helen.

"I love them," said David, warmly. "I don't know why. I've got an old coffer in Chambers—in Lincoln's Inn. Nobody knows where it came from, but it's plainly terribly old. And I can't tell you the pleasure I get out of that old box. I think of the smith who made it and the merchant for whom it was made : the latter in doublet and hose, with the door of the chamber barred and the curtains drawn——"

"Down on his knees," said Helen, "his bearded chin on his shoulder, the candles beside the coffer lighting his shrewd, old face."

"That's right," cried David, glowing. "How did you know?"

His companion laughed her rare laugh.

"I'm afraid we've the same complaint. To tolerant people, like Mo, it's known as romance. It doesn't worry us and it isn't in the least infectious, but if we let it appear, it gives other people a pain. Of course, I'm awful. Do you know Italy?"

The man shook his head.

"I hope to—one day."

"You'll love it. It's terribly old and it's lovely —wherever I've been. You can break your shins over beauty. If six hundred years ago an Italian blacksmith was ordered to make an iron bar to be stuck on the edge of a quay—well, he made a beautiful bar. And Nature plays up. The mountain-sides of Como . . ." The speaker drew in her breath. "Don't think I'm not mad about England. I am, and I always was. But there are some things abroad that you can't have anywhere else."

"Like Chiberta."

"That's right. Chiberta's unique. And half of

it's atmosphere. You can't take Chiberta to bits . . ."

She was standing still, as she spoke, looking down on the town. The eyes of the man beside her were fast on her eager face. Talking of beauty . . .

With a shock, Bohun realized that he found her a lovely thing. For one frightful moment, Rowena stood by her side . . . and Echo breathed in his ear.

Rowena's unique. And half of it's atmosphere. You can't take Rowena to bits.

The man looked away and struck his spurs into his mind. This responded at once. There was nobody like Rowena. She was his wife. Helen Adair would be the first to admit it. Wait till she saw Rowena, and see her fall down and worship, like everyone else. Besides, comparisons were odious. There *was* no comparison.

Bohun began to feel mean. Rowena should have been sharing these shining hours—instead of playing golf with a fellow who couldn't keep his hands to . . . The reflection snapped off short, and that terrible bedroom scene rose up, as hideous as ever, to make the sunlight gray.

Helen saw Bohun flinch—and felt a sudden anger for the woman she did not know. The man was so honest and simple, so grateful, so anxious to please. It was like some brute of a carter thrashing a willing horse.

" Shall I tell you something ? " she said.

The man's head came round.

" I mean, I think you should know why Mo and I are leading so strange a life. You're the first person we've talked to for more than a month."

" I never gave it a thought."

" You wouldn't. That's why we like you. The truth is—I've been through the hoop. I had to divorce my husband . . . six months ago." She shrugged her shoulders. " These things happen, you know . . . And now I'm out of the wood. I'm not even licking my wounds—I've no wounds to lick. At the time I thought that the world had come to an end : but I realize now that I was being tempered— held in the flame. And I'm miles the better for it . . . But that's by the way. Only you've told us all about you, and I thought it only fair that you should know all about me."

David spoke as he felt.

" I'm so thankful you're happy again."

" That's a very nice thing to say."

" You know I mean it," said Bohun.

" You don't have to tell me that."

The smile that went with that saying lifted up David's heart.

Then an aeroplane soared out of heaven, to circle above the town and guide their conversation into the way of flight.

They made their way back to where the car had been berthed . . .

In fact, the car was in sight, when David perceived a florist's a little way off.

" You go on," he said. " I won't be a moment."

He ran to the shop and looked round. Some glorious, yellow roses were diminishing everything else. He bought two dozen forthwith and hurried back to the car. As he got in, he laid them on the top of the locker behind the seat. Then he shut his door, and wiped the sweat from his face.

As the *coupé* stole into the stream—

" Sorry," he said. " I—I wanted to get you some flowers."

Helen Adair said nothing, but, directly the traffic allowed, she brought the car to rest at the side of the street.

" Let me see them, please."

" They're nothing at all, I——"

"I don't care. I want to see my present."

Shamefacedly, Bohun produced it. Whilst he held the stems, Helen withdrew the pins and uncovered the blooms.

She considered them, smiling and holding the paper away : then she bent her head to smell their exquisite scent : then she looked up and round.

"I simply love them," she said. "How could I do anything else ? "

Flushed with pleasure, Bohun laid them away . . .

As they ran into Biarritz—

"When I get home," said Helen, "I'll write a note to your wife. But it's no good my asking you when you know you're engaged. What about dinner to-morrow ? Or are you booked ? "

"Oh, no, I don't think so," said David. "I—I can't be sure, but . . ."

The thought of refusing to dine at *La Belle Issue*, in order that they might be able to run with the crowd, deprived him of speech. ' And another said I have bought *a bunch of baboons* and I go to prove them : I pray thee have me excused.'

"We've got till Sunday," said Helen. " You won't be engaged every night."

"Good lord, no," said David.

"Then that's all right. We've no engagements at all."

She set him down three minutes later, at the mouth of the busy drive.

The fine, blue eyes held his, as the beautiful hand came out.

"Good-bye for now," she said, smiling. "Thank you again for being so good to Tumble and thank you once again for my pretty flowers."

"Please don't," said David. "Don't thank me. I—I owe you so much."

"Don't be silly," said Helen, gently. "I mean, between friends . . ."

She smiled and was gone.

The man stared after the car, with light in his eyes.

* * * *

The two women met and passed on the sunlit road. Neither saw the other, for their cars were going too fast. But each of them was thinking of David Bohun.

Rowena was in high good humour. David's withdrawal had shown that the punch which she had landed had knocked him out. When they met, she had one point to make, before they were reconciled. This was that she stood, like iron, by every word she had spoken before they had gone to bed. If she had spoken bluntly, that was because he had trodden for week after week on what, he ought to have known, was a woman's most sensitive corn. She had said what she had in good faith : to her mind, the charges were proved. If he really wished to disprove them, then he must show her—and show other people, too —that he looked upon her as nothing less than his wife. When he asked how he could best demonstrate this truth, she would explain to him that the obvious step to take was to leave a party that bored him and let her stay on. An almost more obvious step was not to attend . . . In that way, little by little, the loathsome impression created might be removed. ' It'll take time, of course. I want to be fair to you. In view of what you've said, I'll do my utmost to keep an open mind. But I warn you, I shall take some convincing—and so will everyone else.' Mrs. Bohun's wedges had no thin end.

As the *coupé de ville* came to rest, a wistful look slid into her soft brown eyes . . .

All went according to plan. David had a dreadful ten minutes—and would have had more, but Rowena wanted her lunch. She sat in judgment upon him, heard his stumbling excuses and watched him swallow the sentence she presently passed.

The thing was as good as a play.

With his head in his hands, the man rocked.

"That *you* should believe this, Rowena! That *you*, my wife—my darling . . ."

"I'm sorry. It's not my fault. You've done nothing but ram it home. If you mean what you say——"

"I do, I do—you must know it."

Rowena sighed.

"Well, it's up to you," she said, simply.

Then she walked into the bathroom, to wash her hands.

As on a more famous occasion, the act was symbolical. So far as she was concerned, the matter was closed.

Upon her return, however, David was still too much shaken to be paraded at lunch—a vexatious, if sterling tribute to her ability. She, therefore, resigned herself to having her cocktail upstairs and commended a brandy and soda for his infirmity. This medicine she reinforced with a matter-of-fact relation of what she herself had done since she saw him last and then—to fill up five more minutes—she asked him where he had been.

When he said he had 'met some people', she pricked up ears. What could be better? Whilst she was receiving addresses, he could be 'mucking about' with his new-found friends.

"Fancy you." She hardly suppressed the sneer. And then, "Did you get their names?"

"Yes. One's called Mrs. Adair. And her mother ——"

"*Adair?* Not *the* Adair? Oh, it can't be true."

David opened his eyes.

"I don't know about *the* Adair. They've a villa called *La Belle Issue*. They gave me breakfast there, and——"

"They gave him breakfast," said Rowena, and covered her eyes.

Her husband stared.

"I don't know what you're getting at. I can only tell you——"

"Try and get this," said Rowena. "That you have gone and gate-crashed where half the nobility of Europe is fighting and biting and scratching to slime its way in. The 'people you met' this morning were Lady Persimmon and her daughter, Mrs. Helen Adair. Last year she divorced her husband—he's always known as 'Bugle': he used to be in The Tins. But she's still got her income all right. Her grandfather settled that on her and tied it up. Good American dollars. Five hundred thousand a year."

"I'd no idea," said David. "She's very simple and nice. She's writing a note to you, to ask us to go to dinner to-morrow night."

"Glory be," said Rowena. "I give you best. I'll sow the good news this evening. I'm afraid the ground may be stony: but I'll bet it takes root all right. My God, how sick they'll all be. Mr. and Mrs. Bohun are dining with the Adair."

Her glee would have been less rampant, could she have heard the discussion proceeding some four miles off.

Helen Adair was leaning against a table, and Lady Persimmon was sitting up in a chair. Between the two of them, Tumble, in fair round belly, was gazing dejectedly upon the platter which he himself had made bare.

"It's a wicked show," said Helen.

"That's clear as paint," said her mother. "The wolf's gone to live with the lamb. The trouble is that the lamb is in love with the wolf."

Helen Adair nodded.

"No doubt about that. But it's really dreadful to

see. It's cruelty to animals, Mo. I mean, he isn't fair game."

"I agree," said Lady Persimmon. "He's like a sweet-natured dog. He takes for granted that his mistress can do no wrong—a fatal postulate. When she's brutal, he grieves—because he's offended his goddess and caused her pain."

"Oh, don't," said her daughter, wincing. She stooped to pick up Tumble and hold him close to her heart. "Why is it always the best that get so terribly stung?"

"That's easy," sighed Lady Persimmon. "Because they can always be trusted to play the game. If you mean to kick a man in the stomach, the obvious thing is to choose one that won't kick you back. By the way, does he know about—us?"

"I told him something—I thought it might do him good. But it only did *me* good—he spoke so nicely at once."

"That I can well believe. I don't know when I've liked a young man so much."

"And then those roses," said Helen. "He was so shy about them. He's not in the habit of giving women flowers."

"Full marks to you," said her mother.

"In a way. But that's not the point. He'd no idea whatever of paying a compliment. He did it out of nice feeling. It was just the way of his heart. I mean, I could see it all happen. You *can't* abuse instinct like that."

"Oh, yes, you can," said the other. "And you get your millstone all right in the world to come. But that doesn't help your victim. He's got to dree his weird. And now go on. Say it."

"Can't we do anything, Mo?"

"Nothing, my darling. I don't have to tell you that. If he was a dog, we could buy him. If he was a horse or a mule, we could go to the police. But cruelty to loving husbands is one of those states of affairs which we are bound to ignore. Even if you were a man, you couldn't possibly come between husband and wife. But being a woman . . . but being Helen Adair . . . I suppose we must ask them to dinner."

"You needn't worry," said Helen. "Before I asked you, I knew the answer by heart. We can do nothing, and I can do rather less. As a matter of fact, no woman will ever wreck that home."

Lady Persimmon nodded.

"That's a true saying," she said. "His wife may break his heart, but he'll never let her down."

"What a ghastly thought," said Mrs. Helen Adair.

* * * *

That Lady Persimmon and her daughter should both have split so neatly the wand of truth by no means argues that they were unearthly shrewd. There was no guile in Bohun. The man could be read like a book. And that morning the book had been open at a very unfortunate page. That was Rowena's fault. She had hit her husband so hard that the page which should have been turned in two or three hours remained open for twelve. And so it was read—by Mrs. Adair and her mother, without any effort at all. Its report was confirmed by the severally innocent facts which Bohun himself had disclosed. His wife's belief in a game which he did not play . . . their association with people with whom he could not converse . . . his obvious ignorance of the nature and quality of the company which they kept . . . But the greatest factor of all was that *neither the one nor the other had ever seen Mrs. Bohun.* Had they met the Bohuns together or seen her first, I beg leave to doubt that, open book or no, they would have suspected the truth. Rowena disarmed suspicion. But knowledge you cannot disarm. And mother and daughter *knew*. Unknown to Rowena, against her inviolable rule, they had been suffered to pass behind the scenes.

When, therefore, they met the lady upon the following day, they were not only not deceived, but profoundly shocked. Such wickedness had not been dreamt of in their philosophy. The reflection that, but for their private view, they must have been duped, made them feel weak at the knees. Rowena's naïveté, her submission unto her husband, her peeping love for David, her innocent revelation of a self-denying instinct of which she was unaware—these things disclosed a practised treachery which far more than met the requirements of married life. It became immediately clear that Bohun was but a rung, that his wife was proposing to rise . . . on the stepping-stone of his dead self . . . to higher things.

For the man's sake, the two played up : but virtue went out of them, and when the Bohuns left at eleven o'clock, Helen Adair was limp in body and soul.

Her mother shall speak for herself.

" Give me a brandy and soda. I feel all in." She lay back and closed her eyes. " I know I only ' walked on ', but I'm not accustomed to playing in Grand Guignol . . . That woman's a ghoul."

" And the man ? " said Helen, busy with bottle and glass.

" Is doomed," said Lady Persimmon. " Out of his faithful heart. No one on earth can save him. They can have what's left, of course, if that's any good."

Helen Adair said nothing. She dared not trust her voice.

* * * *

As may be supposed, another inquest was opened and held in the *coupé de ville.*

" My dear," cried Rowena, " how priceless ! You've got right off."

" What ever d'you mean ? " said David.

" What I say. The Adair—well, likes you."

(Rowena, who made no mistakes, had almost put a foot wrong.)

" I don't suppose she does for a moment. After all——"

" What I mean," said Rowena, " is this." She slid a bare arm through his. " The Adair is renowned for taking no notice of men. And to think that she's noticed my husband—well, any girl would be proud."

" You're very sweet, Rowena."

He found her hand and put it up to his lips. As he kissed the fingers, he felt them close about his.

" She's worth keeping up with, David—a girl like that. Not for her money—for herself. I'd like to be friends with her . . . more than with any woman I've ever seen."

The man's heart thrilled to the lie.

" I'm so terribly glad, my darling. She—she does show the others up, doesn't she ? "

" They don't exist beside her. But I can't do it alone. You'll have to help me, David—she's more at her ease with you. You'll have to make the running. D'you see what I mean ? "

" Not quite. Why shouldn't we——"

" She's shy of all women—that's why. She can't forget that a woman took her husband away . . . I saw it and felt it the moment I entered the room. It isn't her fault. I'd be exactly the same."

Lie upon lie.

" Can't altogether blame her," said David.

" It's natural. So I can do nothing. I'd only frighten her off. But I think she'll make friends with you, if you put out your hand. And in that way, little by little, she'll come to be friends with me. It may take time, but it's worth it—from my point of view. I've never had a real friend, and she's such a splendid type. She's right up to date, and yet she's decent and stable—just look at those eyes."

The words were the words of David, though the voice was Rowena's voice. The man recognized them excitedly.

"That's just how I feel about her." Rowena almost laughed. "Oh, Rowena, I *am* so glad. And I'll do my very utmost, my darling . . . D'you think they'll ask us again?"

"They'll hardly do that. But you can go and ask after Tumble, while I'm playing golf. Not to-morrow, of course—on Friday. I mean, that's natural enough. You're at a loose end for two hours, and if you drive down with me, you'll be almost next door."

"I don't want to shove myself in."

"D'you think I'd let you do that? But I want you to put out your hand. She'll come to you, if you do. And then, when she's got to know you, she'll come to me."

"I'd love you to be friends," said the man.

"Well, it's up to you."

More was to come. When the car reached the hotel, to Bohun's surprise and relief the lady advised him to send the chauffeur to bed.

"I don't want to go on," she lied. "Not after *La Belle Issue*. The contrast would be too sharp. I know I like running round, but I've still got a palate left. And I can't drink ice-cream soda after a vintage wine. And I'll tell you another thing. If I got to know the Adair, I shouldn't want to go out."

Trust Mrs. David Bohun to drive a nail home.

His heart too full for words, her husband once again put her hand to his lips.

Two minutes later they entered their splendid suite . . .

Alone in the sumptuous bathroom, she set her back

to the door and moistened her lips. Her glittering eyes saw nothing—that was to be seen.

"My trick, I think," she said softly. "And I guess I'll make a few more—you insolent bitch. Didn't like the look of me, did you ? Not good enough for His Nibs, The Sobstuff King ? Well, you try and get him, Pansy. Not his heart—his body, my dear. It'll keep him out of mischief and be damned good for your soul. Nothing like continence, darling. And if you try hard enough—well, you never know. But I guess you'd part with a packet before you'd come into Court."

* * * *

David went to *La Belle Issue* on Friday—after a trying night. (He had left Rowena at one, and she had come in, bridling, at half past three.) Lady Persimmon was shopping, but Helen was there.

"How nice of you to come," she said gently. "Tumble and I were so hoping we'd see you again."

The brown eyes reflected the light which they had lit in the blue.

The two hours went by very fast . . .

As the man said good-bye—

"If you come to-morrow," said Helen, "you'll find Mo here. I know for a fact she'd like to see you again."

"I'd love to come," said David. "Please give her my love."

When he arrived the next morning, Helen Adair was abroad. This, to a disappointment he did his best to conceal. After all, he was due to leave Biarritz the following day. But Lady Persimmon was charming, and Helen returned to the villa at half past twelve.

The half-hour fled . . .

Then David made much of Tumble and threw a look round the haven which he would see no more.

" Good-bye Lady Persimmon."

" Good-bye and good luck, David Bohun. If I know anything of you, you'll be glad to see Lincoln's Inn."

" Yes—in a way. Good-bye."

Helen walked with him through the cool house and on to the smooth, brown drive.

" What time are you leaving to-morrow ? "

" By the evening train," said David.

" If you're free to-morrow morning, why don't you walk down to La Barre. It's only just over there. When the tide's coming in, it's worth seeing. I often walk there on Sundays . . ."

The man's heart leaped.

He saw her on Sunday morning, when he was yet a great way off, standing still on the yellow shore of a fabulous sea. Her head was bare, and the breeze was at play with her curls and her short-sleeved dress : she seemed to belong to the sunshine and gallant air, and the glorious company of rollers seemed to be doing her homage, prostrating themselves before her and creeping to where she stood.

For an hour they watched the pageant—first the unending battle waged between river and sea, and then the long march of ocean against the strand. Three times they saw a rare beauty—fishes at play, darting the length of a breaker the instant before it broke, enshrined, as bees in amber, in the lucid ribbon of water directly beneath the foam.

Rowena was scarcely mentioned in all they said. This was not Bohun's fault. He spoke so handsomely of her that Helen Adair could not stand it and steered the conversation away. She found that he had next to no friends and went no more to his club. ' Now I'm married, I don't have time. Not that I want to, you know.' The decline and fall of the Cadnams was haltingly told. ' They'd been there so long that I'd got used to his faults. Of course, that's a fatal mistake. I'm afraid I'm rather like that—I let things go.' The man was on surer ground when he spoke about Lincoln's Inn. The girl led him on to speak of his life at the Bar. That, at least, was his own. (She did not have to be told that Rowena had never touched it, and never would; that to hear of it bored her to extinction—at one time, to David's distress.) When he found that she cared to listen, he made her free of his Chambers and more than one Chancery Court: they shared the salt of Judges, the whims of eminent Counsel, the mirth of the Junior Bar.

The hour was gone in a moment . . .

When it was time to be going, the man felt suddenly cold.

" I hate saying good-bye," he said slowly. A hand went up to his head. " I can't tell you what it's meant to me to—to be with you like this."

Helen lifted her lovely head to stare at the sky.

" The yoke of idealism is heavy. When two of the oppressed get together, it does them both good."

David produced a smile.

" Mrs. Adair," he said, " is being polite."

The answer came, quick as a flash.

" Perhaps. But Helen isn't. You ought to know by now that she means what she says."

The bruised heart leapt to a note it had never heard.

" I'm too shy. I can't say your name. When I get back, I'll write it."

" I'm ashamed of you, David. If I can do it, you can."

He put out his hands for hers, and she gave him both.

" Good-bye, Helen. Don't forget there's a place called London."

" You must write and remind me. Take care of yourself. Good-bye."

He left her where he had found her, beside the superb allegro of sea and sun, and hastened back through the woods to the country club.

That Rowena kept him waiting, David was ashamedly glad. He needed time to recover. He seemed to have brushed against something—some high emotion he could not share with his wife. Not love, of course—Rowena had all his heart. But something that was stronger than he was—some force, perhaps, that only idealists knew . . .

Obeying a natural instinct, he entered a changing-room and laved his hands and his head.

Ten minutes later the *coupé de ville* slid on to the Biarritz road.

" And how's the Adair ? " said Rowena.

" She couldn't have been nicer," said David.

" Good for you. Have you got to Christian names yet ? "

" Er, just."

" My dear, you're a giddy marvel. And when is she coming to Town ? "

" She doesn't know."

" Never mind. But you must keep her warm. Write to her from your Chambers, but never from Curzon Street. If she thinks I'm on in this scene, you won't see her for dust. I'll lay she sent me no message."

" To be honest, I don't think she did."

" What did I tell you ? All women are off her list. Well, well . . ." Rowena sighed. " As I told you on Wednesday night, if I'm to be friends with her, it's up to you. I give you a free hand, David—I couldn't be jealous of her. You must go your own way about it and take your time. I shall try and forget about her—until you can come and tell me to ask her to dine with *us*."

Receiving such a broadside, a finer reason than Bohun's might well have gone down. The man was given no choice. Rowena had kicked his conscience into the way of peace.

* * * *

While the Bohuns were crossing Paris the following day, a magnificent basket of lilies reached Mrs. Adair.

Helen glanced at the card which was with them and then at her watch. Five minutes later, she and the exquisite blooms were on their way to Bayonne.

The good women to whom she gave them, were vastly obliged—and endeavoured to deny the reflection that the money which the basket had cost would have fed their twenty-five charges for more than two days.

Helen returned more slowly than she had gone. The duty which lay before her was less to her taste than the pleasure which lay behind.

Still, the thing had to be done . . .

Arrived at the villa, she sat down and wrote a short note. This rendered her thanks for the flowers—to the woman whom she detested, whose husband she loved.

CHAPTER V

Consommation Obligatoire

FORSYTH, solicitor, glanced at the clock upon his table and picked up again the report which he had already read.

Private and Confidential.

Mrs. B.

This lady and her husband have been spending some days at Biarritz and are returning to-day.

I am satisfied that any attempt to get in touch with the servants at Curzon Street or even to watch the house would be not only ineffectual but dangerous, for the butler is of Chinese extraction and the other servants have been procured by him. Inquiries in the neighbourhood reveal that he is as silent as he is noticing.

It is unfortunate that the opportunity of surveillance at Biarritz has been lost, but I suggest that careful inquiry should be made there while Mrs. B.'s visit is still fresh in the memory of hotel servants etc.

G. C.

29th April.

As he laid the paper down, Mr. Chater's arrival was announced.

" I'll see him at once," said Forsyth.

Twenty seconds later the agent entered the room.

As a private detective, George Chater was not exceptional. He had no imagination, frequently failed to see the obvious and could have solved no problem which fairly deserved that name. As an inquiry agent, however, he had his points. He was cautious, painstaking and faithful, delighted to do as he was told and reported nothing but the truth. Then, again, he chose his assistants well.

The solicitor smiled and nodded.

"Good morning, Chater. Sit down. First, as regards Biarritz. I'm sorry we missed that chance, but it can't be helped. As you suggest, you must see what you can pick up there without delay. In fact, I haven't much hope, for the French hotel looks ahead. Customers are worth keeping : questioners aren't. So I rather think you'll draw blank—though, of course, you must try. And now what about this butler ? I find him strange."

"He's certainly unusual," said Chater : "and a very great stumbling-block from our point of view."

"Have you seen him yourself ? "

"No, sir. One of my men has seen him, and in view of his report I judged it best that I should keep out of the way."

The solicitor frowned.

"I think you should see him yourself : if you make the most of a taxi, he needn't see you."

"Very well, sir," said Chater, obediently.

"D'you know where he came from ? " said Forsyth.

"Nobody knows," said Chater. "He just appeared. I understand he's been there about two months."

"Before his arrival," said Forsyth, "the Bohuns had a man and his wife. I never saw the woman, but I remember the man. They'd been with Mr. Bohun some time—I should say some two or three years. Get on to them, will you ? And see what they have to say."

"I will indeed, sir," said Chater. "At least, I'll put a man on. I rather think I should go to Biarritz myself."

"Unquestionably," said Forsyth. "What's more, if you take my advice, you'll stay where the Bohuns stayed and spend your time in the bar. Get to know the bar-tender, Chater. He's more likely to help you than anyone else."

"Very good, sir," said Chater. And then, "That's going to cost a good deal."

"That can't be helped," said Forsyth . . .

Within ten days he received a further report.

Private and Confidential.

Mrs. B.

According to your instructions, I visited Biarritz last week and spent three days as a guest at The —— Hotel.

I had no difficulty in encouraging the bar-tender and others to talk about this lady. All were loud in her praise. Her conduct seems to have been above reproach and her devotion to her husband is insisted upon. More than once I was given to understand that sympathy was felt for her because the consideration he showed her did not merit the devotion he received. I was told that he had left her to herself a good deal and was believed to have his own friends. It was said that he had been seen in the company of another woman, but without his wife.

On my return, I found that Mr. and Mrs. Cadnam, who were recently in service at Curzon Street, had been traced and interviewed. It proved easy to get them to talk of Mr. and Mrs. Bohun. For Mr. Bohun they had not a good word to say. It was apparently he who had dismissed them against Mrs. Bohun's will. If they are to be believed, he gave them no reason, except that he wished to make a change. Mrs. Bohun could do nothing with him, but thanks to her efforts they have obtained a comfortable place. According to the Cadnams, she is an ideal wife and always puts her husband before herself. Mr. Cadnam insisted that she had 'spoiled' him.

G. C.

May 8th.

This further report shook Forsyth, as well it might. He had asked for bread, had expected a stone, and had been given a serpent. The paradox plagued him all day and when, after dinner that evening, he gave his mind to the 'labour' which he had sworn to perform, a full two hours went by before that distinguished member had found a way to proceed. The next morning he summoned Chater and thanked him for having done 'such excellent work'. Then he gave him careful instructions, not one of which concerned Mrs. David Bohun.

* * * *

From Rowena's point of view the visit to Biarritz had been an outstanding success. She had, of course, intended to have a good time, and she had expected trouble with which she would have to deal. Not only had she had a better time than she had intended, but the trouble, which had duly appeared, had brought forth most kindly fruit.

Let me put it like this.

Rowena was well aware of the value of compassion. To be generally liked was good—so far as it went : but for people to be sorry for a favourite strengthened the favourite's position beyond belief. To a wife whom everyone liked, for whom everyone was sorry, all things were possible. Very well. Rowena, taking care to be liked, had set herself to achieve sympathy. The trouble was that David was a likable man—not a man for whose wife one would be sorry, in the ordinary way . . . Her underlip caught in her teeth, Rowena had given the problem much anxious thought. She

had herself done what she could. She had scourged
her husband in secret : but the man had steadfastly
declined to reward her openly. She had lied about
him discreetly : she had lost no occasion of putting
him in a bad light : but, though she had made some
progress, she could not get away from the fact that
David could do in six weeks what she might not do
in five years. In a word, the sympathy she hoped to
achieve was his to bestow. *And now, my God, the man
was going to bestow it.* And that, with both hands
. . . To prove that he was not possessive—in a
very unpleasant sense, to disabuse the world (and his
wife) of the ugly belief that he held that her body
was his, her husband was going to ' neglect ' her,
ostentatiously leave her alone. As if that were not
enough, he was going to pursue a liaison—not with
some inconspicuous baggage, but *with the Adair* . . .
Had Rowena been Louis XI, she would certainly have
praised God. (That she did not is scarcely to her
credit. Louis went in unwholesome fear of his Maker,
but Rowena had no such failing. Her conscience had
died young.)

I have said that she had ' had a good time '. This
was a fact—and the lady was hard to please. Whether
she deserved it or not is another matter : what is
quite certain is that she owed her ' good time ' to
herself.

Bursting suddenly upon a workless society which
custom is beginning to stale, any alluring woman who
knows how to dress and dance should meet with
success. But add to sex-appeal the innocence of a
child . . . It will be remembered that Rowena had
achieved artlessness. This was a tremendous asset.
Her naïveté disarmed the women and stimulated the
men. Much of the attention paid her would have
embarrassed a matron who liked her fun and would
have been fiercely rejected by a professed courtesan :
but the *ingénue* accepted it joyously. When she was

outrageously handled, the eager playmate assumed it was part of the game. Mrs. Bohun's performance was faultless : her innocence was impregnable : people supposed that her husband must be out of his mind . . . Rowena enjoyed herself vastly—as knowing nothing, and yet aware of all things.

Returning to Curzon Street, David had the definite feeling that he was off his course. He was out of tune with Rowena, in tune with Helen Adair. But while he thanked God for Helen, he would have dismissed her twice over to be in tune with his wife.

Reviewing his fall from grace, the man found himself to blame. That he knew nothing of women was not, perhaps, his fault ; but ignorance in life, as in law, was no excuse. He had thought that marriage was simple, that, given mutual affection, any fool could succeed in the married state. Punch and Belinda were most happy : it had never entered his head that this was due to Punch's discernment—a prudent understanding which he did not himself possess. The prayer-book, of course, was misleading : it made wedlock look straightforward—a matter of sharing with another and thereby doubling what one had. But he might have known that that was no more than an outline . . . Rowena's words came to his mind —' You've no idea what a change it is for a girl.' It was true. He had had no idea. This, to his shame . . . His teeth clenched hard upon his pipe, Bohun wished to God that he could call back time. His darling, the weaker vessel, had committed herself to his care—and before four months were past, he had let her down. It suddenly dawned upon him that here was the reason for all her *exigence*. Convinced that the man she had married knew only bodily love, that all his attentions were tainted, that she was a glorified mistress and nothing more : hugging her filthy secret. only to read its reflection in strangers' contemptuous eyes : fighting to disabuse them of what she knew was the truth . . . Bohun grew hot with shame. Little wonder that, bearing this cross, Rowena was *difficile*. The man declared with an oath that he would put matters right. Talk about correcting impressions . . . He would blind her and everyone else with the vivid fact that they had been utterly wrong, that he simply had no use for the lusts of the flesh. It would not be easy : but the way of the transgressor was hard. It would be his penance for being a blundering fool.

Remembering Helen Adair, the man was comforted. There was a friend—and more. There was something on which Rowena had set her heart. ' I'd like to be friends with her . . . more than with any woman I've ever seen.' Very well. She should have her wish. It would be his privilege to bring her her heart's desire. He saw the two girls together, making each other free of their exquisite attributes. He saw Helen at Curzon Street, at ease with them both, taking Rowena's side in light-hearted argument. He saw them about together and Lady Persimmon a slave to Rowena's charm . . . By bringing these visions to life, he would atone for the wrong which a fool in his folly had done a sensitive wife. Here was no penance, but rather a labour of love—to improve a precious friendship, to accomplish an understanding with Helen Adair . . . Bohun's heart burned within him and the light came into his eyes. Theirs was a strange relation and one which he would have sworn could never exist. Rowena had all his heart—no doubt about that : yet he was attached to the other —frankly and deeply attached to another girl. And Rowena knew and approved. ' I give you a free hand, David—I couldn't be jealous of her.' How was that for fine comprehension ? Not one woman in fifty thousand would have displayed so rare a senti- ment. By God, he had much to be thankful for. If he was off his course, at least he knew what he was doing and where he was making for. Meanwhile there was Lincoln's Inn—and a longer row of briefs than he had any right to expect.

*   *   *   *

Let who will cast a stone at David Bohun. Of course the man was a fool: but, while honesty obscured his outlook, his blind faith in his darling delivered him into her hands. He made his betrayal so easy that Rowena, often enough, had much ado to conceal her rising contempt. This was, of course, unfair. As well despise the dog that begs for the poisoned cake which his master holds. But, fair or unfair, the curious fact remains. Much as the borrower can never forget or forgive the timely loan, so Mrs. Bohun found it increasingly hard to suffer the fool she was making of her idolater. She had bruised his heart for her good: she continued to chasten her consort partly because the habit had taken hold, but mainly to slake her impatience of his credulity.

*   *   *   *

To return hospitality is, four times out of five, the act of a fool. What shall it profit a mug, if he shall lose the whole world, and keep his own soul? The fifth time it is a gilt-edged investment.

David was not aware of these truths: Rowena was.

" But, my darling, we owe them——"

" What the devil does it matter if we do? If they like to continue to ask us, that's their look-out."

" I know. But I hate being under an obligation."

" You aren't. There's no such thing. Obligations went out with family prayers."

" But——"

" Can you get this? If we were to ask them back, they'd write us off."

The lady knew her world. Because she has been offered a guerdon, many a goose has stopped laying her golden eggs. ' We can't possibly ask the Fenwicks —they'll ask us back.' But give the goose a drink when and where she happens to raise a thirst, and you will increase her output out of all knowledge. ' And the Fenwicks, of course. Who else ? ' What is manifestly so difficult is to be at hand with a drink at the right moment. And the geese that lay golden eggs are as inconsiderate as they are exacting.

Rowena had early perceived that Curzon Street was geographically convenient to the consumption of liquor in the late afternoon. It possessed the inestimable advantage of being more or less ' on the way '. She had therefore set herself to study the ' sherry party ' with infinite care. This must not be too big, yet never too small : the service must be deft, yet unobtrusive : the victuals, rare. The liquor must be first-class—for the sake of the one man in twenty who knew good wine from bad. (This point was of great importance. Tickle the palate of the connoisseur, and he *with a loud voice* will declare his gratitude. Swift to appropriate a judgment they know to be good, all within earshot will later commend that house, and so oblige their host by serving their vanity.) Then, again, there was the question of seating. Where is the man who will stand, if he can sit down ? Yet people stood at such parties—because it was more convenient than to sit down. Rowena determined that at Curzon Street people's convenience should coincide with their ease. And so on . . .

Her plans being cut and dried, preparations were made to carry them out. Fine sherry was collected from sale-rooms—at a third of its retail price. A famous bar-tender parted with two of his best receipts. The thin, two-fronted withdrawing-room gave up its elegant ghost. Anselm was shown the objectives to be attained.

The butler's appreciation of the position was swift and intelligent, predicting the discreet initiative which, when the time came, he displayed. Cadnam, of course, would have been a broken reed. More. The smoking flax of his endeavours would have stunk before all who saw them. As it was, in spite of her husband's arrival at half past six, the first of Rowena's parties was a deserved success.

It was after the sixth in ten days that David saw fit to protest. At half past seven the last of the guests had been sped, and the Bohuns were due to dine out at a quarter past eight. Fresh from a hasty bath, the man stood stripped to the waist, with a brush in his hand.

"My darling, these cocktail shows. I give you full marks, of course: but . . ."

Here he looked up, to meet his wife's eyes in the mirror to which she sat. Her lightly clothed figure was that of the fashion-plate: far less attractive pictures appear every day of the week—and point the truth that the body is more than raiment. But Bohun saw no picture, because he had seen the look in his lady's eyes. This was rock-steady and compelling.

"Go on," said Rowena, quietly.

"It doesn't matter," said David, and fell to brushing his hair.

"D'you want me to wash them out?"

"Good lord, no," said David, rising: "but, er, couldn't you keep them for days when we're not going out? You see, I come back pretty tired, and—and it doesn't give me a chance. If I can sit down for a bit, I'm as right as rain: but—well, take to-night, for instance. Before the last of them went, it was time to go up and change."

"My God," said Rowena, "you win it—and that's His truth. Solely to ease your conscience, I've found out a way to do the impossible thing—successfully

entertain people who only know how to be hosts.
I never wanted to do it : but it meant so much to you
that I made up my mind to try. Somehow I've
brought it off. I am making the sort of return which
is not sick-making, yet is within your means. The
Grainers were here to-night. To date we've cost them
some forty to fifty pounds—that show at Granada
cost them a tenner a head. Their joint *consommation*
to-night cost *us* about three-and-six . . . And they
were just tickled to death—so tickled that they want
us for Ascot. They've taken the Mundays' place."

" Ascot ? "

" A naughty race-meeting, dearie—but that's by
the way. For your sake, I have produced and now
have to play in the shows—fetch and carry and giggle,
until I'm ready to drop. And then you come in
when it's over and say you're tired."

" I only meant——"

" That phrase," said Rowena, " should be inscribed
on your tomb. *He only meant* . . . You know, it
gets you in one."

With tightened lips, her husband stooped to a
drawer. After rigging a shirt with studs, which did
not resist, and cuff-links, which did—a trying operation which Cadnam had been used to perform—he
turned again to his wife.

" Why are you so nasty, Rowena . . . so often . . .
when we're alone ? You're sweet enough, when we're
out."

Dangerous ground, this. But Rowena's foot was
as sure as that of Will-o'-the-Wisp.

" Does it occur to you that I can say exactly the
same ? On parade you're—well, not inspiring, but
at least you're civil enough. Off, you seem to do
nothing but try to tread on my toes. I put up this
show to please you. To have failed would have been
too easy : but, though I was dead against it, I did
my level best to make bricks without straw. I had

to work damned hard to do it. That sherry's worth a guinea a bottle. I got it for six-and-six. But not at the wine-merchant's, love. It wasn't as simple as that . . . To round the nightmare, I have to be on tap for two hours, attending our guests. And then when it's over, my God, you take me to task."

"You know I didn't. I never take you to task. I said, 'Why not have the shows on days when we're not going out?' If I'd known you were tired, I'd have pitched it in stronger still."

"It didn't occur to you, did it? *You* were tired, and that was as far as you got."

"I'm afraid it didn't. I'm sorry," said David Bohun.

Rowena shrugged her shoulders.

"I'm used to that by now. What leaves a mark —what rankles is when you've slaved for a blessing and get a curse."

"Rowena, I tell you——"

"I know. Don't say it again, or I'll scream. I've told you these parties tire me. If that is the truth, why am I such a fool as to give them before going out?"

David could only stare, and Rowena went on.

"Because, by your wish—not mine, I have shown our hosts that we are actually able to make them a fair return. Well, *now we've got to make it* . . . Ask them—not once, my friend, but over and over again. If we don't, they'll start in doing sums—dividing the *Café de Paris* by a sandwich in Curzon Street . . . By your desire, we've woken the sleeping dog: and, now he's awake, he's got to be watered and fed. If he isn't, he'll bite . . . We've put the words into their mouth that we dare not hear used—'The least they can do'."

A little leaven leaveneth the whole lump. David, who believed in full measure and never did things by halves, swallowed it dutifully. He also went to and put his arms round his wife—and begged to be forgiven for treading upon her toes.

"I'll think it over," said Rowena. "You can't kick a girl up the back-side and then expect her to plunk herself down on your knee. It's got to wear off, you know—the soreness, I mean. And what of this Ascot business? I've got to say 'yes' or 'no'."

Both knew what the answer must be.

"I guess we can go," said David. "I can get to Chambers from Ascot as well as from Curzon Street."

"Then you'd better apply for vouchers." Perfunctorily she gave him her lips. "And now for God's sake get a move on. It's eight o'clock."

*   *   *   *

It was natural enough that the drubbings which David endured at the hands of his wife should shorten his temper towards his fellow men. Tolerant though the man was, he had never—as he would have put it —stood any rot. Men and women had proved this again and again. Far down in the soil of good nature, there had always welled in Bohun a sturdy spring of impatience which those who dug too far were certain to strike. Such as uncovered this spring got soused for their pains—and were thereafter careful to bask upon the top of the soil, if, indeed, they were ever encouraged to use that pleasance again. Needless to say, Rowena was never drenched. Though she pierced the soil to the rock, the spring was powerless against its master's wife. But the natural result of her borings was to bring it nearer the surface than it had run before.

It follows that when, the next morning—to be precise, at a quarter past one o'clock, Bohun was appointed to a table at which were one man and two women each of whom plainly considered that they should have been better placed, his sense of humour nodded and something less indulgent reigned in its stead.

The room, which was underground, was unpleasantly warm and contained twice as many souls as it could have conveniently held : what air there was had been breathed again and again and was not so much charged with as merged in cigarette-smoke : the noise was combative—three or four hundred voices were talking against the band which strove to make itself heard above three or four hundred tongues : the movement was that of the ant-hill—guests continually swarming upon an invisible floor, and waiters ceaselessly using the maze which the tables made, meeting and dodging and striving and going all ways : food was served and tasted and presently taken away ; only the wine ran its course, finding a fleeting favour it seldom deserved.

David had meant by now to be on his way home, but he had missed his chance and could not now withdraw for another half-hour. He consoled himself with the hope, which he knew to be faint, that his wife would leave with him at a quarter to two. After trying to see where she was, he surveyed his fellow discards and was surveyed.

He knew all three by name and had danced with one of the women a week ago. The lady had had her day and would have been having it still, could she have masked her hatred for such of her sex as ventured to get in her way. Her resentment was less enduring than that of some of her peers ; but she could not disguise her displeasure when the man for whom she had dressed was seduced by somebody else. In a word, she was a bad loser—and bad losers spoil the game. The voice that shakes, the smile that glitters, the laugh that jars—people fight shy of these things : and Mrs. Jocelyn Garter was gradually reduced to the ranks.

David addressed her quietly.

" Would you like to dance, Mrs. Garter ? "

" I should simply loathe it," said the lady.   " For one thing, look at the floor."

" I expect you're right," said the squire, and turned to his other dame.

" My name's Bohun," he said.   " I think you're Lady Bedew.   Would you care to dance this ? "

The other rose at once, and they fought their way to the floor.

Rich, well-bred, still handsome and too young at fifty-eight, Hilda Bedew had a firm belief in the dance. She did not enjoy the movement, which, because her shoe was designed for a smaller foot, regularly caused her such pain as morphia is prescribed to abate : but she was less able to deny the soft suggestion that she was yet in demand than is the bear to reject the proffered bun.   Born to virtue, she coveted earnestly the worst gifts.   In her efforts to rise in circles upon which she should have looked down, she made of her decent mind an habitual prostitute ; but, physically unattractive, she had never been called upon to make the supreme sacrifice—this, mercifully, for the friction which such a summons must have set up between her chastity and her ambition would surely have fused her soul.   Few things gave her more pleasure than the promiscuous use of her Christian name : she mentally squirmed with pleasure when she was thus promoted by someone of half her age.

Had Bohun been a good dancer, neither Mrs. Garter nor he would have found so repugnant the congestion upon the floor.   This inconvenienced all, but embarrassed him.   And Lady Bedew did not, as they say, handle well.   The latter cared for none of these things : she was demonstrating the truth that she was still in demand.   Her satisfaction, however, died with the dance.   To her surprise and dismay, Bohun made no attempt to detain her as soon as the music had stopped, but, ignoring and even curtailing the generous meed of applause which she was according the assurance of eight American Jews, smiled his thanks and shepherded her out of the press.

As they regained their table, Mrs. Garter made haste to charge the poor lady's cup.

" Back again ? " she said brightly. " You've only just gone."

Bohun let himself frown.

" You were right," he said. " It's too full."

" Did I say that ? " said Mrs. Garter.

" I thought you did," said Bohun. " It is any way."

The Hon. George List put in a fatuous oar.

" A man is as full as he feels," he declared irrelevantly.

Lady Bedew was consumed with laughter.

" Trust George," she said—enigmatically.

" Why ? " said Mrs. Garter, inconsiderately.

The mutual contempt of discards is a terrible thing.

Someone once said of George List that he was beside the point. I cannot better that description. God knows what he had cost to produce, but, except as a presentable ' odd man ', he was of no value. He had never been known to do anything worth doing or to say anything worth saying and was probably the finest argument for Communism in existence. His consumption of liquor approached the miraculous, for, while no one had ever seen him sober, no one had ever seen him offensively drunk.

Here some inferior soup was frantically served.

" Can't take soup on an empty stomach," said List. " Why don't they serve the champagne ? "

" They must have seen you coming," said Lady Bedew.

List produced and lighted a large cigar.

" I could use some wine," said Mrs. Garter. She

turned to David Bohun. "Get hold of some, will you?"

Bohun raised his eyebrows.

"I think that's List's job," he said. "I don't know the Stumms very well."

"I didn't ask List. I asked you."

Bohun's expression hardened.

"I know you did," he said. "But I'd rather not. I don't know our host well enough to do as you wish."

He turned to Lady Bedew and offered her cigarettes. Remembering his late offence, the lady declined.

"Well, I'm damned," said Mrs. Garter.

"Stale news," said List. "I wish they'd bring that champagne."

"Poor George," said Lady Bedew. "It isn't fair. Has anyone heard Moon's latest?"

As the others ignored the question, Bohun felt it his duty to purchase the gem.

"What's that?" he said politely enough.

"He calls Lucinda Curdle 'The Cooling Stream'."

"I wish," said List, "they'd bring us some cooling champagne. Oh, waiter, catch my eye, if you can't catch Reuben Stumm's."

"George, be quiet," gurgled Hilda, and turned to Bohun. "Do you know why?"

"I can't imagine," said Bohun, trying to care.

"'As pants the hart'," said Lady Bedew, triumphantly.

Bohun wrinkled his brow.

Had he known that a rich man, named Hart, desired to possess Miss Curdle . . . that Miss Curdle's price was marriage—a fee Mr. Hart was sure she had never demanded before . . . that bets were being laid upon the issue, Bohun might have recaptured some of the ground he had lost with Lady Bedew. As it was, he lost more.

"I'm afraid I don't see it," he said.

G

"Never mind," said Mrs. Garter. "Ask her to dance, instead. Or don't you like dancing with her?"

Bohun set his teeth.

"I told you just now," he said, "that the floor was too full."

"A man can't be too full," said List. "Nature sees to that."

"George, you are awful," said Hilda, deliciously shocked.

Mrs. Garter sighed.

"Well, if you won't, you won't. After all, youth must be served."

Lady Bedew winced, and Bohun felt the blood come into his face.

He addressed his molester curtly.

"If something's upset you," he said, "I'm sorry for that. But please remember that I'm not a whipping-boy." He returned to Hilda Bedew. "I expect you know Biarritz, don't you?"

The question was singularly unhappy. Everyone knew that two years ago Bedew had fled to Biarritz with somebody else's wife and that Hilda had followed her husband and brought him back.

Even List looked up at the place-name, and Lady Bedew bit her lip.

As Bohun shot a glance round—

"Surely that was unnecessary," said Mrs. Garter, coldly. She looked across the table and smiled at Lady Bedew. "I saw a dress to-day, Hilda, you simply must buy . . ."

The other's face cleared.

"Go on, dear," she said, in evident gratitude.

Bohun felt hot all over.

Thus do the wicked flourish—and all things work together for ill to some unfortunates.

As the champagne arrived, the lights were suddenly lowered and a cabaret-show was begun. Distraction and dusk together suited List down to the ground.

When the lights went up again, the champagne-bottle was upside down in its pail.

*   *   *   *

The seed which was sown that evening, because Mrs. Garter was cross, took definite root. Had she alone let it be known that she had no use for David, his reputation would not have suffered at all : but when Hilda Bedew, of whom it could truly be said that she loved her fellow men, went so far as to say that she didn't care for him much, all who heard her became unsure of Bohun. Suspicion is, I suppose, ten times as hard to allay as it is to confirm. With no idea of what he was doing, David allayed it one day and confirmed it the next. Very slowly it began to be accepted that Bohun ' wasn't too good '. With this acceptance, the springs of sympathy broke ; and the very compassion Rowena so much desired began to flow for her from an unimpeachable source.

CHAPTER VI

Hark to Persimmon

SUCH was Bohun's work that it more often kept him in Chambers than took him to Court. It follows that, had they so wished, Rowena might have lunched with her husband three days out of five. It would, of course, have been a mistake. Lunch would have taken two hours instead of one, and Bohun would have forgone what the finest wife in the world could not have supplied—for when craftsmen break their fast in their own refectory, the cheer purveyed is not that of the body alone. But Bohun was never required to renounce this fellowship, for his wife would as soon have thought of meeting him during the day as of going to shop with a string-bag in Edgware Road. This was as well, for the hour which he spent every day in Lincoln's Inn Hall, which had been agreeable, was now restorative. More. There were times when it was disinfectant.

Indeed, to disclose all at once a truth of which Bohun himself became only slowly aware, his life at the Bar was now the better part, for business and pleasure for him had been counterchanged. Once—long years ago—he had found his Chambers exacting, the Law Courts strict, and though content to be ruled throughout the day, had hugged to himself the thought of the furlough that evening would bring. Often his mind had left the law's delays to dwell with comfortable pride on the little, old-fashioned house which a doting aunt had left to him as it stood, to tell its airs and graces and time-honoured faults, to treasure books

and pictures and the flicker of a fire upon a wall—and
a leisurely bath, and silver laid upon rosewood, and
Cadnam's diligence. Other visions had taken shape—
Punch and Belinda to dinner, a party at the Mayfair,
an evening with Lord Elvin and Forsyth, a rubber of
bridge, or a theatre, with supper to come : but always
there had glowed in the background the quality of his
home. But now all that was changed. As before,
he was bond and free. But now the scene of his
freedom was Lincoln's Inn ; and Curzon Street had
become the house of bondage.

Long ago David had learned not to ask Rowena how
she had spent her day.

" I rose, I ordered the meals and I checked the books :
I went through the linen and saw that the house was
clean : I took the car and went to a frightening lunch ;
I cashed a cheque at the bank, attended a dress-parade
and had my hair done in by a Jugo-Slav who ought to be
dipping sheep : I came home and did the flowers,
which I frankly admit I ought to have done before. I
hope and believe that's all. If you don't believe what
I say, I should have me watched."

The brusque account misrepresented the facts. The
lady never ordered a meal : she merely approved the
menu the cook sent up. She never went through the
linen or checked the books. Anselm did the flowers
and saw that the house was clean. The lunch, in
Half Moon Street, had been a screaming success. The
exclusive dress-parade, to which each guest was
encouraged to bring a man, had been the event of the
week. But, true or false, the statement had its effect.
It reminded David sharply that much that he took for
granted was due to a housewife's care : that he was
spared quite a lot by going to Lincoln's Inn : and that
a display of curiosity regarding what he ought to have
known was a trivial round was liable to be misconstrued.

The sidelight is instructive.

Rowena was merely producing the line she had

started to draw, for her husband to toe : but David was carefully noting the course which it took—*for future reference*.

By the merry month of May, the line was practically drawn. For fear of offending his goddess, David was painfully careful never to put a foot wrong. This, to his own hindrance. There were times, for instance, when the butler, whose wages he paid, seemed to fail to appreciate the orders that Bohun gave. At least, they were not carried out. Rather than cross his mistress, his master held his peace. It is lamentable, but it is true. Mrs. Bohun had got her husband where he belonged.

Let me insist that he went in no fear of his wife. His love was perfect and so had cast out fear. He only shrank from offending the woman he loved.

*   *   *   *

On the day on which Bohun left Biarritz, both Lady Persimmon and Helen Adair had known that the latter would go to London before the season was out. Neither had mentioned this knowledge, which constantly fretted poor Lady Persimmon's peace ; but both were waiting—the one for her daughter to announce her decision to go, and the other until she felt she could wait no more.

More than a month went by, and June came in in splendour, after a week of rain.

Bohun had written twice, and Helen Adair had replied. Nothing in his letters suggested that life was gray : but that may have been because to write to Helen rejoiced his heart. Her replies effected still more : the sight of the French stamps quickened his pulse. But Helen had no use for letters. She wanted to hear his voice and to see the look in his eyes.

Now that summer was in, magic went to the making of the Chiberta nights, and Neighbour Nature's land-

marks were imperceptibly removed. The terrace of
La Belle Issue became a belvedere, from which the
bewildered eye commanded a realm. Foreground was
magnified : background was done away : only a
heraldry of stars denied infinity. All sound was
amplified. The long, slow crush of the breakers crept
from its bed, and every now and again a slant of music,
made by the Country Club, soared into and out of an
earshot that knew no law. Perfumed by wave and
pine, the breathless air seduced the common sense ;
and Lady Persimmon, who liked to retire at eleven,
found herself still upon the terrace at half past twelve.

It was, in fact, this perfection that forced her daughter's
hand. Helen simply could not endure it—because
David, less lucky than she, would have loved it so
much.

On the third such night, she took the bull by the
horns.

" I'm going to London, Mo, for two or three days.
Will you let me stay at the Square ? "

Lady Persimmon resided in Kensington Square.

" Of course, my dear. Where else ? Send a wire
to Beamish to open the house."

" I'll ring you up every day."

" That's a good child. Will you bring me some
bedroom slippers ? Your evil beast hath devoured my
second pair."

" Poor Mo. Of course. I'll be back within the
week."

" That's right. And, er, if you should find that you
want me, of course I'll come." Helen Adair shook her
head. " My dear, one never knows. I might be—
convenient. The bare idea of the journey offends
' my drowsèd sense '; but I'd sooner make it ten
times than—than . . ."

Lady Persimmon hesitated, and Helen set a hand
on her arm.

" I won't do anything foolish."

" I know," said Lady Persimmon. " But three's company—when you're not in a public place. Oh, and please do remember this. *That woman's not safe.*"

The fingers closed upon her arm.

" Poor Mo. Are you very worried ? "

" I wouldn't say that ; but I don't like the look of things. Tigers may eat their young : but that doesn't alter the fact that they don't like being interfered with during a meal."

Helen Adair said nothing and Lady Persimmon went on.

" What I'm trying to say is this. Of course you're not going to trespass—we both know that. You're going to stick to the path. But do remember, my dear, that *the path itself is perilous*—because it runs by the side of that woman's land . . . And now I feel very much better—I've given tongue. I've a great respect for your judgment—because I know you've a great respect for mine. The difficulty was to hand you the strong opinion I'd formed. And now let's go up to bed. But don't omit to give that young man my love. And when I say that, I mean it. He has a most refreshing address, and I shall be very happy to see him again."

" I suppose you know," said Helen, " that you are unique."

" Don't be absurd," said her mother. " Not every tiger likes the taste of its young."

* * * *

From one point of view, Helen Adair's decision to leave for London could scarcely have been better timed. Though she did not know it, the tide of her love-affair was at the flood.

This was the way of it.

Rowena was not wholly inhuman—though such mistakes as she made were seldom of consequence.

She was, for instance, subject to the common, if maddening, complaint of remembering what it was she had wanted to ask her husband only when the latter was no longer within her call. Happily for David, the results of such occasional lapses had never been inconvenient to Mrs. Bohun.

And then in May she fell down.

She had meant to confirm, by inquiry, that David had done as she said and had duly ' applied for vouchers '—for admission to the Royal Enclosure at Ascot in June. Time and again the question had come to her mind, but always when David was absent, never when he was there. Then the month of June came in, and the lists were closed—and at last Rowena remembered when David was there to be asked.

The two had dined alone, for once in a way, and were sitting at ease in a silence which David had come to esteem. Rowena was absorbed in a French periodical whose contents betrayed, to such as had eyes to see, the orders to be issued in August for early autumn wear : and David was thinking of the luncheon which he was to give to Helen the following day. The latter had suggested the Savoy, because it was well within range of Lincoln's Inn.

He had told his wife, of course : and his wife had been patently pleased.

" Splendid. Keep up the good work. But don't ram me down her throat, or you'll frighten her off. Remember—you're playing this hand : and when you're sitting pretty—well, then you can bring me in."

In fact, life was none too bad. For six days—seven days now, there had been no unpleasantness which fairly deserved that name. He seemed to be managing better—to be using the weaker vessel as she had a right to expect. And she was responding to treatment . . . And to-morrow he was to see Helen, who—who looked upon things as he did, who understood.

David knocked out his pipe, filled and lighted another and picked up the *Evening News*.

Suddenly Rowena sat up.

" I've been meaning to ask you for ages." Something within David contracted. " You did apply for vouchers for Ascot ? "

Something within David relaxed.

" I went the day after you'd asked me. On my way to——"

" You *went* ? "

The word fairly flamed, and David repressed a start.

" It's quite all right, my darling. I ordered——"

" *My God in heaven !* " Rowena was on her feet. " *You blazing fool*," she hissed, " *d'you know what you've done ?* "

David, actually trembling, could only stare upon a hatred of which he had only read. Rowena was transfigured with rage—rage with him for his failure to do as she said, rage with herself for her failure to tackle his failure in time. Of the two, her rage with herself was the harder to bear. She added her burden to his with a passion which shook his soul.

" I said ' Apply for vouchers '," she shrilled. " ' *Apply for vouchers* ', you wash-out : not ' Go to some blasted tradesman and order seats '." Her voice rose into a scream. " ' *Apply* ', you rotten idiot. You know what that means—*APPLY*."

Her husband got to his feet.

" Don't go on like this, Rowena. I'm sorry if I——"

" ' If ' ? " screamed Rowena. " ' *IF* ' ? " She covered her face with her hands. " Oh, why weren't you choked at birth ? "

The sentiment, so voiced, made Bohun feel suddenly cold.

After a moment's silence—

" Please tell me what's the matter," he said.

His wife uncovered her face and looked him full in the eyes.

" By God, I will," she said straightly.

With that, she drew in her breath. Then—

" When you said we could go to Ascot, I said ' Apply for vouchers '—I used that phrase. You found it strange. But you never asked what I meant. You preferred to assume that I meant ' Buy some tickets ' or something like that. In fact, I meant what I said."

" What did you mean ? " said David, after a decent pause.

" ' Apply for vouchers '," said Rowena, with burning eyes. " *To a man called The Master of the Horse.*" David recoiled. " *Vouchers for the Royal Enclosure.* D'you think I'm going to Ascot, wearing a Paddock badge ? "

" But, Rowena—The Royal Enclosure ? They'd never give vouchers to us."

" Of course they would have. Why not ? You'd only got to apply. We're a damned sight better than half the crowd that get in."

" In the Royal Enclosure ? Who says so ? Why, you——"

" Don't argue with me. I *know*. If you'd applied, you'd have got them." She clapped her hands to her temples and let out her breath. " My God, what *are* you fit for ? The one thing I leave to you, because I *can't* do it myself——"

" I'll do it now," said David, white as a sheet.

" You can't," spat Rowena, triumphant. " The lists were closed on Friday. You're out of time. And *I* can't attend Royal Ascot, because my peach of a husband has let me down."

" ' Can't attend ' ? " cried David, as one who cannot accept a doom ten times as monstrous as he had thought.

" Can't go . . . attend . . . be present. The thing's washed out. Good God, what else d'you go for—except the Enclosure badge ? What else does anyone go for, you frightening fool ? If you can't get a voucher, you're marked : and if you've got any sense, you damned well take to your bed. You're 'indisposed' that week—but everyone knows what it means."

The man sat down in a chair and put his head in his hands.

"I'm most dreadfully sorry," he muttered. "I'd no idea."

The statements seemed to inflame Rowena's wrath. For more than a minute she railed, lashing her luckless husband with sneer and imprecation and wild abuse. Then the bitter prospect before her advanced its claims, and she flung herself down on a sofa and burst into tears. These were not idle : an idiot would have known what they meant—for she wept as a naughty child, screaming and flouncing and striking in impotent rage.

The spectacle paralysed David. For one thing, he had not known that a woman could let disappointment so rule her soul : for another, he had not dreamed that the self-possessed Rowena could ever give up possession to emotion of any kind : finally, his wife was transformed—that mopping and mowing visage was one he had never seen. He forgot for the moment that he had brought this about. The shocking exhibition obsessed his mind.

He realized suddenly that the scene must be made to stop. Somehow he must do something to make Rowena take up the control she had lost . . .

He had meant to kneel by her side, but she struck at him as he stooped and he caught her wrist.

"Pull yourself together, Rowena."

Her answer was to fight like a fury, to shake him off.

He caught her other wrist, pulled her up and round and urged her into a corner of the sofa on which she had lain.

" You d-dirty bully, you're hurting."

" You're hurting yourself by struggling. I'm not going to let you go."

He tried to hold her lightly ; but this the violence she offered would not allow. For fully a minute she wrenched and dragged and twisted, as though in a vain endeavour to have her way. Then her body went slack and her head fell back. Her eyes met her husband's squarely.

" Have you gone far enough ? " she said.

The man released her at once. His wife was herself again.

" I'm sorry," he said. " I had to do something, you know."

" First you make me cry, and then you knock me about."

" I never knocked you about. I——"

" God bless our home," said Rowena, inspecting her wrists. " You are strong, aren't you, Willie ? No ordinary girl——"

" I'm sorry. If you hadn't struggled——"

" Why don't you say," said Rowena, " that you did it in self-defence ? That's what they say in the police-court—before they're jugged."

" I don't think you know," said David, " how you were going on."

" What d'you expect ? " flashed his wife. " For weeks I've looked forward to Ascot—I've never been. And now you've gone and smashed it—not bitched it, but done it in. I can't be seen there, I tell you. I can't attend. I can't go down to the Grainers'. I can't wear the clothes I've bought . . ."

Again she began to weep—this time restrainedly.

David was at her side.

" Rowena, listen. It can't be as bad as that. If you've never——"

" Of course it's as bad," sobbed Rowena. " And what the hell do you know ? Your idea of a function is going to watch the Boat Race from somebody's private roof."

(This was untrue : but Rowena had not forgotten the leaden hour she had spent in a biting wind, confronting the implicit grace of Hammersmith Bridge and squired by a deaf divine, who rowed for Cambridge in 1878 and knew in his heart that he was a lady's man.)

" I tell you——"

" My God," shrieked Rowena, " d'you want to drive me mad ? You say you'll tell me—*you* ? " She smote the arm of the sofa with all her might. " Ascot is off your map, and you know it as well as I. First on the right past *The Wheatsheaf*—and that's as much as you know. *But I DO know*. I may have never been there, but I've got two ears to my head. I've mixed and stayed and lived with people who've gone . . . who go all the time . . . who'd miss the last 'bus to heaven before they'd cut Ascot out. And why ? *Because of the badge*. Because for four days they *must* display a patent which nobody *can* deny. ' Royal Enclosure ', it says—you can't get away from that. And when they've all got badges, d'you think I'm going without ? To have women like Cullet and Curdle putting it over me ? To be ' left ' at the show of the season, because I'm improperly dressed ? " She clasped her head and began to rock to and fro. " Oh, God, I wish I was dead."

" Well, I don't know," said David, desperately.

" Of course you don't know," raved Rowena. " And, what's more, you'll never learn. God knows what they pay you for at the Chancery Bar. Why, you can't even take an order. I said ' Apply for vouchers '—and you go off and reserve some stinking seats. And when it's too late and I'm sunk, you slobber your blasted opinions all over the place. Opinions ? You ? " She let out an hysterical laugh. " You haven't got such a thing. You're not qualified

to hold one. God knows why you live where you do.
You ought to be digging in Ealing and standing a
typist chocolates on Saturday night.''

There was plainly nothing to be done, and, after
waiting a moment, Bohun withdrew from the room
and left his wife to herself.

* * * *

It is not too much to say that for what had occurred
Rowena was wholly to blame.

In fact, she *had* been to Ascot—not, of course, in
the Enclosure—five years before. She never referred
to—in fact, she denied this visit, which had been
instructive indeed. She had seen—what she had
seen. And then and there she had sworn never again
to attend, unless she could wear on her breast the
coveted badge.

Her outlook may be excused. All sorts go to Royal
Ascot, and her strictures were not unfair to the circles
in which she moved. For them, those four June days
were Days of Judgment, when the sheep and the goats
were divided—for all to see. And to be a goat was too
awful—a mortification, in their eyes, belittling the
pains of Hell. Evil communications had come to
pervert their sight. They could not see that a badge
was a mark of honour : they only saw that its absence
was the mark of the beast.

But, though Rowena knew that you had to apply
for a voucher to get a badge, she knew no more—
and she was ashamed to ask. Of etiquette she knew
little—and loathed her ignorance. She had said
' Apply for vouchers ': and when her husband had
swallowed the cryptic phrase, she had at once assumed
that his knowledge was greater than hers. Had she
pursued the matter, she might have exposed her sores.
And so she had let it go . . . Her present realization
that she had been duped, that, so far from knowing

more, her husband knew less than she did of proud
punctilio, raised her to a pitch of contempt which only
the unconversant can ever attain. The emotion was
genuine. She could have spat upon David—with
right good will.

So, then, she sat upon the sofa, crying with rage,
wild with disappointment, and charged with scorn, yet
all the time laying her plans to make good her retreat.
No one must ever suspect that she had not attended
Ascot because she could not have had on a wedding
garment.

Downstairs, in the dining-room, her husband sat,
sightless and shaken, trying to face the fact that she
loved him no more. At last she had made this clear
to his intelligence. 'Not love—*not even* vanity *took*
love *to* task like that.' After a little, he, too, began
to lay plans—desperate, frantic projects to revive . . .
recapture . . . grapple the love he had lost.

* * * *

Rowena refused to retire until long past three. Her
husband's diffident addresses were met with abuse
and insult, with tears and vain repetitions of truths
which she knew were lies. And when at last they
adjourned to a graying bedroom, for an hour his
mental havoc would not allow him to sleep. Little
wonder his eyes looked tired when he entered his
Chambers, as usual, at a quarter to ten.

Such is the tonic of an accustomed toil, the look
was less apparent in three hours' time. Still, Helen
Adair remarked it, when Bohun came stepping to
meet her at the foot of the busy stair.

People were all about them, coming or going or
seeking or being sought ; spruce footmen stood their
ground ; pages, about their business, were hugging
the wall ; and waiters, bearing cocktails, continually
begged their way. Sound rose out of silence, as a

fountain out of a pool—the leisurely drawl of lift-gates, the sigh of revolving doors, the mirth of an orchestra and the clack of a hundred tongues . . . But David Bohun was unaware of these things. All that he was aware of was Helen Adair.

His hand went out in silence. The sheer relief of her presence was such that his tongue was tied.

Helen smiled very gently.

" I'm ready, David. Why shouldn't we go straight in ? "

" I—I'd love to," was all he said.

Bohun never noticed that, as they were led to their table, she was observed. Nobody claimed her acquaintance, but a number of signals flashed and numerous heads were turned. Not all of her observers knew who she was : they saw only a natural beauty, beautifully dressed. She was wearing dark blue and white —had Bohun but known it, the best-looking dress in the room : a precious fur was sloping across her shoulders : a flourish of diamonds was brooching her fine straw hat . . .

The instant attention of waiters precluded talk.

The man chose food and wine, inquiring her pleasure before he ordered a dish. As the wine-waiter bowed himself off, a very cornucopia of *hors d'œuvres* came slowly to rest by the table at which they sat. Their plates were faithfully charged, and at last they were left alone.

David, no longer wordless, spoke from his heart.

" I'm so thankful to see you, Helen. I can't tell you what it means." The girl's heart leapt. " How's Lady Persimmon ? And Tumble ? I needn't ask how you are."

" Mo said that I was to be sure to give you her love. Tumble's terribly well and perfectly sweet."

" Are you over for long ? "

" I don't think so. I've two or three things to attend to, but nothing much. And now let's talk about you. I saw you were in that curious right-of-way case."

"Did you ? " said David, glowing . . .

When the wine was served, Helen Adair spoke out.

"I'm sure you don't drink this in Lincoln's Inn Hall. Why don't you have a brandy and soda ? You look so tired."

"Do I ? You're very sweet. I don't know. Perhaps I will."

The pleased surprise told its own tale. Since Cadnam had left his service, a personal interest in his welfare was something the man had not known.

Once they had dealt with the law, the clutch of conversation began to slip.

"Tell me all you've been doing," said Helen.

David took a deep breath and did his best to obey. His report was unsubstantial and was haltingly made.

For one thing, the man had done nothing worth telling to Helen Adair : for another, he could not reveal this without involving his wife : then, again, the mere thought of Rowena distracted his wits.

The girl beside him put out a helping hand.

"Tell me about *Many Men*—you've been to see that ? "

"I'm ashamed to say I haven't."

"David ! What are you saying ? Half London's seen it twice."

"I know. I want to see it. But—I don't know. We don't go to the theatre alone, and people seem to be fonder of musical shows. I don't really care, you know : but I'd like to see that."

"D'you go out of Town for week-ends ? "

"As a rule, we do. But I'm not a great week-ender. You see, my time's so short. I can't take Saturday morning, and I must be in Chambers on Monday at ten o'clock. So I'd really rather go out of Town for the day. I rather think we may have a cottage soon. The idea is to share it with someone and sort of take it in turns. Rowena's seen it—I haven't. It sounds all right."

" How is your wife ? I ought to have asked before."

David put a hand to his head.

" She's fairly well. I—I think she's been doing too much. I'm afraid I'm to blame—in a way. You see . . ."

Rowena's version of how the sherry party came to take root was scrupulously retailed. Helen, listening gravely, could hardly sit still. When the spurious recital was over, she spoke of life at Chiberta as much for her sake as for his. At once the strain was relaxed, and both were at ease. Bohun ate her news as a hungry man.

The thing was, of course, fantastic. She had no news. *La Belle Issue* by day and night . . . busy, gray-headed Bayonne . . . the glorious canticle of sun upon sea without end . . . Tumble rampant and couchant—and salient upon a plumber, defiling his mistress' bathroom without his leave . . . back-gammon with Lady Persimmon . . . the lights of a car in the forest, promoting Hans Andersen to a historian's chair . . . Such stuff was not news. Yet the man-about-town devoured it—and asked for more. The girl came to feel a Dives, dispensing the crumbs he had dropped . . .

At last she sat back in her chair.

" I refuse to report any more. I came to hear about you. Besides, mine's a fairy-tale. Chiberta doesn't exist."

David stared over her shoulder.

" It does for me," he said softly. " And the mornings I spent at your villa . . . and then—that hour on the shore. I've got the fee simple of those. And nothing and no one can ever take them away."

Helen felt slightly faint. The man was not speaking to her, but was thinking aloud. His eyes betrayed these facts.   He had no idea at all that he was making love.

As she put her wine to her lips, she first became aware of the resolute beat of her heart.

" David, I've done my best. Won't you tell me your news ? "

The man's face fell.

" I've nothing to report," he said dully. " And that's the truth. Nothing of any interest—from our point of view."

Helen looked grave.

" What d'you mean, when you say ' from our point of view ' ? D'you mean from the idealist's stand-point ? "

David shrugged his shoulders.

" Yes—if you like."

" But that's all wrong," cried Helen. " Idealism's no wear—it's fancy dress. You might as well try to cut ice with Harlequin's sword."

" I know, I know. Never mind. ' The common task '—I've told you all about that. But ' the trivial round ' is too trivial—too insignificant."

Helen Adair inspected a small, clenched fist.

" Don't you ever see Punch and Belinda ? I don't know their other name."

" I haven't seen them lately," said David. " They don't go out a great deal, and we've been rather booked up."

" I thought as much," said Helen. " That's why you look tired. What time did you go to bed this morning ? "

She could not foresee that the question would hit the man over the heart.

David sat deadly still, with his eyes on the cloth. Regarding him, Helen knew that she had laid a hand on the cupboard in which his skeleton stood. She had asked him ' What is in there ? ' Frantically, she willed him to tell her some of the truth.

At last the man looked up.

" Helen," he said quietly, " I'm in a hell of a mess."
Once again the girl's heart leapt. " It's all my fault.
I made it. But that only makes it worse. There's
nothing to be done—it's quite hopeless. I've got to
face that. But if I could tell you about it . . ."

Her impulse was to reply, ' That's why I came to
London.' Instead—

" My dear," she said, " that's what friendships like
ours are for. If I was in any trouble, of course I
should turn to you."

David's eyes were alight.

" My God. Would you really ? Oh, Helen, I'd
do my best. But you'll never be in any trouble . . ."
He glanced about him. " I don't think I'll tell you
here. If we could have coffee outside . . ."

" I don't want any coffee," said Helen. " And
listen. I've got a car here. Let's drive to Lincoln's
Inn Fields. And then we can sit there and talk, till
it's time for you to go back."

" You're terribly sweet," said David, and called for
the bill.

It is not too much to say that both were immensely
relieved—the man because he was now to share his
burden with her, the girl because she was now to share
it with him. Of such is love.

Two minutes later, they rose . . .

As he followed her out of the room—

" Well, I'm damned," said Mrs. Garter. And then,
" My God, she must be hard up."

Her companion ignored the apostrophe—which he
had heard before. His engagement to attend Mrs.
Garter did not, in his sight, include the pursuit of a
topic which made his gorge rise. Damn it, he'd earned
his corn. She'd signed the bill all right, but he'd
sat through the —— lunch.

CHAPTER VII

The Deep End

THE finest square in London was half asleep :
its magnificent plane trees drowsed in the hot
sunshine : traffic was slight.

At rest in the shade, with all its windows open, the
car was pleasantly cool. Helen, who had put off
her fur, was watching her companion and smoking a
cigarette : and David sat back in his corner, smoking
hard and fast and watching the chauffeur strolling on
the farther side of the road.

At last the man opened his mouth.

" If you knew me better, Helen, you'd know I
belonged to a highly dangerous class—as dangerous to
itself as to others . . . the class that *means well*. I
may as well bring that out without any delay. I am
a member of that sect of impossible idiots—blind,
thoughtless, wise in its own conceit and never able to
learn. Our hideous determination is our most ghastly
trait. We mean so terribly well.

" I could give you a hundred examples of my
activity. Since I was married—less than six months
ago—I've let Rowena down again and again. I give
you my word, she's had to put up with a lot . . .
But now I've excelled myself. I've fairly torn things
right up.

" A month ago we had an invitation for Ascot—to
go down and stay for the week. Some very rich
people, called Grainer, have taken somebody's house.
It's frightfully decent of them, although, as a matter
of fact, it's not very much in my line. Placed as I

am, I can't take days off during term. I'll be able to
later on : but at present I can't. And in any event
I shall be in court all that week. But that's by the
way . . . Rowena was very naturally mad to accept.
She's never been to Ascot : and a house-party there
would suit any girl down to the socks. So I said
'All right' . . .

"Well, that was that. And now we come to my
break.

"It being decided that we were to go to Ascot,
Rowena used these words—*You'd better apply for
vouchers*. There's no question of that. I remember it
perfectly well, for I found the expression strange. But
I never asked what she meant, for I thought I knew.
And, meaning well, I left ten minutes early next morning—and went to Keith Prowse on the way . . .

"Well, of course *you* know what she meant. And
so do I—now. She told me . . . last night . . .
after dinner. Till that moment, she'd no idea that
I hadn't done as she said. And now, as, of course,
you know also, I can't apply for vouchers because the
lists are closed."

He stopped speaking there for a moment and put a
hand to his head. Helen Adair said nothing. She
dared not trust her voice.

"Well, there you are. Rowena took it badly—as
any girl would. It seems—I didn't know it ; but,
then, the well-meaning *don't* know——"

"Please don't talk like that, David. It—it does
upset me so much."

The man shook his head.

"It's just as well you should know what I'm really
like."

"I do," said the girl. She set a hand on his arm.
"And I hope you'll never be different in any way."

Bohun turned to gaze at her, knitting his brows.

"But, Helen, I've told you——"

"Nothing to your discredit. Thank God you *are*

well-meaning. The point is, you're not a fool. It's
the fool who means well that sends people out of their
minds."

"But I am a fool."

"Who says so ? I know I don't. And Mo doesn't,
either. And she's a pretty good judge."

"But to go to Keith Prowse——"

"Was a perfectly natural act. What do you know
of Ascot ? You have no time for such things, because
you're better employed. The Royal Enclosure probably never entered your head."

"You're perfectly right," said David. "It never
did."

"Why should it ? To those who don't know Ascot,
the Royal Enclosure—well, belongs to the Court. In
fact, it doesn't—now. It may have once."

Bohun looked down—at the very beautiful fingers
laid on his arm. So for a moment. Then he put his
hand upon them and looked into Helen's eyes.

"Are you saying these things to—to cheer me ? "

"You know I'm not. I never do things like that."

"But Rowena——"

"Is naturally disappointed," flashed Helen Adair.
"She's never been to Ascot, and she wanted to go in
style. All the same, I don't quite understand. I
thought you said that you'd be in court all that week."

David swallowed.

"I know. But—she would have been with a
party. She'd have been looked after all right."

"I see," said Helen. "But why d'you keep saying
' would have ' ? The meeting's going to take place."

"She—she feels she can't go," said David, " unless
she's a badge. It's—it's a matter for her, and she's
made up her mind about that." His hand left Helen's
and went again to his head. "I—I don't think she'll
ever forgive me . . . for letting her down. We've
had—misunderstandings before : but last night it
was . . . more than that. She's been very patient,

you know. But I've done it once too often, and now
—she's through. She didn't say so. She never used
those words. But—well, I gathered it, Helen. And
I saw it—there, in her eyes . . ." He shook his
head, as a pugilist shakes his head—as though to be
rid of the shock of a punch to the jaw. " I'll get
her back—somehow. Somehow, I'll get her back.
But—it's rather a *mauvais moment*. And I felt if I
could tell you . . ." He took out his cigarette-case,
offered it to Helen, lighted their two cigarettes and
pitched the match out of the car. " Will you give me
your hand, please ? " The girl put her fingers in his,
and he put them up to his lips. " I want you to
know I'm grateful . . . that now I'll have five days
to treasure, instead of four . . . that the fifth will
always stand out as the day on which I—dared to
lean on your shoulder . . . and felt feet better, Helen,
because it was yours."

The slim fingers tightened on his : but more than
a minute went by before his companion replied.

If the girl's brain was unsteady, joy and sickness
fought to possess her heart. She had listened to a
shocking indictment of Mrs. Bohun. David had said
quite enough to reveal the barbarous portion which
he supposed was his due. Yet he had no idea that
he had disparaged his wife. She was not to blame—
in his eyes. As that of the ill-used dog, the fault
was his. More. As that of the ill-used dog, his one
idea was to do away his offence and induce his offended
mistress to let him lick her hand. All the time,
though he did not know it, his heart had already
turned to Helen Adair.

A wave of pity and love passed over her soul. She
had a terrible longing to take his head in her hands
and kiss the scales from his eyes . . . But that way
madness lay. The thing to do—the immediate thing
to do was to hale him from the valley of shadow in
which he lay. That this would make his peace with

Rowena could not be helped. His present misery must be resolved—at once.

"Have you pencil and paper ? " she said. " I want to write."

Most men would have asked her intention : but that was not Bohun's way. Besides, he knew where he was with Helen Adair.

Without a word, he opened a little 'engagement' book . . .

The girl wrote steadily, for a minute or more. Then she closed the book on the pencil and put them into his hand.

"Where are your Chambers, David ? "

"Just over there. Not more than five minutes' walk."

"Will you copy out what I've written, and bring me the copy back ? On a sheet of note-paper, please. I'll wait here until you come."

"I will," said David, wide-eyed.

He put the book away and set a hand on the door.

"Sealed orders," smiled Helen. "You really will do as I ask ? "

"Of course I will. I'll be back in ten minutes' time."

With that, he was gone : and she sat looking after, until he passed through the gateway of Lincoln's Inn.

Not until he was in his own room and the door was shut, did Bohun read the writing which he was to copy out.

As he read, the words swam before him, and a hope that he knew was dead rose up incontinent.

Mr. David Bohun presents his compliments to His Majesty's Comptroller . . .

*   *   *   *

Helen watched him coming. At thirty paces, she read the joy in his face. As for the man, he fairly ran the last ten.

' Helen, darling———"

" David, listen," said Helen, and put out a hand for the note. " You must not bank on this. I think I know someone who'll help : but I can't be sure. I'm going to see right away, and you're going back to Chambers to do your work. I'll ring you up before six and tell you how I've got on."

" I don't care. You're so sweet to do something —so terribly sweet. Even if it doesn't come off———"

" Don't be absurd," said the girl. " D'you mean to tell me you wouldn't do this for me ? "

" My God, you wait," cried the man. " You give me a chance to carry you out of the wet. Oh, Helen, I can't ever thank you—it simply won't go into words. I want to *do* something—*something* to show you how grateful I am."

" Be careful. We're not home yet."

" I don't care. It doesn't make any difference. Oh, dear. You're so glorious to look at, I'm half afraid I'll wake up and find it's a dream."

The conceit was not out of reason. Helen Adair rejoicing was ever a sight for the gods. But to see David Bohun so happy and to know she had brought this about set her fine being in a glow. Her eager lips were parted : her magnificent eyes were starlit : the light of her countenance shone—on the man she loved.

" I'm going now," she said. " D'you think you could catch Dixon's eye ? "

David beckoned to the chauffeur and put his hand into the car.

" Good-bye, Helen dear—for the moment. How soon shall I see you again ? "

As she took his hand—

" I don't know," said the girl. " Shall you be away this week-end ? Because, if you won't and you'd like, as you said, to go out of Town for the day . . ."

" I'd simply love it," cried Bohun. As he spoke,

his face was clouded and a hand went up to his mouth.
" But I can't be sure at the moment. Something was
said about Brighton . . . I'll send you a note to-
night."

Helen smiled and nodded. Then she gave an
address to the chauffeur, who took his seat.

" Good-bye, David. I'll ring you up before six."
The man watched the car out of sight.

* * * *

As may be supposed, the girl was sure of her ground.
Not for nothing had she, for two years, been the wife
of a popular captain of the Household Brigade. She
had made many friends at Court, and the favour
which she was to ask was absurdly slight—to consider
a late application : no more than that. As like as
not, if Bohun had asked it himself, it would have been
granted to him. But, though she was going to do it,
in fact it was going to cost her much more than
she cared to confess. For one thing, she dreaded to
revisit surroundings which had neighboured occasions
which she had sought to forget. Ten to one, before
she could open her mouth, the servant who opened
the door would know who she was. She had been
admitted before—when she had been ' Bugle's ' wife.
What she found much harder to swallow was the
clean-cut, glittering truth that she was obliging the
woman who was preying on David's soul. Look at it
how you will, she was doing the slut a service—helping
the treacherous jade to her heart's desire . . . Setting her teeth, she made up her mind to ignore this
poisonous fact. The application was that of David
Bohun. In fact, it included his wife : but that was
nothing to her. The application was that of David
Bohun.

One thing at least she was spared—the belief that
her action might change Rowena's heart. David might

cherish illusions—probably did. 'Somehow, I'll get her back.' But he never would. You cannot recover what you have never had. And he would not try very long—not if he saw much more of Helen Adair.

Any one of her friends at Court would have leapt to serve Helen Adair. She chose a man whose duty was done in the background, a good and faithful servant, who would have been well content with an eight-hour day.

When she sent in her name, he came at once to greet her and ushered her into his room.

"Helen, this *is* a pleasure. We've missed you so very much."

He made her sit down in comfort and stood by her side, inquired after Lady Persimmon and told her how often her name was on people's lips : he deplored her present seclusion, declaring that it was unfair, and when the girl protested that she was wasting his time, he gently corrected a notion so patently false.

"That, my dear, is a contradiction in terms. Helen Adair can waste nobody's time but her own."

Helen gave him a grateful smile.

"You always spoiled me," she said. "But I know you're working too hard, and I'm not going to lengthen your hours. I want you to help me, Colin." She gave him the note. "Such a nice friend of mine proposes to go to Ascot. He'd like to be in the Enclosure, but now he understands that he should have applied before."

"Should he ? " said Colin. "I doubt if they're quite so strict." The letter was not sealed and he drew out the sheet. "Any way, he needn't worry. I'll send it round."

As he glanced at the application—

"He's a great-nephew," said Helen, "of Lord Elvin who died this year."

The other looked up.

"He ought to be proud of that . . . I see he

includes his wife.   Has she been presented or been to
Ascot before ? "

" I don't think so," said Helen.

A thrill of apprehension had quickened her pulse.

" Then she'll have to be vouched for," said Colin.
" I take it you know her . . . If you'll excuse me a
moment, I'll send for a form."

For fifty seconds, perhaps, he was out of the room.
The time was just long enough for his guest to weather
the brain-storm his words had provoked.

The girl felt ready to faint.

She had never dreamed that Rowena would have
to be vouched for.   People did not have to be vouched
for a year or so back.   Their applications were granted
or were refused.   But now a form had to be signed.
And Colin had gone to get one . . . *for her to sign*.
She was to vouch for Rowena.   *She*, Helen Adair,
was to vouch for that poisonous woman, that . . .

" Oh, God, I can't do it," she whimpered.

All the time she knew that she must.   *Must.*   She
could not withdraw now.   There was no way out.

Had she known, she would never have come.   She
would have arranged it somehow—some other way.
Rowena could have found a proposer—no doubt about
that.   It was not that she would not behave : she
would do the Enclosure credit, as like as not.   The
sepulchre was whited all right . . .   Her objection
was *personal*.   She simply did not wish to vouch for
Mrs. David Bohun.   *Wish ?*   The idea was revolting.
More.   It was perilous.   As hating the woman, as
gaining her husband's love, as hoping that somehow
some day the man would belong to her, how could
she put upon record . . .

Helen Adair was no saint.   But no woman likes
recording her treachery.   And when she is not a
traitress, she likes it still less.

A baize-covered door shuddered, and by a tremendous effort the girl recovered her poise.

" I've been thinking," said Colin. " When Barbara hears that I've seen you, she'll give me no peace.
She's at Tapestry now—with the children : and I'm
going down, if I can, on Saturday night. Why don't
you come down for the week-end ? We're all alone ;
and when I say that we'd simply love to have you,
you know, my dear, I'm putting it very low."

" You are a dear," said Helen, " but I've got a date
on Sunday. My nice young man, who, like you, works
all the week, is to pay his debt by taking me out for the
day."

" Then bring him to us," said Colin. " Tapestry's
just the right distance, and the country after Bagshot's a sight to be seen."

" May I leave it open ? " said Helen. " It's really
his show, and he may have other ideas. But I'd love
to see Barbara."

" Of course," said Colin. The baize door shuddered
again, and he raised his voice. " Come in."

A clerk appeared—a proposal form in his hand . . .

As the door closed behind him—

" Come to the table," said Colin. " You only
need sign your name. I'll have it filled in."

The girl did as he said. There was nothing else to
be done. She scarcely glanced at the form. What did
the wording matter ? She, Helen Adair, was vouch-
ing . . . putting on record . . .

As she laid down her pen—

" This is something new, isn't it, Colin ? "

" More or less," said the man. " They tightened
things up, you know, a year or two back." He pinned
together the application and form, pencilled a note on
the former and pitched them into a tray. " There'll
be some excitement, downstairs, when they see your
name. We don't have many favourites, and when
you went . . ."

He let the sentence go, and Helen rose to her feet.

" So many thanks, dear Colin. I'm going now. Give

Barbara my love. If—if I were to come on Sunday,
could I really count on you and her being alone ? "

"Indeed you can," cried the man. "We go into
retreat on Sundays. I actually have the gates shut.
But you'll find they'll open for you. Why, when
they see you coming, they'll lift up their heads."

Himself, he saw her downstairs and into her car . . .

The girl drove straight home.

Long before she reached Kensington Square, she
had made up her mind that, if David met her on
Sunday, to Tapestry they would go. Barbara and
Colin should see the man for themselves. Then, if
anything ever happened, at least they could swear
that he was not such a man as lets his wife down . . .
Of course, that wasn't the point. She, Helen Adair,
had proposed Rowena Bohun.

She rang up David, in Chambers, at four o'clock.

"Just to say it's quite all right, David. They'll
send your vouchers along."

"Helen, you angel——"

"Let me know about Sunday. Good-bye."

She put the receiver back and surveyed herself in
a mirror which hung on the wall.

"I'm going to forget it," she said. "It wasn't my
fault : but the worst-looking things never are. And
I daresay, if I could see it, it's got its humorous side.
Only, I'm badly placed . . . Dear God, what *would*
Mo say ? She'd have a stroke, of course. But it
wouldn't stop there."

With that, she rang up Chiberta and talked with
Lady Persimmon for a quarter of an hour.

No mention, of course, was made of David Bohun.

*   *   *   *

A sherry party was proceeding when Bohun reached
Curzon Street.

The revel was not at all to Rowena's taste : but,

though she had been much tempted to put off her guests, she had sunk her personal feelings to honour the call of her duty towards herself. Such a chance of *suggestio falsi* must not be thrown away—just because she felt more like murder than changing hats. Such as came would see for themselves not only that she was ailing, but that her disorder was due to her husband's ill will.

The events of the night before had left their mark upon her face, and though this could have been hidden, she let it appear. Then, again, she bruised easily. Left as they were, her slender wrists would tell an infamous tale . . .

That she played her part to perfection will be believed : it remained—such is Fate—for David himself to support her, at half past six, by a display of spirits so high as to be almost boisterous—a demeanour so unusual that everyone present supposed it to be assumed. I, of course, except Rowena, who hid the surprise she felt. Such was the man's excitement, he never noticed that he was coldly received ; and when, soon after his entrance, everyone left, he saw in their early departure another smile of the Fortune whose pet he had now become.

He sped the last of their guests and tore back upstairs.

" Rowena ! "

" Go on. I'll buy it," said his wife. " I suppose you've gone one better and taken two seats on a coach."

The satire was lost on David.

" I've got the vouchers," he cried. " At least, they're going to be sent. Helen Adair fixed it. She went to St. James's Palace and——"

He got no further than that.

His wife was laughing as he had never heard her— not with tremulous wails of mirth, but with the honest horse-laughter of one to whose coarser instincts something has made an appeal which must be allowed.

Something within the man seemed suddenly turned

I

into stone. What had been warm and eager was suddenly cold and dead. And he found his wife's laughter offensive . . . very grossly offensive . . . to Helen Adair. Before he knew it was rising, his anger was high.

His voice cut through the guffaws, as an usher's cry of ' Silence ' cuts through laughter in court.

" D'you mind stopping at once ? " The laughter stopped dead. " It doesn't amuse me to hear you laugh like that."

" I beg your pardon ? " said Rowena, her eyes like steel.

Her husband met them squarely.

" I said that it didn't amuse me to hear you laugh like that."

" What on earth d'you mean ? "

" What I say," said David. " And if ever you feel like laughing like that again, I'd be obliged if you'd wait till I'm out of the room."

" My God, he's giving orders," said Rowena. " You did learn a lot at lunch."

" I learned nothing at lunch," said the man. " Except that Helen Adair is a damned good friend. From the moment I showed her the mess, she'd only got one idea—to straighten it out. Well, now she's done it. I see nothing funny in that."

" ' Showed her the mess ', did you ? I suppose you took care to explain that you'd done your little best and I'd spat in your eye."

" I don't do things like that," said David Bohun.

" What *did* you say ? "

" What I thought fit," said David, passing from strength to strength. " You needn't be afraid. I didn't tell her the truth."

Rowena's eyes burned in her head.

" Did you say ' afraid ' ? " she hissed.

" I did," said David. " ' Afraid.' "

" ' Afraid ' of what ? Of her ? "

" Of my telling the truth. I say you need have no fear. I'm not going to give you away. But if——"

" God, give me strength," said Rowena. " He's not going to give me away. The cheapest guy that ever manhandled a woman——"

" That's a rotten lie—and you know it."

" Steady, my son," said Rowena. " I've stood quite a lot from you, but——"

" You know that I never——"

" Look at my wrists," flashed Rowena, and held them out.

" I see them," said David, grimly. " And both of us know how they happen to look like that. In a word, we both know the truth." He threw up his head. " What's the good of lying to me—when both of us *know* ? Lie to your pals, if you like. As like as not, they'll believe you and think I'm a dirty dog. D'you think I care ? D'you think I could ever care—what scum like the Stumms and the Grainers think about me ? "

" St. James's Palace calling," said Mrs. Bohun.

" Sneer if you like," rapped her husband. " I say *we* know."

" The pity is," said Rowena, " you didn't meet her before. Before me, I mean. Then——"

" That remark," said David, coldly, " is in the grossest taste." Rowena choked. " And I'll tell you another thing. You say it's your ambition to be her friend. Well, your ways aren't her ways, and you've got a long way to go. If someone does her a service, she doesn't hoot with laughter behind their back." He brought his hand down on the table by which he stood. " It makes me boil," he cried, " when I think of what she's just done. And you say you want to be friends ! By God, if she rang up now and asked you to lunch, I give you my solemn word I'd warn her off."

" Would you, indeed ? " said Rowena, between her

teeth. "Well, just get this, my friend. *You're married to me.* Your smell may appeal to her, but——"

"What you want is a damned good thrashing," said David Bohun.

It was the contempt with which the statement was quick that made Rowena see red. Only the fear of marking him kept her nails out of his face.

"Get out of the room," she screamed. "Get out of my sight—before I ring for Anselm and have you put in the street."

Without a word, her husband stepped to the fire-place and rang the bell.

When the butler entered the room, he addressed his wife.

"Have you any orders for Anselm ? "

Rowena made no reply. With narrowed eyes, she regarded the graceless glove which Mrs. Grainer had left.

"Well, I have," said Bohun. He turned to the butler, waiting beside the door. "You're fired," he said sharply. "Discharged." He took two bank-notes from his note-case and laid them down on a tray. "There's your money in lieu of notice. Pack your things and be out of the house in an hour."

With that, he walked out of the room, leaving the butler blinking and Rowena open-mouthed, with a hand halfway to her chin.

* * * *

Ten minutes later he left the house for his Club. There he wrote a short note.

Dear Helen,

It's quite all right about Sunday. I'll love to come. When and where shall I meet you ?

Yours ever,
David Bohun.

CHAPTER VIII

Anticyclone

THE quarrel of that June evening shook Bohun far more than his wife. Ministering to herself, the latter was soon revived. A whiff of the handsome vengeance which she was to take was her restorative.

Rowena was well aware of what she had done. She had, in fact, made two mistakes. She had let her contempt for her husband reject control : and she had underrated the charm of Helen Adair. Neither mistake would have mattered, if she had made it alone. Together, as certain fluids, they were bound to cause an explosion such as had just occurred. But, though she was momentarily disconcerted, she was by no means dismayed. Such damage as had been done was negligible. It would be repaired—and paid for . . . Not to have had a badge would have been ten thousand times worse.

Anselm must go—for the moment. But he would soon return. After a week of his substitutes, David would be only too thankful to have the man back. During his absence the sherry parties would have to be suspended : but David would pay for that with a physical and mental inconvenience which had to be seen to be believed. There is nothing like rank service for sending a hard-working master out of his mind . . .

Then, again, from this time on she would have to treat David himself with something more than contempt. Rowena raised her eyebrows—an ominous sign. ' A damned good thrashing ', he had said. Dear, dear—these idle words . . . Her air was that of the expert who has had a fight forced on him by someone who does not know how to handle a sword.

And that was all.

In spite of what she had said, the fact that her lawful husband had ' fallen for ' somebody else, so far from perturbing the lady, failed to arouse her interest. She knew the poor fish too well. Though he loved the Adair to distraction, David Bohun would never let down his wife. All he had done was to add a whip to her rack. Of course their marriage would crash—in her own good time. She had always proposed that it should. But she, by God, was the pilot : and she would crash their marriage when and where and as it might happen to suit her book.

The reflection that the woman who loathed her had gone to some pains to procure her her heart's desire continued to afford Mrs. Bohun infinite joy. ' Better is a dinner of herbs . . . ' ? Solomon slipped up there. ' The stalled ox '—every time. And a man with six hundred wives might have been expected to know that hatred is a hell of a sauce.

Half a mile off, her husband sat very still in his old-fashioned Club, now exalted in spirit and now aghast, digesting the startling truth that he was body and soul in love with Helen Adair.

* * * *

Bohun need not have dreaded returning to Curzon Street. Neither need he have rehearsed the line he was going to take with Rowena, his wife. Such rehearsal was vain. Rowena, his wife, made it so— by the simple, well-worn process of taking the wind from his sails.

He returned at eleven o'clock, to find her reading in bed. As he entered the room, she addressed him —exactly as though they had parted ten minutes before. And that, in amity.

" I'm afraid you were right about Anselm. He's gone, of course. He was getting above himself. In fact, to tell you the truth, I'd have asked you to fire him last week, but for the hideous prospect of finding another man."

David, of course, was dumbfounded, as she had meant him to be. As in a dream, he heard himself make answer—

" I'm glad you take it like that."

" I've many faults," said Rowena, " as you should know. But, at least, I know how to admit that I've made a mistake. And I'll tell you another thing— there's something wrong with my nerves. I'll have to have treatment or something. I'm all right now —for the moment : but you must have noticed—*I* have—that my sense of proportion's all wrong. Things get me on the raw, when they oughtn't to get me at all. And I go off the deep end for nothing—because I can't help myself."

Her husband bit his lip.

" I'm afraid," he said, " I'm afraid I get on your nerves."

" Everyone does," said Rowena. " But you're the only one I can sock. It's damned unfair, of course : but I can't turn round on the others—you must see that. And so I rub your nose in the mess they make . . . This evening old Love-in-a-Mist broke one of our plates." (The sobriquet, which was at once Mrs. Grainer's and inappropriate, was due to that lady's interpretation of the game of ' sardines '.) " The Spode ones, of course. Just bunged it down on the ground. Well, I damned near called her a cow. Instead, I wrung out a smile and talked about something else. And when you came in, you met it . . . We can't go on, of course. If I must, I'll start a baby —that ought to trim the ship. But I think I'll try treatment first."

" What sort of treatment ? " said David.

Rowena observed with interest that he did not pursue her suggestion that she should bear a child. The fact was illuminating. Hitherto he had continually begged her to do him a favour on which he had set his heart. And, as may be believed, Rowena had always refused.

"I don't know," she said lightly. "Rays or massage, or something. They tickle the spinal cord, and you're born again."

"All right," said David, slowly. "It—it might be a good idea. All the same, until you're better—I mean, I think perhaps we've been together too much." He swallowed desperately, striving to paraphrase the downright sentences which he had intended to use. "Let me put it like this. At the moment, I don't think my presence helps. In fact, Rowena, I think it irritates you."

"I don't blame you," replied his wife. "Nerves aren't too funny, when you're standing as close as you. But don't sheer off too much, or people will talk."

"I shan't sheer off," said David. "But—well, to-night, for instance, I've been at the Club. And I think it's done us both good, to tell you the truth."

Rowena nodded sagely.

"No doubt about that."

"Well, there you are," said David. "If that's going to help us, we'd better try it again. As I've said, I can't go to Ascot, because I'm in court that week. That being so, there's no point in my going to the Grainers'—except for you. And as things are, I think I'd better stay here. You see, apart from anything else, to go up and down every day——"

"Let me at once admit that, if our positions were reversed, I shouldn't break my neck to spend every evening with you."

The man put a hand to his head.

"As long," he said, "as long as you understand . . . I mean, I think it is better that we should be sometimes apart. I don't know about next Sunday. I think you said that the Mockets had asked us to Brighton."

Quick as a flash—

" I shouldn't come," said Rowena. " If Helen Adair will have you, I'd take her out for the day."

" All right, I will," said David, as casually as he could . . .

Had the man been asked, and consented, to say what had just taken place, he would have declared that ' things had been patched up '. That was, of course, his belief. The correct answer would have been that the lion and the lamb had been discussing a *modus vivendi*—a pretty exercise which, in the absence of the millennium, seemed likely to prove abortive.

* * * *

Soon after eleven on Sunday Helen Adair's black coupé was stealing up the Hammersmith Road. By her request, Bohun was driving. The two had the car to themselves.

Neither said very much, for both were shy—the man, because of his secret : the girl, because she knew what his secret was.

When they came to the Great West Road, David took pleasure in giving the car her head. To his delight the coupé went like the wind.

" She's a corker," he said, easing up for some traffic-lights. " And where shall I take you, Helen ? I know I asked you before, but you only said ' West '."

" Ask me again at Bagshot. I've got a blow for you, David. You've been invited to lunch."

" Damn," said Bohun. " I wanted you all to myself."

" You needn't go," said Helen. " I left it open, all right. But they're very quiet and simple, and I think you'd enjoy yourself."

" D'you want to go ? "

" Not if you don't, David. But it isn't a party,
you know. Just a hard-working man and his wife.
They're very like us."

" They can't be like you," said the man . . .
And then, " All right. Let's go. I don't know where
to take you : so it's better that you should take
me."

From Hartley Row they idled—the summer's day
was so brilliant, the pageant of the country so rare.

The roadside oaks and elms, bloodstock of Shakespeare's England, became the King's highway : gates
in the blowing hedgerows disclosed deep meadows,
compassed by glancing woods : rose-red manors
peered between great-hearted timber, older than
they : the breathless green of chestnuts defined the
gray of towers : after the way of Æsop, sunshine and
shadow were sharing a rolling park, where a leisure of
cows was pointing an artless fable that was before
alphabets were : and, every now and again, a crest
would command a landscape that filled the heart—
such stuff as Georgics are made of . . . and Englishmen remember, as they die.

" Makes Chiberta seem cheap, doesn't it ? " said
Helen Adair.

Makes Rowena seem cheap, doesn't she ? thought
David Bohun. But he said—

" I love Chiberta—and always shall."

They came to Tapestry's gates at a quarter to
one.

As they stole up the drive, the girl told Bohun of
Colin and Barbara.

" They belong to my other life : and I'd never meant
to open that book again."

" But you did—for my sake, Helen."

" David, my dear, get this. By making me open
that book, you did me a first-class turn. There are
damned few Colins about, as you'll see for yourself.

To cut him out was absurd. I mean, he's a type to grapple. And Barbara, too. Yet, but for you, I might never have seen them again."

" I don't care. You did it for me."

With his words, they sighted the house—an exquisite Caroline mansion, asleep in the sun—a place of flags and mullions and the beauty of chiselled stone, of winking lattice-windows and the refrain of doves.

As they left the car, their hostess leaned out of an oriel, over their heads.

" Helen, darling, how are you ? "

And Colin, in pipe and shirt-sleeves, had opened the door before the servants arrived . . .

The afternoon slid by as a sunlit stream, whose unfrequented waters reflect, one after another, the scenes of natural beauty by which they pass—lunch within panelled walls . . . coffee upon the velvet of an Horatian lawn . . . children playing at a fountain whose seventeenth-century basin made them a bathing-pool . . . Barbara holding a spaniel, while Helen withdrew a thorn from one of his pads . . . the two men surveying the meadows, to see if they could be used as a landing-ground . . .

The four agreed together, as Helen had known that they would. Though their lines were so very different, they felt the same about things.

So, till four o'clock, when Helen caught David's eye and said they must go. The others protested, of course ; but the two stood firm. They proposed to wander awhile, before returning to Town.

When David tried to thank her, Barbara smiled.

" We had you for Helen's sake. Come again for your own."

As the coupé slipped out of sight—

" That's a hard case," said Colin. " I suppose his wife's a wrong 'un. They mostly are."

Barbara took his arm.

" I'm afraid you're right. Poor Helen."

"She deserves a square deal," said Colin, "if anyone ever did."

"We've helped them to-day," said his wife. "Why shouldn't we do it again?"

"No reason at all," said Colin. "They're both all right. So far as I'm concerned, Tapestry's at their disposal from this time on."

*   *   *   *

Bohun picked his way through the country for more than an hour, careless of his direction and only taking pains to keep to the lesser roads. To the two, thus asking nothing, the countryside gave of her best; and the vagrants had to themselves such beauties of wood and pasture as tourists have sought in vain.

They were talking easily now.

"You don't know the relief," said David, "of sitting down to a meal with people like that. I don't mean being with you. That's far more than relief: it's like being raised from the dead."

"David"—protestingly.

"It is. But that's by the way. To play for two or three hours with people who feel as you do, who think and talk as you do . . ." He let the sentence go, drew the car to the edge of a beechwood, threw out the clutch and switched the engine off. "You see, the people I meet are not like that. They're the truly idle rich—the type that makes a Communist out of an honest man. So far as I know, they do nothing but muck about. From their point of view, conversation must be flippant, scandalous or foul—if possible, all three. If it isn't one or the other, then it isn't worth listening to. To have sat through that lunch to-day would have bored them stiff. It would have been *above* them: but *they would have thought it was below them*—beneath their contemptible contempt. They back horses and think they're sporting: their

hair-dressers give them tips. They're either familiar
with servants, or else they treat them like dirt . . .
I don't ask much. I'm not high-brow; I'm not a
prude. I don't think I'm intolerant. If they like to
behave like baboons, that's their affair. But they
ought to be behind bars : and when they're not, and
you're thrown with them night after night—well, it
makes you critical." He threw himself back in his
corner and mopped his face. " I'm probably being
unfair : but it's such a relief to let go. They're civil
enough to me—God only knows why."

" There are—others, David."

" I know. Millions. But I don't happen to meet
them. It's not surprising. They won't muck in with
baboons . . . You see, I can't choose our friends.
I have to leave that to Rowena—I've too much to do.
And she seems to stick it all right. She's no more
like them than I am, but she's a big success."

Helen Adair bit her lip.

Then—

" It's a frightful pity, David, to run with that crowd.
They're nothing new, you know. They've always
been there. But—well, the others won't have you, as
long as you run with them."

" I know," said the man. " I know." He turned
on her almost roughly. " You're one of the others,
Helen. And yet . . . you've—taken me up."

" I've not. Don't use that phrase. People like me
don't ' take up ' people like you. We just made
friends—and you know it. Oh, David, how could you
say such a rotten thing ? "

Helen Adair could act, but she was not acting now.
The sudden flash of anger—on his behalf, the look of
reproach that hung in those glorious eyes—these things
belonged to a kindness which Bohun had never known.
Little wonder, his love took charge . . .

Somehow, her hands were in his, and his head was
bowed, and his lips were brushing her palms.

" I suppose you know I'm mad about you," he said. The cool fingers closed about his face.

" I know—and I'm thankful," said Helen. " You see, I love you so much."

The man started up.

" Helen ! "

Helen Adair nodded, staring out of the wind-screen and down the green and gold lane.

" It's perfectly true," she said.

She was in his arms, and her face was pressed tight against his.

" Helen, my darling, my darling."

" That's why I came to London," she heard herself say.

" Oh, I can't believe it," cried Bohun, holding her off, and searching her clear, blue eyes with the fire in his own. " That I should love you is natural : you are so sweet and lovely—so very beautiful, Helen, from head to foot. I've never seen anyone like you—nor's anyone else. But that you should . . . love . . . me . . . Are you sure it isn't just pity ? "

The girl answered steadily.

" Quite sure, my darling. I loved you that day at Bayonne."

" Helen, Helen." As he drew her towards him, the starlit eyes were veiled and the beautiful head went back. " My God, I'm afraid . . . you're so lovely." He kissed her lips and her arm went about his neck. " Oh, Helen, my sweet, my darling, why can't I die on this moment ? I've touched the top of the world."

" Ah, if we could—together." She caught her breath. " And start again—together . . . at the foot of the world to come."

" Adam and his beautiful Eve . . . their great adventure before them, and nothing behind."

" Oh, David, my blessed . . ."

Letting the world slip, they played with their pretty

dream, each holding the other close, as though of such
physical contact the vision might come to life . . .

For a handful of shining moments a good-natured
Time stood still. Then the man kissed her eyes and
lips, and then sat back in his seat, with her hand in
his lap.

"My darling," he said very quietly, "what do we
do?"

"What can we do, David, but wait? I—I don't
think your wife loves you. If she did, this wouldn't
have happened. I mean, I don't believe in wrecking a
home."

"When did you know it, Helen? It's true, of
course."

"When she came to dinner that night. But don't
let's talk about that. You know it now, too—thank
God. It was so awful to see you . . . worshipping
something that—didn't worship you back."

Bohun looked out of his window.

"Men make prize fools of themselves."

The hand in his lap clasped his.

"It wasn't your fault, my darling. You are so
faithful yourself that you're terribly easy to bet—
deceive. That's always the way, you know."

"You knew it the moment you saw her. And I've
only just found out—on Wednesday evening, the day
before we had lunch."

Helen looked straight ahead.

"What's happened since then, to—to change you?
On Thursday, in Lincoln's Inn Fields, you were crazy
to 'get her back'."

The man looked down.

"She killed it dead that evening, when I got home.
I told her—your telephone message . . . how terribly
sweet you'd been. I could hardly wait to tell her,
until those—those wasters had gone . . ."

"What did she say?" said Helen.

"Nothing at all," said Bohun. "She laughed . . ."

and laughed. Laughed as I'd never heard her . . .
And something shivered inside me—the golden bowl,
perhaps. I guess it was cracked before, but I didn't
know that."

The girl put a hand to her head.

" I'm sorry it came through me."

" What does it matter, my darling ? "

Helen raised her eyebrows.

" Oh, it doesn't really, I suppose. Never mind.
Let's leave it there. I'm sorry I dragged her in. But
don't tell me anything else. Don't ever mention her
to me. I mean, it does no good—and we don't want
to talk about her behind her back."

" Oh, my God," said David, " I can't let her down."

" Listen, my darling," said Helen. " You must
understand one thing. I know quite enough to know
this—that nothing you chose to do would be ' letting
her down '. We're going to behave, of course—for
both our sakes. But, *even if we didn't,* you wouldn't
be letting her down."

" But——"

" David," said Helen Adair, " do get this straight.
If you feel that, so long as you're married, we oughtn't
to meet again—well, then, we'll part to-night. That's
a point of view which I can only respect. But I
cannot sit still, my darling, and hear you accuse yourself of letting her down. It's a hideous contradiction
in terms—and it makes me want to scream." She
caught his arm and shook it—as that of a sleeping man
who must be awaked. " Oh, for God's sake, sink that
idea. If I'm never to see you again, at least let me
open your eyes. She's been so brutal to you . . ."

The last six words did the trick. As Helen spoke
them, David's compunction died. It was true, what she
said. Rowena *had* been brutal—kicked kneeling Love
in the face . . . And Helen knew this was so. No
one had ever told her, and yet she knew . . . Wisdom
like that showed how much his judgment was worth.

"You're perfectly right," he said quietly. The grip on his arm relaxed. " I can't think how you know, but you're perfectly right. I don't . . . owe her . . . any duty. She's . . . put me through it . . . too much."

There was a little silence.

Then Bohun sought and recaptured the delicate hand on his sleeve.

" Ought I to tell her ? " he said.

" She knows," said Helen, quietly. " That's why she laughed."

There was another silence. Scale after scale was falling from Bohun's eyes.

At length he laughed lightly enough.

" It's my turn now," he said. " How cheap and small it all seems—my life with her—I mean, beside *our* show." With a sudden movement, he drew the girl into his arms. " Oh, Helen, my beautiful darling, I love you so. And to think that you love me back . . . Nothing matters now—any more. Nothing can ever matter . . . except the light in your eyes." She put up her mouth, and he kissed it tenderly. " But I've less than nothing to offer. You're sure you've not made a mistake ? "

" Not this time, David. You needn't worry, my darling. I'll never love anyone else."

" My sweet, my sweet . . ."

Together they dandled the present, as its parents a first-born child. Then a bicyclist stole round a bend, and a future they could not dandle loped by his side.

Fear laid the tip of its finger upon the man's heart.

" When must you go back, my darling ? To France, I mean."

" I'm not going back," said Helen. " I'm not going to leave you now."

Bohun looked out of his window. He dared not trust his voice.

After a little space—

K

"Now I know that you love me," he said. "I'd been making myself believe it : but now I know. The thing's fantastic, of course. But that doesn't matter at all, for I know it's true."

"It isn't fantastic," smiled Helen. "To tell you the truth, I think we make an excellent pair."

"Oh, don't be blasphemous . . ."

For another handful of moments, they laughed in the future's face.

Then—

"This waiting business," said David. "It's got to be faced, of course. There's nothing else to be done. We can't possibly have a scandal . . . But—you're much wiser than I am. How long shall we have to wait ? "

The girl laid her head on his shoulder.

"My darling, I've no idea. It's going to be fright-fully hard : but I have a feeling it's not going to be very long. I can't tell you why. I've nothing to go on at all. As you say, we can't have a scandal. For one thing only, I think it would break Mo's heart. For that reason, we've got to be careful—a loathsome phrase. But Mo will be over next week, and she'll be a present help."

"We can see one another, Helen ? "

"Of course, my sweet. And I can write to your Chambers and you can write back. But I don't think we'll telephone . . ."

"You say," said David, slowly, "you don't think it'll be very long. Supposing . . . you're wrong, darling . . . Supposing time goes on, yet nothing— takes place . . . How long can we stick it, Helen ? Watching our happiness wasting . . . the glory that we've discovered just draining away ? "

The girl put a hand to her eyes.

"Don't talk like that, my darling. We've *got* to manage—somehow. Divorce doesn't worry me : but I couldn't be—on the wrong side."

She felt the man's muscles contract.

"My God, no," he breathed. "Not that."

"Don't look ahead, David dear. It doesn't do any good. At least, we've found each other. And love has, sometimes, to live from hand to mouth."

"I know, I know. But, now that I've got you, I don't want to let you go. We're going to part this evening, in Kensington Square. I'd like to be going home . . . to hand the car over and follow you into our house . . . to lie on the bed and talk to you while you were changing . . . to call to you from the bathroom . . . to sit opposite you at dinner—and keep on losing my place because of how proud I am and how lovely you look."

She was in his arms again now, and her head was back. Her eager lips were parted, her eyes were shut.

"One day," she whispered, "one day . . . We'll keep this day—every year. We'll lunch at Tapestry, and come to this very place . . . And then we'll drive home . . . and change . . . and dine alone together . . . just as you said."

The man pressed his lips to her throat.

"One day, my darling, one day."

* * * *

The band had retired for refreshment, and thirty or forty revellers, their occupation gone, were languidly supporting the silence, lolling about the tables at which they had dined and holding more general conversation than the discipline of the saxophone ever allowed.

Mrs. Jocelyn Garter, however, was concluding a private report, which the man to whom she had made it seemed scarcely prepared to believe.

"I tell you, I saw them, Boney. Of course she's going to seed, but she showed him up. And you ought to have seen his face. He could hardly wait to get out."

" But I thought——"

" And I saw, my friend. I was lunching with
Teddy Bemuse. I'll lay his wife doesn't know : but
we'll soon find out." She leaned across the table and
raised her metallic voice. " Rowena."

The man was aghast.

" Oh, I say, Jocelyn, you can't."

" Shut your face," snarled Mrs. Garter, returning to
Mrs. Bohun. " D'you know the Adair, Rowena ? "

The answer came pat.

" I've met her once. She asked us to dinner at
Biarritz. I think she's most awfully sweet."

" D'you ever lunch with your husband ? "

Rowena shook her head. The bracketing of the
inquiries appeared to mean nothing to her. Everyone
else at the table was holding his or her breath.

" Never," said Mrs. Bohun. " He lunches in Lincoln's Inn Hall. You see, he can't spare the time.
He only gets half an hour." She looked round the
table, wide-eyed. " What's she laughing for ? " she
demanded. " What have I said ? "

Mrs. Garter's gossip threw himself into the breach.

" It's very simple, Rowena. Jocelyn proposes that
your husband shall ask her to lunch."

Rowena laughed her very attractive laugh.

" I'll bet he doesn't," she bubbled. " If he can't
have lunch with me, it isn't likely he'll go and have
lunch with her."

A roar of laughter succeeded these simple words.

Could artlessness go further ? (If you remember,
Rowena had achieved artlessness.) Mrs. Garter had
been reduced—at the mouth of a babe. The hearts of
her audience warmed towards Mrs. Bohun.

But when the band had returned and Rowena took
to the floor, the others approached Mrs. Garter and
asked her what she knew.

CHAPTER IX

News Reel

AFTER ten bloodshot days, Anselm returned to
his duty in Curzon Street. This, by David's
request. The latter had been brought to his knees
by the service which he had suffered since the former
had gone. He had, of course, no idea that Anselm
had selected the butlers whom Rowena installed in his
place.

The first was a total abstainer—or so he said. It
may have been true. He may have practised in secret
some form of abstinence. The fellow reported for
duty at five o'clock, and David saw him for a moment
at a quarter past eight. His demeanour was then
inspiring : his carriage was that of a prelate upon
parade. Whilst the Bohuns were dining out, Anselm
ministered to his protégé's needs. Shortly before midnight, David escaped from a party which was raging
in the bowels of the earth and, leaving Rowena to
follow, made his way home. With a sigh of relief,
he let himself into the house, to find his *maître d'hôtel*
supine in the hall. He was, as they say, dead drunk.
The stupor in which he was folded was impregnable.
Kicks and cold water could not touch him. The man
was not of this world. The other servants, when
summoned, refused to come. Yet, something had to
be done—for Rowena's sake. David had to deal
single-handed with a carcase of thirteen stone. What
was worse, the man had been sick. Had it not been
pouring with rain, David would have lugged him into
the street. The next morning he wished he had—for

the drunkard arose captious, not to say bellicose.
The charge of intemperance was furiously received :
declarations of independence were raved : fantastic
rights were asserted : all manner of threats were
belched. Upstairs Rowena lay listening, on her face
the smile of the producer who looks upon his pro-
duction and sees that it is good. By eleven o'clock
the man was out of the house. David, short of his
breakfast, reached his Chambers one hour and three
quarters late.

The second was temperate : but if he had other
virtues, they did not appear. He was slovenly, de-
structive and rude. He smoked while laying the table,
ate while answering the bell, and, finding the telephone
a nuisance, swore at his correspondent and left the
receiver off. He cleaned neither shoes nor silver, rose
too late to serve breakfast, used his employers' bathroom, was insolent under rebuke. After ninety-six
galling hours, Bohun was summoned from Chambers,
to turn the man out of the house. His expulsion took
time—as a dog with a bone in his mouth, he was
on a good thing. Finding his protests vain, he fell
back on abuse. He packed leisurely, whilst David
was chafing below. More than once he interrupted
his packing and came to the head of the stairs, to
make his master free of the further and better re-
proaches which he had just composed. Rowena, upon
the first floor, could hardly control her mirth. He
left at last—in a flurry of animadversion which drew a
small crowd. David returned to his Chambers, short
of his lunch.

The third was amorous. Devoid of all physical
attraction, he lived for love. Two hours after he
came, the housemaid left. Not to be frustrated, he
looked again at the cook. It is not too much to say
that the latter could have hiked with impunity in
shorts and Afghanistan. *Quot homines, tot sententiæ.*
A man of no ordinary perception, Anselm's latest

detected sex-appeal in the cook. Called upon to defend her virtue for the first time in fifty years, the woman raised the house and about an acre of street. David returned from Chambers, to find Rowena arguing with the police. In the end, no charge was made : the man was cast out, neck and crop : the cook was fetched by her sister at half past ten.

The house stood empty of servants for thirty-six hours. Then Bohun threw in his hand, and Anselm came back. The housemaid returned the next day, and the cook, still breathing out threatenings, the day after that.

It must, I think, be conceded that Mrs. Bohun and Anselm had won, hands down.

* * * *

It was, of course, a great pity that Chater was unaware that Anselm had been dismissed. The interregnum, though brief, had offered a golden chance. All three pretenders would have talked. If they had said nothing else, they would have disclosed that Anselm had procured them the throne. And Rowena had related in detail the lengths to which she had gone to run them to earth. But Chater was otherwise engaged.

A letter which Forsyth received on June 15th suggested that the detective considered his client's purse.

. . . The most that can be said is that the definite lines of inquiry are now reduced to three. I think there is no doubt about that. But the cost of following up only one of them might well prove prohibitive. I mean, it might easily run into four figures . . .

Forsyth replied by return—in his own hand.

Dear Chater,

Please go ahead. I don't care what it costs. She's got to be found.

Yours very truly,
J. G. Forsyth.

* * * *

We know that Mrs. Bohun detested Mrs. Adair, and we know that she had determined to twist her husband's tail. When, therefore, the lady learned that Helen Adair was not to return to France, she made no attempt to disguise the pleasure she felt.

To herself she said—

" They're off. Oh, goody goody. My God, how I'll make them sweat."

To her husband she said—

" David, how priceless. I am so glad. It's going to be so terribly nice for you."

As though rejoicing with him, she blew him a kiss— and watched him wince in spirit before an address which would lately have lifted his heart.

Rowena was nothing, if not artistic. She could turn a whip into a scorpion.

Uxorious as ever in public, she began to cherish her husband when they were alone. This, to the man's distraction . . . Deeply in love with Helen, Rowena's spurts of ardour revolted him, body and soul.

To Helen, herself, she sent flowers—and more than one invitation to dinner in Curzon Street.

She lunched at the Savoy without warning. ' I looked out for you and Helen : I don't think you can have been there . . .' She accepted invitations for Bohun likely to clash with arrangements which he had made . . . She was seized with a sudden faint-ness five minutes before he was leaving for Kensington Square . . . She referred to Helen in public—when

David was there. 'He knows her much better than I do. Do tell them about *La Belle Issue*—I only saw it by night . . .' Asked, at Colin's instance, to dine 'on guard', David could not find his dress-studs—and was half an hour late . . .

It was just as easy as not to tread on the lovers' toes.

Helen Adair felt like murder, and David began to lose weight.

Here, perhaps, is the place to insist once again upon the fact that Rowena knew no law. She was untrammelled by any decency. She consulted her own convenience, and nothing else. She could—and did—pull out at will the meekness of a St. Francis, the inhumanity of a Danton, the wanton malice of an unruly child. Provided it served her turn, no act was too common or unclean. Herein lay her strength. Not even Helen suspected that she had removed David's studs—which, according to her, the laundry returned the next day. The thing was too low—and, therefore, incredible. Rowena had on the breastplate of unbelief : she went in the mail of her fellows' incredulity. The advantage of this armour was quite inestimable. She could—and did—take action, of which so much as to suspect her would have cost her luckless husband his self-respect. She did things of which, had she been charged, a jury would have found her not guilty without ever leaving the box—because they would have known that civilized people do not do such things. And there they would have been wrong, because Rowena did.

But, though she tormented her husband and, through him, Helen Adair, such devilry was by the way. She never once lost sight of the main idea—to increase the flow of compassion for Mrs. David Bohun. Under her skilful direction, the rill swelled into a stream.

Of course, as her stock rose, so David's fell. Everyone knew he was 'crazy about the Adair'. Nobody dreamed that she knew this far better than they. Notorious evil-livers described it as ' damned unfair '. Men who were committing adultery swore it was dirty work. Women who were doing the same declared that they ' drew the line '. There was some excuse for the men. One spoke for all—in his cups. " Who the devil's Bohun ? " he hiccoughed. " I could do with the Adair myself."

David Bohun was unaware of these things. It sometimes occurred to him that people were more off-hand than they had been before, but the notion worried him less than the dust on the soles of his shoes. He had come to despise so much the circles in which he moved that, if he was used cavalierly, he merely supposed that they felt and resented his scorn. Baboons will be baboons . . . He would, of course, have sold his soul to withdraw—to decline all invitations and make himself scarce. But Rowena kept him up to the bit.

" We must put up a show, my friend, or people will talk. I mean, you know what they are."

" By God, I do," said David, bitterly.

" Exactly," said Mrs. Bohun. " I can shout ' It's nerves, you fools ', till I'm black in the face. I can yell ' He's no use for you, and that's why he's pulling out '. But they'll only wink and nod—and whisper behind their hands. That's the worst of a one-track mind. They're ready to see a girl-friend in every bush . . ."

The jab was more than enough. It was not to be thought of that the name of Helen Adair should be mouthed by baboons.

" I wish to God *you'd* pull out," said David, desperately.

" No doubt you do," said Rowena. " If I did, you'd be spared the pain of meeting my common friends."

" For your own sake," said David—and wondered if that was true.

" I see," said his wife, slowly. " And what should I do with myself when you dined in Kensington Square ? "

The discussions always ended in some such way— his sword on the ground, and Rowena's point at his throat.

There was nothing for it, of course. He simply had to go on. If he was to stroll with Helen, he must parade with his wife.

How much Rowena suspected he did not care. His conscience was clean. She had trodden his love under-foot, and he had picked it up and offered it—some-where else. The trouble was . . .

David had often wondered what was the domestic relation between a husband and wife who loved one another no more. Well, now he knew. It was in-tolerable.

His case would have been far less evil, if they could have lived apart. Helen would have been no nearer : but she—Rowena, his wife, would have been further off. The idea was more hopeless than he dreamed. Rowena would never have agreed. Pity be damned ı it wouldn't have suited her book.

* * * *

When Helen Adair took a furnished house in the country, some forty-five miles from Town, Lady Per-simmon praised God.

Since she had returned to London, David had come three times to Kensington Square. There was no harm in that, of course. In fact she had been very glad to see him again. But she had a hideous feeling that each of his visits was watched—and re-ported to Mrs. Bohun. And Mrs. Bohun, in her eyes, was about as trustworthy as a cobra bereft of its mate.

Her mind was broad. If David had had just cause

to divorce his wife, she would have danced at his
wedding with Helen Adair. He had nothing to offer
her daughter, who had so much. But he was honest
and decent, and, what was just as important, the
two were in love. The man would make her happy
as she had never been. But the protasis was the
snag. *If* he had had just cause to divorce his wife . . .

It was more than likely, of course, that, in fact,
he had just cause. What was perfectly certain was
that he had no proof. And he never would have any
proof, unless or until Mrs. Bohun desired to be free.
What was so dangerous was that she might desire to
be free, yet not be divorced.

Lady Persimmon frowned.

From what she had seen of the man, Bohun would
watch his life crumple—and Helen's, too, before he
allowed his wife to divorce him without just cause.
It was certainly done—every day. She understood it
was 'gentlemanly'—a very beautiful thought. But,
then, gigolos' interpretations of the laws of chivalry
were always beautiful.

" But, Mo——" said Helen.

" Don't interrupt," said her mother. " I'm just a
shade wiser than you. Besides, at the moment, I'm
inspired . . . If I can perceive these truths, why so
can that woman—his wife. Which brings us to the
mouth of the gun. Let's look down the barrel, shall
we ? She's not going to fire it just yet.

" His wife desires to be free, yet not be divorced.
She knows he will never help her, either by being
guilty or by pretending to be. It is, therefore, as
statesmen say, ' up to ' her. If she wants what she
wants enough, she will seek to prove him guilty of
something he has not done. She may or may not
succeed. But people who stick at nothing can get a
very long way.

" Well, there you are. I don't say it's going to
happen. When the time comes, she may not mind

being divorced. But if it does—well, I do not like the idea of your being concerned."

Helen regarded the end of her cigarette.

"Isn't she rather more likely to turn to black-mail ?"

"That," said Lady Persimmon, "depends upon the solicitors she employs."

"I think she'll think twice," said Helen, "before throwing bricks at me that were made without straw."

"I'm sure," said her mother, "she'll give it much anxious thought. But I'd like you to keep out of range. You know. Just in case. That's why I'm so glad you've taken this pretty place. Of course I knew Bluemantle before you were born. It used to belong to the Clarets—he was a dear. He had a shocking stammer—to which he would never give in. He'd burn his mouth at table and then he'd fight with a *B*. When we could bear it no longer, some-body'd offer him *Blast*. 'No, not *blast*', he'd say, and start off again. Of course everybody broke down, and he used to laugh himself till the tears ran down his face."

"I don't believe you," smiled Helen. "It's too good a tale."

"It was I," said Lady Persimmon, "who offered him *Blast*. Never mind. Don't go and steal it. I'm going to tell David myself. I must say I like his laugh. It's so unaffected and hearty. When do we move ?"

"What about Monday, darling ?"

Lady Persimmon frowned.

"Make it Saturday," she said. "And ask him to lunch on Sunday. The country will do him good."

* * * *

Royal Ascot had come and gone. Combining busi-ness with pleasure, Rowena had made the most of a gorgeous time. Parading for four whole days with those whose social standing was higher than that of her friends, she studied their style and their manners with infinite care. She compared them with the best of her peers, determined to define that sometimes indefinable difference which man can never miss, which his Maker can never perceive. It was a valuable exercise. She marked, learned and digested a great many things. Then, again, she was careful to watch the impression which she herself made upon men who belonged to circles in which she did not yet move. Her conclusions were satisfactory. She was remarked.

When the day was over, it was a relief to relax. Out of a rousing programme, the hour and a half of 'strip' poker on Saturday night lifted the week's entertainment to a level seldom attained and won for Mrs. Grainer the blue riband of hospitality. The spectacle of Love-in-a-Mist, who had already lost heavily and now had been dealt a full house, torn between a desire to beggar her neighbour and a natural reluctance to show forth the awful havoc which forty-five years of good living can make of the female frame, was unforgettable.

Next week, the prey of reaction, Rowena considered the claims of a clinic at Potter's Bar. The institution, which was above reproach, dispensed electrical treatment to such as were drooping or fancied that that was the case. Beneath its roof the sick were certainly healed. Whether, as was claimed, the treatment accorded could neutralize 'those demands upon the nervous system which are so disturbing a feature of modern life' is questionable. After discussion with David, who failed to disguise the truth that he did not care, Rowena announced her intention of 'having a stab'.

"If you take a course of twelve, you're up on the deal. Go as you please, of course. When you feel you're about run down, you stagger into the shrine and the acolytes wind you up."

" It sounds all right," ventured David.

" I'll say it does," said his wife. " If I glory in you next week, you'll know what it means. The instinct's there, you know : but it's been like an over-fed pug. Now we're keeping it short, it's beginning to open its eyes. I nearly wired you from Ascot. Would you have come ? "

" I don't know," said David, shortly. " We've got a long way to go."

" That's more like it," said Rowena. " A month ago you'd have said ' Why didn't you, darling ? ' and kissed the back of my neck. But now you never press. Did Helen Adair put you wise ? "

" I don't discuss you with her."

" Well, do. She might be a help. And if she was to mend the lute, I'd—I'd get the Mockets to ask her to Brunskill Towers."

Rowena was mistress of the gibe which rings in the ear. She was always saying things at once offensively pregnant and painfully inconvenient to attack. For twenty-four hours in the day, she had her tongue in her cheek.

The idea, for instance, of the Mockets' consenting, under pressure, to admit the Adair was post-impressionistic : the suggestion that the latter would prize such condescension was almost slanderous : over all, the stark proposal that Helen's good offices should be invoked to help Rowena and David into each other's arms was, in the circumstances, indecent.

Yet what could the man reply ? To demolish three such conceits, he must either speak at some length or else employ the bludgeon of vulgar abuse.

Neither method was practicable.

He would not have been permitted to speak at some length. As for more direct action, David had let fly—once. And when he had said his say, his wife had put her arms round his neck.

"Give me guts," she had murmured, and rubbed her cheek against his.

*   *   *   *

All the world's stage was still : a July sundown was playing her lovely rôle : dusk stood in the wings, waiting : night was at hand.

Pacing the lawn at Bluemantle, David and Helen were trying the bars of their cage.

"I could have it out," said David. "Tell her that we've—got off ; and say that, that being so, we'd be better apart."

"What good would that do, my darling ? If she thought you'd be better apart, you would not be together now. Besides, she knows about us. She knew what had happened before you knew it yourself."

"But what's she getting at, Helen ? I'm less than nothing to her : so why shouldn't she let me go ? "

"I can't answer that question," said Helen. "I only know that she doesn't want you to go. It follows that, if you went, you'd do something she didn't want. And I can't recommend that procedure. I mean, I think you'd pay for it, David . . ."

The man put his hands to his face.

"God knows I'm paying now. I mean, we—don't fit any more. That's putting it very low. Quite apart from you, we've nothing whatever in common—I see now we never had. And she doesn't make it easier—somehow . . ." He dropped his hands, to frown on the precious turf. "When I was leaving this morning, she told me that Punch and Belinda were coming to lunch. Well, that's damned awkward, you know—my not being there. I thought she'd arranged to play golf . . . Any way, she might have known——"

"Let's leave it there," said Helen, shakily. "It's the devil and all, I know, but——"

"It's worse than it was," said David. "I'll hang

on somehow, of course. I can't do anything else. But the—the blasted mockery gets me under the ribs." The girl took his arm. "I want to be rid of it, Helen. Life's not meant to be acted : it's meant to be lived. Well, sometimes you can't live it. Fate's against you or something, and so you stand back to the wall. But you don't try and *act* it, because you're an honest man. But I *have* to act it, my lady. I have to strut and spout on a pinchbeck stage . . . And all the time, you're waiting here. Day and night I see you, waiting to live our life."

A cool hand closed upon his.

"We must stick it somehow, my blessed. It—it won't be long."

"God send it isn't," said David. "I give you my word there are times when I'm damned near through." He raised a prisoner's eyes to the painted sky. "Is there no way out, my darling ? I mean, we both know in our hearts that it may be . . . years."

The girl caught her breath.

Then—

"I know it won't, David. Not years. I couldn't stand that. As it is, there are times when I feel that we can't go on. I know you're under fire and I'm out of range. But that doesn't make any difference— because I love you so much."

Foliage harboured them now, and he held her close.

"To hear you say that to me ! "

"Listen," said Helen. "You're going in half an hour. If I did the natural thing, I'd ask you to stay. Spend the night here with me, get your things to-morrow and leave with me for Chiberta in two days' time. That's what I'd love to do : and I'll go so far as to say that I don't even think it would be wrong. But I'm not going to do it, my darling—for it wouldn't be fair to you, it wouldn't be fair to Mo, and it wouldn't be fair to myself. Look at it how you will, our names would be mud—and they don't deserve

to be mud . . . Now it may come to that—in the
end. I recognize that. I mean, there's a breaking-
point. We cannot go on—indefinitely. At least, if
you can, I can't. So it may come to that. But I
. . . don't want it to, David—*for my own sake*. It
would be the death of Mo, but let that pass. Your
wife would name me, of course—in her petition, I
mean. And I don't . . . particularly want . . . to
be named by your wife."

"You never will be," said David. His tone was
low and vibrant. Helen had hit him hard. "You
never will be, my darling. I couldn't stand that.
And I'm damned if *I*'ll take the stick by the dirty
end. God knows she's forcing it on me, if ever a
woman did. But I will not have it said that I let
her down. I couldn't plead provocation. I couldn't
shout ' Yes, I did. But I had good cause '. I'd have
to sit still and submit to my own dishonour . . ."
He threw up his head and laughed. " My God, how
people would scream, to hear me talk like that. It's
done every day—every hour. And it means no more
to them than—than wearing a dress-shirt twice. I
don't think it means as much. You see, somebody
might suspect that the shirt had been worn before.
And that would take a lot of living down. But to
be divorced is an adventure. It's rather like crossing
the line. I've heard a man cheered when he showed
his face at a party, because his wife had got a decree
that day. Of course I'm pure Albertian . . ."

This was untrue. In fact, his mind was diseased.
The cancer of self-respect had eaten into his brain.
Had it been taken in time, he might have been spared :
but the stride of social science had passed him by.
That man had come to make manners, he did not
appreciate. For him, as for William of Wykeham,
manners would always make man.

Helen put up a hand and touched his hair.

"Be Albertian for me," she said gently.

The man smiled into her eyes.

" There's something wrong with you, Helen. To come to care for me is peculiar enough : but, having committed that folly, to want me to stay as I am . . . It's just as well, of course, for I don't believe I could change. My God, when you look like that, it sends the blood to my head. The world fades out, and there's only the firmament left. I know that's there, for all its light is caught in your wonderful eyes. Did you ever know Ben Jonson ? I don't think you can have—he was before *my* time. Perhaps he dreamed about you." He held the girl off and set his head on one side. " You know you're —illustrative. Sonnets have meant something quite different, since I set eyes upon you."

An Eve laughed back, and he drew her into his arms.

" My blessed Nell," he said quietly, and kissed her excellent lips.

" I love that name," breathed Helen. " No one but you has ever used it before."

For a moment they clung together. Then the man braced himself.

" Time I was going," he said. " They say life's what you make it. I think they're wrong. You see, you make my life . . . Where's Lady Persimmon, Nell ? I must say ' Good-bye '."

* * * *

Bohun was nearing Slough, when Belinda Leighton frowned.

" I'm not sticking up for him, Punch : but I think it's so unlike him—that's all I said."

" You went much further than that. You said there was something behind it—or some such bilge."

" Who says it's bilge ? "—furiously.

" I do," raged Punch. " And I know what I'm talking about. I'm a man, and——"

" Just because——"

" Will you let me finish ? " howled Punch. " I'm a man, and D.B.'s a man. And men know the why and the wherefore of what men do. The Adair, who-ever she is—she can't know how to behave, or she'd ask his wife—has taken a fancy to him. She's out of his ken, of course, and his vanity's tickled until it's tied up in knots. He's dazzled to hell and he can't see anything else. The sun, moon and stars rise and set in the small of her back. His best friends coming to lunch ? Well, let 'em come. He's something better to do. And there's Rowena trying to iron it out . . . She was damned near crying, you know, when we first came in. I wish he was here. I'd tell him what he was fit for . . . And then you stick up for him."

" All I said," said Belinda, " was that, knowing D.B. as I do, I cannot understand his doing a thing like this."

" That's because you're a woman," said Punch. " I tell you, men know men. God knows what's going to happen. But D.B. doesn't care. He's on a good thing."

Belinda sighed.

" I suppose you're right," she said. " But I must confess I find it hard to believe."

Her husband shrugged his shoulders.

" It's been done before," he said, and picked up a pipe. " Oh, and what about his Dulcinea ? There's a bitch, if you like."

Belinda frowned—and picked up *The Sunday Times*.

CHAPTER X

Snob

ROWENA was not a climber. For such a mode of progression she had a hearty contempt—the scorn which the card-sharper keeps for the man who earns his living at bridge. When the time came, she proposed to go up in a lift.

She had always intended to rise : but what she had seen at Ascot had turned her intention into an instant desire.

In those four days she had seen what Elsie Baumer had seen . . . in all the echoing squalor of a parish hall . . . before the indecent exposure of a beggarly Christmas Tree. She had seen herself looked down on by women who were mentally and physically her inferiors, whose clothes she would not have been seen dead in—*because of the company she kept.*

And something else she had seen—that it was not a question of rising, of going up. Such terms were grotesque. They suggested that she was *below* that welter of ill-dressed fools. It was not a case for a lift, but a case for a bridge.

Rowena had come back from Ascot, red-hot to embark. And not upon her adventure—*upon her voyage.*

Time was short. In a little more than a month, the London Season would end. But a start could be made. Possible bridges could be considered and surveyed.

When her husband had used the words ' I wish

you'd pull out', he little dreamed that the process had already begun.

*   *   *   *

Since the world began rolling, in 1901, the compartments into which society is divided have never been water-tight.   More or less percolation takes place.

As might be expected of her, Adela, Countess of Churt, put it higher than that.

" For thirty-six years," she snarled, " I've been trying to hold the bridge, and for all the good I've done, I might just as well have married the pastry *chef*.   Not that I've failed.   I've been facing the wrong way round.   I've been keeping the enemy out, when I should have been trying to keep the garrison in."

Her bitterness may be excused.   Her grandson, the Earl to be, had just announced his engagement to a lady of ill report.   The future Countess of Churt would be able to boast that she had been the daughter of a usurer, the wife of a bookmaker and the mistress of the leader of a band.

The dowager had many faults, but the statements she made were usually founded on fact.   Out-and-out desertions apart, when the day's parades were over, some of the garrison fraternized with the foe.   Among them was Henry Sinbad, fourth Earl of Juliot, now rising sixty-two.

' Now Naaman was a great man and honourable : but he was a leper.'

Juliot was worse than a leper : he was a bore.

Bred to wealth and position, he well and truly discharged the trust which his birth had imposed.   He had governed a province : he was Lord Lieutenant of his County : he had presided over committees innumerable.   He administered his estates : he spoke in the House of Lords : he wrote to *The Times*.   But he cared for none of these things.   His heart's desire was to be a social success. Grimaldi's heart's desire was to play Richard the Third.

A figure-head, pure and simple, Juliot could not unbend. His efforts to be free and easy would have sobered a drunken man. Determined to entertain, he was repulsively facetious. Resolved to be gallant, he was copious to distraction. His interpretation of the dance inspired his unhappy partners to pray for death. Festivity sat ill upon him. Even a false nose failed. His inadaptability was impregnable. Youth at once attracted and fled before him. But no one was ever rude—his dignity saw to that.

It was no good not asking the man. He haunted night-clubs and restaurants after ten. He would chafe at a Lord Mayor's banquet, because the speeches would make him late for his tryst. And when he appeared, beaming, strong men said ' Oh, my God ', and women's hearts failed them for fear.

That he would in the end have ' got it ', there can be no doubt. He had already remarked that a singular malaise was abroad—that settled as a butterfly upon its victim, to make her listless and tongue-tied until it rose. Sooner or later, he must, I think, have perceived that the ailment's visits coincided with his. But it never came to that, for one night, in desperation, somebody introduced him to Isabel Stumm.

The presumption angered Juliot, who was a particular man. But he was far too gentle to take it out on the girl. He asked her to dance . . .

Before the music had stopped, he had tasted the sweets of success. No malaise was afflicting Miss Stumm. Lord Juliot's lumbering addresses were rapturously received. He danced again with the girl, who fairly extended herself. Then he followed her to her table—and met Mrs. Stumm. He felt ashamed of himself, but he had the time of his life. He set the table on a roar. The old jokes he misquoted from *Punch* came into their own.

After that, there was no looking back. Night after night, Juliot would visit some table where his welcome was warm.

An understanding arose. Nothing was expected of him. His condescension was without prejudice. He was never invited to come. Much was made of him, if he did. The arrangement was not so one-sided. Juliot was seen at the table—and Juliot was a great man.

He was also a proper man. The fault which has been exposed was the worst he had. His morality was active. People watched their tongues, when he was about. He was a confirmed widower. Thirty-five years before, he had bored his wife to death.

And then, at the end of July, he met Mrs. David Bohun . . .

Rowena knew who he was and had taken his measure before she had seen him twice. Before she had seen him three times, she had made up her mind that here was the man she required. Her husband was a rock. Very well. Lord Juliot should be a bridge—to carry her over the gulf which was fixed between, say, the Grainers and Adela, Countess of Churt.

Of course her choice was good. Juliot would make a stout bridge. What was still more to the point, he would land his passenger not only within the city but in the citadel. His brother (and the heir to his title) had married the only child of the Marquess of Wells. The union was blessed with twins—a son and a daughter of parts. Aged twenty-four, these two were, bluntly, 'the goods'. They went everywhere worth going to. And the 'shiny' papers starred them—wherever they went.

Rowena was well aware that to have her way with Juliot was going to be very hard. The man was scrupulous. If he liked to dance with Miss Stumm, that was his affair : but he would have cut off his hand before he would have asked her to meet his nephew and niece. Still, Mrs. David Bohun was not Miss Isabel Stumm.

Twice she could have met him, before she did : but when she knew he had observed her, she took her leave. When he was introduced, she poured him her sweetest wine, but before he could ask for more, she had made herself scarce. A week went by before he saw her again. Then she looked up to find him beside her and to hear him deliver a jocular compliment, after the way of a vicar commending a jumble sale.

That evening Rowena was sad. Her lip trembled more than once. When she danced with Teddy Bemuse, Juliot could have sworn that she shrank from the common touch. It occurred to him that she did not belong to her crowd. She was perfectly charming to them—she knew how to behave. But her manners were cleaner cut. She was out of a different drawer.

That night, as she was going, he cleared his throat.

" Were," he declared, " were I endued with the audacity which, if we may credit the simple-minded rhapsodes of ' this blessed plot ', distinguished a certain, ah, connoisseur, I should be sorely tempted, Mrs. Bohun, to borrow a curiosity which has always seemed to me less impertinent than excusable, and to repeat the time-honoured query which, I dare swear, a few years ago you were invited to memorize."

Rowena managed to give him her frankest smile.

" Please yield to the temptation, Lord Juliot."

" Then," boomed the Earl, " I shall make bold to inquire—if not with the somewhat, ah, fleeting gallantry of my candid prototype, at least with a disinterested duty which I beg you will do me the honour to accept, where are you going, my pretty maid ? "

To his overwhelming delight, Rowena bobbed.

" I'm going to Curzon Street, sir, she said."

While the man was simmering with an appreciation so lively as to deny him the concentration requisite to speech, she spoke for a moment of her home. Then, with the sweetest sorrow, she bade him good night.

The next time they met, he styled her his 'pretty maid'.

Rowena was off.

*   *   *   *

Nobody grudged her her conquest—not even Isabel Stumm. When she was rallied upon it, she said 'You can't be unkind'. She introduced David to Juliot— and David, as usual, played faithfully into her hands.

For the purpose she chose an evening when her husband was not at his best. The man was tired and had fought to be left at home : but his wife had put pressure upon him . . .

"Just as you like. Of course I accepted for you, but that was because you were asked. And as long as we use the same bathroom, you will be asked. I mean, that's the way of the world. I've not the slightest desire to spoil your fun, but—well, it pays to advertise, Pansy, now and again. You know. *Blue Riband of Married Love : Rock of Ages Left Standing— so sucks to you.* It cramps the scavengers' style. Of course, if you'd rather confirm the entirely unwarrantable notion that you're all over someone who isn't all over me . . . I mean, one does one's best : but one cannot ignore the fact that when one goes out alone, the talk has a knack of straying to Kensington Square. *I* know she's down in the country, mother and all, but . . ."

She waited until her husband was just about to withdraw. Then she brought the two together, and disappeared.

David was suitably polite. Juliot, who could not turn quickly, was slightly disconcerted at meeting without any warning the man before whose hearth he had been warming his hands. Automatically, he reached for his rod and his staff—that is to say, the remembrance of who he was. As he did so, it came to his mind that the loyalty of his pretty maid had been more than tinged with a sorrow which she had done her best to conceal. He began to look Bohun up and down. And when Henry Sinbad, fourth Earl of Juliot, Viscount Gatacre of Mountjoy, Baron Pommel of Guige, Hereditary Keeper of the King's Great Ring, looked anyone up and down, it was a major operation.

Now David had been prepared to render him such respect as his age and his standing deserved : but when he was deliberately measured, as though he were a footman who had answered his master back, he began to examine his measurer's claims to respect. At once he perceived that eminent, elderly peers, who revel for nothing with people they would not ask to their house, deserve rather less respect than their less fortunate hosts. He began to measure Juliot—as Juliot had seldom been measured, since he left Eton for Oxford in '92.

By the time Rowena returned, Juliot disliked David Bohun very nearly as much as he pitied his wife . . .

Though the lady was making good progress, she was not deceived. Fortresses, such as Juliot, were not reduced in a month : and at the end of July the siege would have to be raised. The most she could do in the time was to make such a breach in the walls as would still be there in October when people came back to Town. Then, if the man was alive, she would have her way with him before the winter was out. Grainers, Mockets and Stumms would be dropped with a resolution which only one of their kind could ever display ; Curzon Street would reflect a gaiety more refined ; and Mrs. David Bohun would move with admired discretion in that corrupt old borough which only the sansculottes will ever close.

Possunt quia posse videntur.

On the twenty-fifth day of July, Lord Juliot invited Rowena to lunch with him at his club.

To say that she was elated in no way describes her glee. Self-confident as she was, Rowena had never supposed that she could have got so far in so short a time. No rose without a thorn. At once she began to fear for the next three months. Would the iron be still hot in October—the iron which she had heated so fast and so well ? She fobbed off the apprehension and set her regular teeth. On Wednesday her chance would come—the chance she had hewn for herself in the sweat of his brow. My lord was to try her reins— in the Ladies' Annexe of the Carlton Club. It was up to her not only not to fail, but to exploit to the utmost that elegant hour and a half . . . to heat the iron so hot that it would not grow cold. There and then she began to consider the line she would take.

There can be no doubt that Rowena had cause to be proud. Never before had Juliot done such a thing. He stretched no points : he was a high-principled man. Excellent though she might be, his pretty maid was on the wrong side of the fence and, so, not eligible to be entertained by him at the Carlton Club. And yet he was going to do it—the word had gone forth. He had said to her ' Friend, go up higher '. He had taken two pages to say it, but that is beside the point —which is that he would not have said it, unless he had felt quite sure that his maid would not let him down. Rowena had cause to be proud. Though weighted out of his ken, she had satisfied the conditions which her admirer imposed.

Upon that fateful Wednesday another encounter took place.

For the first time since leaving London, Helen had come up to Town. She was going to meet David for lunch at a quarter past one. Belinda, too, was lunching at the Savoy—with a young-hearted uncle of hers, who knew very well that a girl does not care for a club. And Belinda and David were early, but the uncle was late. Since Helen Adair was ' on time ', the three had two minutes together which bore some remarkable fruit.

Before David could introduce her—

" I know you're Belinda," said Helen, and put out her hand. " My name's Adair and I've wanted to know you for months."

Belinda fell for her flat.

More. Looking at David and Helen, she knew that her husband's strictures were simply grotesque. The two might well be in love, but, whether they were or not, they were incapable of letting anyone down. Her instinct had jibbed at the notion, and her instinct had been perfectly right. There was something behind the proposition which Punch had so violently solved. She began to weigh Rowena—the perfect wife.

Had Rowena known, she would not have cared two hoots.

* * * *

Lord Juliot never spoke out. He liked his own voice too well. And so he spoke round and about, swaddling his point in periods which served to distract the attention and tear the patience to threads. It follows, of course, that when he set out to be subtle —to convey a certain impression or drop a delicate hint, only the keenest eye could see the wood for the trees. But Mrs. David Bohun was on the look-out : and when, in the comparative seclusion of an attractive drawing-room, her host set down his cup and spoke for two minutes of time in a voice which was earnest and low, she was able to wrest his meaning from the monstrous garlands of irrelevance with which it was hung. The man had sought to suggest

that she was too good for the company which she
kept.

This was, so to speak, the joker—the card of all
others which she would have wished to be dealt. She
played a beautiful hand as well as it could have
been played. The impressions which she conveyed
stood out as sharp as mountains against the rising
sun.

Speaking well of all men, she made it perfectly clear
that she was acquainted with grief. Commending
her nearest and dearest, she proved that she was
oppressed. Her spirited defence of the Grainers disclosed the fact that she loathed the sound of their
name. From her affection for the Mockets emerged
the bitter truth that she despised herself whenever she
broke their bread. Out of her belief in the Stumms
issued the sickening horror they never failed to inspire.
Her loyalty was devastating : her loving-kindness dis-
embowelled. Her love for her husband came gushing
—to show that it was misplaced. In fact, it was a
famous betrayal—with faith and hope and charity
speaking the lines.

Juliot was deeply moved. He patted his pretty
maid's arm, delivered himself of such slush as screams
are made of, and, when she rose to her feet, begged
her, as a personal favour, to be in no hurry to leave.

Rowena would not be persuaded. She knew when
to stop.

She left on the crest of the wave, with Juliot out
on the pavement, bowing and smiling and lifting a
pompous hand.

When her taxi had disappeared, he made his way
back to the members' side of the club. For over an
hour he sat in the library, priding himself on his
perception, muttering ' Poor little woman ', and chew-
ing over and over his savoury cud. Then he got up
and walked to the House of Lords.

Rowena had gone straight home and up to her

room. There she slept for two hours. She fully deserved her rest. Virtue had gone out of her.

* * * *

"She's sweet," said Helen. Belinda was being discussed. "And now I want to meet Punch. Can't we get them to Bluemantle?"

"I don't see why not," said David, thoughtfully. "I'll tell you what, my darling. Why shouldn't I take this place, Hautboys, and ask them down? Punch only gets three weeks, and I know they've nowhere to go."

"No reason at all," said Helen. "As a matter of fact, I think it's a big idea."

"By God, I will," said David. "If Rowena doesn't like it, she needn't come."

"What about these people, the Sewlers?"

"The Sewlers can go to hell. They will—eventually: they're a perfectly poisonous pair. Hautboys, with Punch and Belinda, will do well enough. If I can't be happy, at least I shall have some peace."

Helen changed the subject—in some uneasiness. It was perfectly clear that David Bohun's patience was wearing thin. This was dangerous. His and her only chance was for him to hold on. A battle could have but one end. Rowena's little finger was thicker than David's loins.

Hautboys was the Northamptonshire cottage of which Rowena had heard and which she had been proposing that the Bohuns and Sewlers should share. Much against his will, David had been to inspect it one Saturday afternoon. It was not a cottage at all, but a decent house, with three or four acres about it and woods to screen it from winds and from curious eyes. Its owner, ordered abroad, had built it with one idea—to cut domestic service out of his life. If he had not succeeded, at least he had got a long way.

The place was a striking example of what electrical energy can be induced to perform. Luxury leapt from the switch-board in an astonishing way. Power could not lay the table or make the beds, but it was not too much to say that, unless there was food to be cooked, servants at Hautboys could barely have earned their keep.

After a little, David returned to the charge.

" I'll ring up this afternoon. I remember the agent's name. They won't let for less than a year, but that can't be helped. Besides, it'll make a fine bolt-hole— I wish I'd had it this month."

" I should certainly do it," said Helen. " And then ring up the Leightons and fix that up. And, David darling, don't scrap—you know what I mean. If there's trouble about the Sewlers, say nothing at all. Don't—get going, my darling. When people like you get going, they—they sometimes go over the edge."

The man put a hand to his head.

" Why shouldn't I leave her, Helen ? "

" I can give you no reason, my dear, but I know it would be a mistake. You're not dealing with— with an ordinary woman. Take that from me. I'm not thinking at all of myself—I'm thinking of you. You've got to look after yourself : but, so far as you can avoid it, you must not cross her, David—it isn't safe."

" But what can she do, my darling ? "

Helen Adair clenched her fists.

" That I can't tell you, David. I'm like a dog that takes hold of his master's coat. My instinct tells me to stop you. That's all I can say."

" I expect you're right," sighed David, and called for the bill . . .

While Rowena slept that day, her husband agreed to take Hautboys from August the first, and Punch excitedly accepted ' the best invitation I've had for twenty years '.

For all that, when Belinda told him that she had met Helen Adair, his indignation returned and was fiercely expressed. He would hear no good of Helen, charm his wife never so wisely.

"D.B.'s a damned fool—I put it no higher than that. Men do go off the deep end. But she's a rotten woman—and that's God's truth. She's got the whole world to choose from, and then she goes and picks on somebody else's man. And because she's rich an'—an' powerful . . . It's a case of Naboth's vineyard—that's what it is."

"Wait till you see her, Punch."

"I don't want to see her," snapped Punch. "If I was asked to meet her, I'd —— well turn on my heel. And that's what you should have done. God damn it, there's Rowena, his lawful wife, eating her little heart out, because of what's going on, an' all the time doing her best to pretend there's nothing doing an' save his face . . . An' then you roll up an' swear she's one of the pets."

Belinda left it there. There was no doubt about it—Punch was Rowena's man.

* * * *

Work kept David in Chambers till seven o'clock.

As he made ready to go, he determined to dine at his club. He was not in the mood for endurance, but rather for letting fly. If he went home and Rowena referred to Hautboys, he would have to announce that he had taken the place. And then, of course, Rowena would twist his tail . . . Remembering Helen's entreaty, he felt that he would be wiser not to go home. So he told his clerk to ring up and say that Mr. Bohun was going to dine at his club.

Then he passed out of his Chambers and, presently, into the bounty of Lincoln's Inn Fields. The summer evening favoured a leisurely walk. By the time he turned into St. James's Street, he had strolled his distemper off.

* * * *

Twenty-four hours had gone by, and Bohun was dressing for dinner at half past eight.

People were coming to dine—for once in a way. Nothing so solid as the Leightons—a jerry-built crowd : ' Undy ' Bauch, the Sinoples—husband and wife, the Cullets—father and daughter, and ' Boney ' Belong. Still, the Bohuns had been to their parties and David would have supped with the devil, to pay off a debt.

Striving to fasten his collar, he spoke to his wife. " Are we going on after, Rowena ? Or shall we stay here ? "

" After what ? " said Rowena, at work on her lips.

" Well, after dinner," said David.

" I don't care a damn," said Rowena, addressing her glass.

" Well, it's up to you," said David. " If they're content to play poker—well, that's all right."

Still busy with her mouth—

" If who's content to play poker ? " said Mrs. Bohun.

" Our guests," said David, shortly. " The Cullets, Belong and the rest." He swung about, tie in hand. " Or is it washed out ? "

Rowena put her head on one side, regarding her lips.

" You've got your dates wrong," she said. " That show was last night."

" Last night ? " cried David, staring.

Rowena picked up a towel.

" That's right," she replied. " Last night. Which reminds me—you owe ' Pa ' Cullet a tenner. I took them on to Granada, and then I had no money to pay the bill."

There was a little silence, while David felt the blood come into his face.

He saw his guests arriving the night before : he heard Rowena's excuses and saw their looks : and he saw himself oblivious, reading whilst he was dining, a mile away.

The thought of the brick he had dropped was disconcerting enough. That his wife, in her spite, had deliberately let him drop it made him see red. Her present, studied casualness was, so to speak, the cracker at the end of the lash.

With all his might, he strove to control his voice.

" You must have known I'd forgotten."

Rowena shrugged her shoulders.

" I don't see why. You do pretty much as you please."

" I don't ask people to dinner and then dine out."

" Only to lunch ? " said his wife.

" I don't do it at all," said David. " You got my message last night at seven o'clock."

" Thereabouts," said Rowena, inspecting her nails.

" What did it say ? "

" ' Mr. Bohun has been detained and is going to dine at his club.' "

" Well, why didn't you ring up the club ? I'd have found your message waiting and come straight on."

" I don't ring up men's clubs—to see if they're there."

" You knew I was there," said David. " And you knew I'd forgotten that people were coming to dine."

" Steady over the cobbles. How did I know these things ? "

" Because you know me," said David. " But you wouldn't ring up the club, because you wanted to let me down to your friends."

" Tripe for two. Never mind. I should point that out to Pa, when you send him a cheque."

" Not tripe," said the man. " Dirty work. And you know it as well as I."

Rowena turned.

" You forgot they were coming," she said.

" I made a mistake in the date."

" Was that my fault ? " said Rowena.

" I never suggested it was."

" So far, so good. And yesterday, if you remember, dear Helen was up in Town."

" I gave her lunch, as you know."

" Yes, and if you'd been giving her dinner, you wouldn't have been at the club ? "

" But I said——"

" I know. So does everyone else. But can't you get this, darling ? If I had rung up the club, *and you hadn't come in*—well, that sort of thing isn't fair on the nuptial lute. We've, er, dropped it once or twice in days gone by : but now that it's perking up and we're drawing closer together ev-er-y day, it's no good looking for trouble and doing the bastard in."

" I see," said David, shortly. " If I'm deceiving you, you'd rather not know ? "

" I'd far rather be deceived than let it be thought I was trying to catch you out."

" It comes to this—that you thought I was dining with her."

" Fifty-fifty, duckie. I couldn't make up my mind. But I didn't dare ring up, in case you were."

Bohun stepped to a wardrobe to take out a tie.

Rowena was lying, of course. But the lies which she told were fair and round and polished, affording no sort of grip. What was so incredibly offensive was that she did not pretend to be telling the truth. Her manner was that of the conjurer doing his tricks, desiring his audience to watch him and see for themselves—' You see, there's no deception '—and deceiving them while he was speaking, as both of them knew.

" We can't go on like this," said Bohun, thickly.

" I beg your pardon," said his wife.

The man started. He had not realized that he had

spoken aloud. Then, tie in hand, he stepped to a looking-glass.

" You must see for yourself," he said, " that we can't go on like this ? "

" Like what ? " said Rowena, wide-eyed.

" As we are," said Bohun, shortly. " To add another lie to the bunch, we've got on each other's nerves."

" You're not on my nerves," said his wife.

" I know. I said it was a lie. Never mind. Let's put it like this. You know as well as I do that the ' nuptial lute ', as you call it, is irretrievably smashed. You seem to take pleasure in kicking its wreck about. But I——"

" Are you asking me to divorce you for Helen Adair ? "

The savage punch hit Bohun over the heart.

" Good God, no. Of course I'm not. And you've no right to talk like that . . ."

" I'm sorry, lovey. What is it you're trying to say ? "

" You know better than I do. Take it as said."

" I'm afraid that won't do," said Rowena. " Besides, I've made one mistake."

Bohun buttoned his waistcoat and picked up his coat.

" You make me feel," he said, " that I want to walk out of the house. And I think I'd better do it —I'll tell you why. We don't get on any more, and we never shall. Well, that to me is a pity : to you, it's a hell of a jest. I'm ready to submit to what is to me a misfortune : but you put your arms round its neck. I'm out to make the best of the business : you make the most. You actually exploit the position : you actually use it against me . . . Now that you've killed my love, you pick it up and stroke it and say how lovely it is. You feed on mockery, and ram the filthy beastliness down my throat . . ." He stopped there, panting with emotion, turned again to the glass and dragged on his coat. " Well, all these things being so, I can't help feeling that we'd be better apart."

Rowena raised her eyebrows.

" I find it hard to believe that Helen Adair approved that felicitous speech." David stood very still. " She's not such a fool as you are . . . Never mind. You want to walk out. *Well, you go on and do it* . . . Oh, and since you raised the point, there's just one question I'll ask. You say that I killed your love. Where did you lunch on the day that *I* gave it the *coup de grâce* ? "

" You can make what suggestions you please," said David Bohun. " We both of us know the truth, and that's as much as I care. And now I've a question to ask. Will you sign a Deed of Separation ? You'd have this house, of course, and—and all you could want."

Rowena smiled slowly.

" No, I shouldn't," she said. " *Not if you went.*" She turned again to her glass and patted her hair. " Don't think I mind your asking—I know the feeling so well. You knew what the answer would be, but you *had* to ask. I felt like that on Sunday—you'll never guess when. When I asked if Helen Adair had sent me her love."

As white as he had been red, her husband made no reply . . .

After perhaps five minutes he followed his wife downstairs.

CHAPTER XI

Breaking-point

WHEN Rowena learned that her husband had taken Hautboys, she hid her delight. There was no reason why he should know that he had pulled her chestnuts out of the fire.

She desired to be rid of the Sewlers—whom Juliot would have deplored even more than the Stumms. But 'Koko' Sewler was not a lady to cross, and the joint occupation of Hautboys had been as good as agreed. And now David had cut the knot —in the best of all possible ways. What 'Koko' would say about him would startle the fowls of the air.

That there might be no mistake—

"Well, you can tell them," she said. "I'm not coming in on this deal. Scratch dear Koko, and God knows what you'll find. But it won't be milk and soda—I'll lay to that. Of course she'll never believe that I knew nothing about it until you'd signed the lease."

"You needn't worry," said Bohun. "I'll see she does."

The man was as good as his word.

If 'Koko' had any doubts, Rowena's tearful confusion resolved them at once. The letter which Sewler wrote David made this abundantly clear.

To the latter's surprise, Rowena did not oppose —much less attempt to imperil the visit which he had invited the Leightons to pay.

"I see. That will be nice. Two rooms between

183

four people—we can't have anyone else. I suppose you're quite sure you want *me*—at your country place. Or were you banking on my absence ? Of course, if I'd done as you wanted and signed a Deed, you'd have had a spare bed . . ."

But that was all. In fact, by her invitation, Belinda came down before Punch. (Much of Rowena's success was due to the simple fact that she did with all her might what she had decided to do.)

Bohun was right when he said that Hautboys, with Punch and Belinda, would bring him peace. For the first time for months, the man was allowed to relax in body and mind.

August was commendably hot : a bathing-pool swayed in the garden : Anselm, who slept in the village, made life very smooth. And Rowena was, as she called it, upon parade. This, from morning till night, because the Leightons were there. And even by night, conjugal disaffection was never enlarged : the quarters were much too close—two double rooms and two bathrooms, all linked by connecting doors.

So, though he hungered for Helen, and shrank from his wife, Bohun's case was far less evil than it had been in Town. What was more, his hunger was fed. If the rations were slight, they kept the wolf from the door.

It was Belinda Leighton who gave him to eat.

The Leightons had no car, but the Bohuns had two. Since both of these were two-seaters, whenever the four went out, David drove with Belinda, Rowena with Punch. On such, but no other occasions David would talk to Belinda of Helen Adair. Delighted to listen, Belinda learned a great deal. But things went further than that. Rowena took Punch to luncheon at Brunkskill Towers : but David declined to go—and took Belinda to Bluemantle, forty miles off.

At dinner that night Punch's manner was something brusque—except, of course, to his hostess, who gave a finished performance from first to last.

" And now, Belinda, do tell us about the Adair. I hardly know her, you know. She's David's friend. I think that's a good idea, really—for us to have different friends. And when I did meet her, she was most awfully nice. Of course, you know, she's terribly good for David . . ."

Three such visits took place.

Then September came in, and the Leightons returned to Town.

It must be confessed at once that these two charming people were not as good friends as before. As we know, the crack had been there : their visit to Hautboys had turned it into a cleft. Upon ' the Bohun business ', the House of Leighton was divided against itself.

This need not have happened. Such a husband and wife might well have done better than that. But it must be borne in mind that for every hour which Belinda had spent with David, Punch had spent sixty minutes with Mrs. Bohun. And the latter had not wasted her time—it was not her way.

Attempts to discuss the question made matters worse, for Punch would begin to see red before Belinda had fairly opened her mouth. In a way, he may be excused, for while he was nursing a grievance, Belinda was not.

Belinda knew that Rowena was false as hell. Punch believed in Rowena, heart and soul. *But Punch resented Belinda's belief in Bohun.*

* * * *

Forsyth, deep in Scotland, considered a letter from Chater which, with other urgent papers, one of his clerks had brought from Lincoln's Inn Fields.

Private and Confidential.

Sir,

Mrs. B.

According to your instructions, close observation was kept upon Hautboys for a period of seven days. No attempt was made to get into touch with the servants, because the Eurasian butler was there from morning to night, only leaving for his room in the village after the cook had retired.

The property is sheltered by woods and though the two men I employed could not get up to the house, they were able to command the house and most of the garden without being seen.

Since the weather was very fine, Mr. and Mrs. B. and their two guests spent most of their time out of doors, and the windows were always wide open when they were within. This favoured observation, which, with the help of binoculars, became at times very good —particularly, as you will see, when use was being made of the bathing-pool.

I enclose a copy of their diary, which records exactly what the two agents saw.

From this you will see that from first to last they saw nothing to suggest that Mrs. B. is anything else than a loving and dutiful wife, but that, on more than one occasion, her husband's manner suggested that he was impatient of her attentions.

I beg respectfully to remind you that these conclusions confirm the opinions so strongly expressed not only by the bar-tender at Biarritz, but by Mr. and Mrs. Cadnam four months ago.

In these circumstances I have felt that no useful purpose would be served by further observation of such a delicate kind.

I should add that Mr. and Mrs. B.'s guests were a Mr. and Mrs. Leighton, a lady and gentleman of very good report. They have been married for more than three years, live in a flat in Chelsea and are ideally happy.

Mrs. M.

In view of the attached statement from Mr. Edwin Bowles, there can be, I fear, no doubt that this woman sailed for Australia in 1922. This being so, I can hardly believe that you will wish the matter pursued, for this would mean my going myself to that country and, I think, taking a man with me. And in view of the fact that the scent is now fifteen years old, such an undertaking would have a small chance of success, and a very great deal of good money might well be thrown after bad. At the same time, if you so wish it, I am perfectly ready to go and to do the best I can to run the woman to earth.

Yours faithfully,
George Chater.

J. G. Forsyth Esq.

It will be observed that fortune favours the base. Had Chater's two men stayed on for a second week, Mrs. Garter, Bemuse and the Cullets would all have swum into their ken. What is very much more to the point, they would have had cause to revise their opinion of Mrs. Bohun. The field-glasses which had revealed a loving and dutiful wife, would have disclosed the startling and pregnant truth that, when no guests were present, the lady's demeanour could be less amiable.

To Chater, such information would have been welcome, indeed. All he had learned so far had gone to show that Forsyth had made a mistake. As he had fairly said, Biarritz, the Cadnams and Hautboys bore one another out. These three declared that his patron's conviction was wrong. Forsyth had said that the lady would be hard to unmask. Three several inspections had shown that the lady was wearing no mask . . . The detective was scrupulous. He hated giving a stone, when he had been asked for bread. But, when he had proved that there was no bread to be had, to consent to continue to seek it offended his moral sense.

But, if Forsyth was disappointed, he hid his dismay —and summoned his clerk forthwith, to take down his reply.

> *Dear Chater,*
>
> *I am much obliged. As I have said before, the woman has got to be found. So please arrange to sail as soon as you can. Take a man with you, of course. Let me know when you leave and cable me when you arrive. I am crediting your account with another five hundred pounds.*
>
> *Yours very truly,*
> *J. G. Forsyth.*

* * * *

Rowena raised her eyebrows.

"Then you should have said so before. It's too late now."

Her husband set down his cup and shook his head.

"I'm not going to Dioni," he said.

"It was fixed six weeks ago."

"By you—not me," said David, lighting a cigarette.

"I see . . ." Rowena nodded. "Why won't you go to Dioni—darling heart ?"

"Because I prefer to stay here."

Rowena sighed.

"All right," she said slowly. And then, "It can't be helped. I confess I'm disappointed. Besides, I'd have liked a change. Those treatments are all very well, but——"

"D'you mean to say you're not going, if I don't go ?"

" Of course I'm not," said Rowena. " I'm going to stay here with you."

There was a little silence, while David's cigarette went gradually out.

Since, four days ago, the Leightons had taken their leave, life at Hautboys had been less gray than red. On the first day, soon after breakfast, Rowena had left for London, *via* Potter's Bar : half an hour after her going, Mrs. Jocelyn Garter and Teddy Bemuse had arrived : because he could do nothing else, David had entertained them until Rowena's return—at a quarter to eight. The visit realized the worst misgivings of The Litany. The guests, who hated their host, resented the fact that their hostess had let them *down* : the host, who hated his guests, resented the fact that Rowena had let him *in*—an emotion which was inflamed by the maddening belief that the lady had *not* forgotten an engagement which, for some reason, it did not amuse her to keep. (The belief, of course, was sound. The Garter-Bemuse combination was to be ' faded out '.) On the second day the Cullets had come to lunch and, yielding to their hostess' persuasion, had stayed the night. ' Pa ' Cullet and David had had to use the same room—an arrangement which suited the former, for by the time he retired his wine had become a burden which he was glad to share. Worst of all, for the benefit of her guests, Rowena's love for her husband had been naked and unashamed.

" Yes, I thought that'd make you think," said Rowena Bohun.

David looked up.

" It has," he said shortly. " I'm ready to live and let live. But that's not your way."

Rowena regarded him, over the rim of her cup.

" I rather like being married. It seems you don't."

" It serves your turn," said David, with narrowed eyes.

" Don't be so material, Willie. Besides, quite a

lot of wives would object to dear Helen Adair. I mean, if that's not letting live—well, I don't know what is."

The man rose at once.

" You know as well as I do there's nothing wrong."

Rowena opened her eyes.

" Of course. So does Lady Persimmon. That's what we like about you—the way you beat down Satan under your feet."

" D'you mind not talking like that ? "

" I've finished now. Do we go to Dioni or not ? "

The man reflected, chafing. If he did not go, Rowena would make it her business to drive him half out of his mind. If he went, it would be like Biarritz —without *La Belle Issue* and Helen Adair.

" Why d'you want me to go ? "

" Because, if I went there alone, it would be assumed that I was a prostitute. You see, I'm not joining a crowd. As far as I know, there's nobody there that I know. And I don't want a queue of dagoes outside my room . . . Once you've been seen with me there, you can go to hell. Be wired for from Chambers, or something—whatever you like. But I can't arrive unattended, my bonny boy."

There was another silence.

" All right," said Bohun, at last. " I'll take you out. But I warn you, I shall be wired for. I'm damned if I'll stay."

Rowena blew him a kiss.

" I'll do without you somehow. Her need is greater than mine."

* * * *

Two hours later David slid under the gate-house which kept Bluemantle's approach . . .

The butler was plainly pleased to make much of an honoured guest. As he led the way to a bathroom—

" Mrs. Adair is out riding, sir. She should be in in about a quarter of an hour. If you'd like to sit on the terrace . . . Lady Persimmon's away, sir. She's spending two nights in Town. May I bring you something to drink, sir, as soon as you're down ? "

" Is Mrs. Adair in the park ? "

" Yes, sir. If you went down by the orchard . . . She always comes in that way."

" I'll go and meet her, Parsons. Don't bother about the drink."

He saw her before she saw him—a slight, bare-headed figure, astride of a glorious roan.

The horse was standing up where the turf swelled into a knoll, surveying the prospect before him and pleased with what he saw. His rider was sitting straight, with her lovely head in the air, and her eyes were fast on the flash of an aeroplane, playing its elegant tricks in a cloudless sky. For a moment of time, the two might have been one statue, the beauty and grace of which were almost too rare to be true. The eager port of a huntress, her heart lifted up by the sight of the sport she loved, the pride of the thoroughbred, the noble background of English earth and heaven made up so striking a picture that Bohun stopped in his tracks. So Actæon may have stood still, before the hounds that loved him leapt for his throat . . .

Then the roan stooped, to prove the grass at his feet, and Helen Adair leaned forward and then looked round.

As she came up—

" I'm in love with an immortal," said David. " I saw her just now—with her eyes on her proper home. Why don't you fly again, sweetheart ? Your heart's in the air."

" I'm waiting for you, my darling. I love it so much that I want to share it with you. But we can't do it yet. If we were to fly together, the papers would pick it up. But tell me—why are you here ? I'm simply thankful to see you, but Mo will breathe through her nose—you know she's away ? "

" Parsons told me," said David. " But if I hadn't come to-day, I couldn't have come for a week. The day after to-morrow Rowena's going abroad. I'm not going to stay, but she wants me to take her out. She's gone to Town to-day, and I'm going to-night."

" Abroad ? Where to ? "

" Dioni," said David. " I only just know where it is. But I'll love the journey back. A fortnight at Hautboys alone ! You'll have to come over for lunch."

Helen slid down from her horse and took the man's arm. Temper lurked in his tone—the fret of a sea that the idle wind has lashed, that broods upon its drubbing and will not be comforted. There was no help in talk : only her touch could dry his resentment up. After all, it was natural enough. The virtue of physical contact is old as the hills. She pulled off a glove and laid her bare hand on his wrist.

" I'm terribly glad you've come. I miss you more than ever, when Mo's not here. I can talk about things with her . . . The Leightons have left you, of course : and I'm sorry for that. D'you think, if I asked them nicely, they'd come down and spend a week-end ? Belinda's one of the best, and I'd love to meet Punch."

" I wish you would," said David. " I think Punch suspects our relation. I'd like to get that put right." He stood still there, and a hand went up to his head. " How damnably helpless one is in a case like this. As a rule in life, as in war, you can either fight or retire. But I can do neither, Helen. I've got to sit still where I am—and take what's coming to me. My best friend thinks me a blackguard : but what can I do ? I can't tell him the truth without exposing my wife."

" I'm sure Belinda knows," said Helen Adair.

" I know," said David, " I know. But I very much doubt if Punch'll take what she says. He's an obstinate bloke is Punch : and he thinks the world of Rowena—she's seen to that."

His words made Helen uneasy. It showed that the man was beginning to notice things. He was quite unaware, at the moment, of what she was certain was true—that the whole of the Bohuns' acquaintance (for what it was worth) already regarded him as a first-class cad. When he found this out, it would shake him, as nothing had shaken him yet : the honest contempt of ' outsiders ' would hit him over the heart. As yet he had no idea that his wife was proving him guilty of that which, vile as they were, her friends would never have done—of abusing the simple faith of an artless child.

" I'll put it right," said Helen, drawing him into a walk. " While you're away, I'll go to Kensington Square. And I'll ring up Belinda from there and ask them to dine."

" Yes, do do that," said David, abstractedly. Then he continued slowly, after the way of a man who is thinking aloud. " I believe I shall have to leave her, when Term begins. I don't think I can go on. Take this Dioni business—why am I going out ? Because she said that if I did not go, she'd stay at Hautboys with me. Before that threat I gave way . . . Can you be surprised that I'm losing my self-respect ? "

" Don't look at it that way, my darling. Try to remember you're playing a terribly difficult game. And that, if you keep on, you'll win."

" I expect you're right," said David. " I'm not much good at these things. But I do know this— there's a limit to human endurance. And I am approaching that limit, hand over fist." He threw up his head there and took a deep breath. " I don't think you've any idea what I have to stand. Quite

N

apart from anything else, my position is hideously false. And that offends me—like hell. Pretence, to me, is loathsome. I'd rather break stones by the road. Then, again, it's ignominious. Rowena despises me, and I share her contempt. She's only to show me the whip, and I do as she says. Finally, it's wearing —and that's a very mild term. I am constantly expending more self-control than I've got. I'm not the kind that breaks down, but you can't do that sort of thing and be the same. For one thing only, it's going to affect my work . . .

"Well, there we are. I shall go on as long as I can. And when I can go on no longer, I shall clear out. After all, what can she do? Write and ask me to come back. And when I refuse, then she can petition the Court. Restitution of Conjugal Rights." He let out a laugh. "Well, let her damned well do it. It may do me some harm, but it won't do her any good."

"And then?" said Helen, quietly.

"The Court would order me to return to her. I shouldn't, of course. And there the matter would end. A petition like that is only a gesture now. It had its uses once, but they're out of date."

There was a little silence.

Then—

"You've put it fairly," said Helen. "So very fairly that I have nothing to say. When you can stand it no longer—well, then you must go. If I'd had my way, you'd have left her two months ago. It sends me half out of my mind to think of her twisting your tail. I lie awake sometimes, till the dawn comes up, thinking, thinking, thinking, and hammering on the cold iron that Fate has given to us, when we asked for bread. And all that keeps me going is your amazing strength."

"My strength?"

"Your strength, my darling. No man I ever met could have stuck it so long. And when I consider the

hell that you're going through, for very shame I pluck
up courage again. I don't know how you do it, and
that's the truth. But I *do* know that *not* to do it
would be a frightful mistake . . . As you say, the
position is hellish. It's very hard to see how it could
be worse. But, if you left her, I think she might
make it worse. For God's sake don't ask me how,
for I've no idea. Only my instinct warns me against
such a course. You see, she is—not like us. She does
things we would not do. But the terrible danger is
this—that *she can think out things that never would
enter our heads.*"

"That's very true," said David, heavily. "I've
learned a hell of a lot in the last eight months. I
never knew . . . anyone living . . . could stoop so
low."

In silence they passed through the orchard and so
to the stable-yard . . .

The girl had spoken no more and no less than the
truth. She was afraid of Rowena, for Bohun's sake.
Because she could see more clearly, her position was
almost more dreadful than his. Herself in comparative
safety, she saw the man she loved within range of a
poisonous snake. He could not scotch the serpent :
neither could she. All she could do was to beg him
to stand very still . . . until help came . . .

That their spirits should rise with luncheon was
natural enough. The meal was prophetic—an earnest
of what was to come. For the first time, they sat
down alone in a private house. Facing each other,
at a table which might have been theirs, waited upon
by servants who knew very well that the man was no
ordinary guest, they broke the bread of illusion and
rose refreshed.

Six comfortable hours slid by . . .

Together, they drove to see Tumble, making the
best of quarantine, seven miles off—the scrap professed to know David and played with the two in

a paddock until he could hardly stand up : then on to a market-town, where Helen had shopping to do : and so again to Bluemantle, whose venerable lawns and timber and sculptured yew offered the peace of the world in a lordly dish.

The stable-clock struck seven.

It was the chill of depression as much as the cool of the day that made them turn to the warmth of the 'short' saloon.

This was an intimate chamber, far taller than it was broad, where famous men had nodded and statesmen had put off state, whose clock had been advanced to get a King to his bed. A fire of logs was flaring upon its hearth, turning the dusk to darkness and breathing the room's defiance of winter nights ; and indeed the scene seemed set for the two to take up and play out the *rôles* they had played at lunch.

But Bohun's car was waiting, out in the drive . . .

He stood, surveying the chamber, hand to chin, marking well its detail, as one who means to remember a place he has cause to love : then he turned, too quickly for Helen, and met her eyes. These were fast upon him ; her lip was caught in her teeth ; and her beautiful hands were cupping a tragic face. At once she looked away at the leaping flames : but the man came straight to her side and held her against his heart.

" I feel the same," he said quietly. " This room was made for our leisure—before going up to bed." She made no answer, but hid her face in his coat. " And in ten minutes' time I'm going . . . back to the woman I married . . . who hates me . . . as I hate her."

Helen cried out at that.

" Oh, don't, my blessed, don't. You're only making it worse."

As though she had not spoken, the man went on.

" Is it worth it, my darling ? That's all. Is anything worth the misery we're going through ? "

" I—I think so, David."

"So do I. But I am not sure. So far we've obeyed our instinct, which tells us to do as our people have always done. So far we've obeyed it blindly, and I'm not going to say we've been wrong. But, before we go any further, I want to examine this instinct—to see if it's worth obeying at such a terrible cost."

He kissed her and let her go : then he made his way to the sofa and took his seat on its arm.

"It really amounts to this—that we're putting the bubble reputation before our love. The door to heaven is open : but, for the sake of our names, we propose to sit tight in hell. And that, indefinitely."

"Not indefinitely, David."

"Till our hearts are broken, then : or we can't stand the pain any more . . . Well, is it worth it, Helen ? Is the bubble reputation worth such a frightful price ? It was, fifty years ago—no doubt about that. But is it worth it to-day ? Everywhere traditions are tumbling, and the die-hards who cherish their ruins are called damned fools for their pains. The golden age is over : and the age of nickel is in. What is divorce to-day ? It's the outward and visible sign of common or garden sense. If I could divorce my wife, we'd both go mad with joy : it's the one thing we're praying for—that God will give me the chance. We'd give up a year of our lives for me to be free. But we want to be able to say, 'She did the dirty on us, and we didn't do it on her. We've got our cake all right ; but please, sir, we never pinched it ; she put it into our hands.' That is the noble path which our instinct commands us to tread."

Helen lifted her head.

"Be fair to yourself, my darling. Be fair to us both. You've every right to leave her, and I have every right to take you away. But we cannot proclaim these things. And so we should be——"

"—debarred from one of those ruined courts

which the die-hards keep. At the moment we've got the *entrée*, but do we ever go in ? Never. Because we're too broad-minded. We don't cross off men and women because they have been divorced—*unless we know that they're rotten*. If I had deceived Rowena, if I was out for your money, if you had pretended to be Rowena's friend——"

A telephone-bell whimpered, to snap the sentence in two.

" That's Mo," said Helen, rising. " Don't go, my darling. She just wants to know I'm alive."

While mother and daughter talked, Bohun strolled on the terrace under a fading sky.

So for, perhaps, five minutes. Then he turned to see Helen coming, over the flags.

He went to meet her at once and took her hands.

" I'm all right now," he said, smiling. " I think that room went to my head. One can make out a hell of a case, but when all's said and done—well, I'm used to the bubble reputation, and if I were to bust it, life wouldn't be quite the same. You feel as I do, I know—if you didn't, I shouldn't be here. And it does us no credit at all. In fact, I'm not at all certain we're not damned fools. But we've just been born narrow-minded *where we ourselves are concerned*. And now I must go. Kiss me, Nell. When I get to Dioni, I'll wire you—to say that I'm coming back."

As his car moved down the drive, Helen stood still as death at the foot of the famous steps. Straining her ears, she heard it slow up for the gate-house and then its snarl as it leapt at the open road . . .

Five minutes later Bohun was four miles off, and Helen was lying, weeping, face downward upon her bed.

* * * *

Bohun was taking no chances.
He had hardly arrived at Dioni before he received

his telegram of recall. He had, of course, composed it himself, and had left it, with strict instructions, in the faithful hands of Minter, the Hall Porter of his club.

He held up the sheet to Rowena, unpacking a wardrobe-trunk.

The lady raised her eyebrows.

" Don't rush your fences, Willie. Bluemantle won't run away."

The man set his teeth.

" I'm leaving to-morrow," he said.

" Why not ? Who wants you to stay ? But what in thunder's the use of a fancy wire, if nobody sees the joker but you and me ? "

" What d'you want me to do ? " said Bohun.

Rowena sighed.

" Well, why did you have the wire sent ? "

Bohun frowned. Then he folded the paper and put it away.

" All right," he said. And then, " What a farce it is."

Rowena shrugged her shoulders and turned again to her trunk . . .

That evening he played his part, with the telegram in his hand, ' breaking the news ' to his wife, who was sitting with friends she had made in a lively bar. The performance he gave was wretched : Rowena's, of course, was superb. If Forsyth had seen it, the man would have thrown in his hand. Her sherry untasted, she left the bar halfway to tears . . .

She saw David off the next morning, and then returned to put a brave face on the business and take up her shattered life. It was a forlorn, if exquisite, little figure that, half an hour later, ran down to the brilliant surf.

As she came to the edge of the water, Rowena stopped dead. Something—a definite impulse bade her turn round and look back.

She did so—to see Lord Juliot, fifty yards off.
When he saw that she saw him, he raised his panama
hat.

For the very first time in her life, Rowena felt weak
at the knees. *She, whom nothing escaped, had failed
to perceive the gift which the gods had thrust under her
nose.* The man should have been in Scotland—so
much she knew. But because *she* was at Dioni . . .

"God in heaven," she breathed. "And I called
the old —— a bridge . . . If I can smear dear David,
I've only got to walk in. And he shouldn't last more
than two years—with care. Rowena, Countess of
Juliot . . . Oh dear, oh dear."

As hard as she could, she ran straight to where he
was standing, after the way of a child.

CHAPTER XII

Force Majeure

SIX weeks had gone by, and London was filling up. The autumn was over and gone, and the voice of the eunuch was heard in the band, fluting its tearful reproach, *You might have left me the dreams which I found in your arms.* The canticle was the rage. People who thought well of Shakespeare took care to learn it by heart. Somebody called it ' The *Te Deum* of Foot and Mouth Disease.'

Barristers were in Chambers, the Bohuns in Curzon Street : Helen Adair was at Bluemantle, Juliot at Carlton House Terrace : the Court page of more than one journal announced the return of the Grainers to Rutland Gate.

Such was the state of things when David Bohun decided to leave his wife.

It was to his fortnight at Hautboys that this decision was due. The immense relief of being without Rowena for fifteen days, the taste of that blessed freedom which he had so lightly exchanged for a bondage that put out light, the luxury of waking each morning to sixteen full hours of grace—it was the loss of these things by his wife's return that made cohabitation seem insupportable.

As a matter of hard fact, his case had been worse. The man was at work all day, attended next to no parties, frequently dined at his club ; and though Rowena went out much less than before, there were days when he scarcely saw her, except in bed and asleep. Such time as they spent together was certainly none too sweet, for, though he did not know it, the sins of Juliot were visited on his head ; still, though Rowena laid on, it was not the burden itself which could not be borne, so much as the gnawing remembrance of those few, glorious days when he had no burden to bear.

And so, one Monday morning, Rowena returned from the country to find her husband gone.

The note he had left for her was downright enough.

Dear Rowena,

This is to say that I've left you. I find it hard to believe that you'll be surprised. Personally, I think we should have a Deed of Separation. I mean, it's more regular. But if you're against such a thing, I really don't care. You can always write to my Chambers, if you should change your mind. Meanwhile, I shall pay a hundred and twenty pounds into your account on the first day of every month.

Yours,
David.

Reading this letter, the lady was not amused.

* * * *

It is an old saying that the man who is his own lawyer has a fool for his client. To this may be added another, far stranger, truth—that the lawyer who acts for himself will assuredly let himself down.

If Bohun had not been a lawyer, he would, of course, have gone to Forsyth for help. But, because he was a lawyer, he knew *well enough* what should (or should not) be done. The letter which he left for Rowena was wholly correct. He had assured her an income, told her where to address him, advised the execution of a Deed. If and when she agreed that a Deed had better be signed, then he would go to Forsyth

and ask him to draw one up. Otherwise, what was
the point of washing linen so foul before *anyone's*
eyes ?

Such reluctance was natural. Confessions of failure
are never easy to make ; but when they involve the
exposure of highly intimate sores and the laying of a
grisly indictment against the most excellent image
which you yourself have set up, the impulse to hold
your tongue is powerful indeed. What Bohun lost
sight of was this—that it is to receive such confessions
that family lawyers exist and that their offices are
laundries, where linen, no matter how foul, may be
conveniently washed.

That Rowena did not go to a lawyer cannot be
charged against her as the act of a fool. What is
sauce for the gander is not always sauce for the goose.
Lawyers—and David among them—believed in the
law : but Mrs. Bohun did not—except as a means to
enforce her especial desires. She needed no guidance,
thank you, much less mealy-mouthed interference—
from some pettifogging gelding, about as well qualified
to advise her as would have been a curate to advise a
Borgia.

She considered the state of affairs with all her
might. Separation was out of the question. Somehow or other, of course, the man must be made
to return. The sweets of living alone were toothsome
indeed, but the time for these was not yet. If the
lady had had a motto, it would have been ' Business
First '.

Separation was out of the question, because separation would be a spoke in her wheel. When a man
leaves his wife, *yet goes to no other woman*, suspicions
are bound to arise which, charm she never so wisely,
the wife can never allay. And the Countess of Juliot
must be above suspicion. If she was not—well, she
would not be the Countess of Juliot. That went
without saying. Juliot knew as much about women

as he did about the sole of his foot : but where his
wife was concerned, he had large ideas.

*   *   *   *

She told nobody what had happened : she did not
write to her husband : in fact, for three days, she
took no action at all.

David was equally discreet. He certainly wrote to
Helen ; but that was all. And Helen wrote three
replies—and tore each of them up. No counsel was
better than bad. She did not tell Lady Persimmon,
because she wished to spare her the frown which the
news would provoke : and her mother was worried to
death, because she was well aware that matter of some
importance was being withheld.

Rowena was waiting : Helen was waiting on Rowena :
and David saw more and more clearly that what he
had done was good. And the morning and the evening
were the third day.

*   *   *   *

The one good thing which had come to David Bohun
out of his conjugal wreck was the fact that he turned
again to his old-fashioned club. As a member of five
years' standing, he had more than a nodding acquaintance with some of the pleasantest fellows that ever
sat wide of a fire : but when he had married a wife,
this relation had come to an end ; for, from then
until June, he had hardly set foot in the house. Two
or three times he had entered the Ladies' Annexe—
when a hasty dinner had suited Rowena's book ; but
in the Ladies' Annexe members were ladies' men.
And then, as we know, from June on, Bohun had
made good use of his old-fashioned club : and with
his return, of course, the pleasant relation revived.
Be sure he valued it as never before. Once, it had

passed the time : but now it was meat and drink to a fainting man.

When he left his wife, he had taken a service flat—any port in a storm. He slept and breakfasted there, lunched in Lincoln's Inn Hall, and dined at the club. By the time three days had gone by, he felt a new man.

This was no more than natural. The prisoner had burst his bonds.

On Wednesday evening, he strode through the glittering streets, conscious of work well done and a kindly leisure at hand. He warmed to his surroundings—to the mighty rivers of traffic, the gleaming banks of the shops : he snuffed the smell of London —that faint, peculiar scent which the old jade always wears, thrilled at her boisterous catches, boasted her infinite variety, swore there was no one like her in all the world.

In high good humour he came to St. James's Street, to the topless, mahogany doors and Minter's respectful smile. A gentleman-at-ease passed into his faithful mansion at seven o'clock . . .

Three-quarters of an hour had gone by, and Bohun was making one of a quiet-voiced group, discussing its glass of sherry, before going in to dine.

"To my mind," said Onslow, "the thing's unarguable. Consider the case of France. In that enlightened land a 'thirsty' can get a drink at any hour of any day in the year. There *is* no closing time. *Cafés* and bars keep open as long as their customers like. And how much drunkenness is there ? *None at all.* I have never seen a Frenchman the worse for wear."

"Neither have I," said Charing. "But that is the nature of the beast. Frenchmen just don't get tight. But Englishmen do. And so, to preserve the decencies, the English must be controlled."

"It's a matter of climate," said Barham. "If

Frenchmen lived in England, they'd drink to forget the fact."

"What's Bohun think?" said Twysden. "He's got a legal mind."

"I'd like to see it tried," said David. "All liquor restrictions suspended for one full month. And the country told in plain terms that if——"

"Mr. Bohun, sir?" piped a voice.

David turned, to regard a diminutive page.

"Yes. I'm Mr. Bohun. What is it?"

"Your guest is waiting in the annexe, sir."

With that, the boy was gone, and Bohun looked round.

"My guest?" he said. "But I haven't invited one." He turned and lifted his voice. "Boy!"

The boy came back at a run.

"Yes, sir?"

"There's some mistake. Who sent you?"

"The Hall Porter, sir. They telephoned through to him."

"Go and tell him they've got the name wrong. I'm not expecting a guest."

As the page scuttled away—

"That is the worst," said Barham, "of an aristocratic name. What I go through——"

"To be aristocratic," said Onslow, "it is not necessary to be misleading. Besides, I knew a nigger called Barham."

"The old school tie," sighed Barham. "D'you still keep up?"

David did not join in the laughter. A frightful suspicion had fastened upon his mind. Supposing Rowena . . . With an effort, he shook off the notion, as being absurd. Not even Rowena would come unasked to his club. Ring up, perhaps: but not come. No woman, however abandoned, would do such a thing as that.

Barham and Onslow were sparring, but, though he

smiled with the others, his mind had no room for their jests. Somehow, he must be ready—in case the page came back and said that a lady was there. He wouldn't, of course. There had been a mistake in the name : Beaumont or Burn had been given, and Bohun received. Still, just in case . . .

He decided to leave the group and stroll to the porter's lodge. Then, at least, if it *was* Rowena, he would not have to carry it off. Onslow and the others would never give the matter a thought. He had not said he was dining : and, if he did not come back— well, he might have gone home.

As he made to turn—

"I appeal to Bohun," said Onslow. "He knows the law. I submit that to desire a fellow member to take and bestow an article of his faith—not in safe custody, but in that fabulous inclosure which a certain mammal is commonly alleged to have preferred . . ."

My God, would the man never stop ? The page would be back in a moment : and then, if it *was* Rowena . . .

". . . I submit that such a request is not only out of all order, but falls well within the category of ' conduct likely to lead to a breach of the peace '."

David heard himself answer.

"Speaking off-hand, I'd say ' no '. Your remedy would be to sock him. If he took you to Court, they'd certainly let you off."

With that, he turned—to see Minter, a pace away.

"It's quite right, sir. It's Mrs. Bohun."

There was an awkward silence.

Then David put a hand to his head.

"She's—she's made a mistake," he faltered. "She's made a mistake in the day . . . All right, I'll go across, Minter. I'm much obliged."

I have said that the man was no actor. His words would have passed : but his manner gave him away.

Stiffly, he left the hearth and crossed the echoing hall, sure that the others' eyes were fast on his back.

In fact, they were not. Charing and Onslow were looking into the fire. Twysden had picked up a paper. Barham was regarding his shoes. The four had seen something private, something not meant to be seen. It would not have mattered if each had seen it alone. That they had seen it together had put the four out of face. What it was they had seen they neither knew nor cared : but the glimpse had embarrassed them. A fellow member had committed an unforgivable sin.

* * * *

Making his way to the annexe, David stood still in a passage and wiped the sweat from his face. The man may be forgiven : he had his back to the wall.

When he tried to face what was coming, regret and shame refused to vacate his mind. If only he'd gone himself, instead of sending the page . . . If only he'd gone to the lodge and whispered to Minter to say he was not in the club . . . That was what Minter was for—to save a member from being molested like this. As it was, the worst had happened—worse than the worst. He had shown his dirty linen where dirty linen must never, never be shown—and that, to four good fellows he hardly knew. That it was not his fault was wholly beside the point. An unwritten law had been broken, and that was that. The finest excuse in the world was inadmissible. Besides, it *was* his fault. Only a fool would have failed to carry it off—to deal with that pregnant silence which had succeeded the sentence which Minter had passed.

Again the sweat broke on his face, and he entered a lavatory . . .

The cold water did its work. When he came to the drawing-room, he had himself well in hand.

The room was agreeably full. People who had dined early were taking their coffee, before going on to the play. Others were drinking cocktails, before going in to dine. Members were being attentive ; guests were being gracious ; servants were being discreet. Manners were conspicuously 'party' ; smiles were bright ; mirth hung upon a hair-trigger ; to speak was to entertain. Yet, there was no clack of tongues : converse was confidential, laughter was low. And all were in evening dress—except a forlorn, little figure, seated beside a pillar, on the edge of a high-backed chair.

Her husband found the pose startling. Here was play-acting with a vengeance. Artless, artful or downright, Rowena was not of the type that sits upon the edge of its chair.

She had, of course, attracted attention. As Bohun moved towards her, he saw two women whisper and then look round. The sweat which the water had staunched began to break out once more.

He was sure that Rowena had seen him, but, until he was two paces off, she never looked up. Then she started to her feet with a cry, swayed, drooping, into his arms, and hid her face in his coat.

Beside himself with horror, he sought to make her stand off.

" Rowena, not here—I beg you."

Her knees were giving, and he had to hold her up

" Oh, David, David," she whimpered, " you're all I've got."

The man went white to the lips.

" Hush, Rowena—I beg you."

" I'm sorry I was cross about Helen. I take it all back. You can do what you like with her : but don't leave me alone."

His teeth fast clenched, the man jerked out a command.

" My God, Rowena, *stop* it. You can't do this here."

The room was in such a confusion as it had never known. Some people were sitting dumbfounded, others were trooping out. In the doorway new arrivals were huddled, as though uncertain whether to come or go. A servant was standing open-mouthed, with a tray in his hands. A party close to the pillar was up on its feet, and an elderly, hawk-eyed woman was plainly steeling herself to interfere.

"I've been so frightened," wailed Rowena. "And the servants laugh in my face."

"*Rowena, for Christ's sake, stop it.* You're giving offence."

"Am I? I'm sorry." She let him go, and a hand went up to her head. "I'm awfully sorry. I think I'm going to faint."

A girl cried out, as she swayed, and David caught her somehow and laid her down. Then he was brushed aside, and the hawk-eyed woman took charge.

Being in, she enjoyed herself. Admitted to the club on sufferance, she had become its ruler, whose word was law. Be sure she made the most of the power she had seized. She snapped out orders and, under the guise of efficiency, was quite inexcusably rude. She looked up and spoke to David, as though he were something unclean.

"I should go away," she rapped out. "Wait outside or something. If you're wanted, I'll see you're told."

He felt the blood come surging into his face. Then he turned on his heel and made his way to the door.

The slender hall was crowded—with people who should have been using the drawing-room. Most had nowhere to sit, and servants were hastening with chairs from the dining-room. The place was creeping with whispers, alive with shrugs.

All eyes left the doorway, when David appeared. The shrugs and whispers gave way to attempts to make conversation, too obvious to be a success. Only a thin voice held on—that of a very old member, whose back was turned, expressing the humble duty of a forgotten age.

"I am so very sorry that such a thing should have occurred. That any guest of mine should have been subjected, in what I have always looked upon as my own house, to so distasteful an experience . . ."

Someone drew him aside, to give David room to go by. The latter passed out of the hall and began to go down the steps which led to the vestibule.

A party was coming up, with a member whom David knew—a cheerful fellow, cursed with a carrying voice.

"Hullo, Bohun, how are you? Thank God there's someone not dressed. Come and have dinner with us —or are you engaged?"

As though he had not spoken, David passed on: and the other stood staring after and then swung round, to stare up at the crowded hall. Then he cried to his guests to wait and passed to the head of the steps. Another member was there, and he touched his arm.

"What the devil's the matter, Hillock?"

The other spoke in his ear.

"A frightful show. His wife broke down and fainted. They're bringing her round. Some other woman, of course. It's a shocking bad case. I mean . . ."

David sent for a taxi. Whilst it was being fetched, he stood by the side of the lodge, with his back to the wall. What he had suffered had numbed him. That more degradation was coming left him unmoved. A harridan might use him as a leper, but she would only be flogging a horse that was dead. She would only be robbing a bankrupt. From him that had not, had been taken even that which he had.

People were leaving the annexe. The party he had passed on the stairs was the first to withdraw.

The carrying voice reached David, before its owner appeared.

"We'd better go to a grill-room. There's been an upset of sorts. I'm really frightfully sorry . . ."

Few of those leaving saw David, standing back in the shadows, out of the glare of the light. Unaware of his presence, they spoke of what they had seen.

"I can't tell you how sorry I am . . . it wasn't your fault . . . did you see how he looked at her . . . a most awful show . . . my God, I am sorry for that kid . . . Montmartre if you like, but not in St. James's Street . . . well, I've been a member now for thirty-two years, but . . . no, you go on. I really don't feel I can face a musical show . . . and yet she's mad about him . . . a first-class swine . . ."

A servant came down the steps, as fast as he dared. He spoke to the annexe-porter, busy with the speeding of guests.

"Where's Mr. Bohun?"

The porter jerked his head.

"Just there, by the lodge."

The other peered for a moment. Then he came up to David, still standing against the wall.

"Mrs. Bohun is ready, sir."

"Say that a taxi's waiting—if she will come down."

"Very good, sir."

People had stopped talking. Their one idea seemed to be to get out of the place.

From the head of the steps, the harridan's voice rang out.

"Where is the man? He's wanted. Will nobody do as I say?"

Her brief reign was over. Nobody did as she said. A servant was addressing Rowena.

"Mr. Bohun says will you come down, madam. A taxi is there."

With a very ill grace, the harridan swallowed her gruel.

" I'll come down with you, my dear. After all, if he likes to give orders . . . You know, I'm only a guest."

With her arm about Rowena, she urged her charge to the steps . . .

As they came to the vestibule, Rowena started forward, clasping her hands.

" Oh, David, you will come with me ? "

" Yes, I'm coming," said Bohun. He jerked his head at the doorway. " The taxi's there."

Rowena returned to her champion.

" I can't ever thank you enough. You've been so terribly sweet."

But the other's eyes were on David. She spoke with a shaking voice.

" I only wish, my poor child, that my son were here. He's a very short way with cads. And he would have seen you home."

Only two servants were there to hear the elegant speech.

Turning his back upon contumely, David followed Rowena out of the club.

As the door of the taxi was slammed—

" Poor old trout," said Rowena. " She thinks he's back in the Army. The voice that breathed o'er Quetta. But I do wish she'd clean her teeth."

* * * *

Ten minutes, perhaps, had gone by, and the Bohuns were home.

The man had not opened his mouth, since leaving the club.

Rowena was at ease on the sofa, sipping a glass of sherry and reading *The Evening News*. David, his hands behind him, was looking into the fire.

After a little he turned—

" I'm not going to kill you," he said : " but that

is only because I don't want to be hanged. For what you have done to-night, you deserve to die."

Rowena looked up.

"I know just how you feel," she said.

"I don't think you do," said the man. "I think if you did, you'd be frightened—out of your life."

Rowena shook her head.

"Nothing doing," she said. "I shouldn't have taken your name, if you'd been that sort. Never mind. It's all over now. But I shouldn't do it again —lest a worse thing befall."

Her husband stood very still.

"What on earth d'you mean?" he said. "You can't imagine I'm coming back to this house."

Rowena shrugged her shoulders.

"I hoped you would."

"After this evening? I see. Well, you've got me wrong, Rowena. So far as I am concerned, you've shot your bolt."

The lady considered her sherry.

"Quite sure?" she said.

"Quite sure," said David, quietly. "You see, you broke me this evening. I've no more to lose." He glanced at his watch. "And now I'm going. I shouldn't go back to the club, for I shan't be there."

As he stepped to the door—

"What a fool you are," said Rowena. "D'you want what happened to-night to happen at Lincoln's Inn?" Her husband stopped in his tracks. "Yes, I thought you'd forgotten that. On the steps of Lincoln's Inn Hall—I saw you come out to-day, though you didn't see me. Or would you rather we splurged . . . *and gave the Press a treat . . . at the Savoy*?"

"My God," said Bohun, hoarsely.

"Think it over, my friend. If you come back, you can go as you —— well please. But if you don't, you're for it—*and so is she*. Meet where you like—I'll find you: you're painfully easy to watch."

There was a sinister silence, whilst Bohun stared upon his wife, with a hand to his mouth.

A scene rose up before him, even more awful than the nightmare from which he had just emerged. He saw the restaurant which his wife had named, he saw the suspended animation, he saw three figures standing, the cynosure of all eyes : he saw himself turned to stone, he saw and heard Rowena mouthing her deadly lies, he saw the stricken look upon Helen's face . . .

When he spoke, he spoke very low.

" This is—blackmail."

(In fact, it was bluff. The future Countess of Juliot could never have gone so far. But how should her husband know that ?)

" It's God's truth," said Rowena. " Of course, if you like to chance it, that's your affair : but this evening ought to have shown you that I am—shall we say ' minded ' to have you back."

She picked up her paper again.

" If I were you," said David, " I'd be afraid to die."

" That I can well believe. But I am of ' sterner stuff '. Besides, you're not going to kill me. You said so just now."

The man spoke through his teeth.

" You know that Helen's dead white. But to force my hand, you threaten to paint her black . . . to rope her into a filthy, vulgar brawl . . . to broadcast——"

" More or less," said Rowena. " More or less. And if you want me to do it, *sleep out to-night*." She drank what was left of her sherry, set the glass on a table and got to her feet. " And now I'm going to change. You heard me order dinner for nine o'clock."

With that, she was gone.

For full two minutes, the man stood still, as she had left him, with sightless eyes. Then he took a deep breath and looked round. Perceiving the sherry, he filled a glass to the brim and emptied it at a draught. Then he passed downstairs and out of the house.

* * * *

Rowena dined alone and went early to bed.

Late that night her husband posted two letters.

One tendered his resignation to the secretary of his club. The other was addressed to Helen Adair.

> *Nell darling,*
> *This is just to say that I'm going back.*
>
> *Till Sunday.*
> *David.*

When Rowena heard his taxi, she put out her light.

As she curled herself up, she spoke to herself.

" Twelve o'clock of a hell of a night," she said. " And all's well."

CHAPTER XIII

No Reply

IT is said that, though he survived, to live to a good, old age, a man who had once been racked was never the man he had been before the torture was done. This may or may not be true : what is quite certain is that David Bohun was changed. He was, as I have shown, a highly sensitive man : and the scene in the Ladies' Annexe had left its mark upon his soul.

He was more reserved than before ; worked longer with less result ; avoided the fellowship to be found in Lincoln's Inn Hall. He was very quiet with Helen —plainly most glad to be with her, but very quiet, after the way of a man who has been bereaved. And nothing that she could do could bring the light into his eyes.

The girl never knew what had happened. He could not bring himself to tell her : and Helen respected his silence and never asked. But in case she addressed him there, he had to tell her that he had resigned from his club—and thereby lifted a corner of the curtain he would not draw. The glimpse was more than enough. Helen tried not to pray for Rowena's death.

That night, for the very first time, she knew that she was afraid . . .

The position was grave. The lot of a prisoner who has escaped and has been recaptured is proverbially grim. David had need of her, as never before. And she was beyond his reach. David had need of his club, as never before. And he had resigned Having no one to turn to, he now had nowhere to go. Unless something happened soon . . .

When at last she went to her bed, Helen had made up her mind to return to Town. What if the woman was trying to drive him into her arms? Better a living sheep than a dying lion.

The next morning her maid came to tell her that Lady Persimmon was ill . . .

The doctor, summoned from London, was downright enough.

"She'll be all right in ten days, but she mustn't stay here. The South of France, Mrs. Adair, as soon as she's well. That is my prescription. I know I'm right."

It is written, 'To obey is better than sacrifice.' Remembering the saying, Helen felt ready to scream . . .

When Lady Persimmon was mending, she rang up Belinda Leighton and asked her to meet her in Town. Relations were none too easy—Punch had flatly refused to meet her at all. Belinda said nothing to Punch, and went to lunch with Helen in Kensington Square.

After lunch Helen spoke out.

"He's in deep water, Belinda—and I've got to leave for Chiberta in four days' time. I told him yesterday. And when I told him, Belinda, he bowed his head. He never said anything. His head went down—that was all." Belinda's eyes filled with tears, but the other held on. "For pity's sake, Belinda, do what you can. I'm going to make him promise to turn to you two: but it's the Sundays that I'm afraid of. You see . . ." She stifled a sob there, and Belinda put out a hand. "He'll spend his week-ends at Hautboys: but I cannot bear his being there all alone. I mean, I think it's—serious . . . If he asks you two down, will you go? And write to me and tell me—about the look in his eyes? I hope to

God I'll be back in a fortnight at most, but I cannot leave my mother, until she's herself again."

A shocked Belinda swore to do what she could . . .

On the day that Helen left England, Bohun went about his business, as a man in a dream. God knows what errors he made in his paper-work ; but, to his clients' horror, he mixed two ' motions ' in court and dealt in vain with the other as though it had been the one. By the registrar's help, the tangle was straightened out, but by that time the Judge was hostile and would not make the orders which Bohun had sought. A consultation followed at which he let Beaver down : the law which the latter was expecting was not on his junior's tongue. Bohun left Chambers that evening, more dead than alive. Sunk in a sea of troubles, he trod the familiar pavements, took the familiar turnings, crossed the familiar streets. Subconsciously he waited on the traffic and picked his way between vehicles, standing still. His body moved as a horse, with the reins on its neck. And, as a horse makes for its stable, his body made for his club. Before he knew where he was, a page had swung open a door and he was within the house. He turned to nod to Minter, as usual—and saw the look on his face . . . It was an arresting look, and Bohun stopped in his stride. For a moment he stared at the Porter he knew so well : then he shot a glance round, and a hand went up to his mouth.

" Oh, my God," he said, and turned on his heel.

Blind with shame, he blundered into the street . . .

That night a record was broken. For the first time since he left Oxford, Bohun went to his bedroom the worse for drink.

* * * *

Since he had come back to her, Rowena had left him alone. She watched him carefully, but she left him alone. Not knowing how to use him, she held her peace. Sometimes two days would go by without their exchanging two words. She knew she was right to wait : but she wondered at Helen Adair. If the bitch was in love with the man, why didn't she take some action, to stop the rot ? Then the Leightons came to dinner . . . It was from Belinda that she learned that Lady Persimmon was ill and that she and her daughter had left for the South of France.

" When's she coming back ? " said Rowena.

" I've no idea," said Belinda. " I think it rather depends on her mother's health."

Rowena summoned a sigh.

" Poor old boy," she said gently. " It must have hit him *très* hard. She's terribly good for him, and we both of us owe her so much." Belinda felt slightly sick. " I wish I'd known that Lady Persimmon was ill. I'd have sent some flowers. I saw her house last week—the one in Kensington Square. She's let it to some people called Vintner. It wasn't so nice as I'd expected. I didn't care for the——"

" I don't think she has," said Belinda.

" She has, indeed," said Rowena. " They've been there nearly——"

" But I *know* she hasn't," cried Belinda. " Only last Monday I lunched there with Mrs. Adair."

" Well, that's extraordinary," said Rowena. " I heard Mrs. Vintner say . . ."

She rounded the lie, before turning to something else. She had learned what she wanted to know— that Helen had asked Belinda to care for David Bohun.

* * * *

Winter came heavily on.

A second attack of bronchitis, far worse than the first, put Lady Persimmon down before she had been at Chiberta for forty-eight hours : and though she weathered the storm with something to spare, it left her spent and shaken—the prey of convalescence for weeks to come.

God knows when I can leave her, wrote Helen Adair. *Belinda, what have we done, to be treated like this ?*

Belinda replied by return.

The week-end at Hautboys was a complete success. He picked us up on Saturday after lunch, and got us down in plenty of time for tea. Punch was in very good form—I'm afraid because he thinks that you've taken your leave—and David was looking better before we got in. It was marvellous having no servants—you know the house runs itself : and all that we had to do was to wash up and make the beds. David, of course, had brought enough food for ten, and Punch had got some champagne . . . We got to bed about two, had breakfast about eleven and went for a four-mile walk in a sunshine as good as yours. And David was his old self—I can't say more. He quietened down a bit, when we had to pack up after tea : but, even when he left us in Chelsea, you simply wouldn't have known him for the man who had picked us up. He's giving me lunch to-morrow, and next week-end we're going to Hautboys again.

Cooped in *La Belle Issue*, Helen read over and over the comfortable words . . .

Rowena went about her occasions, much as a hot-house gardener whose heart belongs to his work. She did not spare herself : all she did, she did with the greatest care. Her ' sherry ' parties were suspended : the Cullets were dropped : the Leightons were nursed : the Grainers were ' faded out ' : the Mockets were loosely held ' at the end of a string ' : the Stumms were abased : the Earl of Juliot was exalted.

My lord was crazy about her—the time they had spent at Dioni had settled that. The two had been

together from morning to night.   No longer, of course.
Indeed, their idyll could have been submitted to a
committee appointed by the Lords Spiritual with
every confidence.   For all that, the resemblance which
it bore to a honeymoon was brutally close.   When
Rowena kneeled before him, fresh from the waves,
a dripping bathing-dress insisting upon her symmetry ;
when she sat by his side in the dusk of a balcony,
listening to the crush of the breakers enfolding the
strains of a valse, the velvet sky above them sewn
with a million stars, the wanton touch of zephyr
seducing her scented curls—at times like these Juliot
could have moved mountains, if mountains had stood
in his way . . .   As one tends a delicate plant,
Rowena tended this delicate state of mind.   (It was,
after all, a question of temperature.)   Be sure it put
forth leaves.   From being desirable in his sight, she
was becoming indispensable to his existence.

To my mind, her greatest triumph was won in
Curzon Street.   Incredible as it may seem, her relations with David himself began to improve.

' When the devil was sick, the devil a saint would
be.'   Rowena was not such a fool.   Her remorse was
reluctant and surly—that of the gangster who, proposing to bump his man off, has inadvertently con-
demned him to everlasting torment.   ' And barbarism
itself *had* pitied him.'

As was natural, the man rejected the ' dope '.

" It's too late, Rowena.   I want no attention from
you.   It—it only revolts me now.   I suppose that's
why you do it—to make me feel sick."

" As a matter of fact," said Rowena, " I do it to
please myself.   That show at the club, you bought.
You had been warned.   Although, I must confess, I
didn't know it'd hit you as hard as it did.   Still, you
had to be brought back somehow.   What I did not
foresee was the Adair's going south . . .   You see,
I'd banked on her.   If I twisted your tail, at least

you'd always got her, to kiss it and make it well. And then—you hadn't got her . . . In their ruder moments some people might call me harsh : but I'm not unconscionable. I frankly admit I'd take some melting to-day, but I know what it used to feel like to have a heart."

Some men would have turned and rent her, as she deserved. But David's reply was to get up and leave the room.

Rowena looked after him, with a hand to her chin. " ' And some '," she murmured, " ' some fell on stony ground '."

The quotation was apt. But if the ground was stony, at least it was not ' the way side '. The seed took root of sorts and throve upon the casual attention which it received. The handing of a paper, the turning on of a bath, the making welcome of the Leightons —such things could be ignored ; but they could not be denied. Imperceptibly, relations improved.

* * * *

December came in, and Helen was still abroad.

Once she had left for London—on forty-eight hours' leave. And a fog had stopped all flying. And, because she had fought to fly, she had missed the train. To continue her journey was futile. Before she could get to London, it would have been time to start back.

A letter which David sent her shall speak for itself.

All right. I promise. I won't stay there alone again. I admit it's a curious sensation. The absence of any servants makes it seem strange. Of course, if the house was smaller . . . But I can't ask too much of the Leightons, and Rowena's said something to Punch. What, I don't know : but I think he's got an idea that she will not go to Hautboys because of something I've done. What the hell does it matter ? Any

*way they're coming down on Saturday next. If they
can't come the week after that, I shall have to go
somewhere else. I MUST get out of London for
twenty-four hours in the week—because that gives me
the strength to face London again. I used to love it
so much, but I dread it now. It's grim and hostile
to me. I don't belong any more.*

*For some reason or other, Rowena leaves me alone.
She promised she would, you know, if I returned. I
think it's come to this—that my jailer pities me.
Belinda is sweetness itself. What I'd have done
without her, I simply don't know. She is the true
confidante. The trouble is, I don't see her enough
alone. We can talk about you at lunch : but Punch
is with us at Hautboys, which makes it impossible.
Of course the whole thing is impossible. The
moment you come back, it's got to come to an end.
What end, I don't know : and that's what I want to
discuss. I think I had better see Forsyth : he was
my great-uncle's lawyer and is an exceptional man.
But I'd like to talk to you first.*

*I know you'll come as soon as ever you can. I'm
living to see you, Nell. I have nothing else to live for.
I'm afraid to look at the future : I try to forget the
past : but the thought of you keeps me going . . .
my darling Nell.*

*Think of me at Hautboys on Saturday evening next.
If only old Punch wasn't there, I could ring you up.*

That letter was written on Wednesday.

On Friday evening Belinda rang David up.

" Is that you, D.B. ? My dear, I'm so dreadfully
sorry—I've just had a wire from Punch. You know
he's at York, and he was to have left to-night. Well,
now he can't get away. *Hope to leave Sunday evening*
is what he says. My dear, I'm so terribly sorry . . .''

Slowly the man made answer.

" That's all right, Belinda. It . . . can't be helped.''

His voice made Belinda frantic.

" My dear, my dear, I'm so sorry. Don't you think you can get someone else ? I mean, is there no one —no man in your Chambers, or something ? "

" I'm afraid there's no one," said David. " But it doesn't matter, Belinda. Another time."

He put the receiver back, as a man who is very tired. Rowena looked up from the sofa.

" What is it ? " she said.

David stiffened at once.

" Nothing," he said. " The Leightons can't come to-morrow. Punch can't get away."

" That means Belinda can. Why don't you ask me ? "

David stepped to a table and picked up a book.

" All right, all right," said Rowena. " I'm not out to gate-crash, Willie. I know where I get off. But if you want Belinda, I can just as well sleep at Hautboys as Brunskill Towers."

David looked up.

Hautboys, as arranged . . . without Punch . . . with Rowena, just for the night . . . He could telephone to Chiberta . . . And Belinda and he could talk to their hearts' content.

" D'you mean that ? " he said.

Rowena raised her eyebrows.

" Take it or leave it," she said. " It's nothing to me. From Brunskill Towers to Hautboys is thirty-five miles : and if seventy miles will take that look off your face . . . I drive over after tea and I drive away after breakfast—perhaps before. It's so much eye-wash, of course. You're not going to sleep with Belinda, because she's not Helen Adair."

The man hesitated. Then he went to the telephone and picked the receiver up . . .

" I say, Belinda, Rowena says she'll come. She'll be staying at Brunskill Towers, and she'll drive over from there and spend the night at Hautboys, to save our face."

P

" D.B., how priceless ! I was almost in tears about it. What time will you pick me up ? "

" Between two and half-past, my dear . . ."

David put the receiver back and turned to his wife.

" I'm much obliged," he said.

" Don't be a fool," said Rowena. " It happens to suit my book. *I particularly want to be casual with Ruby Mocket.* And I'd like to see the guy who can show me a better way."

* * * *

The next day broke full of promise. An overhead fog in London argued that breathless brilliance which only Winter can add to the countryside. High and low fled the city, to make the most of the glory that lay without. And Belinda and David with them. Rowena had left already for Brunskill Towers.

" As soon as we're in," said David, " I'll ring her up. I may take some time to get through : but Rowena won't fetch up before seven o'clock. You'll speak to her, won't you, Belinda ? "

" Of course I will. You can't ring up from Chambers ? "

The man shook his head.

" Lincoln's Inn calling Chiberta would never do. The sensation would be terrific. You see, the clerks run the switchboard. They'd not only listen in, but they'd talk about it for days."

" I'd ring up Punch," said Belinda, " if only I knew where he was. But he's staying with a partner, or something, and I don't know the name of the firm. I do hope it's fine with him : he would have enjoyed this so much."

By the time they came to Hautboys, a noon of blue and silver was giving way to an evening of red and gold . . .

Less than an hour later, David was speaking to Helen—on the shore of the Bay of Biscay.

"Helen, my darling, I can't hear you awfully well."

"I'm not surprised. We're having a frightful storm. No thunder, you know. But I never saw such a gale."

"How strange. It's still as death here. Helen, darling, how are you?"

"I'm splendid, and Mo's much better."

"Oh, Nell, does that mean——"

"It does, indeed. If she goes on like this, I'll be able to come next week."

"My God, how marvellous? You see what I say in my letter. Or haven't you had it yet?"

"I got it this morning, my darling. And I think what you suggest is a great idea. But tell me, David—you're not alone at Hautboys?"

"No, no. I gave you my word. Belinda's here. Punch couldn't get away, so we thought it was off. And then Rowena stepped in. I told you she'd been —more human, the last few days. And when she heard I was stuck——"

"She's not there now?"

"Good lord, no. She's driving over from Brunskill Towers. She's staying there, you see. And to-morrow morning——"

A definite, ruthless 'chunk' cut the sentence in two. Strangely enough, it never reached Helen's ears. But David heard it plainly and knew what it meant. He let out a roar of fury that brought Belinda running, teapot in hand. He was flicking the hook to and fro.

"Exchange," he was crying, "*Exchange!* You've cut me off."

Unaware that the line had gone, Helen Adair was speaking low and vibrantly.

"David, listen. I don't like the sound of this. You say you're alone with Belinda and that she, Rowena, is coming to spend the night. Well, that's all right—*if she comes.* But for God's sake be careful, David, *in case it's a plant.* You see what I mean? Don't wait a moment later than eight. If she hasn't come by then, take Belinda away and leave her at some hotel. Have you got that, David? *David!* . . . Oh, my God, *we're cut off.*"

Five minutes went by before she could get her exchange. And another five minutes went by before she was told that the line to Bordeaux had ' gone '.

She spoke to the postmaster at a quarter past six.

" This is *La Belle Issue* and I am Mrs. Adair. I *must* get through to England at any cost."

" *Madame,* I am desolated——"

" At any cost. I mean that. I don't care how much I pay."

" *Madame,*" wailed the other, " what will you? It is, without doubt, the tempest. The line to Bordeaux is down."

" Then take me round by Toulouse. Get me through by seven, and I'll give you five thousand francs for every minute I talk."

The man was squinting with emotion.

" *Madame,*" he screamed, " I cannot. The line to Toulouse was broken ten minutes ago."

" I see. Can I send a wire? "

" Impossible, *Madame.* All communication is cut. For the moment only, of course. You may rest assured that——"

" Where is the break in the line? This side of Dax? Or beyond? "

" Beyond Dax, *Madame.* I know no more than that."

" You know the number I want—Bell Harry (England) 42. Get me that number by seven, and I'll pay twice the figure I said. But I can't wait longer than seven—I'm going out then."

Helen put back the receiver and moistened her lips.

" Two hours and a half," she murmured. " I ought to do it in that. God knows what I'll say to Mo :

but it can't be helped. If I'm not through by seven, I'll have to go to Bordeaux." She stepped to the bell and rang twice—for her personal maid. " Of course, he may have got it—I never heard us cut off. Or when she doesn't fetch up, they may have the wit to clear out." As though in fervent entreaty, she clasped her hands. " Oh, surely they will—they *must*. If I can see at this distance . . . Oh, how could they be such fools ? After all that's happened, how *could* they ? " Here a knock fell on the door, and her maid came into the room. " My things for one night, Thérèse : and yours as well. Be ready in half an hour. We leave for Bordeaux together at seven o'clock."

" Bordeaux ? On a night like this ? I beg that *Madame* will——"

" It's got to be done, Thérèse. If you'd rather not come——"

" It is not for me. I will go to hell with *Madame*, as *Madame* knows. But it is not right——"

" In half an hour," said Helen. " Tell them to open the garage and put up some food. Just tea and biscuits will do. We can dine at Bordeaux."

" I will do as *Madame* says, but I beg and pray that *Madame* will hire a car. It is not a night for *Madame* to drive herself."

" No, no. As Dixon isn't here, I must drive myself."

At seven o'clock she spoke to Bayonne again.

The postmaster was desolated—and was immediately cut off.

Two minutes later, the coupé was on the road.

* * * *

Neither maid nor mistress will ever forget that drive : but only the latter knew the height and the breadth and the depth of the risks she took. Weather and night be damned—she drove as a strong man drives

on a beautiful summer's day. Forty-five miles to the
hour, and a hundred and ten to go . . .

Some things stood out of the effort, as peaks from a
mountain range—a ribbon of black and silver, bordered
by bending trees . . . the tireless sweep of the wipers,
fighting the ceaseless rain . . . the savage buffets
of the tempest upon the hull of the car . . . the roar
of the forest about them for miles on end, a sound of
the utmost fury—the bellow of beasts enlarged . . .
and then a lamp being waved, and a frantic face at
a window, running with rain and sweat.

" *A tree is across the road, and you cannot go by.
Two men have been killed already, but twenty minutes
ago. They are lying there, on the verge . . . You
will have to go round by Bielle. Ten kilometres back,
madame, and turn to the left.*"

The check was serious. Bielle was hard to find, and
the roads were narrow and winding and none too good.
Twice the girl had to stop and study the map. Fifty
precious minutes went sliding into the draught. And
then at last they were back on the broad highway.

At a quarter past ten exactly, they made
Bordeaux . . .

Helen drove to the nearest hotel, ordered rooms
and dinner and put through her call.

" Will it be long ? It's urgent."

" I do not know. You will have to take your turn."

A dinner of sorts was served . . .

Every ten minutes, either Thérèse or her mistress
rang up the exchange.

At eleven o'clock a furious slattern gave tongue.

" You must show patience, as others. If you do
not, you will go to the foot of the list. It is not our
fault, I suppose, that only one line is working instead
of three."

Not until a quarter to twelve did the call come
through.

Helen fell upon the instrument.

" Yes ? "

" Your call is waiting. Why have you not replied ? "

" I am here," said Helen. " The bell has just gone."

" Stay there. I will try again."

The girl was trembling so much that she could hardly keep the receivers against her ears. All sorts and conditions were talking—of course, in French— and a nasal voice was continually crying ' Allo ! ' And then, at last, came England . . .

" London here. Speak up, Bordeaux."

" London," cried Helen. " *London !* I've asked for Bell Harry 42."

" That's right, madam. I'm sorry there's no reply."

The girl's heart gave one bound.

" Are you quite sure ? " she panted. " Quite certain ? Oh, will you please ring them again ? "

" Just a moment, madam . . . Is that you, Bell Harry ? . . . Still no reply from 42 ? . . . I'm very sorry, madam . . . Half a second . . . I'll put you through . . . You shall hear the bell ringing yourself."

From the woods and meadows of Northamptonshire, piercing the roar of London, threading the surge of the Channel, skimming the endless plains of slumbering France, came the steady, regular thresh of Hautboys' telephone-bell.

Helen Adair praised God. The eyes of the two had been opened and they had had the sense to be gone.

The operator was speaking.

" Did you hear it, madam ? "

" Yes, yes. Oh, thank you so mucn."

" That's quite all right, madam. I'm sorry you couldn't get them. It's rather late, and I daresay they've gone to bed."

* * * *

Helen went to her bed, but not to her rest. The good-hearted operator had murdered sleep.

Without, the gale was still raging : the windows of her room were shaken by the force of the wind. She had brought no book to read : she was tired to death ; and uncertainty fed upon her senses, as vultures feed upon the dead. Not until nearly four did she fall asleep. Then Youth and Nature took charge, and she slept till ten. Five minutes later, she asked for ' Bell Harry 42.'

Perhaps because it was Sunday, the call came through before twenty minutes had passed.

" This is London speaking. I'm sorry there's no reply from Bell Harry 42."

So great was her relief, the girl had much ado not to burst into tears . . .

The tempest was over and gone, and a sovereign sunshine was healing a battered and dripping world. In the best of spirits, mistress and maid drove back the way they had come. The roads were open : the car moved as a bird : Thérèse, who was sick of silence, chattered as any brook.

They came to *La Belle Issue* at a quarter to five. Helen left the car and entered the hall.

" How's her ladyship, Parsons ? "

" Splendid, madam. The doctor's so pleased with her, he's not coming to-morrow at all."

" Oh, isn't that good ? Are there any letters for me ? "

" No, madam. Nothing at all. But Mr. Bohun rang up at a quarter to two." Helen stood very still. " He was very sorry to miss you, madam. I said I thought you'd be in by about five o'clock : but he said he'd be gone by then—that he had to get back to Town."

CHAPTER XIV

Meet the Adair

"GO on," said Forsyth.

David crossed his legs and folded his arms. "We got in, I suppose, about five—Mrs. Leighton and I. We had some tea and unpacked and I put through a telephone-call to Mrs. Adair. It was nearly seven o'clock when the telephone went. It was my wife speaking. I can't remember her words, but she said she'd been talking or something and hadn't noticed the time. She said she was starting *then*—she was speaking from Brunskill Towers—and that if we wanted our dinner, we'd better not wait. Well, I was more relieved than anything else. As I've told you, things are different, when she's around. But we couldn't very well dine, until she got in. And then at a quarter to nine she rang up again. I said, ' Good God, where are you ? ' And she said, ' There's nothing doing. I'm back at the starting-gate—and devilish lucky to get there. You shouldn't have let me start.' I asked her what she meant. She said, ' I suppose you'll tell me it's clear round you.' I said I hadn't looked out. She said, ' Well, you needn't bother. I wouldn't go out again for a million pounds. There's a fog like a fleece round here, and I've been off the road four times and done six miles in two hours.' Of course I said I was sorry. And she said, ' Damn your sorrow. If you were a little less selfish . . .'

"I cut off there, and shoved the receiver back. I simply couldn't bear it. I felt like murder, Forsyth. Anyone would . . . Well, Belinda calmed me down and we had our dinner at once.   And now let me make this plain.   *The idea of our turning out never entered my head.*   It may have hers—I don't know.   But, if it did, she never said anything about it."   He sat back there and stared upon the palms of his hands.   " That may seem strange to you, so I'd better deal with it now.

" That it didn't enter our heads is one of those things that seems to me so natural and yet is so hard to explain.   The idea of *going* to Hautboys, we two alone —well, we both knew we couldn't do that.   Instinctively, as I've told you, we turned it down.   Then an arrangement was made for somebody else to be there. Well, it wasn't our fault that that arrangement broke down.   We'd, so to speak, done our bit.   Well, that's one thing . . .   Then, again, in these days, Forsyth, when camels are swallowed whole by everyone every day, to strain at a gnat is to make a fool of yourself. And to strain at *such* a gnat would have been to insult us both.   We've been like brother and sister, Belinda and I.   And she knows Hautboys as well as I know it myself . . .   Finally, I was furious.   Rowena had made me see red.   If she had left when she had promised to leave, she would have been at Hautboys without any fuss.   And then to be cursed for her failure to do as she'd said—to do me a favour for which I had never asked . . .   Well, I was damned thankful to think she was forty miles off.   And when one is smarting like that, the idea of further punish- ment—for that's what it would have been, to turn out at that time of night : and Belinda, too, of course : I couldn't have left her alone—further punishment, mark you, for something I'd never done . . .   Such ideas are provocative, Forsyth.   And if you have them at all, you laugh a nasty laugh and put them where they belong."

" I entirely agree," said Forsyth, " with all you've said.   You've put it very fairly, and I think it more than likely that I should have done the same.   But

I'll tell you something which I'm afraid you know. Your wife is no ordinary woman. She *meant* to make you angry. You know the phrase ' blind with fury '. Well, she *meant* to make you blind. She had spread the net in your sight : so her only chance of success was to make you blind."

David stared at the lawyer, finger to lip.

At length—

" You're right, of course," he said slowly. " I wish to God I'd come to you months ago."

" So do I," sighed Forsyth. " Never mind. You had dinner, you said. And then ? "

David took up his tale.

" Well, I don't know when we turned in. Soon after eleven, I think. We wanted to be up early and get the best of the day. I know I slept like a log . . . We breakfasted about nine and went out on foot about ten. Thinking it over, Belinda seemed a bit quiet. I can't swear I noticed it then : but, if I did, I probably put it down to her husband's not being there. Leighton's quite mad about the country—on a sunshiny day. I suppose we got in about one. After lunch we took it easy, until it was time to push off. Then we tidied up, more or less. We stripped the beds and washed up—well, you don't wash up, really : there's a machine that does that : all you have to do is to wipe the stuff. And somewhere about half past three we left for Town. I dropped Belinda in Chelsea about a quarter to six and got to Curzon Street about six o'clock. My wife wasn't there, of course. I supposed her to be at Brunskill Towers.

" I was just going up to change, about a quarter to eight, when Belinda rang up. She could hardly talk straight : she was in the most frightful way. As far as I could make out, Punch had been there when I dropped her—I hadn't gone into her flat, so of course I hadn't known that. He'd come back early from York. He'd wired on Saturday night, but of course she'd never got it, because she was out of Town. Well, he wasn't too pleased to find his wire unopened, but when he found that she'd been at Hautboys with me, he went off the deep end. When she told him about Rowena and how she should have been there, he called her a —— liar and worse than that. Apparently he maintained that he'd caught her out, that she'd banked on his not coming back till the time he'd said—that is to say, Sunday night—and that if he had not come back and got in before her, she would never have told him that she had left the flat. And he seems to have said that he had suspected us —that we'd been too thick for his liking for quite a long time . . .

"Well, I said I'd come round and see him there and then : but when I said that, Belinda screamed that he'd gone. 'Gone?' I said. 'But where to?' 'God knows,' she said. 'But he's packed some things and cleared out.' 'D'you mean he's left you?' I said. 'Mean?' she cried. 'He's done it! And he swears he's going to divorce me' . . .

"Well, I don't know what I said : but I told her that that was hot air and swore I'd get hold of him somehow and put things straight. But she kept saying, '*It all depends on Rowena.*' And when I asked what she meant, she said, ' Oh, my God, I'm so frightened,' and then rang off." He sat back and wiped his face. " I didn't see, even then. I don't defend myself, Forsyth. My brain's not as good as it was . . .

" Then I went upstairs to change, and on my bed was this note."

With the words, Bohun got to his feet, stepped to Forsyth's table and laid an envelope down.

Looking extremely serious, Forsyth withdrew the sheet.

And I trusted you as myself. If somebody else had told me, I would have laughed in their face. I suppose you'll think I was spying. I can only say that when I found I'd made a mistake and that Ruby's party was at Lyndhurst and not at Brunskill Towers, I drove to Hautboys so happy at the thought of being with you and us being alone. I couldn't go fast enough. And then—well, you know what I found. Of course, that's the end. Please don't try to approach me. I hope I never see you again.

Rowena.

Oh, David, how could you? I'm so frightfully sorry for Punch.

Forsyth laid down the paper and fingered his chin. "Anything else?" he said. "I've one or two questions to ask."

"No, that's all," said David, and took his seat on the arm of the chair he had left.

"She offered to go to Hautboys. Did anyone know of that offer, except Mrs. Leighton and you?"

"No one. Yes—wait a minute. I did tell Mrs. Adair."

"When you rang her up at Chiberta. I see. But nobody else?"

"Nobody else," said David.

"Very well. Now she rang you up twice that evening—your wife, I mean. And each time she said she was speaking from Brunskill Towers."

"That's right," said David.

"Try to remember those calls. When you picked up the receiver, were you asked for your number or did you at once hear her voice?"

"My impression is that I heard her at once."

Forsyth sighed.

"I was afraid so," he said. "I'll have it checked, of course. But it's ten to one that those calls were local calls."

"Good God," said Bohun, rising. "You mean——"

" What's the name of your village ?   Bell Harry ? "

" That's right."

" Any public telephone-boxes ? "

" I know of one."

" Well, if she used that, I think it more than likely there'll be no trace of those calls. I don't want to break your heart, but it's no good not facing these things. I'll have a man down there to-night, to find out what he can. She may have been seen by some-one—you never know."

" But she'd never get home, Forsyth, without far more than this. She can file her lying petition and rope Belinda in : but when we tell our story——"

" She's got to tell hers first. And I've got an uneasy feeling that it's going to be—well, red-hot. Still, it's only her word against yours. Is there anyone you can think of she might have suborned ? "

David was very pale.

" Only the butler," he said. " I never liked the man, and I fired him once."

" Is he with you now ? " said Forsyth.

" Yes."

The solicitor pointed to the telephone.

" Get on to him now," he said. " Tell him to leave his work and to come straight here. We must have a statement *at once*—before he's been approached by the other side. Once they've made him their witness . . ."

The two men waited in silence, until the connection was made. Forsyth picked up the spare receiver.

" Is that you, Anselm ? " cried David.

It was the housemaid that answered.

" I'm sorry, sir. Mr. Anselm's been called away."

" Where to ? D'you know where he's gone ? "

" He didn't say, sir. I think he was sent for, sir. I heard the telephone go, and then he came running upstairs and said he was wanted at once."

" All right," said David, and put the receiver back.

" Too late," said Forsyth. " They've got him. It can't be helped. But I'd give a hat full of money to see his proof."

* * * *

In an office a mile away, Anselm was sitting up straight, with his hat on his knees. By his side, at a little table, a shorthand-writer was taking down all he said. Opposite him sat his mistress, a pale-faced, shrinking figure, twisting her hands. And Mr. Ernest Crowner, of Messrs. Crowner and Growth, was sitting back in his chair, with his eyes on the butler's face.

" And then ? " said Mr. Crowner, encouragingly.

Anselm took up his tale.

" It was just about half past three that the tele-phone went. It was Mrs. Bohun speaking. She said that she was speaking from Brunskill Towers."

" You were then at Curzon Street ? "

" Yes, sir."

" What did she say ? "

" She said, ' Anselm, my travelling-case is not in the car. Are you certain you put it in ? Or is it up in my room ? ' I said I couldn't be sure and I asked her to hold the line while I went to see. I put the receiver down and ran upstairs, and there was the travelling-case at the foot of her bed. I came down and told her so. ' Thank heaven for that,' she said. ' I was afraid that someone had taken it out of the car. But I've got to have it, Anselm. You'll have to bring it down.' I said, ' Certainly, madam. I'll catch the first train I can.' She said, ' I want you to. But listen, An-selm. Don't take it to Brunskill Towers. There is no house-party here—I've made a mistake. So I'm going to join Mr. Bohun—he's gone down to Hautboys, you know. So catch a train to Bell Harry and take a taxi up.'

" Well, I changed as quick as I could and I caught the four-fifteen. That got me down to Bell Harry at a quarter to six. I didn't take a taxi, because it wasn't worth while. The distance was under a mile, and I wanted a walk . . . It was dark, of course, by then, and when I was nearing Hautboys, I saw the tail-light of a car drawn up by the side of the road. I didn't think anything of it, except that I supposed it was somebody come to Hautboys and, that being so, it seemed funny the driver hadn't gone in. I mean, from the gates to the house is about a hundred yards. And then, coming closer, I noticed the number-plate . . . And then I knew it was Mrs. Bohun's car.

" Well, I did think that was funny—her leaving the car in the road : and then it occurred to me that, being alone, she perhaps couldn't manage the gate."

" What d'you mean by that, Mr. Anselm ? "

" Well, you can't drive through that gate, sir, without it's latched back. And the latch is very awkward and very stiff. So it entered my head that she'd given up trying to latch it and walked on up to the house to get Mr. Bohun. And then I heard somebody crying . . .

" It was Mrs. Bohun, sir, hunched up on the step of the car. She was crying terribly, with her head in her hands. I went to her at once and stooped down. I said, ' It's Anselm, madam. What is it ? Can't you get in ? ' She didn't answer me, but only went on crying and rocking herself to and fro. So I said, ' Madam,' I said, ' you can't stay here, or you'll catch your death of cold. Does Mr. Bohun know you've arrived ? ' But she wouldn't answer me, so I put down her case, went in by the wicket-gate and ran to the house."

" With what object ? " said Mr. Crowner.

" To fetch Mr. Bohun, sir. I could see the lights in the house, so I knew he was there. Of course I knew something was wrong, but I'd no idea what.

" Well, the quickest way to the house—to the front door, I mean—was to leave the drive halfway and go by the lawn. That took me past the morning-room windows. One of these was open, and, as I was going by, I heard Mr. Bohun's voice."

There was a little silence, and Rowena covered her eyes.

" Could you hear what he said ? " said Mr. Crowner, softly enough.

Here it must be made plain that up to this point the butler had told the truth. His mistress had rung him up from Brunskill Towers and he had gone down by train with her travelling-case : he had found her car in the road (according to plan) and he had left her there and had stolen up to the house. Only, she had not been weeping . . .

If perjury is to be committed, then perjury must be composed. Though David did not know it, his wife had procured and studied a standard work on divorce. She knew, even better than he, exactly what straw was required to make her infamous bricks : and she knew that the straw which was used must not be furnished by her *and nobody else*. In a word, corroboration was vital, in such a case. Very well, the Court should have it and have it strong. She arranged with the butler exactly what he was to say. She told him what he had heard and what he had seen, and she made him repeat the lies till he had them by heart.

Palpably embarrassed, encouraged by Mr. Crowner, who knew how to grease a reluctance to say what cannot be said, Anselm dictated the filth which was to bring to ruin a faithful husband and wife . . .

When the monstrous fiction had been transformed into fact, the butler described how he had returned to the car and had induced his mistress to drive away. Once she was in the car, she had, he said, insisted upon returning to Town, and he had driven with her, because he thought it not right that she should be left alone.

"Did you tell her what you had seen?"

"Oh, no, sir. We hardly spoke. But when she left the house the next morning, of course I knew why she had gone."

"In fact, until now, you've said nothing—to her or anyone else?"

"That's quite right, sir."

"A very good policy, Mr. Anselm. Please keep it up."

"Very good, sir."

"And if anyone questions you, refer them to me."

Half an hour later, Rowena put out her hand, and the lawyer took it gently in both of his.

"Try not to worry, Mrs. Bohun. What's done is done, and, if I may say so, you're taking the wisest course. It's very, very unpleasant, but you must try to look upon it as a surgical operation, the sooner which is done, the better you will be."

"Shall I have to give evidence?"

"I'm afraid so. But that'll be made very smooth. And the case is quite clear. You're very fortunate in Anselm. He'll make a perfect witness."

"Will he have to go to Court, too?"

"I expect so. But don't you worry. Come and see me to-morrow at three o'clock, and I'll have the documents ready for you to sign."

Rowena averted her head.

"It does seem so dreadful," she whimpered. "I know it's always happening, but it never entered my head it could happen to me."

Mr. Crowner, for all his experience, was deeply moved.

*   *   *   *

So much for Monday morning.

On Monday afternoon, Mrs. Adair reached Croydon

at three o'clock. She drove direct to Chelsea, as fast as she could.

A haggard, wild-eyed Belinda opened the door of her flat.

" Punch has left me," she whispered.

" I know," said Helen. " I've come to get him back. Pack your things. Don't argue. You're coming to Kensington Square."

" Have you seen David ? "

" No. I've come to see Punch. What time does he leave the City ? "

" At half past five, as a rule."

" Then be as quick as you can. We can talk to-night."

Without a word, Belinda did as she said. She saw in the other's eyes a resolution to which it was best to give way. Not that she had any hope. Only Rowena could save her. Only the thief could restore the stolen goods.

By half past four the two were at Kensington Square, and forty minutes later Helen Adair was in the City of London, regarding a doorway which would have admitted her car and wondering why a blind alley, some thirty feet wide, should go by the sounding name of Firmament Square.

Her chauffeur left his seat and opened the door.

Helen Adair leaned forward.

" Listen, Dixon," she said. " You know Mrs. Leighton. Well, Mr. Leighton works here. His firm is Carruthers and Tulip—I see the name there. Now, I've simply got to catch him, as he comes out. But I don't know him by sight and I don't want to send in my name. D'you think you could get hold of someone who'd tell you when he was coming and point him out ? "

" I'll manage it somehow, madam. You wish to speak to him, madam, when he appears ? "

" I want him to get into the car. And then we'll get out of the City as quick as we can."

" Very good, madam."

The chauffeur entered the building and, after a glance about him, made for the lift . . .

Perhaps ten minutes went by. Then Dixon reappeared—on the heels of a good-looking man with a fair moustache. As the latter stepped on to the pavement, he found the chauffeur beside him, with a hand to his hat.

" Mr. Leighton, sir ? "

Punch started.

" Yes, Leighton's my name," he said.

" Would you speak to my lady a minute, sir ? She's here in the car."

Before Punch could say ' yes ' or ' no ', the chauffeur was gone, and the door of a car was open, three paces away.

The very soul of suspicion, Punch came slowly up to the side of the car. As he reached it, the lights went on, and Helen Adair leaned forward with shining eyes.

" How d'you do, Mr. Leighton. My name is Helen Adair. I've come seven hundred miles to have five minutes' talk with you. After such a journey, please don't send me empty away."

Punch was staring upon her. Never before had he seen such wonderful eyes. And her face was the face of a goddess—not that of a bitch. It occurred to him that she ought to be on his side. If she was in love with Bohun, Belinda had let her down.

Before he knew where he was, he had entered the car.

The door was shut, and the chauffeur had taken his seat.

As the car moved off—

" Where are you taking me ? "

" I should like to take you," said Helen, " wherever you want to go."

Punch sank back on the cushions—which were better than those of the Tube.

"Well, if it's not out of your way, I've got to be in Half Moon Street by half past six."

"*Sherry with Rowena*," thought Helen. "*I'm much obliged.*" Then she put the tube to her lips. "Half Moon Street, Dixon," she said.

The chauffeur's hand went to his hat.

Punch was seized with a sudden suspicion.

"I'm sorry to be so blunt. Have you seen my wife?"

"I had to see her," said Helen, "to get your address. Otherwise, I'd have come straight here."

"Have you seen . . . Bohun?"

"No, I haven't," said Helen. "He's no idea I'm in Town. I tell you, I've come to see you—from the South of France. I want to tell you something that happened—on Saturday afternoon."

So she *was* on his side. She thought he didn't know and she'd come to tell him that his wife . . . . No, that was wrong. A girl with eyes like that didn't do people down . . .

"What happened," he said slowly, "on Saturday afternoon?"

"I was at Biarritz," said Helen, "and I had a telephone-call. David Bohun rang up from Hautboys . . . Now when he rang up, I supposed that he was alone. And I wasn't pleased about that, because, from what I've heard, it isn't a house for a person to stay in alone. But when I asked him, he said that you couldn't get away, but Belinda was there . . . and that his wife, Rowena, had promised to join them later, to take your place."

"Yes, I've been handed that slush," said Leighton, violently. "To begin with, it's pretty small beer for a worldly man. Then——"

"I entirely agree," said Helen. "It's pitiably thin. But why was I handed it . . . at a quarter to five . . . on Saturday afternoon? I was six hundred miles off . . . so I couldn't see into the house. If David had liked to say that he was alone . . . or that you were there with Belinda . . . I mean, what was the point, Mr. Leighton, of telling me, at Biarritz, so—so painful a lie ? "

The man shrugged his shoulders.

" I've no idea," he said. " And to tell you the truth, I don't care. The fact remains that my wife——"

" I know, Mr. Leighton, I know. But don't you find it strange that he rang me up ? If a man takes a quiet week-end with somebody else's wife, does he improve the occasion by making a long-distance call to another girl ? "

Punch turned, frowning, to meet his questioner's eyes.

" Forgive me, Mrs. Adair, but what are you getting at ? "

" I'll tell you in a moment," said Helen. " But won't you please answer my question ? *Why did he ring me up ?* "

The other fingered his chin.

" I don't know," he said. " How should I ? I suppose he had some reason . . ."

" This letter will tell you," said Helen, and put a sheet into his hand. " Don't forget—it was written on Thursday. Read it all, if you please : but read the last paragraph first."

Punch took the sheet with a frown.

Think of me at Hautboys on Saturday evening next. If only old Punch wasn't there, I could ring you up.

Leighton stared at the words—as a man does stare at something written about him which he was not meant to see. Then he turned over the page and read the letter right through.

I won't stay there alone again . . . But I can't ask too much of the Leightons, and Rowena's said some-

*thing to Punch . . . Any way they're coming down
on Saturday next . . .*

*For some reason or other Rowena leaves me alone.
She promised she would, you know, if I returned. I
think it's come to this—that my jailer pities me.
Belinda is sweetness itself. What I'd have done
without her, I simply don't know. She is the true
confidante. The trouble is, I don't see her enough
alone. We can talk about you at lunch : but Punch
is with us at Hautboys, which makes it impossible.
Of course the whole thing is impossible . . .*

Helen was speaking again.

" Listen, Mr. Leighton. I got that letter at Biarritz
—the day before yesterday. And that afternoon he
rang up . . . and handed me what both of us
know to be slush . . ." Punch looked at her sharply,
but Helen was regarding her hands. " Well, when
he said . . . what he did, what do you think I
replied ? "

" What did you reply ? " said Punch.

" I said something *which he never heard* . . . because at that vital moment we were cut off. A
frightful gale was raging south of Bordeaux : and a
tree was blown down on the line and broke it in two.
And so, though I never knew it, we were cut off.
But, of course, when he didn't answer, I knew there
was something wrong : and, an instant later, I found
that the line was dead."

" What did you say," said Punch, " that he never
heard ? "

" One moment, Mr. Leighton. I'll tell you before
I'm through. But I want you to see my position.
He might or he might not have heard . . . the very
important statement which I had made. I knew that
the line had gone, but I didn't know *when* it had gone.
It might have gone in the middle : it might have gone
at the end : or it might have gone at the beginning

—before he had heard one word. And the line to Bordeaux was gone . . . so I couldn't make sure.

"Well, I waited for the line to be mended till seven o'clock. Then I took my car and drove through the storm to Bordeaux. That's more than a hundred miles—and I don't want to do it again, on a night like that. I think all Hell was loose . . . But I dared not take the risk that he had not heard what I said.

"The elements were against me. I didn't get in till past ten. And then other lines were down, and I never got on to Hautboys, until a quarter to twelve. And then . . . there was no reply. I could hear the bell ringing, five hundred miles off : but they couldn't hear it, Mr. Leighton, because they were fast asleep."

"Well, I give you best," said Punch. "I happen to know that way on a dirty night. When the wind comes into those forests out of that bay . . ." He sucked in his breath. "You might have been killed, you know. Popping along those roads . . . You only want a tree down—on the other side of a bend . . . And now, if you please, will you tell me ? What was it you said to Bohun that he didn't hear ? "

"I'll tell you now," said Helen. "I'll give you my very words. I said to him, *David, listen. I don't like the sound of this. You say you're alone with Belinda and that she, Rowena, is coming to spend the night. Well, that's all right—IF SHE COMES.*" The other started, and a hand went up to his mouth. "*But for God's sake be careful, David, IN CASE IT'S A PLANT. You see what I mean ? Don't wait a moment later than eight. If she hasn't come by then, take Belinda away and leave her at some hotel.*"

"My God," said Punch, hoarsely. He caught the girl by the arm. "D'you mean to say you think you were right ? *That Rowena framed this business . . . to get them down ?* "

"I know it," said Helen, looking him full in the

eyes. "The moment he told me, I knew it. That's why I drove to Bordeaux. She's been laying for me for weeks: but I didn't happen to fit—and Belinda did."

"But——"

"She wants to divorce her husband. She's done her level best to drive him into my arms. But he wasn't standing for that, and neither was I. His life has been hell for months. And when I had to leave England, I begged and prayed Belinda to—to do what she could. And she's been too marvellous, Punch. If it hadn't been for her, I think he'd have taken his life. She's written to me twice a week—I've got all her letters here."

The man wiped the sweat from his face.

"My God, these women," he said . . . "D'you think you could take me to Chelsea?"

"If you want Belinda," said Helen, "I think she's at Kensington Square. When I went to get your address, she wasn't looking too good; so I——"

"In that case," said Punch, "will you take me to Kensington Square?"

Helen gave the order to Dixon.

Then—

"What about Half Moon Street?" she said.

"No —— fear," said Leighton. "If half what you say is true, I'm well out of that. But I want to be honest with you. I'm not *sure* yet. You've got some damned good cards: but I find it hard to believe that Rowena would do me down."

"It's up to you," said Helen, and put out the light. "And now d'you mind if I doze, till we get to Kensington Square? I haven't closed my eyes for thirty-two hours."

CHAPTER XV

Stock-taking

IT goes, I think, without saying that if Leighton had
kept his appointment with Mrs. Bohun, he would
have filed his petition as soon as ever he could. Once
he was aware of the statement which Anselm had
made, he would have heard no reason, though one
rose from the dead. That, of course, was Rowena's
idea : and, but for Helen's action, it must have been
realized.

To the latter full credit is due. In fact, the cards
she held were not very good : but by sheer personality,
she had induced a man she had never met to swallow,
though not to digest, a frightful report of a lady with
whom he was well acquainted, to whom he was deeply
attached. When she said she must doze, she meant it.
The effort had left her faint.

Still, personality cannot work miracles. It was Mrs.
Bohun herself who had paved her enemy's way.

When Rowena had rung up Punch—at half past two
that day, at Firmament Square—the man had been
slightly surprised to receive her call. It was not quite
decent, somehow. True, they were in the same boat,
and no doubt it was wise and convenient that they
should exchange their views : but she might have
waited a little . . . Rowena knew better. Once the
iron, which she had waiting, had entered into his
soul, Punch Leighton was hers. Action so swift
might seem crude : but it was going to be damned
effective.

She was, of course, as usual, perfectly right. She

could hardly have been expected to foresee that a girl who did not know what had happened, would come seven hundred miles to put a spoke in her wheel. It was by no fault of her own that she played into Helen's hands.

When Punch did not come to Half Moon Street, she did not know what to think. For the first time for years, she was gravelled. She passed a very bad evening. The check was ominous.

At last she went to her bed and wished for the day. When the morning brought her no letter, she tried to decide what to do. After long hesitation, she rang up Firmament Square . . .

"Oh, could I speak to Mr. Leighton?"

"Who is that speaking, please?"

"It's Mrs. Bohun."

"I see. I'm afraid Mr. Leighton's not in."

Rowena replaced her receiver, with narrowed eyes. That day she wrote to Juliot.

My dear Friend,

I have written to no one at all, but I must just tell you that I cannot dine with you to-night. I shall never dine with anyone again. For one thing, no one will ever ask me: and if they did, I should be far too ashamed to go. I simply don't know how to write the words, but I have had to go to a solicitor and he says I must divorce my husband at once. It has been the most awful shock to me: I trusted them both implicitly, and when I think that it was by the merest accident that I found out . . . As soon as I can, I am going to disappear. I simply can't face the scandal. But the solicitor says I must not go until the case has been heard. I am so ashamed—so terribly ashamed. Don't dream of answering this letter. If I can find the courage, I'll write again one day.

Your unhappy
Pretty Maid.

Summa ars celare artem.

Within a quarter of an hour of receiving this ingenuous letter, caution had been flung to the winds and the doting peer had been carried to Half Moon Street.

He was, of course, expected.

For two hours he did his utmost to comfort a frantic child. In a word, he extended himself. His explanations were interminable. The quality and the quantity of his platitudes passed all comprehension. Flatulence knew no law. In the end, his monstrous labour met with a certain success. His pretty maid permitted herself to be very slightly reassured.

* * * *

Though nobody had been told, the news was out. Mrs. Garter had it that evening—and let it go : and a wave of rare indignation swept through the garish circles which Rowena had lately adorned. Grainers, Cullets and Stumms jumped at this explanation of her untimely withdrawal from their society. Harsh thoughts which they had harboured turned to their condemnation and her renown. Illuminating memories were hysterically exchanged. Ruby Mocket, who had drunk herself into a melting mood, burst into tears and had to be taken home. David, of course, was violently and vulgarly abused. Even Hilda Bedew let fly. And ' Koko ' Sewler's comments were quite unprintable. Rowena's stream of sympathy burst its banks.

(It was, in fact, two or three weeks before the news was received at what had been Bohun's club. There it would have been ignored, in the ordinary way : but the scandalous scene in the annexe was still in everyone's mind, and the sequel attracted attention because of that. Members shrugged their shoulders—and drew another line through the name they had blotted out.)

* * * *

Alone at *La Belle Issue,* Lady Persimmon was rapidly
gaining strength. There can be no doubt at all that
the knowledge that the blow had fallen—yet not upon
Helen Adair, had done her more good than could have
any prescription that chemists make up. For the
first time for months, her beloved daughter was safe.
More. Horrified as she was at such iniquity, she was
human enough to allow that she had been right, that
her prediction of June had been exactly fulfilled.
A letter from her reached London on Thursday.

*I entirely agree. Belinda must have the best lawyers
that money can buy: yet she and her husband must
be put to no sort of expense. Of course they won't
take it from you: but if you can get them to Bagot,
he'll do the trick. George Bagot, you know—not
Charles. After ten minutes with George, his point of
view will be theirs. God knows which way things will
go, but I have a dreadful feeling that that woman
knows what she is about. If I were handling the case,
I should concentrate upon finding out her motive.
Why does she want to be free? In other words,
their best defence is attack. At least, that is how I
see it. I may be wrong.*

Mercifully, for her peace of mind, she had not the
faintest idea of the line which her daughter was taking
with all her might.

* * * *

It is, I think, common knowledge that continuous
enemy action to which he can make no reply will go
a long way towards breaking a warrior's heart; and
that when at last his turn comes, though it be but a
losing battle, the sheer relief of being able to fight
will add to him a mettle which bodes no good to such
as stand in his way.

So it was with Bohun.

Now that the crash had come and his hands were free, his brain cleared, his heart leaped up and his resolution hardened to a will of the coldest iron. Rowena might have her way : but, by God, her lies should be paid for : his turn would come in Court, and, before he had done, she should bleed from the mouth and ears.

There was no holding the man. Forsyth found him an equal. Against her will, Helen had to sit at his feet.

" But David, darling——"

" Lady, be good. For what you did on Monday, I take my hat right off and put it under the seat. Only you could have done it : and you could only have done it on Monday afternoon. If Punch had got to Half Moon Street, we should have been sunk."

" Don't put it too high," said Helen. " That's the mistake I made. I even toyed with the conceit that Punch's secession might hit your wife so hard that she'd throw in her hand. But that was because I was tired . . . In fact, by snatching Punch, I saved the Leightons' marriage from going bust." She threw up her lovely head and covered her eyes. " It's just as well that I did—for all our sakes. Belinda was doing my job : and if Punch had turned her down, I'd never have smiled again."

" Don't put it too low," said David. " The Leightons apart, Punch's allegiance is a very valuable card. Rowena's hand was upon it. And then you whipped it away and gave it to us. If Punch had filed his petition, I really believe Belinda would have thrown up the sponge. Any way, she'd have gone to pieces, and it wouldn't have been worth while to put her into the box."

" Whereas, now . . ."

" She'll fight like hell. She's going to be named, because she's got to be named. And she'll intervene, as they call it, for her own *and for Punch's* sake. You've given her something to fight for. You've given her *everything* to fight for—and, in fighting for Punch and herself, she'll be fighting for me."

"But the battle royal will be between you and your wife?"

"Yes. The matter before the Court will be Rowena's prayer that her marriage may be dissolved—on the score of my misconduct with somebody else."

"It amounts to this," said Helen, "that Belinda is going to give evidence on your behalf. Well, that's all right: but you can't get away from this. Her evidence will be tainted—to this extent . . . that it's very much to her interest to tell the same tale as you."

"You can't call that 'tainted'," said David. "Her evidence won't be independent. You can't put it higher than that."

"My evidence would be independent," said Helen Adair.

David took her hand and put it up to his lips.

"Quite so, Madonna," he said. "But that you should give it is quite unthinkable."

There was a little silence.

Then—

"Look at it this way," said Helen. "You will not let me be called because, though I can help you, you will not let me 'lay my head on the block'. Well, that's your funeral: but where does Belinda come in?" She smote the arm of her chair. "David, darling, I *must*. Remember this—I asked her to do as she did."

"You did nothing of the kind," said David. "A trap was laid for us, and we walked slap in. The moment you knew we were there, you risked your life and your limbs to get us out. And that was more than we had any right to expect. I mean, we bought it, sweetheart."

"I don't care about that," said Helen. "The point

is this. I besought Belinda to care for you. In doing me that favour, she walked bung into the muck. Well, that's quite bad enough : but d'you mean to say that I am to sit quite still and watch her go down ? "

" I hope she won't go down."

" It's fifty fifty," said Helen, " and you know it as well as I. What's the good of my paying her costs ? She wants my evidence . . . to pull her out of the hole."

" She'd never accept it," said David. " Not in a thousand years."

" If Bagot said I must be called, she'd never give it a thought."

" If you told Bagot to say so, I'm perfectly sure he'd refuse. For one thing only, my sweet, the evidence you would give would be a two-edged sword. You'd be an ideal cock-shy. Your cross-examination might get Rowena home. Pure prejudice, of course. But, of course, she'll ask for a jury : and that's what juries are for. Here's the sort of thing you'd be asked.

" In fact, it amounts to this—that you requested Mrs. Leighton to keep your lover warm, whilst you were away ? Are you quite sure that she didn't exceed her instructions ? And wasn't it because you felt that she was exceeding her instructions that you made such frantic efforts to telephone to Hautboys that fateful Saturday night ?

" Well, you can say *No, no, no.* But counsel will look at the jury and tell them they're ' men of the world '. And, as like as not, they'll believe him."

" What about the letters ? " said Helen. " You can't get away from them."

" The letters," said David, " would do more harm than good. They'd certainly bear you out ; but the prejudice they would create could be weighed by the pound. A is reporting to B the efforts which she is

making to comfort the husband of C. My darling,
counsel would eat them.

*"Tell me this, Mrs. Adair. You disliked Mrs.
Bohun? Disliked her so much that you would not
meet her at all? Yet, behind her back, you encourage
a young married woman to cherish her lawful husband
on your behalf? Have you ever heard of the saying
'hoist with his own petard'?"*

"And now I'll be frankly brutal and brutally frank.
Men will be men: and the men on the jury will con-
form to that deplorable rule. They'll be against me
from the start—because Rowena's attractive and
Belinda's a peach. They'll say, 'This isn't fair. This
bloke's had too good a show.' Well, that's quite bad
enough. But if, on the top of that, *you're* going to
enter the box *and quietly declare that you are in love
with me*, I shall have to have police protection between
the acts. The jury's one idea will be to get me down.
The merits of the case won't count. All they will
know is this—that 'no man on earth has the right to
have three such women as these'."

Helen fought not to laugh. The matter was serious.
Yet how could she not rejoice, to see David at the
top of his form?

"I'm thinking of Belinda," she said.

"I'm sure you are," said the man. "But Belinda
and I are roped together, my sweet. If they send me
down, she'll have to go down with me."

"In view of her letters to me, I do not believe any
jury would let her go down. Punch is a man of the
world, and he was extremely bitter against you both.
He also loathed my name. I came to him out of the
blue and told him the truth. I spoke for ten minutes
—and shook him. Then I showed him Belinda's
letters and did the trick. And if I could do that with
Punch . . ."

R

" One moment," said David, quietly. " Don't forget this. *Punch hadn't heard Anselm's statement.* But the jury *will* have heard that, before you open your mouth. *And* they will have heard Rowena . . . speaking with the tongue of an angel upon parade."

The girl bit her lip. She had expected to be opposed, but not discomfited. But here was a David that she had never seen—with the swift, sure speech of a master, quietly showing a pupil where and why she was wrong. Looking upon him, she perceived how crushing had been the burden which he had borne. Rowena's hold upon him had been like some frightful curse. But now the curse had been lifted, and he was himself again. Whichever way the case went, never again could Rowena ride on his neck.

Then she remembered Belinda, and turned again to the breach—which she had not made.

" My darling, put yourself in my place. Say that I do as you say and keep out of Court. *How shall I feel, if Belinda Leighton goes down?* I shall always, always feel, to the end of my days, that if I had done my bit, she—might—have—been—saved. And this is not Quixotry. Belinda's my very good friend. It was for my sake that she came in on this show : and it was in doing my job that she walked into the trap. Now, I don't want to be a cock-shy. But, at least, what they throw at me will be light enough stuff. But *in any event* Belinda is going right through it—right through the sordid hoop. And if she goes down, she'll be marked for the rest of her life. Well, how would you like that ? And how would you like it, if you were in Punch's place ? Your faithful wife degraded . . . found guilty by a jury of infidelity . . . branded for ever, as having passed through the Divorce Court by quite the most shameful path. I mean, David, even to-day, the woman co-respondent's is—well, not a coveted post . . . As like as not, she's for it, whatever I do. But can't you see that if I do go to Court, at least I'll have the satisfaction of knowing that I didn't fail her in her extremity ? "

" You've put it damned well," said David. " But neither Belinda nor I would allow you to do such a thing. I know I can answer for her. It's not because I love you : it is the fellow-feeling, which even strangers have, that simply will not permit so wanton a sacrifice.

" If you had the case in your pocket, if your evidence was such that, when you gave it, Rowena's case must collapse—well, then you would have to give it. No doubt about that. But you haven't got the case in your pocket—or anywhere else. And counsel would never dare call you, because your evidence *is* tainted—founded upon the liaison which you have been having with me.

" Remember this—we're in it together, we four. You and Belinda and Punch and I. And Belinda and I are for it. What keeps us going is that you and Punch are behind us, heart and soul. You are, so to speak, our seconds—our second selves. *And we have nobody else.* Well, the bare idea of either of you stepping in . . . chucking the precious duty which means so much to us . . . involving yourself in the mess, to turn from which to you is our great relief—well, can you be surprised, my darling, that before such a ghastly prospect my heart sinks down ? I rank you with Punch, because Punch has come back to the fold. In fact, as you know, you are for Belinda and me the opposite number to Rowena, with whom we can be ourselves, because you are *outside* the business, yet have that understanding which only an *inside* knowledge can ever acquire."

He put out his hands for hers and drew her out of her chair and into his arms. For a moment he held her close, smiling steadily into her questioning eyes. Then—

"My perfect Nell," he said gently, and kissed her beautiful lips.

* * * *

A copy of Rowena's Petition was served upon David Bohun in Lincoln's Inn. Anselm was present at the service, to point his master out to the hangman clerk. When David looked up and saw him, the perfect servant immediately took off his hat.

Belinda was 'served' the same day, as she was leaving Chelsea to go to Kensington Square. She had been warned, of course: but the shock was great. Trembling from head to foot, she retraced her steps, the telltale document clutched in a desperate hand. Once in her flat, she pushed it into a drawer and fell on the telephone . . .

"Bagot and Bagot speaking."

"Oh, can I speak to Mr. George Bagot ? "

"Who is that, please ? "

"Mrs. Leighton."

"Just a minute, please."

Then came a pleasant voice.

"How d'you do, Mrs. Leighton. This is George Bagot speaking. I think I know what's happened. Won't you come down right away ? And we'll introduce ourselves and have a short talk."

"I'd love to."

"Splendid. I'll expect you in a quarter of an hour. I shouldn't look at the paper, but bring it along."

* * * *

Thus set in motion, the Law's machine took charge. Appearances were entered and presently the cause was set down. It seemed unlikely that the case would be reached before June.

All parties chafed at the delay—Rowena, most of all.

There were times when she wondered whether she could endure. Alone, she could have managed admirably : but the Earl of Juliot's support was insupportable. Kind hearts may be more than coronets : but the Juliot amalgam of the two would have suffocated a Caliban. The peer himself was in ecstasy. Duty and love slobbered over each other.

Belinda and David were very much better placed. Forsyth and Bagot told them to go as they pleased. ' Above all things, be natural : and do as you've always done.' The good advice cast out fear. A merry Christmas was kept at Kensington Square. Curzon Street, swept and garnished and once again in the hands of a man and his wife, saw comfortable dinners for four. In February, Helen and Belinda left for *La Belle Issue*, and Punch went to stay with David in Curzon Street. When Easter came, the two men drove down together, to join the girls : the Leightons stayed at the villa, and Bohun slept at Bayonne. The four passed a care-free week and forgot the world.

Lady Persimmon took pains to hide her disquiet. She was not so sure as she had been that Helen was out of the wood.

* * * *

It was in the month of April that George Bagot dined with Forsyth, one Saturday night—and talked across the rosewood for more than an hour and a half.

" This blasted case," said Bagot. " Forsyth, I'll tell you something. I'm worried out of my life."

" So am I," said Forsyth. " That's why you're here."

There was a little silence.

Then—

" What sort of a witness," said Bagot, " will Bohun make ? "

" He'll be very bad under fire. He has that flagrant

honesty which will take no sort of cover, but marches straight on. He's going to be fouled—not once, but over and over again. Well, I don't want him to foul back, but, when that happens, he ought to go into a clinch. But he won't—he's too damned honest : and that's the truth."

"I know," said Bagot. "I know. Mercifully, Mrs. Leighton's all right. I think she'll do very well. But I don't like the look of things. Mrs. Bohun's a *rara avis*. And I have an uneasy feeling that in the box she is going to be irresistible."

"I'm sure she is," said Forsyth. "What is almost worse, while she has accumulated a formidable store of material for cross-examination of Bohun, he has practically nothing for us to use." He slewed himself round on his chair and crossed his legs. "Let me give you an illustration . . .

"Last autumn she went to Dioni, and nothing would do but that Bohun should take her out. He consented under pressure, but gave her to understand that the moment they got there, he should turn round and come back. To this she agreed, suggesting that he should be wired for, to cover his precipitate return."

"Oh, my God," said Bagot.

"Well, there you are," said Forsyth. "Before he left London, he actually wrote out a wire, purporting to come from his Chambers, signed with the name of his clerk, and gave it to the Hall Porter of his club to dispatch in three days' time."

"Oh, it's not true," mouthed Bagot.

"It is, indeed," said Forsyth. "And, what's more, I'll lay a monkey she's got that original wire. And, just to round the picture, before he left Dioni, he wired to Mrs. Adair, to say he was coming back."

"Oh, I can't bear it," said Bagot. "They're going to vivisect him before our eyes."

"And bear this in mind," said Forsyth. "What I've just told you emerged, as it were, by accident. The man is incorrigibly honest. For him to recognize evil, it's got to be nude.

"And now look at the other side. What have we got that we can use against her?" He brought his hand down on the board. "Next to nothing, Bagot—except a host of suggestions which she will flatly deny."

"What did she do at Dioni?"

"I wish I knew," said Forsyth. "I sent out a man, of course. But the scent was gone. The hotel she stayed at was closed and the staff dispersed. You and I and our clients know that she is as wicked a woman as ever was foaled : but we have nothing to show that she's ever put a foot wrong."

"Servants no good?"

"Hopeless. Butler, cook and housemaid—they're solid for her. And Bohun's got nothing to give me—except, as I said just now, the lie direct. And a jury gets sick of that before five minutes are out. 'I put it to you that that is untrue?' 'No.' 'That what really happened was . . .?' 'No.' Well, that sort of stuff will do us more harm than good."

"No doubt about that," said Bagot. He finished his brandy and picked up a cigarette. "In fact, the truth is this. As the matter stands at present, we're going to help her home. If half what we say is true, the woman's a fiend. That is our case—we can't say anything else. But juries don't believe in fiends. Cats or vixens—yes. But not fiends. And they'll find our suggestion offensive—to their intelligence . . . Take those two telephone-calls. We know that she made them all right, though they can't be traced. But when we suggest that she made them, we are, in fact, submitting that she is a ghoul . . . And from what I'm told she doesn't resemble a ghoul . . . Then, again, juries do not believe in ghouls . . ." He laid down his cigarette and took a deep breath. "It's no good pretending, Forsyth. If we're not to go down plunk, we've got to have Helen Adair."

There was another silence.

At length—

"I never remember," said Forsyth, "a decision so hard to make. Unless we call Mrs. Adair, we're bound to go down. If we call Mrs. Adair, we *may* pull it off. You can't put it higher than that. We *may* pull it off. Is it right, on such a chance, to allow her to make such a terrible sacrifice?"

"Of course it's not right," said Bagot. "In fact, it's extremely wrong. But is it right to deny to Mrs. Leighton a very fair chance of escape?"

"No, it isn't," said Forsyth. "No doubt about that."

"Well, there you are," said Bagot. "That is my daily beat. Round the vicious circle, like the hopeless squirrel in his cage. To my weary mind, there is nothing whatever to choose between those alternatives. Each of them would be a crime. The question is, which to commit."

"I think," said Forsyth, "that you should take her statement. I'd do it myself : but if Bohun knew that I'd done it, I think he'd throw in his hand. Taking her statement doesn't commit us at all. But then we shall be ready . . . in case we do decide . . . to put her into the box."

"What about counsel?" said Bagot.

"They mustn't see it," said Forsyth, "until we've made up our minds. And if we decide not to call her, they'll never see it at all. This is a matter for you and me to decide : and I will not have my hand forced by someone less qualified than we are to make this accursed choice."

Bagot leaned suddenly forward.

"I believe you've made it," he said.

"Yes," said Forsyth, "I have. Subject to your approval, I've decided . . . that if we cannot shake the petitioner's case, Mrs. Adair should be called, to support our own. That's why I want you to take her statement. But I have a hope of shaking the petitioner's case. In a way it's forlorn. But I've drawn a bow at a venture, and at the present moment the arrow is on the wing."

"Go on," said Bagot, wide-eyed.

Forsyth fingered his chin.

"It's a curious story," he said, and sat back in his chair. "You remember old Elvin? Well, he was Bohun's great-uncle and only relative. A few hours before he died, he altered his Will and left me a sum of money upon a secret trust. Now the trust was this—to unmask Mrs. David Bohun and set his great-nephew free."

Bagot stared and stared. At length he moistened his lips.

"How on earth did he know?" he whispered.

"This is what he told me," said Forsyth. "Very shortly before his marriage, Bohun had brought to Jeffreys his future bride. Old Elvin had liked her at once. 'She took me by storm,' he said. 'And where the boy's concerned, I'm hard to please.' But the moment he saw her he knew that he had seen her before. Not her herself, but her double: a girl exactly like her—same face, same figure, same ways . . .

"Well, he believed, as I do, that those alike in body are always alike in mind: and so, when the two were gone, he began to try to remember—for curiosity's sake. 'Not that it mattered, Forsyth—understand that. That she was sterling stood out.' Out of pure curiosity, therefore, he went to work . . .

"Well, the days went by and the marriage took place, while, sitting alone at Jeffreys, the old fellow drove his thoroughbred memory . . . And then at last he remembered—I'll never forget his words. *I tried her for perjury, Forsyth, some twenty-nine years ago—the foulest, most treacherous lies that ever a woman told . . . The jury let her off. They couldn't withstand her charm and her angel face. And they hadn't*

*before them the proofs that lay on my desk. They were
not 'evidence'. And so she went free—in this world.
But if I had done as she had—out-Judased Judas, put
out the eyes of Truth, I say to you, Forsyth, I'd be
afraid to die.'*

At the third attempt—

"God Almighty," said Bagot. "But what an
amazing thing."

"For me," said Forsyth, "it will not go into words.
It wasn't second sight : it was something far greater
than that . . . a secret law of Nature, which Elvin,
of his wisdom, was able to read and apply. Be that
as it may, it was because of this writing upon the
wall that the old fellow sent for me and imposed his
secret trust. That same night he died ; and with his
death, of course, my duty began."

Forsyth paused there, to wrinkle his brow : but
Bagot sat very still, with a hand to his mouth and
his eyes on the other's face.

"Well, I took the obvious steps . . . But, to cut
a long story short, every inquiry I made not only
did the lady no harm, but actually went to show
that old Elvin was utterly wrong. Bohun's own servants, for instance, gave her a marvellous chit. 'In
all respects,' they said, 'a loving and dutiful wife.'
And they very plainly liked her better than him.

"I confess that I was shaken. My inquiries were
not so much fruitless as bearing the opposite fruit to
that I had been led to expect. And then . . . my
eyes were opened : and all of a sudden I saw that
this universal esteem, in which the lady was held,
was not proving Elvin *wrong*, but proving him *right*.
*Everyone, high and low, was being well and truly deceived
by Mrs. David Bohun.*"

"I give you best," said Bagot. "How obvious
these things are—when once they've been pointed out."

The other smiled.

"No cause for pride there," he said. "I ought to

have tumbled before.   Never mind . . .   My inquiries
had satisfied me that Elvin was perfectly right.   But
they had done more than that.   They had satisfied
me that further inquiry was futile—*unless it was made
of someone too cunning to be deceived*.   I mean, that
was mathematics."

"Very high mathematics," said Bagot.   And then,
"Go on."

"Well, the question was how to discover a person
sufficiently shrewd to see through Mrs. Bohun . . .
Suddenly I thought of her double—the woman whom
Elvin had tried some twenty-nine years before."
Bagot started, and the other laid a hand on his arm.
"If she could be traced, and was living—*there was
the woman, Bagot, to study Mrs. David Bohun.*"

There was an electric silence.

Then Bagot sat back in his chair and covered his
eyes.

Forsyth continued slowly.

"She was found on Tuesday," he said.   "At a
village in New South Wales.   She is—proving difficult,
Bagot.   The idea of returning to England doesn't
appeal to her.   But I think she will be persuaded—
five hundred pounds a month is pretty good pay.   I
said it was a bow at a venture—but I want her to be
in Court when Mrs. David Bohun goes into the box."

CHAPTER XVI

Bohun v. *Bohun and Leighton*

ROWENA was being examined.
The impression which she gave was quite painful. It was so pathetically clear that she was not meant for such things. A frightened child had come to ask for justice—an ordeal not fit to be suffered by such as she. The look of her inspired indignation against Bohun. 'Whosoever shall offend one of these little ones, it is better for him that a millstone were hanged about his neck.' A simple, black silk dress suggested that she was in mourning for her virginity.

"Was your married life happy, Mrs. Bohun?"

"I'm afraid I can't say it was."

"How soon after your marriage did it begin to be unhappy?"

"Oh, at once."

"Why was that?"

"I—I made a discovery."

"What did you discover, Mrs. Bohun?"

Rowena threw a hunted look round.

"It's so difficult to say," she whimpered.

The Judge leaned forward and down.

"You have nothing to be afraid of," he said kindly. Rowena looked gratefully back—with faith and hope in her eyes. "Just answer Counsel's questions as best you can."

"I'll try, my lord."

"What was it you discovered, Mrs. Bohun?"

"I found that I had married . . . a terribly sensual man."

268

A rustle ran through the Court. Everyone seemed to expire or shift in his seat.

David, white to the lips, was staring directly before him—and seeing nothing at all. He had known what to expect : but this was hotter and stronger than anything of which he had dreamed. Foul, cold-blooded lying—the filthiest perjury : and that, upon a matter to which no human being but he and she could speak. He could, of course, deny what she said . . .

The Court was crammed. There was no standing-room. The two aisles were packed with spectators—counsel, clerks and witnesses, waiting for other cases in other Courts. The June day was hot : and the atmosphere within was unpleasantly close. The jury —nine men and three women—were facing Rowena across the well of the Court. But they were not looking at her—they had not the heart to stare upon such distress. One of the women was holding a hand to her eyes. Up on his bench, the Judge was steadily writing—with a pair of spectacles on and his brows drawn into a frown.

"So you had no one that you could go to ? "

"No one."

"Having no one that you could turn to, did you try to help yourself ? "

"Yes. I tried to go out at night as much as I could. People were very kind, and we were invited a lot. So I always stayed as long as ever I could, and sometimes he would get tired and go home first . . ."

Mrs. Grainer, perspiring freely, was sitting with Mrs. Stumm. The two disliked each other and were suffering a discomfort of body which they had never conceived : the rude, oak seats were committing one long, indecent assault. But if the flesh was fainting, the spirit was resolute. For no consideration would either of them have moved. ' Pa ' Cullet and Mrs. Garter were sitting, jammed together, at the end of a row. People had thrust their way past them time and again,

disordering Mrs. Garter and ruining Cullet's shoes :
but though the latter writhed and the former employed
a lip-language which, if a mute had read it, would
have startled him into speech, nothing short of violence
would have made them vacate their seats.   (In a sense,
Mrs. Garter was taking a ' busman's holiday '.   Three,
several times, she had ' been through the Court ', herself.   Whilst others lapped it up, she rolled the wine
of evidence round her tongue.)   ' Undy ' Bauch, another expert, was breathing predictions in Freddy
Sinople's ear, while, a bench or two further forward,
Vi Sinople was nudging Lucinda Hart.   Ruby Mocket
and ' Koko ' Sewler were squired by Boney Belong.
Bemuse was standing somewhere.   Miss Cullet and
Isabel Stumm were right at the back.   And others
also were there.   ' For wheresoever the carcase is,
there will the eagles be gathered together.'

" I think you have no children, Mrs. Bohun ? "
Rowena shook her head.

" My—my husband wouldn't have one : it was . . ."
Her mouth was working pitifully.

" Yes, Mrs. Bohun ?   ' It was . . .' ? "

" A very great grief to me.   I—I wanted a baby
so much."

One of Forsyth's managing clerks was sitting with
David Bohun.   Directly behind them was sitting Tris-
tram, K.C.   The latter leaned forward, to whisper in
David's ear.

" Any truth in that, Mr. Bohun ? "

" It's a —— lie," breathed David.   " It was I that
wanted a child : but she flatly refused."

" All right, thank you.   That's all I wanted to know."

Tristram had the row to himself—for the moment,
Belinda's ' leader ' was out of Court.   Behind Tristram were sitting the ' juniors '—two counsel for Mrs.
Leighton and two for David Bohun.   Two of the four
were taking down every word : this, of course, in long-
hand—their ' leaders ' would cross-examine from these

full notes. Behind the junior counsel, Belinda, cold
with fury, was supported by Bagot and Punch.

"D'you remember anything happening in June last
year?"

"My husband sent the butler away."

"Was that by your wish?"

"Oh, no. He just told him to go. I think he gave
him an hour to be out of the house."

"Why did he do that, Mrs. Bohun?"

Rowena hesitated. Then—

"Well, you see, he was hurting so. And I said,
if he didn't stop, I'd have to cry out. And then I
said, 'You don't want Anselm to hear.' And he
said, 'Oh, is that the idea?' And then he rang for
Anselm and told him to go."

Talk about a broadside . . .

Again, that telltale rustle ran through the Court
. . . and an usher called for silence . . . and the Judge
looked up at the public gallery . . .

Forsyth was standing in an aisle, with his back to
the wall. His eyes were fast upon a woman who was
sitting between Chater and Allen, his confidential clerk.
The latter, pencil in hand, had a pad on his knee. And
the woman's eyes were fast on Rowena Bohun . . .

The likeness was still amazing. The woman sitting
there was what Rowena would be—at fifty-six. Only
the expression was different: but that was because
the one was only watching, while the other was being
watched.

* * * *

Mrs. Ellen Morris had been a hard nut to crack.
The very soul of suspicion, she had cost Forsyth a
fortune in cables and telephone-calls. Won at last,
her consent was grudging—to enter the solicitor's service *at eight hundred pounds a month*. The contract
was for one year only: but it took at least two years

off Chater's life. The detective loathed the woman, as well he might. When he found her in New South Wales, she was keeping the books of an unpretentious hotel. Had she not seen that he was up against time, she would have come to England for the run of her teeth. As it was, no beggar-on-horseback was more exacting than she. When Forsyth explained her duty, she stuck in her toes. 'I don't like law courts—or lawyers, for the matter of that.' It took him all he knew to get her down to the Strand. And then . . . *she had seen Rowena* . . .

Looking upon Mrs. Bohun, the woman knew she was looking upon herself . . . upon what she *should* have been . . . upon what she *would* have been—if only that bitch of a servant had held her tongue. Silk and satin and brooches and patent shoes . . . manicured hands and a toff to hold open the door . . . as like as not, a house full of servants, and crystal glass on the table, and scent in her bath . . . all the things *she* was made for—*ought* to have had . . . that dirty, young slut had them all—while *she*, Mrs. Ellen Morris, was earning a pound a week in a backwoods joint.

What was it Forsyth had said ? 'I'm much afraid she'll be too clever for you.'

A hideous look came into the shifty eyes, and Mrs. Ellen Morris had set her discoloured teeth.

* * * *

Rowena's examination proceeded.

"In other words, Mrs. Bohun, he left you to go your way and began to go his ? "

"Yes."

"Was that what you wanted, Mrs. Bohun ? "

"Oh, no. I was very upset. You see, we were asked together, and I didn't care about going if he didn't come."

"Why didn't you go his way?"

Rowena dropped her eyes and looked ready to cry.

"Well, I wasn't . . . asked."

Bildew, K.C., could have kissed the hem of her dress. Never had he had such a witness. As he led her up to a point, she stepped right out and made it—and made it well. He had but to place a nail, and she drove it, fair and square, clean into the other side's coffin—no doubt about that. Best—far best of all, it was so transparently clear that she had not the slightest intention of trying to score. Her naïveté was —well, devastating. There was no other word.

"Were you ever ill, Mrs. Bohun?"

"Oh, no. Not ill. I sometimes felt very tired."

"Mentally or physically?"

There was a painful silence. Then—

"I think it was both."

"I see. Did you tell your husband that you were feeling tired?"

"Sometimes."

"What did he say?"

"I don't think he believed what I said."

"So you just went on?"

"Yes."

"Did things get so bad that you had to have medical attention?"

"Not medical attention, exactly. He said I could have some treatment."

"At a clinic?"

"Yes."

"Was that his suggestion or yours?"

"Mine."

"Why did you suggest it, Mrs. Bohun?"

"I saw an advertisement of a nursing-home, where electrical treatment was given, to—to tone the system up. And I thought perhaps if I had some, it might be a help."

"Towards going on?"

s

" Yes."

" With your married life ? "

" Yes."

" Did you have it ? "

" Yes. Whenever I felt all in, I used to go to the home."

" And they used to brace you up for the next ordeal ? "

Tristram was up on his feet.

" My friend must not put words into the witness' mouth."

But Rowena knocked him out.

" I was very happy to do it. I didn't want our marriage to crash, *because I'd failed.*"

As Tristram himself said later, the only wonder was the Court didn't get up and cheer . . .

But Forsyth missed the triumph—*for Mrs. Morris had whispered in Allen's ear.*

The woman was plainly excited : and Allen, for all his training, looked startled by what she had said.

Forsyth tried his best to keep calm. Ten to one on a mare's nest : these things never came off. Besides . . .

Mrs. Morris was looking at him—a long, inscrutable look, with the ghost of a smile . . . And Allen was writing . . . and tearing a sheet from his pad . . .

Forsyth watched the note coming—being passed down . . . And then it was safe in his hands, and once again he was standing with his back to the wall.

With a pounding heart, he opened the envelope.

Sir,
The witness used these words :—
Whenever I felt all in, I used to go to the home.
Mrs. Morris made this comment :—
It's a lie. She was never there. Go to the home, and they'll tell you they've never seen her. How's that for perjury ?

J. A.

Forsyth stared at the writing, until this seemed to retire and become very small. Then he looked up, to meet Mrs. Morris' eyes . . . The triumph inhabiting these was not of this world. No doubt there is joy in hell over one sinner that descendeth.

The solicitor gave a slight nod. Then he put the note in his pocket and turned to the witness-box.

" Did your husband consult you, before he invited these guests ? "

" Oh, no. He just said they were coming. But I was only too glad. I'd always—liked them so much. And Mrs. Leighton was terribly sweet to me. Of course, I'd not the faintest idea there was anything wrong."

" While you four were at Hautboys, were Mrs. Leighton and your husband ever alone ? "

" Oh, yes. Again and again. But I never thought anything of it."

" Because you believed that she was your very good friend ? "

" Yes. And then, you see, her husband was his best friend. I knew he didn't care for me any more : but it never entered my head that he was—well, caring for her, or she for him."

Forsyth glanced at the clock. The Court would rise for lunch in less than an hour. He could then have a word with Tristram—behind closed doors. Then a glass of port and a sandwich, and back to Court. Bildew ought to have finished by half past three. And that would give Tristram nice time—to lead the horse up to the water . . . before the Court rose for the day. And then . . . he could put to the proof the almost incredible charge which the woman had laid. ' Go to the home.' Bohun had certainly mentioned that his wife had had treatment of sorts : but neither of them had looked any further than that. *But Mrs. Morris had . . . because she had eyes to see . . . because she herself would have practised the same duplicity.*

" You had hopes of Dioni, Mrs. Bohun ? "

" Yes. I was almost sure there'd be nobody there that we knew. And I thought he'd like the place, and that if he and I were alone together there . . ."

The tremulous voice faded, and a hand went up to cover the quivering lips.

Everybody in Court averted their eyes.

" Yes, Mrs. Bohun ? " sighed Bildew.

" Well, you see, we'd never had a real honeymoon. At Biarritz there was . . . somebody else. And I thought that perhaps, at Dioni . . . we might come together again."

" Was . . . that dream realized, Mrs. Bohun ? "

Rowena bowed her head.

" No."

" How was that ? "

" The very day we got there my husband received a telegram, calling him back."

" Did he tell you who it was from ? "

" Oh, yes. He showed it to me. It was from his clerk—from his Chambers, saying he must return to deal with some case."

" And you believed it, Mrs. Bohun ? "

" Of course. I wanted to go back with him, but he said I must stay."

" In fact, am I right in saying that it was not until you had consulted your solicitor that it first occurred to you that that telegram might have been faked ? "

" Yes."

" Did he reply to that wire ? "

" I thought he did. I went to the Post Office with him and I know he sent a wire off."

" Presumably to his clerk ? "

" I thought so, naturally."

" But do you now know that in fact he was wiring to another woman, advising her of his return ? "

A general movement succeeded this rude disclosure of barefaced treachery. But Forsyth did not heed it :

his mind was obsessed with the charge which Mrs. Morris had made. *My God, if she's right,* he murmured. *My God, if she's right. The very vice I've been trying so hard to unearth. A secret lover—met when she felt that way . . . And Bohun would never have it—' she's not like that'. But she is—I always knew it. And she swears her husband's sensual, because she's sensual herself.* With an effort, he forced his brain to lay speculation aside and return to the hay which Mrs. Bohun was making—and making so devilish well.

* * * *

Tristram rose to cross-examine at exactly a quarter past three : but half an hour had gone by before he led the witness on to the ground upon which he wished her to play.

" I can't help feeling, Mrs. Bohun, that you have put some things just a little bit high."

" I've tried to be fair."

" Of course. But naturally you feel very strongly. And haven't you—well, shall we say ' exaggerated ', now and again ? "

" I'm afraid I haven't—really."

" D'you seriously maintain, for instance, that your husband, sitting there, is a sensual man ? "

" I wouldn't have said it, if it wasn't true."

" ' A terribly sensual man.' Is that right ? "

Rowena twisted her hands.

" Oh, I do hate saying it so, but I can't say anything else. And I've said that he did get better—at least, towards the end he left me alone."

" Too much for your liking, Mrs. Bohun ? "

" I think I'd have stuck anything, to save our home."

" Short of downright infidelity ? "

Rowena looked round helplessly.

" When I found that out, I knew there was nothing to save."

" I see. Well, now, tell me this. Your plight was such that at one time during last summer you felt that you couldn't go on ? "

" I said I used to feel very tired."

" ' Mentally and physically ' ? "

" Yes."

" And that it was because of that that you went to some clinic or other to get tuned up ? "

" That's right."

" Come, come, Mrs. Bohun. You're a young lady of fashion, as we can all see. Didn't you go to that clinic, because to go to a clinic was the fashionable thing to do ? "

" No, I didn't—really."

" A fashionable, West-End clinic——"

" It wasn't in the West End."

" Well, fashionable, then. Where was it ? "

" At Potters Bar."

" A very charming locality. Where all your friends resorted, ostensibly to be fortified against the demands of night-life, but, in reality, because at the moment it was the thing to do."

" Indeed, that isn't so. None of my friends had treatment, as far as I know."

" Perhaps you were setting a fashion, Mrs. Bohun ? "

" I didn't go with that idea."

" What idea did you go with ? "

" I hoped it would do me good."

" I see. Did it do you good ? "

" It kept me going—I can't put it better than that."

" I see. Your married life was such hell, that you actually had to pay a whole series of visits to a nursing-home——"

The Judge put in his oar.

" She has said as much, Mr. Tristram, more than once. I have it down in my notes. Her husband's conduct was such as to make her feel very tired : and whenever she felt that she was at the end of her tether, she used to visit the home. There she received some restorative treatment which made her able, or at least made her feel able to go on with her married life." He turned to the witness-box. " Now once for all, is that right ? ."

" That's quite right, my lord," said a tearful, wide-eyed child.

" I'm obliged to your lordship," said Tristram—and meant what he said.

Ten minutes later, the Court adjourned for the day.

* * * *

David put a hand to his head.

" I'm sorry," he said. " But there's nothing doing, Forsyth. She's had the treatment all right. I've got the bills."

For the first time, Forsyth, the tireless, noticed that he was tired.

" The bills ? " he said dully.

" The receipted bills," said David. " The bills which the clinic rendered and which I paid. I rather think I've got three. Each for a dozen treatments, at two guineas a time."

" Printed bill-head ? " said Forsyth.

" Oh, yes," said David. " *The Boldre Institute.* And I sent off the cheques myself, and got back the receipts. It's the devil and all, but you can't get away from that."

Forsyth raised his eyebrows.

" No," he said, " you can't. That's perfectly clear. Mrs. Morris herself was so certain, she raised my hopes. To be painfully candid, I thought we were on a good thing. But now I see I was wrong." He put his hands to his eyes. " I might have known it was all too good to be true. These things don't happen,

Bohun, to honest men. It can't be helped. That's
that." His hand went out to a bell. "We may as
well have her in and see what she says."

Perhaps a minute later, Mrs. Morris, followed by
Chater, entered the room.

Perceiving her, David stiffened. His wife was standing before him—his wife, grown old . . . *the wife of
his bosom, whom no one living, but he, had ever seen*
. . . hard-bitten, ruthless, shrewd, making no effort to
mask her profound contempt. The sight was unspeak-
ably repugnant. In spite of himself, he shuddered,
and a hand went up to his mouth.

"Mrs. Morris, this is Mr. Bohun."

The woman took his measure, as if he had been
some wax-work at Madame Tussaud's.

"I see."

"Bohun, this is Chater. Sit down, if you please.
Mrs. Morris, I'm afraid Mr. Bohun has broken your
theory down. Mrs. Bohun must have been at the
home, for accounts for her treatment were rendered
to Mr. Bohun. He paid them by cheque to the home
and received the official receipts."

"I don't care about that. I say she was never
there."

"But she must have been, Mrs. Morris. Mr. Chater
tells me that the home is above reproach. That being
so, it's hardly likely that, to do Mrs. Bohun a service,
they would consent to commit a serious criminal
offence. If she was never there, they have been
obtaining money by false pretences—and that, if you
please, in the crudest possible way."

The woman sat up.

"Look here," she said. "There's eight of you trying to down her—you an' Bagot and six other jokers
in wigs. Eight against one—an' she's wiped the floor
with the lot. You know that's true. Judge an' jury
—she's got them where they belong : an' the more you
fight her, the more indignant they'll get. When she'd

been in that box ten minutes, your case was dead.
. . . Well, I'll give you this—at least, you saw it
coming : and that's why you sent for me. But, now
I'm here, you won't have it. Twelve thousand miles
I've come, to do your job : and the first time I open
my mouth, you tell me I'm wrong. ' Her husband's
got the receipts . . . a respectable house . . .' " She
smacked the arm of her chair. " Of *course* he's got
the receipts. Of *course* it's a respectable house. Don't
you think she'd see to that ? She's not going to deal
with a brothel . . . And just in case you *should*
wonder whether it's all O.K.—well, as you say, *there's
the receipts* . . . sent direct to her husband . . . to
speak for themselves."

" You mean——"

" I mean what I say. All day I've sat in that
Court and watched her lie. And this is the only
bouncer of all the thousands she's told that you can
put your foot on an'—an' get her down. You never
smelt it—you can't even smell it now. But I've got a
nose for such things. Stand me out, if you like—I
don't give a damn. But if you *want* to break her,
go to that home."

" We're going now," said Forsyth, and got to his
feet. " And you must come, if you please, to keep
us straight. Quite frankly, I'm out of my depth.
But tell me this, Mrs. Morris, before we start. If
Mrs. Bohun was not in fact at the home, *where was
she*—on all those many occasions on which she says
she was treated at Potters Bar ? "

A scornful leer slid into the woman's face.

" Where d'you think ? " she said slowly—and left
it there.

* * * * *

As Chater had said, the place was above reproach.
But the matron was reticent, as Forsyth had feared

she would be. The institute was jealous of its patients, found it improper to discuss them with anyone else. Visits were privileged occasions.

"Our position is that of a doctor. Without Mrs. Bohun's permission, I have no right, Mr. Forsyth, even to admit she was here."

"Madam," said Forsyth, "you are, of course, perfectly right: but this is Mr. Bohun, her husband, who paid your fees. He, therefore, has some standing, so far as the accounts are concerned. Two of your receipts he has with him." The papers passed. "He thinks that there should be a third, which he cannot find. All I ask you to do is to show me the books from which those accounts were compiled."

The matron hesitated.

Then—

"As he paid the bills," she said, "I see no objection to that."

The ledger was sent for. Whilst it was being brought, the lawyer was able to discover that the matron's only brother, a curate, was about to leave on a cruise. He took out a note-book at once.

"If I may have his name, and the name of the ship. I know so many directors. You've only to ring one up—it's nothing to him. But what he says goes, you know . . ."

"You're awfully kind."

She dictated names and dates.

"I'll see to that to-morrow," said Forsyth.

The ledger arrived.

After a careful inspection—

"There's nothing wrong there," said David. "Of course I can't swear to the dates, but here, in September last year, there's a gap of three weeks. Well, that works out. That's when she was out at Dioni. And then, on the first of October, she starts again."

Forsyth returned to the matron.

"Miss Ulick," he said, "I'm going to ask you one

thing. Unknown to you, these entries *could* have been made by someone who wished to suggest that Mrs. Bohun was here on these particular dates. I mean, that is possible. Can you, of your own knowledge, swear to the fact that Mrs. Bohun was here ? "

The matron opened her eyes.

" As it happens, I can," she said. " I am informed the moment a patient arrives. And I always go to see them before they leave. That is a rule, Mr. Forsyth, I never break. More. The entries that are made in this ledger are made from the ' treatment slips '. Whilst I am with the patient, I always look at the slip. And unless my initials are on it, no entry in the ledger is made."

There was a moment's silence.

Then—

" Excuse me a moment," said Forsyth. " I want to think this out."

He stepped to the open windows, which gave to a pleasant lawn, and stood looking into the garden, where a man of many summers was leisurely using a hose.

There could be no doubt at all that the matron was telling the truth : yet Forsyth knew in his heart that Mrs. Morris was right. The matron had seen Mrs. Bohun time and again : yet Mrs. Bohun was never at Potters Bar. The two conflicting statements were, each of them, true. This meant that there was a catch : at least, not a catch—a simple explanation of this inexplicable fact.

(Miss Ulick was speaking quietly, as though she was anxious not to disturb his thoughts.

" Won't you sit down, Mr. Bohun ? You look so tired."

" Oh, thank you. You're very kind. It's—it's been very hot in Town. You're better off here.")

Of course, he could go back to that woman, sitting outside with Chater, smoking her vile cigarettes. But, unless he was much mistaken, she'd shot her bolt. She couldn't solve this problem. All the way out he'd pressed her—with no result. ' That's up to you. I've told you she wasn't there : but I'm not the Witch of Endor . . .'

My God, how tired he was. And Bohun was like a dead man. No wonder their brains wouldn't work. Continuous concentration had run their batteries down. If only he had to-morrow to think things out . . . But he hadn't got to-morrow—not even to-night. If they couldn't bring this off, Bohun would have to be told about Mrs. Adair. And then there'd be the devil to pay . . . And when he'd been made to see reason, his proof would have to be altered, to let her evidence in. They'd be lucky if they'd finished by midnight—a nice introduction to another critical day . . .

And now, once again to this cursed paradox—these two irreconcilable statements which really agreed. ' Go to the home, and they'll tell you they've never seen her.' ' As it happens, I can swear to the fact that Mrs. Bohun was here.' Diametrically opposite statements—and both were true . . .

Miss Ulick was talking quietly with David Bohun.

" Oh, are you really ? My father was at the Bar. But I don't think he did very much. He hung on, you know : but he made his living by writing, under another name."

Forsyth swung about, staring.

" My God," he said weakly, and Bohun got to his feet.

" What d'you know ? " he said hoarsely.

The matron stared at them both.

" I think I've got it," said Forsyth. " I think we're home. Oh, of course, it's obvious—as usual. . . . Please tell me this, Miss Ulick. *What's Mrs. Bohun like ?* "

The matron moistened her lips.

"Neither dark nor fair, blue eyes, of average height
——"

"I'm much obliged, Forsyth," said David, and put
out his hand.

"But I don't understand," said the matron.

"How should you?" said Forsyth, smiling. "That
wasn't Mrs. Bohun, Miss Ulick. That was . . . *her
deputy.*"

BOHUN v. BOHUN AND LEIGHTON   285

" Neither dark nor fair, blue eyes, of average height
——
" I'm much obliged, Forsyth," said David, and put
out his hand.

" But I don't understand," said the matron.

" How should you ? " said Forsyth, smiling.   " That
wasn't Mrs. Bo.... .... was ....
dappy.

CHAPTER XVII

Achilles' Heel

MR. CROWNER was in excellent fettle. He
loved escorting Rowena down to the Courts.
She was so—extremely effective. Never that he could
remember had a client done him such credit—in every
way. And yesterday . . . What a triumph ! And
what an advertisement—for Messrs. Crowner and
Growth ! Just what they wanted, too : a snow-
white case. *Bohun* v. *Bohun and Leighton*. This
ought to settle those rumours that the President had
his eye on a well-known firm.

As the car slid into the Strand, he glanced at his
watch.

" I, ah, think I should advise you, Mrs. Bohun, that
when we arrive at the Law Courts, ah, two or three
may be gathered together, to, ah, welcome the pretty
lady and wish her good luck."

Rowena was laudably distressed.

" Oh, dear. I never imagined . . . I don't believe
I can face them."

" There, there," purred Mr. Crowner, patting her
hand. " It's nothing at all, I assure you. And I
shall be there."

The lawyer was perfectly right. As the car came to
rest, some twenty or thirty women were crowding
about the door. His protecting arm about her, Mr.
Crowner conveyed his client out of the press.

Had he been less engaged, he might have observed
three ladies, with Chater and Allen beside them,

standing a little apart and regarding Mrs. Bohun with all their might.

With one consent, the three ladies were shaking their heads.

"Gawd be praised," said Allen—and ran after Mr. Crowner, treading the steps . . .

"Oh, excuse me, sir, but this is from Mr. Forsyth. He thinks it highly important that you should read it at once."

A long, flat envelope passed—and a cloud which was very much bigger than any man's hand rose over the rim of the earth into Mr. Crowner's sky.

He had the envelope open before he had entered the hall.

Messrs. Crowner and Growth.

Dear Sirs,

Attached is the statement of a witness who will be subpœnaed on behalf of the respondent within the hour. It is the statement of the matron of the clinic to which your client has sworn that she often repaired. I have thought it right that you should be put in possession of the facts which this lady will prove.

I may add that she will be supported by the two members of her staff who actually treated the patient whom they believed to be Mrs. David Bohun, of Curzon Street.

Yours faithfully,
J. G. Forsyth.

With starting eyes, Mr. Crowner turned to the statement . . .

After a frantic perusal, he clawed his cuff out of the way to glare at his watch.

A quarter past ten.

His heaven now black with clouds, he stumbled after Rowena, moving like a nun in her cloister along the echoing hall . . .

But Rowena did not feel like a nun.

Although she had given no sign, she had seen the envelope pass and had heard what Allen had said. And she knew that the sleeping dog, Danger, had opened its bloodshot eyes.

It was Anselm that had mentioned the clinic—God damn his soul: six months ago, or more, at one of those sleek consultations at which their proofs had been polished by Crowner's loving tongue. And Crowner had pounced upon it, as a dog on a rat : and nothing that she could do would make him let go. 'My dear little lady, allow me—you don't understand. A fact of the utmost value, corroborating your story up to the hilt. Such was the unhappy condition to which, by your husband's behaviour, you had been reduced that you actually had to have treatment, to give you the strength to go on.' From that hour she had been uneasy : with no idea of what he was doing the man was bent on exposing Achilles' heel. More than once, with the greatest caution, she had returned to the charge—of course, to no avail. 'My dear, you must be advised. I know so well the reluctance which must be yours to have such a matter referred to in open Court. Medical attention is, to a sensitive young married woman, her, ah, Ark of the Covenant. But of my ripe experience—and Counsel agrees with me . . .' Rowena could have screamed the house down . . . All through the crawling months, the worm of apprehension had been feeding upon her heart. At times it had sunk to nothing— a lifeless smear : and at times it had swollen into a thick-set snake that had the power to bring herself to ruin and turn her pleasure-garden into a wilderness. Yesterday Tristram's questions had shortened her life. Was it by chance or design that the man had forced her to put the rope round her neck ? And that doddering fool of a Judge had adjusted the cord . . . Well, now she knew the answer. Somehow or other,

that poker-faced bastard, Forsyth, had got ideas . . .
told Tristram to ask those questions . . . and, when
the Court had risen, had driven to Potters Bar . . .
For the first time that she could remember, Rowena
felt the definite stab of fear. Then she heard Crowner
coming—and braced herself for an effort beside which
her other efforts should seem beneath regard. Was
it not written ' And a little child shall lead them ' ?
Somehow—*somehow* she would wrest her fortune out
of the jaws of that dog with the bloodshot eyes.

Five minutes later, she was sitting, facing Bildew,
in a private consulting-room. Crowner was sitting
between them, streaming with sweat, and one of her
junior counsel was standing by Bildew's side. All
three looked extremely grave—and Crowner's eyes
were bolting, and his face was a rich gray-green.

Bildew went straight to the point.

" Mrs. Bohun, forewarned is forearmed. Here is
the statement of a witness whom your husband is
going to call. I want you to see what it says."

The paper passed.

Bohun v. *Bohun* (*Leighton intervening*).

*I, Agatha Ulick, of The Boldre Institute, Potters
Bar, am the matron of that establishment.*

*Almost a year ago, a lady who gave the name and
address of Mrs. David Bohun of Curzon Street,
arranged to receive a course of electrical massage.
The course consisted of twelve treatments, administered
at the clinic. The lady took this course. I never
knew when she was coming, until she telephoned—
usually the day before—arranging to be at the clinic
at such and such a time. An account for the twelve
treatments was rendered to David Bohun Esq., of
Curzon Street. This was paid by cheque. Three
such courses were taken, and three such cheques were
paid. I, myself, saw the patient thirty-six times, that*

is to say, on every occasion on which she visited the home.

I have this morning had pointed out to me the Petitioner in this case. She is not the lady I knew as Mrs. Bohun and, until this morning, I had never set eyes upon her.

　　　　　　　　　　　(*signed*) *Agatha Ulick.*

11th June.

Rowena laid down the statement and lifted the face of a seraph, accused of blackmail.

" But what ever does it mean ? " she demanded.

" That, Mrs. Bohun, is what we want to know. And I must tell you this—that this witness will be supported by two *masseuses* . . . the two who, between them, administered every treatment which this lady received."

" They're all going to say they don't know me ? " Rowena looked ready to cry.

But Bildew was taking no chances.

" They *have* all said they don't know you, Mrs. Bohun."

" But I don't understand. How can they ? They know me quite well."

" And you know them ? "

" Of course."

" Did you see them outside the Courts . . . this morning, when you arrived ? "

A wide-eyed child shook her head.

" I'm afraid I didn't look. You see, there was rather a crowd."

" If you had seen them, would you have known them ? "

Rowena put a hand to her head.

" Well, I think I should. Of course, up to now I've only seen them in uniform."

" But they've seen you in plain clothes ? "

" Yes."

" As you are to-day ? "

" Yes."

" So that their failure is inexcusable ? "

" I don't think they *can* have failed. Perhaps they were all three looking at somebody else."

" I'm afraid that . . . isn't likely, Mrs. Bohun."

A horrified look stole into Rowena's eyes.

" D'you mean to say," she whispered, " that they've been given money to come here and lie."

" That's out of the question," said Bildew. " Subornation of perjury is not Mr. Forsyth's way."

For the twentieth time, Mr. Crowner wiped his face.

" Well, I can't help it," said Rowena. " If they like to be so wicked, it isn't my fault."

Bildew leaned forward.

" Let me put it like this, Mrs. Bohun. Yesterday you said *upon oath* that you had been at this clinic again and again : to-day three people who are in a position to know, are going to get up and swear that you never were there. Well, somebody's lying, Mrs. Bohun : you can't get away from that. And somebody's *going to prison*—for wilful perjury."

" Well, they jolly well ought to," flamed Rowena. " If it *was* me they saw, then to get up and say they don't know me—just out of spite . . ." Her voice was trembling : tears were plainly at hand. " I never heard anything so wicked. I suppose it's because I complained—the last time I was there. I didn't like the manner of one of the girls . . . And I said I shouldn't come back . . . And I never did."

With a shaking hand, she sought for a handkerchief. Bildew recoiled.

The statement had hit him hard, and Crowner's discomposure had left little doubt in his mind that once again Crowner and Growth had been greasing the wheels of injustice to win their case. But this— this outburst put his suspicions to shame. The words were guileless words : and the way was the way of a girl who has nothing to fear. And Crowner was staring upon her—not with the air of a shepherd, but with that of a sheep.

He began to finger his chin.

If the girl was lying, there was an end of the case. But if she was not—well, Alexander Bildew might have his faults, but, cost what it might, he would never abandon Innocence . . . standing with her back to the wall.

" It's three to one, Mrs. Bohun. Don't forget that."

" I don't care if they're six. I say it's a beastly shame. And of course they're standing together— backing each other up. That's just what Miss Ulick did, when I made my complaint. She took the girl's part against me . . . That's why I wouldn't go back."

Bildew looked at Crowner, and Rowena glanced at the junior, standing by Crowner's side. His wig was all out of shape, and he had the silliest face she had ever seen. And that man was at the Bar. He ought to have been ' on the halls '. He'd only have to come on—and look like that.

" What do you think, Mr. Crowner ? "

Crowner put a hand to his throat. A little colour had struggled into his face.

" From what Mrs. Bohun says, I think it's clear that these three women are, ah, seeking to be revenged. Mr. Forsyth no doubt approached them, as I might well have done—just to check the petitioner's state-ment that she had attended the home. And seeing their chance of, ah, vengeance . . ."

He broke off and shrugged his shoulders, and Bildew got to his feet.

" All right," he said. " And now we'd better get back. The Judge will be getting impatient. I sent him word, but—Yes ? "

The fool of a junior was whispering in his ear.

The words seemed to make him think, and, once

again, a hand went up to his chin. Then he looked again at Rowena.

"One moment, Mrs. Bohun. Before we go, just tell me. *What is Miss Ulick like?*"

Rowena put a hand to her head.

So that was what that scum had suggested—that drivelling, loose-lipped half-wit, with a wig that looked as if he kept it in the seat of his pants. He was sucking a pencil now, like a comic scholar unable to do his sum. God knew why Crowner had engaged him—a man with a face like that . . . and a foot *designed* to blunder on to forbidden ground.

My God, Bildew's eyes were widening. She must say something at once. But that damned, congenital idiot was putting her off. He was smiling now, actually smiling—looking at the end of his pencil and smiling fondly upon it, as though he had done a fine thing.

Desperately, she moistened her lips.

To be tripped like this by a wash-out—a caricature of a man . . . that should have been choked at birth. Not Tristram, not even Bildew : but a filthy, half-baked book-worm, that knew as much of life as a cuckoo-clock. By God, was that what he was paid for ? To let his employer down ? To bite the hand that fed him ? What was it to do with him what Miss Ulick was like ?

My God, how Bildew was staring. His eyes were like points of steel. If she didn't speak in a moment, he'd . . . get ideas. And that god-damned slab of vomit was sucking his pencil again. Sententiously sucking his pencil. Just about what he was fit for. To suck a pencil he'd found in somebody else's desk . . .

"So, it's true," said Bildew, quietly. "You never were there, Mrs. Bohun. And when you swore that you were, you committed perjury."

Rowena was breathing hard. Her lips were ready and waiting : but the words would not come. The thing was absurd, but—she could not think of an answer. She, Rowena Bohun, had nothing to say.

In her bag was a note from Juliot, comparing her to an angel, as good as promising marriage—when she was out of the wood. *I am told that your demeanour was perfect . . . that you have come with all honour out of your great ordeal . . . I look forward with that confidence which only the fires of tribulation can ever forge, to a future which will be worthy of your delicate understanding, to which I am determined, so far as in me lies, to contribute, or endeavour to contribute—for, of course, the acceptance of my contribution must be a matter for you . . .* He wasn't tongue-tied. He didn't know what it meant. But she, Rowena Bohun, had nothing to say.

Bildew continued—still quietly.

" Perjury, Mrs. Bohun. And you meant to go back to-day, and commit still more. To swear ' by Almighty God ' that those three women were lying . . . had come here to do you down . . . when all the time you knew they were telling the truth."

Rowena began to tremble—against her will. Her brain, like a horse, was refusing. She could not lay her tongue to the words which should carry her over the jump.

Why the hell didn't Crowner say something ? The fool must see she was crashing . . . crashing for want of a sentence . . . dropping a —— fortune, because, for a moment, she had no answer to make. It was all his fault—the greasy, white-livered swine. But for him and his ' ripe experience ', she wouldn't have been . . . tied up. And now, when, thanks to him, she'd got her back to the wall . . .

Bildew was speaking again.

" I'm going back now, Mrs. Bohun—to throw up your case. I shan't . . . give any reason. You're free, of course. You can take what action you please. But if I were you, I'd get out—while the going is good. And lie very low for a while . . . unless you want to appear in another Court, where the atmosphere is less sympathetic, and wilful perjury sometimes comes by its own."

As he turned, Rowena stopped trembling.

Now that it was too late, her brain was docile again. Now that the words were useless, she knew what she might have said.

In a flash, she had turned upon Crowner. At least, if he'd brought her down, he should go down, too.

"You rotten coward," she flamed. Before this savage onslaught, Mr. Crowner, whose heaven had fallen, caught his breath, and Bildew swung about, with a hand on the door. "I've waited for you to speak : but you didn't like the look of the weather, and so you held your tongue. You *know* I never wanted to say that I was at Potters Bar. I begged and prayed you not to make me, with all my might. But you swore it was just what was wanted to round my case. Corroboration, you called it. You said the jury'd eat it . . . the fact that I'd had to have treatment, to carry on."

The unexpected perfidy hit the unfortunate lawyer over the heart. His face a wet mask of gray, he stared upon his traducer, incapable of movement or speech—and Rowena, with twitching nostrils, stared upon him as though he were something unclean.

It only remained for Bildew to deal him the *coup de grâce*.

"By God, Crowner," he said, " you ought to be struck off the Roll."

Then he and his junior passed out, and the door of the room was shut.

* * * *

The Court was more crowded than ever. Word had gone round that no ordinary case was ' part heard', and the tipstaves were holding the doors against two determined bands of hopeful, would-be entrants, for whom there was no possible room.

Within, an irregular murmur declared the suppressed excitement which everyone felt, and the eagles, who were there in full force, made no attempt to disguise the relish with which they were awaiting a still more succulent feast.

Mrs. Grainer, whose hams were still stiff from the gruelling which they had received on the preceding day, was suffering the added torture of being so tightly sandwiched between neighbours she did not know that she was denied the relief of occasionally shifting her weight, and, although resolved to endure, was already wondering whether, in three hours' time, she would, short of medical assistance, be able to walk. Consumed with indignation, Mrs. Garter was forced to stand—she who had a prescriptive right to a seat —and to watch Mesdames Mocket and Sewler comfortably ensconced behind counsel in places to which, of course, they had no shadow of claim. That was that—— Boney. As like as not, he'd sworn they were witnesses. ' Pa ' Cullet was standing, too : he was jammed with Isabel Stumm in the opposite aisle : but, though the future was grim, the absence of Mrs. Garter encouraged his drooping heart. The vials of bile were all right : but you didn't want a close-up for five solid hours. An occasional glimpse of his daughter and Teddy Bemuse very well placed and *seated* a short ten paces away awoke a clumsy resentment against the flesh of his flesh. He wondered what his father would have said, if one of the girls had sat down before he was seated, and seated well.

Mrs. Morris was there, with Chater, at the end of a row. A sardonic smile seemed part of her countenance : and now and again, as though amused at her thoughts, she moved in her seat and bared her discoloured teeth. Allen was standing beside her, with his eyes on the nearest door.

Belinda was sitting with Bagot in the well of the Court, and David was standing beside them, talking to Tristram, who had an eye on the clock. Forsyth was in his old place—in an aisle, not far from the doors, with his back to the wall. And the Registrar was standing on the leather seat of his stall, speaking the Judge's clerk, who was leaning down from the bench.

It was past half past ten now, but the Judge had not taken his seat. And Rowena and Bildew and Crowner had not appeared. But no one thought anything of it—except the parties concerned.

"He's late," explained Boney Belong. "Missed his tram, or something. Or else he hasn't finished his paper—these Judges do as they like. And they won't bring her in till he's ready : they want to spare her, you see. Old Erny Crowner's rubbin' her down with champagne. They'll be doin' that to Bohun to-morrow. And I wouldn't be him for something. Bildew's goin' to smear him all over the —— floor."

"Goody, goody," said Ruby Mocket. "I hope he squirms. When I think . . ."

The especial desire expressed by 'Koko' Sewler was characteristic of her and so must not be set down, but it found great favour in her companions' ears. Her violence may be passed over, if not excused. Hautboys should have been *her* wash-pot : and that dirty, deceitful satyr had snatched it out of her hands, *to make it his*.

As the sniggers subsided—

"What's the paramour doing ? " she added. "She's not going to die to-day."

"Coming up to the gate," said Boney. "Where's Leighton gone ? "

"End of this row," said 'Koko'. "He's playin' up all right, but I guess he's feeling swotty under the arms."

Here one of the swing-doors shuddered—and caught the practised eye of the Judge's clerk.

"I think this is them, sir."

The Registrar turned his head.

As he did so, the door was opened, and Bildew thrust into the crowded mouth of the aisle.

The clerk was gone in a flash, in search of the Judge.

"Here they are," said most people in Court, including Boney Belong.

Such was the press that Bildew and his junior, behind him, had fairly to fight their way through. Before they had reached their places, an usher was crying 'Silence!' and the heavy, oak doors were open, and everyone, except Mrs. Grainer, was up on his feet.

As Bildew gained the row reserved for 'silk gowns', the Judge stepped out of his corridor on to the bench.

"Where is she?" breathed Ruby Mocket. "She hasn't come in."

"She'll be here in a second," said Boney. "They can't begin without her."

With his words, the Judge took his seat, and all who had risen sat down.

Deliberately Bildew rose—and everyone held his breath.

In a deathly silence the King's Counsel looked at the Judge.

Then—

"My lord," he said slowly and firmly, "I can carry my case no further. Circumstances have arisen which make it impossible for me to proceed."

With a swish of silk, he sat down.

Tristram was up and was speaking.

"In that case, by your lordship's leave, I will put the respondent in the box."

As David stood up—

"But what's it mean?" breathed 'Koko'.

"I'm damned if I know," said Boney. "They

must have bluffed her, or something. She's not going on."

"D'you mean to say she's not coming?"

"Well, you heard what he said. She's not going on with the case."

"Not going *on*? But *why*?"

Misconduct was formally denied, first by David and then by a flushed Belinda, looking her best.

Under the Registrar's direction a formal verdict was returned.

And then, at Tristram's instance, Mrs. David Bohun's petition was formally dismissed.

As the Judge left the bench, a subdued pandemonium broke out.

"But what's it all *mean*?" spat 'Koko'. "Who the devil knows what it means?"

"They've got her down," said Boney. "Frightened her off. After yesterday's show, they knew they were —— well sunk. Their only chance was to 'work' it—behind the scenes. They probably got at Crowner—'Five thousand paper pounds, if she doesn't go on'. Well, what does she know? Nothing. He simply says, 'Look here, I don't like the look of things: and havoc's booked for to-morrow—that Tristram fellow'll rip the skin off your back.' An' she says, 'Oh, what shall I do?' And he bungs in the towel. It's easy enough, you know. It's been done before."

Outside, Mrs. Garter was likewise expounding the truth.

"Dirty work. You can take it from me. I never saw such a case. She'd got 'em dead and stinking, yesterday afternoon. Of course, if you're such a fool as to go to Crowner and Growth . . ."

Mrs. Grainer was yet in Court. She had fought her way to an usher, declared that she was a witness and asked for information upon that score.

"Well, you won't be needed," said the usher. "The case is done."

" But I don't understand——"

" You must see the solicitor, madam. It's nothing to do with me."

" But is the case really over ? "

The usher left her standing, to speak to a shorthand writer shuffling his notes.

After waiting for him to return, and waiting in vain, Mrs. Grainer, breathing out threatenings, lumbered towards an exit, after the way of a bear that is robbed of her whelps.

*　　*　　*　　*

A quarter of an hour had gone by, and Mrs. Ellen Morris was looking at David Bohun and sucking her teeth.

" Tell me this," she said. " Can you think of any man that you warned her off ? And when you'd warned her off, she didn't argue about it, but turned him down ? "

Subduing a feeling of nausea, David knitted his brow.

" No," he said shortly. " No one. I didn't like the people she met, but she gave me no cause to complain of her conduct with any man."

" I didn't ask you that."

David looked at Forsyth : but the latter was regarding the ceiling. Plainly he saw no reason to interfere.

By the door was standing Chater, with his eyes upon Mrs. Morris and a hand to his chin.

" I thought you meant that," said David.

" I didn't. I meant what I said. Was there ever any man that you warned her off."

" She gave me no occasion to do so, from first to last. Once—oh, ages ago, I remember a frightful outsider asked her to dance : and, as we were going home, I said he was really too thick and we'd better not know him if ever we saw him again. But she quite agreed

with me. And it wasn't her fault—she couldn't help
dancing with him, because it was a private party in
somebody's flat."

" You say she agreed with you ? "

" Entirely. I remember it well. The moment I
started, she said, ' I know what you're going to say.'
And then she let fly about him and said how revolting
he was. I remember her saying that she could have
spat in his face."

Mrs. Morris leaned forward.

" But she didn't . . . did she ? "

David recoiled.

" I assure you——"

" Who was he ? "

" I believe he was a dress-designer, or so he said.
But we never saw him again."

" *You* didn't," said Mrs. Morris, and showed her
teeth.

David drew in his breath.

" There's nothing there," he said. " I'm certain of
that. She wouldn't have been seen dead with him.
I mean, he was a Whitechapel Jew—of the filthiest
type."

" I see. D'you remember his name ? "

" I believe it was Leta."

Forsyth picked up his receiver.

" I want the telephone-directory," he said.

In obvious impatience, David crossed his legs.

" I hold no brief for my wife, but the thing is impossible. God knows she has her faults, but she agreed
with me that the man was—rank. And she was
damned annoyed with the people whose flat it was. I
mean, I don't care. But this is a waste of time."

Again Mrs. Morris leaned forward—this time with
fire in her eyes.

" The trouble with you is this—that you'll never
learn. You've been proved a non-stop fool—not once,
but again and again. Your wife's made rings round

you : and, but for me, you'd be sweating blood in that
Court at this very time. But now I've downed her
. . . by seeing what you couldn't see. Right under
your nose for a year : but you couldn't smell it—you
couldn't see nothing wrong. But I got it all right,
my friend—and got it in one. Yesterday afternoon,
you stuck me out in this room that it couldn't be
true. But it *was* true, wasn't it, Smarty ? "

David was white to the lips.

" Yes," he said, " it was true. I told you, I gave
you best."

" An' the next time I try to help you, you shove
in your toes again and as good as call me a —— fool
to my face."

Allen came in with the directory, laid it on Forsyth's table and left the room.

" I only meant," began David . . .

" *You—only—meant*," sneered the woman. " If I
were you, I'd have that cut on your tomb. I mean,
it gets you in one. *He only meant.*"

David was staring upon her, as a man who stares
upon proof of the supernatural—a practical man, who
has always refused to believe. That Rowena had
spoken was nothing. *The words were Rowena's words.*

" Look here," said Mrs. Morris. " I've saved your
bacon—and you know it as well as me. Well, that's
good enough, I should say : but it seems I'm not
through yet. Forsyth here asks for more. ' I want
to free him,' he says. ' He don't want her round
his neck for the rest of his life.' And so I start
in again . . . to look for the man . . . the man to
whose bed she went, when you thought she'd gone
to the home. Well, from what you say, it's Leta.
It mayn't look pretty to you, but he's just her type.
And I'll lay she's not cut him out. But you'll have
to be quick. If she can talk French like you say, it's
Lombard Street to an orange she'll fetch up in France."

Forsyth looked up from the book.

" *O. Leta, Dress-designer.* Is that the man ? "

" It must be him," said David. " There can't be two."

" Yes, I think it's him," said Forsyth. " You see, he lives at Melham . . . and Melham is less than a mile from Potters Bar."

* * * *

Alone at Half Moon Street, Rowena lay flat upon her bed, watching the wanton flies which were ceaselessly circling and swooping about the alabaster which veiled the electric light.

For once, she was making no plans. Her mind ran free. And as one of those wanton flies, it ceaselessly swooped and circled about her catastrophe.

To and fro, back and forth it roved . . . and round and round and round.

Anselm had lit the match, and Crowner had lighted the fuse : and now the dump had gone up, in a sheet of blue flame. She had had a million chances of cutting the fuse : but that would have meant trusting Crowner—making him free of the secret that she wasn't as sweet as she looked. And that was unthinkable.

And Forsyth . . . She'd left him out. Forsyth had taken the fuse and shoved it into the dump. Anselm, Crowner, Forsyth—they were the three that, between them, had brought her down. And only one of the three had known what he was about. Forsyth.

He knew—he'd got it somehow, though God knew how. Dioni—yes, if you like. If he'd pointed at Dioni, that would have been natural enough. Or Ascot, or Brighton, or even Brunskill Towers. Red herring after red herring . . . But Forsyth had turned them down—and gone to the home. A bow at a venture, of course. But how many men would have drawn it, when *David had paid the fees* ?

And she'd damned near pulled it round. Once back

in Court, she'd have done it. Once she'd set eyes on the bitches, she would have been safe. Their word against hers—that's all. And the bills and cheques and receipts all waiting, to back her up. But that half-baked stiff had bent it . . . Bildew was round —she'd got him . . . and then that frightening wash-out had put in his filthy oar.

Anselm, Crowner, Forsyth, a village idiot . . . each of them doing his bit . . . to smash her world.

All her hard labour on Juliot—just chucked away. A —— certainty—sunk in the bright, blue sea. And a warrant for perjury waiting . . . on Forsyth's whim. She hadn't staked anything—and she'd lost the lot. She'd never put a foot wrong—and she'd crashed for good . . . thanks to Anselm, Crowner, Forsyth—and a rotten, moth-eaten super, who didn't know how to live.

How Leta would laugh, if he knew. Call her ' a greedy fire-fly ' and laugh in her face. But he wouldn't know. He couldn't. He didn't even know who she was. He could have found out, if he'd cared to look at her car. But he wasn't like that—Leta. As long as he got his fiver, he didn't care.

By God, how hot it was—not a breath of air. But those damned flies seemed to like it. Or else, perhaps, like Leta, they didn't care. She supposed they knew what they were doing . . . ceaselessly swooping and circling about a light that was out.

CHAPTER XVIII

Harvest

JUNE slid into July, and Lady Persimmon was sleeping as she had not slept for months. Juliot, however, was actually losing weight. Sunk in his Lincolnshire seat, he spent his time afoot, pacing the cheerless park or the pompous library. The exercise saved his life—from which the savour was gone. His sparrow was dead. The daughter of musick had been brought low.

Mrs. Morris was enjoying herself. Every morning, at ten o'clock, she reported to Forsyth's office in Lincoln's Inn Fields. There she drew her expenses—two pounds a day : and after that she was free to do as she pleased. She saw all there was to be seen and much that was not. Her favourite resort was the lounge of a busy hotel.

Rowena was out of England. She was, in fact, at Veilleuse, which boasted a little-known *plage*, some thirty miles north of Bayonne. She passed her days on the sands, entirely alone. The sun and air and sea-water made her rather fitter in body than she had ever been. But she had no plans. Her brain had its teeth in the past and it would not let go. Hour after hour she brooded—over her poisonous luck.

She had made plans—good plans. Before she had left Half Moon Street, she had them all cut and dried. Up or down, she was still Mrs. David Bohun—a fact not at all to the liking of David and Helen Adair. And the latter was fantastically rich . . . It would have to be carefully done, but the proofs which her husband required would be for sale—at a price. She had had the whole thing worked out . . . And then . . . at Victoria Station . . . she had been 'served'. Served with her husband's petition—*Bohun* v. *Bohun and Leta* . . . by a man she had never seen . . . whilst her luggage was being weighed.

And so her plans were back in the melting-pot.

To defend was out of the question, for the women from the home would be called. And if she gave them the lie, a warrant for perjury would issue, sure as a gun. They'd got her cold—this time : Forsyth had got her cold. By God, that man . . . with a statue's face and the scent of a hound of hell.

Face downward, upon the hot sand, Rowena wandered in spirit over her wilderness. As in a dream, she heard the petulance of children, the wail of an ice-cream vendor, the lackadaisical surge of a mill-pond sea. These things were not her portion. Her portion had been taken away.

* * * *

Summer slid into autumn, and Bohun decided to leave the Chancery Bar.

During the year that was past, his work had fallen away. *Bohun* v. *Bohun and Leighton* had done him no good. The case had made demands on his time which had to be met, and clients had been inconvenienced again and again. These offences were remembered against him not only by those inconvenienced, but by his clerk. (This was natural enough : the clerk's fee went with the brief.) And Beaver was dissatisfied : Bohun was breaking the only rule that he knew. All were, of course, aware of the impending divorce. And all who were cross with the lawyer, began to measure the man.

Of course the case had collapsed : *but not until Rowena had said her say*. More than one Chancery gownsman had been in Court—and had been deeply impressed by what he had seen and heard. For the last six weeks of that term, luncheon in Lincoln's Inn Hall had not been the same : no man was short with Bohun, but conversation had faltered when he had appeared.

And so he decided to leave the Chancery Bar.

After all, he'd two thousand a year : and, when Curzon Street had been sold, he would have considerably more. And the Bar took too much of his time. With all the world before them, what was the sense of his sitting in Lincoln's Inn ? All the same, to give up his Chambers hit the man hard. The Bar was his profession. And, until Rowena had queered it, he'd put up a decent show.

A thing that hit him much harder should have been beneath his contempt. One day, in Christie's doorway, he ran into Hilda Bedew. He took off his hat at once—and she cut him dead.

Until that pregnant moment, the man had had no idea that people might still be believing in Rowena, his reprobate wife. And though now, for one fleeting instant, the bare possibility flamed, he dismissed such a notion at once as being absurd.

Lady Bedew had not liked him—none of them had : and, now that Rowena was gone, she saw no reason for admitting an acquaintance which she did not desire. Then, again, it was a scandalous business—' the Bohun affair ' : and people fought shy of scandal, preferred to watch from a distance, were quick to deny that they had been on terms with the parties . . . ' And again he denied with an oath, I do not know the man.' All the same, it was damned unpleasant. And the fellow she was with had seen it—and stared like hell. It was one of those things you tried to forget and couldn't : and when they recurred to your mind, you got hot all over again.

Mercifully for Bohun, he never knew the truth—that

the stone which he had rejected was in fact the head of the corner . . . that Grainers, Mockets, Sinoples—the whole of that pinchbeck crowd, believed, heart and soul, in Rowena, his reprobate wife.

Feeling had run very high—on ' the Bohun affair '.

As I have shown, Rowena was very much liked, while David was not. And as I have also shown, long before things came to a head, Rowena was an object of pity, while her husband was an object of scorn. Then Rowena had filed her petition—and so had confirmed suspicion up to the hilt. And then she had gone into the box—and had confirmed confirmation, rammed certainty home. It is not too much to say that that day she had lighted a candle which should never be put out.

And then, without any warning, her case had collapsed . . .

When people had recovered their wits, they sought for an explanation of this phenomenon. The thing was not logical. A copper-bottomed cutter had foundered before she was fairly launched. Everyone was immediately sure that ' dirty work ' must have been done. Crowner and Growth had been got at. Rowena had been frightened off. The Adair had put up the money for someone to scupper the ship. Surreptitious inquiries were made—of course, without any result. Rowena dared say nothing : remembering Bildew's warning, she lay very low. Having tasted her treachery once, for no consideration would Crowner have opened his lips. Counsel kept their own counsel. Forsyth, Bagot and Bohun were hardly likely to talk. Such silence alone was suspicious. When justice has been made to miscarry, the subject is best not discussed. And then David had filed *his* petition . . .

The hoot which had greeted this action may well have been heard in hell. ' Leta cited as co-respondent ? Rowena charged with misconduct with a Wardour-Street Jew ? ' The thing was grotesque, fantastic, not

to be borne. It was not so much incredible as it was
insulting. Cullets, Sewlers and Stumms shouted each
other down—and may be excused . . . Let me put
it like this. Mrs. Garter had little to lose : but she
would not have touched Leta with the end of a ten-
foot pole. And Rowena was not Mrs. Garter. She
was the eager playmate, that knew no wrong.

Ruby Mocket, if incoherent, made herself plain.

" This damned well proves it—if anyone wanted
proof. A filthy, stinking ramp, from beginning to end.
Noblesse oblige, I don't think. If you want an emetic,
study the upper ten. The Adair wants Bohun ; but
she doesn't want Bohun divorced. Wouldn't look well,
don't you know. It'd give Persimmon a pain : an'
Court Circles'd notice a smell and pull in their horns.
While she's out of the country, Bohun gets going with
the wife of his oldest friend—an' meets it good and
proper, as he deserves. Of course he tells the Adair
it's a bucket of bunk—he's got a perfect answer, an'
all the rest. An' then the case comes on, an' Rowena
goes into the box. Well, that's enough for dear Helen.
Bucket of bunk or no, it's got to be stopped. If it
isn't, Bohun's sunk . . . and Persimmon will have a
pain . . . and when she rings up the Palace, the
number will be engaged. And so it *is* stopped—
somehow . . . God knows how it was done : but
Crowner's banking account might give us a line. And
then she says, ' Well, we don't want no more of this.
I've had enough shocks, dear David. Let's make a
job of it, dearie, and push her over the edge.' An'
Bohun says ' Every time. Just show me where to
sign an' tell me what I'm to say.' Well, we all know
what Leta is . . . Five hundred not to defend—
that's more than enough. Here, give me some more
champagne. I want to wash out my mouth." She
did so—thoroughly. " Say I'm wrong if you like,
but I'll tell you this. *Those two swabs 'll be married
before he's been free six weeks.*"

And there Mrs. Mocket was right. A *decree nisi* was granted to David before December was out : and he and Helen were married in the second week of July.

There was next to no talk at the club—to which David had lately belonged. But clubs are places where the papers are faithfully read, and the several announcements were noted—as echoes of a scene in the annexe which no one would ever forget. And when, one summer evening, Onslow and Charing and Barham were sitting waiting for Twysden to make up a four, Onslow glanced over his shoulder and lowered his voice.

" D'you see that fellow Bohun's got married to Helen Adair ? "

Charing nodded abruptly.

" How did he get rid of his wife ? "

" Didn't she divorce him ? " said Barham. " I seem to remember——"

" No," said Onslow, " she didn't. That was snuffed out. And then, about six months later, he divorced her."

" And she never defended," said Charing. " How did he do it ? That's what I want to know."

" My God, these lawyers," said Barham. " An' then they say they're cleaning up the Divorce Court. Hullo, Twysden, how's Sandown Park ? "

" Make it Caxton Hall," said Twysden. " I'm going there in future. I daresay I shall be bored, but I shan't be robbed."

The others made no attempt to conceal their mirth.

Almost at the same moment, a harridan was sitting at Vichy, regarding an English paper with smouldering eyes.

HONEYMOON ABROAD

Mrs. David Bohun (better known as Helen Adair, the beautiful daughter of the late Sir Chantrey Persimmon Bart., and one of the world's greatest heiresses) and her husband watching their car being shipped for the Continent.

So much for the legend. The photograph which it was serving was almost more eloquent.

The harridan sucked in her breath.

"When I think of that poor, wretched child . . . how she clung to me that evening . . . and how, in spite of all, she worshipped that callous blackguard . . ."

Here malevolence o'erleaped itself, and the apodosis was lost.

* * * *

Nobody knew how old old Niccolo was: but for quite twelve years he had been too old to work. His eye was not dim, but his natural force was abated. He was by no means helpless—still did most things for himself: but the muscles of his back had failed, and though he could walk pretty well, he could neither sit down nor rise up without assistance.

All his life had been spent at Creva, a tiny hamlet commanding the Lake of Como, with terraces for meadows and flights of steps for streets. He could neither read nor write—which was all to the good—and had never entered a car or a railway train: but he had seen many things denied to such as travel and had so applied his heart unto wisdom that, though he had no money, he was immensely rich.

Only his mother had known that he was the son of a famous English house, that his father had longed to be an artist, but had been cast at birth for another rôle. But Niccolo knew very well that he had faculties which his fellows had not, and though he was always careful to hide this knowledge away, he treasured those faculties in secret and had of them a pleasure such as no money can buy.

Among them was a sense of beauty.

No wonder old Niccolo was rich. For nearly one hundred years, at every hour of the day, he had been in a position to consider one of the most exquisite prospects this rolling world can afford. He had seen it created each morning, with pomp and circumstance: he had watched the lake put on its colour and the mountains take up their order and the dayspring etch the detail into their royal flanks: noon after noon he had seen the mutual worship of heaven and earth—the radiance of the snow upon the summits, the magical blue of the water, the emerald green of the pastures, the vivid, clean-cut shadows which all things threw: and evening after evening he had marked the miracle of sundown and watched a gorgeous fable change to a mystery.

The older Niccolo grew, the more he valued these things, for, though he had known seven priests and had respectfully listened to all that they said, in his heart he very much doubted whether the heaven they commended would be so fine as his earth: then, again, these things had not altered, as had the work of men's hands: they were as lovely as ever, while ships and dress and buildings had all grown more and more ugly as time went by, and even men and women had no longer the grace which was in them when he was young.

And so it came about that, since he was good for nothing except to sit still, on fine summer afternoons one of his many descendants would lead him down out of the village and settle him under an olive on one of those pleasant linchets which he had so often mown; and there he would be left to himself, until evening came in, to take the pleasure with which he was so familiar, which never grew old.

David and Helen never saw him: but he saw them —climbing the meadows below him, until they stood upon the linchet directly below his own. He could, of course, do nothing but sit where he was, but, for the first time for ages, Niccolo felt it his duty to get to his feet. He was, he knew, in the presence of quality. Although their backs were turned, he took off his hat.

He almost prayed that they would stay there, where he could see them so well, for both of them were so goodly and each loved the other so much. Not for longer than he could remember, had an idyll one half so sterling swum into his ken.

There was a thorough-bred maiden, bare-headed, slim and shapely and dressed as a maid should be—with her bare, brown arms and legs and a slip of a fair linen frock and two little white shoes. Look at the hand she had laid on her lover's shoulder : look at the pointed fingers and the beautiful shape of that thumb . . . Look at those wrists and ankles, and look at those clean, straight legs . . . And her head was set on her shoulders as heads were meant to be set, and her glowing curls were natural—no barber's irons had made them, but God himself, and the sun itself had lit them, when she was a baby child . . .

She was looking round now, and was showing him such a profile as made the old man feel young. The chiselled features, the pride of that aquiline nose, the curve of that delicate nostril, that great, blue eye—so wide and kind and fearless, and then that most excellent mouth . . . Here was a natural beauty—the stuff that belonged to legends, that only old men could swear to . . . and be laughed to scorn for their pains.

And the swain beside her was worthy—no doubt about that. Tall and broad and upstanding, and as good as stripped to the waist. Strong, too—a proper man : look at those arms and those shoulders and the depth of that lusty chest. And he held his bare head well, and his eye was clear. There was an honest face—she was safe with him : frank and brave and faithful—he'd never change : the same yesterday, to-day and for ever—like the picture upon which they were gazing . . . lake and grove and pasture, and the eternal hills.

Here, to his infinite pleasure, David took Helen's fingers and put them up to his lips. And then they sat down together, with their backs to their old admirer and their eyes on the peerless prospect he loved so well.

" Chiberta to Como," said David, " in just two years and three months. And the very hell of a passage. I should have done better than that."

Helen laced her fingers about an exquisite knee.

" I know just how you feel," she said : " but I've looked at it every way and I can't for the life of me see how, placed as you were, you could have done anything else. Anything better, I mean, than what you did do."

David wrinkled his brow.

" I ought to have left her, my darling. The moment I realized that she had no use for me and I was in love with you, I ought to have just cleared out."

" But you did leave her, my blessed—with what result ? "

The man bit his lip.

" I know. But I ought to have taken a very much stronger line."

" That," said the girl, " would have been more fatal still. Cunning will leave strength standing—it always has. She would have turned against you the strength you showed. She *did* turn it against you. You fired Anselm that evening—and look at what you went through. D'you think those butlers she found, she found by accident ? If any woman did, she deserved to be thrashed. Think, if you *had* thrashed her, how she would have used against you what you had done."

" I gave way too much at first."

" So does every man who's in love with his wife."

" But, Nell, I went too far. Take the Cadnams, for instance. If I'd said they were to stay——"

" She'd have had them out just the same. She was —inexorable. She was also terribly clever and knew no law. Against that a husband is powerless, if he is an honest man. And you of all men, my darling —that's why she picked you out. And so you were at her mercy—I knew it far better than you. I could only implore you to stand it—stand anything. And that was because I knew what you couldn't appreciate —that she would stick at *nothing*, to gain her ends.

" You needn't pick up any stones to throw at yourself. You were up against something abnormal—the very powers of evil, *against which only evil could ever prevail*. If you want proof of this, take Forsyth. He knew that all his wisdom—and he is terribly wise— would go for nothing against her wickedness. *And so he turned to evil*, to bring her down. He enlisted that wicked woman on your behalf. And she—*and nobody else*—knew how to withstand your wife."

" I should have gone to Forsyth before."

" There I agree," said Helen : " although I very much doubt if it would have done any good. You see, I tore everything up. Things were pretty well bent before, but I tore them in two. By falling in love with me, you played straight into her hands. Together, we made her a present of a brigade of guns . . ." She hesitated there, and a hand went up to her hair. " Your work at the Bar and me . . . You were never up to her weight, but, with those two things round your neck she'd only got to flick you to send your head back." Again she hesitated. Then, " If that woman hadn't come off, you know I was going to be called."

David started.

" You weren't ! "

" Yes, I was. It was all arranged. Bagot and Forsyth agreed that, if her case couldn't be smashed,

I simply must be called for Belinda's sake. They were perfectly right, of course : it's no good watching and praying—with a gun hanging up on the wall. Of course, it might have burst in the hand : but we had to risk that. I was waiting at Kensington Square, and they had my proof."

There was a little silence.

Then—

"We've a lot to be thankful for," said David. "No doubt about that. And as we're opening our mouths—you remember that I left her that autumn. Didn't you ever wonder how it was that I came to go back."

"Yes," said Helen, "I did."

"But you never asked me, did you ? "

"No, my blessed, I didn't. I—I knew it was pretty bad."

"She came to the club," said David, with his eyes on the topless hills. "Came to the Ladies' Annexe and sent in her name. Caught me bending, of course —I hadn't expected that. And when I went round— I had to—the place was full. And she . . . made a scene there, Nell . . . in the drawing-room . . ."

The statement cried out for comment : but the girl said nothing—she dared not trust her voice. Presently Bohun continued.

"Well, that was all right : I could take my name off the club. But I didn't have to go back—to Curzon Street. And then she said, if I didn't, she'd—well, repeat the performance . . . at the Savoy . . . And I knew she meant what she said . . . and so I went back."

Helen was twisting her hands.

"And after that I left you—went out to the South of France. Oh, David, my darling . . ."

"What else could you do, my sweet ? It wasn't your fault. Never mind. It's all over now. But you see what I mean—it should never have come to that.

She'd got me down. She had her foot on my neck. And you can't be surprised if I despise myself——'

" I don't despise you," said Helen. "Neither does Forsyth, nor Bagot—I know that's true."

" Mrs. Morris did."

" She would. She despised you all, because a woman like her was able to beat the lot of you all ends up. But Forsyth and Bagot and I are decent human beings who know the facts. You can add Mo in, if you like—and Belinda and Punch. All of us know the story : and everyone of us knows that an honest man was doomed from the moment he took her on. Every one makes mistakes : but you only made one that mattered—and that was when you gave her your name. The rest didn't count—if you made them. I mean, it didn't matter whether you made them or not. And what of Lord Elvin ? Who saw the whole thing coming . . . and left a fortune to Forsyth, to ' catch out that she-devil and free my boy ' ? No, my darling, you've nothing to be ashamed of from first to last. You'd chained yourself to something that was not human. And if you want proof of that—well, I wish you could see the difference between yourself then and now. Even at Chiberta, that April—and that was early on—you looked so terribly tired : and later on your face was often so gray : and at times your eyes were so hopeless . . ."

" That was what got me," said David. " You've put your foot on the truth. The moment I saw you that morning, when I was carrying Tumble and you fell out of that car—the moment I saw your eyes, I knew that I'd made a mistake. Well, there was nothing for it. That's the sort of mistake you've got to live down. And then I saw you in London . . . And then I knew that I couldn't live down that mistake. And so . . . I looked round for hope. And hope wasn't there. *I had no hope.* I tried to pretend, of course. We both of us tried to pretend. But we had no hope—*no hope.* That was what got me, Nell. The present was bad—damned bad . . . those last three months . . . But the future was—frightening . . . *because I had got no hope."*

" I know," said Helen, quietly. " And now shall I tell you something ? *If she hadn't struck when she did, I was going to throw in my hand.* I was coming to London that week, to beg and pray you to leave for Chiberta with me. I meant to *make* you do it— by hook or by crook. I'd have done it the week before, if Mo hadn't been ill . . . for we were past breaking- point . . . Although your wife didn't know it, she'd got me down."

" And I should have gone," said David ; " *and never forgiven myself* . . . Instead of which . . . here we are . . . on the very top of the world . . . with no regrets at all . . . and a future so very shining that I am afraid to look."

He put his arm about her and held her close, and she laid her head on his shoulder and found his hand.

" This country," he said, " these surroundings—I never imagined such beauty in all my life. I didn't know it existed, in any world. And to sit with you, in its midst . . . My God, I suppose I'm alive—not been translated or something, before my time . . ."

" And me ? How d'you think I feel ? "

The man shook his head.

" Not the same for you. It can't be. You love me, I know. For some astonishing reason, you seem to love me a lot. But I am an ordinary man, with nothing whatever to me that other men haven't got ; while you are——"

" Helen Bohun. I love my name."

" —a famous beauty and—I can't better Forsyth's words—' the very finest lady I ever saw '."

" I don't want to be that. I'm Nell . . . sitting in a meadow with David . . . admiring the view. It's paradise, of course : but that's not because of the mountains or the staggering blue of that lake : it's because my head's on your shoulder, and you've got your arm about me, and I'm your wife."

Again the man lifted her fingers and put them up to his lips. And then they sat still, in silence, as though contemplating the kingdom which now was theirs.

At length Bohun glanced at his wrist-watch and got to his feet. Then he put out his hands for Helen's, and drew her up to her feet and into his arms.

"What can I say ? " he breathed. "What can I say or do, to tell you how much I love you . . . how terribly proud I am of my darling wife ? "

The girl put her arms round his neck.

"No good asking me, my blessed. Let's stay inarticulate. At least, I can sympathize. I feel exactly the same."

For a little the two stood, smiling—into each other's eyes. Then the man bowed his head, to kiss her beautiful mouth. For a moment they clung together —and Niccolo's heart was full. Then they turned to go down, as they had come up . . .

They never knew that an old man's blessing went with them : they never knew of the light which they had brought into his eyes : and nobody else knew, either, for Niccolo held his peace. He was wise—in his generation. His descendants would only have reproved him—for failing to suggest to the strangers that they should give him an alms.

*　*　*　*

Less than an hour later, Mr. and Mrs. Bohun reentered their proud hotel.

As they passed through the hall, a man touched his neighbour's arm.

"Did you see who that was ? "

"No. Who ? "

"Helen Adair that *was* : now Mrs. David Bohun.

That must have been Bohun with her. He's done all right for himself."

His neighbour regarded the speaker.

" Not too good, eh ? "

The other shrugged his shoulders.

" Well, he'd got a wife already : so something had to be done."

" Good lord," said the neighbour. " Not really ? "

The other nodded his head.

" A shocking show," he said. " I happen to know. The poor girl didn't see it . . . the way he did. But there you are. She wouldn't put him away, so he put her away, instead."

The neighbour sighed.

" Well, he's got what he wants," he said. " What's happened to her ? "

" God knows," said the other . . .

He need have had no concern.

Rowena had had a good year.

Juliot's letters alone had brought her five thousand pounds.

THE END